# FURY OF AGGRESSION

## COREENE CALLAHAN

# 1

Standing in the lobby of a glossy Manhattan high-rise, Theodora Romanov stared at her reflection in the elevator doors and wondered, not for the first time, what had possessed her. The ghost of good deeds past, perhaps. The devil of righteous indignation, no doubt. A lifetime spent in the muck, surrounded by filth, sure enough. Still...

She never should've done it.

Stupid.

Seriously *stupid*, given she already walked a razor-thin edge.

Was uncovering the corruption and turning him in the right thing to do? Yes. Was it the wisest course of action under the circumstances? Not even close. And yet she'd taken the plunge anyway. Listened too closely. Paid too much attention. Become one with the covert crowd as she stuffed documents into a manila envelope, then committed a cardinal sin for someone like her—slipped the entire mess into a dented blue mailbox standing on a New York City street corner.

Anonymously, of course.

No name or return addresses on the envelope.

Postmark originating far from the neighborhood she called home.

An excellent strategy for a girl with nothing to gain and everything to lose.

Not that truth and justice wasn't important, but...

She didn't want the attention. Or any of the accolades. And depositions? Standing on polished granite tiles waiting for the elevator doors to open, she breathed around the tight knot sitting in the center of her chest. Being a legal secretary meant she witnessed the leashed violence simmering beneath the surface on a daily basis. Veiled threats. Hateful innuendos. Slimy tactics. Her boss used every weapon at his disposal to intimidate, cajole, and scare those seated across the table from him.

He'd never been on her side.

Never would be, either.

He was, after all, part of the problem. Or, in actual fact, the main one. Which shoved legal options right off the table. Now and in the future.

She might be a secretary, but that didn't mean she didn't understand the law. And no matter how prestigious the firm she worked inside, she wanted to avoid lawyers as much as her three-year-old tried to avoid getting her hair brushed. Problem was...

She'd mailed the package.

No going back now.

Her fingerprints were all over it.

Not literally. Theodora might lean toward her better angels, but she wasn't a moron. Rubber gloves worked great in all kinds of situations...keeping her prints and DNA off incriminating documents shipped to the U.S. attorney for the Southern District of New York being just one of them. Taking steps to shield her identity, however, might not be enough, given the shitstorm bearing down on her boss and the firm.

The signs were clear. It was only a matter of time before everything fell apart.

All the more reason for her to run. Hide. Make herself scarce for, oh, say, the next fifty years. A lesser person would've hightailed it to places unknown, but leaving now would leave her vulnerable.

Much as she hated to admit it, she needed her next paycheck, and the financial padding. The little bit extra that would help her move on to the next spot. Help her get set up. Help her put food on the table.

Closing her eyes, she drew a fortifying breath. Four days. Just four more days until the money landed in her account. The second it did, she'd be ready. Packed, prepared, and able to get on the road. She'd stayed too long anyway.

Dangerous.

Ill-advised.

Stupid, given the trouble that dogged her trail.

The elevator doors opened.

Steeling her nerves, she played it cool, did what she always did: murmured good morning to those already standing shoulder to shoulder and walked inside. The ride up to the fifty-third floor was smooth. Her thoughts were not. Jagged and jumbled, her mind ran through all the possibilities. Tension curled at the base of her skull. Already taut muscles reacted, tightening another notch, reacting to the coil of unrelenting stress.

She closed her eyes.

God.

So many unknowns. Too many variables. All of it out of her control.

"Excuse me," a man murmured, brushing past her.

Theodora startled, then realized the doors stood wide open. Her gaze lit on the familiar line of raised block letters. Fancy script. Premier placement. *The* law firm in a city known for the best—*Umbridge, Carter, Stern.* Her floor. Her place of employment the last nine months.

Stiletto heels clicking across hard tiles, Theodora stepped out onto the fifty-third floor. With a nod to Norma, she strode past the reception desk and, navigating the wide hallways lined with plush carpet, rounded the end of her low-walled cubicle. She glanced toward the wall of glass she sat outside every day. Corner office. Sleek leather furniture. Expensive art hanging front and center. Signed baseballs from hotshot clients sitting in Plexiglas cases on the ledge under a bank of windows that overlooked the city skyline.

On the phone, Samuel Umbridge looked up as she sat down in her ergonomic office chair. The skin around his eyes and mouth tightened. Not at a lot, just enough. A tell. *His tell.* One that signaled unpleasant things to come.

Theodora looked at her watch. Seven forty-five a.m., and already the guessing games had begun. Most days she teetered on the edge, wondering what he'd do or say to her next. Since mailing the package, however...

She rolled her shoulders, attacking the tension and readying herself for the unpleasantries, then set her knockoff Gucci handbag on the desktop. One eye on Umbridge, she fired up her computer. As the screen flickered, her boss flicked his fingers, summoning her into his office. Not for the first time, she wondered if she should warn him. Say something about the murmurs coming from accounting. Might be a good cover. Might put her on the outside of suspi-cion. Might save her some grief, buy her some time in the—

"Olivia!"

His voice pierced through the quiet.

Her stomach tightened as the fake name on the fake identification papers she'd used to land her job clawed over her skin. Never failed. Every time she heard it—answered to it—all the reasons she fled Seattle four years ago came rushing back to the surface.

Dread settled in the pit of her stomach.

Her boss snapped his fingers.

Smoothing her hands over her pencil skirt, she tucked her purse into the bottom draw, locked it, then left her chair. No sense delaying the inevitable. Zero advantage to giving herself away, so until she moved on to the next place, she needed to playact. Make like it was just any other day. Nothing out of the ordinary. Same despicable boss, different set of minutes in the *very* long month she'd worked for him. If she'd known then what she did now, she never would've agreed to the transfer.

Memphis Alexander (her former boss) had been, well—*the Boss*. Straight as an arrow. Kind to her inside the office. Generous with bonuses. A true pleasure to work alongside, until her wife got sick and she took a leave of absence. As a senior partner, Memphis could do that. As managing partner, Umbridge owned the right to poach Theodora. Which he did, precisely five seconds after Memphis announced her decision.

A compliment to her professionalism, some said.

A power trip engineered to put Memphis in her place, Theodora knew.

Yeah, Umbridge was just that big of a dick.

"Close the door," Umbridge said the second she stepped inside his office.

Theodora wanted to argue. Glass wall or no, being alone with him never felt good—but instead of protesting, she grabbed the elegant handle and swung the door closed.

Hinges sighed.

Reflections flashed in the pristine surface. A junior associate walking past her desk. The fat green leaves of a plant sitting across from her cubicle. The line of elegant wall sconces lining the hallway. Squaring her shoulders, she folded her hands in front of her and turned back toward him.

Umbridge tossed his phone on his desk and picked up a stack of papers. He wagged the pile at her. "What did I tell you?"

Oh, so many things. None of it good.

She opened her mouth to answer.

Umbridge thundered on. "I warned you what would happen if you didn't stop."

"I'm sorry," she said, watching his piggy snout curl with displeasure. Taking a measured breath, she faced the beast head-on. "I don't know what you're—"

"Do you know what this is?" Taking a step toward her, he flapped the documents.

Her gaze jumped from the pages to his face. Tension ratcheted up another notch as she shook her head.

"Phone logs." A sneer twisted his face as he flung the stack at her. Printed pages flew. Paper seesawed, settling like battle lines between him and her. "Did you think I wouldn't find out? Did you think that spying on me would get you anything but—"

"Hold on a second. What exactly are you accusing me of?"

"You're still calling her!"

"Of course I am," she said, crossing her arms, refusing to be intimidated now that she knew the darkest of her secrets was safe. "Memphis might no longer be my boss, but she's my friend. Her wife is sick. She needs support."

"I don't give a shit what she needs. You work for me now."

Her spine stiffened. "Let's get one thing straight, Mr. Umbridge. You may be my boss, but you don't own my time outside the office. Where I go and who I talk to is none of your business."

A malicious gleam entered his dark, close-set eyes. "Except you didn't call her from home, did you? You sat"—he paused to point at her desk outside the glass panes—"right there and called her, *betrayed* me...from my own fucking office line."

Shit.

She saw her mistake. Immediately.

The snake was a stickler for the rules. Worse, he was detail-oriented, which made outsmarting him almost impossible. Memphis, with all her charm and alpha female energy, could do it. Back Umbridge off. Make him slink away. Force him back into the slimy vestiges of his evil little corner. Always fun to watch, but Theodora couldn't match her former boss's ferocity. She didn't possess the power—and perhaps the stomach—to beat him back with brutality.

She went on the attack anyway. "I'm not spying on you."

"Bullshit."

True. Though not for the reasons Umbridge suspected. Memphis didn't know about the embezzlement from client trusts. She was already in enough pain watching the woman she loved die.

"Look," Theodora said, keeping her tone even, chanting, *Four more days, four more days, four more days,* inside her head. "I'm not—"

The phone on Umbridge's desk rang.

He scowled at her. "One warning. *One,* Oliva, that's it. I'm telling you, straight out, stop. Stop calling her. If Memphis wants to know what going on, she can get off her ass and come back to work."

His callousness shocked her. Why? No clue. After all she'd witnessed, all she'd grown up seeing, all the muck she'd waded through to come out clean on the other side, his cruelty shouldn't have fazed her. Somehow, though, it did.

She stared at him.

He glared back.

The phone stopped ringing.

And started up again.

"Mr. Umbridge—"

"Answer the phone," he said, turning away. "Then get me some coffee."

Sick to her stomach, she pivoted and grabbed the door handle. Outwardly calm, inwardly seething, she swung the glass panel wide and, with practiced ease, hid her fury as she rounded her cubicle and picked up her phone.

"Umbridge, Carter, and Stern. Olivia speaking."

"You're blown," said a voice, one she hadn't heard in six months.

"What?"

"Your cover, Theo. Blown. You gotta move, and do it now. He knows where you are."

"Bea—"

"Don't think. Move. Pick up Violet from daycare and go. Don't stop at the apartment, just *go,*" her sister said, sounding out of breath. The quick click of high heels came over the line. Fast tapping, as though Beatrice was running downstairs. "You set an escape route?"

White-knuckling the phone, Theodora nodded. "Go-bag's good to go. I've got a car stashed, too."

"Good. Meet me at our spot."

"I—"

"No time, sis. Do it."

"Three or four days. It'll take me—"

"I know. You gonna be there?"

"Yes."

"I'll arrange everything. Get you a new fleet of identities."

"You on a burner?"

"Yes. Memorize the number. Call on a secure line once you're away. Let me know you made it out clean."

"Okay," she whispered, unlocking her desk drawer. "Three days, Bea."

"Three days, Theo."

"Love you to pieces."

"Right to my marrow, babe. Now, *move!*"

Wasting no time, shielding her movements from Umbridge, Theodora tucked her purse under her arm. A second later, she was walking down the hall toward the elevators. Straight out of one life, careening headlong into another. On a collision course with her past and the last place she wanted to go—home.

**2**

———————

The night promised to be an interesting one. Not in good ways, but an idiot deserved what he got, and Sloan refused to stand on ceremony. He called it like he saw it. Sometimes too bluntly, much to his brother-in-arm's chagrin, but... whatever. A spade was, and always would be, a spade, and in the scenario about to unfold, he was without a doubt the joker.

Combat boots thumping on polished concrete, Sloan shoved the door to the stairwell open. Cinder-block walls and floating dust motes greeted him, but all he could think was—*the joker*. Nice play on words. A smooth way of saying his night was about to go down the crapper, but some things couldn't be avoided.

No one cared that he wanted to stay underground, in his computer lab, dancing his usual dance with the dark net. The shift in routine was his fault. In a moment of sheer madness, he'd given his word and now, no matter how screwed up things got, refused to break it.

Lives depended on him. The Nightfury pack's future hung in the balance. Sloan didn't need to be told what the failure of his mission would bring. He understood the importance of the task better than anyone, but still...

Sometimes volunteering to help backfired.

Primary case in point? Agreeing to become Angela Keen's mentor on top of all the other shit he had to do. The female was fast becoming a pain in his ass.

No surprise, really.

A homicide detective in her former life, Angela embodied smart and strategic. He liked that about her. No matter what he threw at her—mostly books right now—she mastered the techniques and passed every test. The problem, believe it or not, began and ended with her iron will.

The she-devil possessed sharp edges, the kind of stubbornness most males didn't know how to confront. He'd spent the last two days trying, attempting to slow her down...with very little success. How Rikar (her mate, the Nightfury pack's first-in-command) kept her contained, Sloan didn't know, but...

Goddess.

Guess love really was blind.

Sloan gave the door another shove. Steel slammed against cinder block. The bang reverberated up the stairwell before the door edge whipped back in his direction. Sidestepping the backlash, he crossed the landing, then jogged up the first rise of treads.

One story down, six more to climb.

Most of the time, he avoided the aboveground lair. Tonight, however, wasn't one of those nights.

He'd been summoned less than sixty seconds ago. A whole half an hour ahead of schedule. Why? Bastian didn't say, but Sloan could guess. *Angela.* He clenched his teeth. Total pain in his ass. Especially since he wasn't ready to be topside. Not yet. He needed the extra time to even out, find emotional balance, and contain the rage that always bubbled close to his surface.

A remnant of the past.

Part nature, mostly nurture. The residual left over from devastating loss.

Moving at a steady clip, he rounded the next landing. Eleven years, and the wound remained fresh. Gaping and open. Oozing mental and emotional poison. Reminding him every day of his mistake and all he could've done differently.

So many things.

Too many things.

All of which he should've done.

The guilt alone slayed him. The grief, though...

His pace slowed. The echoes of his footfalls stalled. Silence descended as memory took hold, dragging him back. Gripping the railing, he closed his eyes. Like a pack of hungry piranha, anguish ripped into him. Day after day. Night after night. Tearing vital chunks of him away as the pain of losing Simeon cut deep.

He'd dug the graves himself, refusing to allow the groundskeeper to do his job, laying mother next to newborn babe. His penance. A way for him to say goodbye. The only way he knew how to do right by his son after it had all gone so horribly wrong.

Clenching his teeth, Sloan opened his eyes. Yeah. No question. Given his state of mind, the extra half an hour inside his subterranean greenhouse mattered. Lounging in the shadow of mature trees—the sights, sounds, and scents of nature all around him—soothed his vicious side.

As an earth dragon, he had plenty of brutality to spare.

Unlike other Dragonkind, the magic in his blood aligned with the rhythms of the planet. The automatic connection plugged him into the Meridian—the electrostatic bands ringing the earth, source of all living things. Not all the way. Just enough to boost his power, making him more dangerous than most as he tapped in, becoming one with the wilderness, absorbing what he needed to stay healthy and strong.

A lovely trait to deploy.

An unusual skill.

A game changer in many ways, a true gift in others.

Unlike other warriors, he didn't need to feed at regular intervals. His connection to the earth stabilized his magic, allowing him to go months between energy feedings. A great perk, though most of the time, the link wasn't stable...or anywhere near safe. Over the years he'd learned to navigate the ebb and flow, knowing when to plug in to earth energy and when to disconnect.

The Meridian was brute force amplified. Pure power. Majestic in intensity. Only a fool played in that pool without knowing the risks. He took calculated ones, sure, following the jagged curve when energy leaked from the electrostatic bands, skimming thin layers off the top, absorbing the excess through a shadowy channel most males never detected.

Unfortunate for them. Good for him, given he spent an inordinate amount of time thinking up ways to avoid energy feedings with human females.

His brothers-in-arms thought he was crazy.

Most nights, Sloan agreed.

He enjoyed sex as much as other males. Loved the softness. Got off on the sight and scent of an aroused female. Lived for the sounds she made while he built her pleasure to a crescendo, then drove her over the edge. The carnality fed his soul—the earthiness in him—as he connected to the Meridian through her and mainlined her energy to nourish his dragon half.

No better feeling in the world.

The beauty of the experience, however, never changed the facts: loving something didn't always mean it was good for you.

Sometimes, the thing you wanted most left you empty, standing under the eaves, lost to the shadows, nothing but a hollow husk in the aftermath. His history proved that well enough. He'd never forget what happened in El Paso. Would never forgive himself for losing control and causing her death. *Amanda*. His best friend for years. A female he never should've touched, no matter how readily she welcomed him.

What his brothers-in-arms believed about him didn't matter. Sloan knew the truth. Understood the brutal hook of his nature. He'd learned his lesson the hard way. Getting too close to a female—letting his guard down—was a bad idea.

Dangerous for him.

Lethal for her, so...

"Not gonna happen," he growled, turning the corner around the last landing.

He took the steps two at a time. Halfway up, he came fully aboveground. He felt the pull and claw as the subterranean cocoon cradling him ripped wide open. Static crackled down his spine. He flinched. His dragon half hissed. And Sloan understood, mourning the loss of soothing vibrations as invisible tendrils let him go one talon at a time, making him twitch in denial.

A wave of anger rippled through him.

"Settle," he murmured, tamping down volatile instinct, soothing himself with the knowledge he'd be airborne soon. In dragon form. Wings spread in open skies. "Breathe."

Sloan drew air in through his nose and exhaled through his mouth as he reached the top and crossed the upper landing, a large, open area spread across a concrete platform. Reinforced steel door dead ahead. Electronic keypad installed to one side. He murmured his wishes. Magic frothed in front of him. The lock clicked. Heavy-duty hinges groaned as the security door swung wide. Dipping his head beneath the lintel, he stepped over the threshold into the corridor.

Concrete floors transitioned to dark hardwood. The scent of pine floor cleaner hit him. Boot soles squeaking across the wide planks, he eyeballed the male stationed across the hall.

Shimmering ice-blue eyes narrowed on him.

Sloan stopped short.

Arms crossed, expression set to "pissed off," Rikar pushed away from the wall. "You're gonna look after her."

"You know I will."

"First flight, man. It's—"

"I know." Flexing his fingers, Sloan prepared for the fight about to unfold. "And you're not coming."

"I fucking am."

"No, you're not. I've been given strict instructions from B."

*For good reason.*

Bastian wasn't commander of the Nightfury pack for nothing. The male was razor sharp, lethal in all the right ways, and knew his warriors well. Hence the *strict instructions* when it came to Angela. B didn't want her mate involved. Sloan agreed and, as her mentor, would make sure Rikar wasn't part of her dragon combat training team.

Period.

End of story.

Zero wiggle room for the pissed-off frost dragon gearing up to shove ice down his throat.

"You're nowhere near the mountain tonight, Rikar," he said, laying it out, leaving no room for misinterpretation. "You push it, I'll lock you down."

"Fuck," Rikar said, scrubbing a hand over his blond hair—a skull trim, shorn almost as short as Sloan's. "Who're you taking?"

"The Metallics."

"Not Gage."

"Yes—Gage."

"Sloan—"

"He's a brutal motherfucker," he said, squaring off with his first-in-command.

Not his first choice.

Going toe to toe with Rikar presented a plethora of problems. Death by a million ice daggers topped the list. Something a smart male worked hard to avoid, but...shit. He couldn't back down. Not tonight. Not about this. Angela deserved his best. All he could give her.

Refusing to give ground, Sloan widened his stance. "Gage won't baby her, Rikar. He'll make sure she gets the training she needs to fly free. You want her to become a valued member of our pack, she needs to be treated like any other warrior. No coddling. We take our time with her. We do it right. She needs to be able to fend for herself no matter the situation or enemy combatant involved. I'm not sending her out into the world unprepared. So yeah, Gage is part of Ange's dragon combat training team. And you're—"

"Sloan—"

"Going to suck it up and, as much as it kills you, step off."

"She's not an ordinary fledging, man. She's the first female Dragonkind in centuries. She's extraordinary. She's everything. She's—"

"I know, brother."

"*Mine.*" A muscle jumped along Rikar's jaw. "She's mine. I love her. I can't live without her. If something happens to her, I just... I can't... Fuck."

Raising his hands, Rikar cupped the back of his head. A rough sound left his throat. One fueled by agony.

Sloan's chest tightened. Understanding pulled the cord, strengthening the bond he already shared with his brother-in-arms. Rikar might be one of the strongest males he knew, but he wasn't immune to heartache. His posture broadcasted his anguish. All the worry. Every bit of his concern. The strain over the last couple of days as he fought to bring Angela through her *first shift* intact—healthy and whole. The fact she hadn't died counted as a miracle, one made manifest by the male standing in front of him, so... yeah. Rikar's fear was justified. Real. All consuming. Something no other Dragonkind male had had to deal with in centuries.

So...nothing left to do but power through. Through the fear. Through the pain. Through all the shit ahead of him to get Angela where she needed to be—Rikar's opinion be damned. Still...

He hated to see his friend suffer. Something must be done. Assurances needed to be made and promises kept. Otherwise, Rikar would lose his mind.

"Rikar." Stepping in close, Sloan reached out. His

hand landed on the first-in-command's shoulder. "Hey."

Rikar dropped his arms and lifted his head. Intense ice-blue eyes met Sloan's.

He held steady, taking the scrutiny, absorbing the male's pain. Adjusting his hold, Sloan gave him a squeeze. "I get it, man, I do, but Ange needs you to trust her. You know how you do that?"

Rikar shook his head.

"By trusting me."

"You're good, Sloan, one of the best, but it's hard for me to trust you with this."

"I get it," he said, holding Rikar's gaze, giving him time, waiting for him to accept what he couldn't change.

"Christ." Dread lining his face, Rikar shook his head. "So many things could go wrong."

"Nothing's gonna go wrong."

"I can't lose her, Sloan."

"You won't."

A furrow between his brows, Rikar stared at him. "You got her?"

Sloan nodded.

"Really got her?"

"Yeah, man."

Rikar released a pent-up breath. "Okay."

One word. Devastating impact. Wholehearted trust packaged inside the least amount said.

The realization rocked him. He wanted Rikar's trust. Hell, he needed it, but under the circumstances, given the gravity, hadn't expected it. Not really. The stakes were high. Astronomical by Dragonkind standards. Angela's life hung in the balance, along with Rikar's sanity if he didn't get it right.

A huge responsibility. A challenge he must meet, match, and best.

"Okay," Sloan murmured.

Understanding the underlying message, his friend nodded. The icy blast of his eyes warmed a little. "You bring her home to me in one piece."

"A little battered and bruised, maybe, but—"

Rikar shoved him.

Sloan grinned as he slid backward. "She'll be good, brother."

"She better be."

"At least until she crash-lands in the backyard," he said, his grin morphing into a smile.

"Shit," Rikar grumbled, throwing him a dirty look. "Learning to land always sucks."

Didn't it, though? First flight was always difficult, but once airborne, a fledging warrior got the hang of things quick. The problem always arrived when putting paws back on land. Crash landings were common. Ripped wings and broken bones weren't unheard of as a warrior spun out of control, tearing up great swaths of landscape in his wake.

Always fun to watch.

One hundred percent popcorn-worthy.

Not that Sloan would be bringing any tonight. He'd be too focused on making sure Angela survived the outing.

Rikar was right. She wasn't a normal Dragonkind fledging. She hadn't been born with an ounce of dragon DNA. She'd been gifted with it. Kidnapped. Drugged. Forced into compliance. Injected with a serum by Ivar—commander of the Razorback pack, madcap scientist, out to change the course of Dragonkind's future. An interesting goal. Maybe even a noble one. Problem was, he'd done it without Angela's permission, changing her into something she wasn't meant to be and didn't know how to control.

Sloan had spent *hours* researching, talking to human scientists on the web, trying to understand how Ivar had done it. Lots of questions. No answers. Which meant he needed to keep his guard up and instincts sharp. Start to finish, the whole thing was a crapshoot. An experiment that could, and probably would, go wrong.

Shoving his friend back, Sloan put his feet in gear. Pace steady, he strode down the hallway. His destination—Black Diamond's garage. His mind—on the mission ahead.

Hanging a left into a wider corridor, he went over the parameters. High place. Lots of open space. Friendly winds. Not too many obstacles for her to avoid. All necessary elements until he catalogued Angela's strengths and weakness.

He'd done his recon. Knew the best place to launch her, so—

"Where're you taking her?" Rikar asked, footfalls beating in tandem with Sloan's on glossy floorboards.

Sloan threw his friend a sidelong look, wondering about the wisdom of answering the question. "Am I gonna have to lock you down?"

"Comes to that, B'll do it," Rikar said, looking uncomfortable in his own skin.

Sloan studied him a second. He shouldn't tell him. Really, he shouldn't. Rikar knowing the when and where was a bad idea, but...

"Screw it," he muttered, uncaring he'd be in for an ass kicking if Bastian found out.

Rikar was her mate. The pair shared an unbreakable bond, one embedded with magic and fueled by the Meridian. He had a right to know the ins and outs, every detail of her training and progression.

"Where?"

"The cliffs."

"South side of the mountain?"

Sloan shook his head. "North. Stronger updraft there."

His friend grunted.

"Your word."

"How long—an hour?" Rikar asked, sounding like he'd swallowed hot coals.

"Make it three."

Looking uncomfortable, Rikar rolled his shoulders.

"*Rikar,*" Sloan said.

"Fuck, all right. I'll stay put."

He hoped so. Otherwise, Angela wouldn't get the training she needed, and the Nightfury pack would end up eyeballs-deep in nothing good.

## 3

F og spilled across the blacktop, merging with the dark, making it difficult to see as Theodora drove deeper into the woods. Snaking two-lane mountain road. Narrow gravel shoulders. Massive white pines and jutting rock walls on either side of the rural route.

Up and down hills.

Around sweeping corners and rolling S-curves.

Too many dented guardrails fencing in the steep drop-offs, broadcasting where others had lost control on the slick asphalt.

A road she knew well, but hadn't traveled in four years—the first time she'd fled Seattle and made the trek to Aunt Jean's. Not a good memory. Even worse now for the fact she didn't want to be back in a place with so many secrets. Too many shadows. Real and remembered ones.

Flexing her hands on the wheel, she steeled her nerves and accelerated out of another turn. She trusted her twin. Beatrice knew what she was doing. After years of dealing with monsters alone, her sister navigated the chasm between their family and the real world with surprising ease, keeping herself and Theodora safe despite the danger.

A tightrope act.

Much like the last three days driving across country. Nothing but back roads. Lots of gas stations without cameras situated in small towns. Ten-hour days spent in the car. Most of it driven at night while Violet slept, a sacrifice Theodora made so her daughter didn't feel the squeeze of being cooped up in a car during the day.

She glanced in the rearview mirror. Buckled into a secondhand car seat, Violet slept like only a three-year-old could: deep and unworried. Little chin dipped down. Dark lashes kissing her cheeks. Hands open, fingers curled in her lap, dreaming sweet dreams. No way to know for sure, but it was a good guess.

Unlike her, Violet wasn't afraid of the dark.

Theodora had made it that way, providing her daughter with solid and steady, moving only when it became too dangerous to stay. Making it her mission to give her daughter what she'd never gotten. Loving Violet was easy. Keeping her child carefree, given how often Theodora needed to pull up stakes to keep them safe, wasn't. Somewhere along the way, though, she'd succeeded where her own father failed.

Her daughter wasn't scared of anything. She ran straight into danger. No fear. No hesitation. No worry of being hurt by the unknown. Her three-year-old spirit knew no bounds. She sought out shadowy corners, instead of shying away, enthralled by the possibilities along the path.

Braking at a stop sign, Theodora looked both ways, flipped her blinker on, and turned right. While she drove, she pictured Violet at the playground that morning moving full steam ahead, curious about everything she encountered. Kids. Dogs. Bugs, and the plants each made homes inside. Hell, she'd spent more time examining an anthill than digging inside the sandbox.

Such a huge imagination. One Theodora didn't share. No need for her to wonder. She knew what lived out in the world, was well acquainted with the kind of violence most adults, and the children lucky enough to be in their care, never experienced firsthand, but...

She *knew.*

Bad things happened at night. While darkness spread its wings and others slept snug in their beds.

Her teenage years had provided all the proof she required. The second her uncle decided to raise her and Beatrice, all ignorance stopped. He didn't shield them from the violence. He ensured they learned early and often what the family business entailed.

Most people believed monsters existed in picture books. Theodora knew the truth. The human variety were far more dangerous than the ones found in those pages. She'd lived the horror. Breathed the brutality. Smelled danger on the wind everywhere she went.

Even now, it bobbed on the ribbon of pine-scented air coming through the window she cracked the second she crossed into Washington state, filling the car she'd stashed in a run-down town outside New York City. On the edge of Nowhereville, New Jersey, a place no one cared enough to ask questions. The perfect distance from her old apartment—not too close, just far enough away to remain anonymous and safe.

Renting the storage unit had worried her. Turned out to be the good decision. She'd been able to reach the impossible-to-kill 1992 Chevy Impala fast. Untraceable wheels. Easy to overlook on the highway. A gas guzzler that stuck to the road in bad weather. A slick bit of luck sold to her by an ancient Asian man with a gentle face and kinder eyes.

Her salvation. Her one shot at getting out of New York without her uncle's hunters catching her scent before she blew town. Nothing but her purse, the go-bags with clothes, the leftover cash her sister gave her years ago in the trunk, and Violet (most precious of the three) as cargo.

"Thank God," she whispered.

She'd been lucky to escape, fortunate Beatrice found out about her uncle's plans and warned her in time. Otherwise, her trip home would've been a very different one. A much more painful one.

Giving in to a shiver, she eased up on the accelerator. A death grip on the wheel, she rounded the winding S-curve and spotted the first landmark. Covered by thicket, the cracked boulder sat where it always had—ten feet from the side of the road. Pink quartz with a white vein slashing through the top.

Weak light thrown by her headlights sliced over stone. She pressed on the brake, slowing to a crawl, searching for the mailbox. A minute later, she found it. Dented, neglected, number no longer visible, the faded blue box leaned like a drunk against a tree. Scanning the dark woods beyond it, she turned the wheel. Her tires rolled off asphalt onto gravel. The soothing hum of rubber on blacktop changed to a jagged crunch.

Violet shifted in her car seat. "Mommy."

Creeping up the bumpy drive, Theodora glanced over her shoulder and watched her daughter rub her eyes. Her heart clenched as fierce pride engulfed her. Her baby—so unbelievably precious. A gift, pure and simple. An unexpected addition that changed the course of her life.

Her uncle had not approved. He took one look at her daughter's daddy and said, "No fucking way." But no one could deny Anthony had gifted Violet with all things bright and beautiful: his sharp intelligence, his steely determination, the kind of curiosity Theodora both adored and feared. His warm sienna skin, light brown eyes, and all that soft, curly hair in little-girl form—the dominance of his genes was stamped all over Violet.

Beauty in all its bounty. A gorgeousness Theodora thanked God she woke up to every day.

"Mommy."

"Hey, honey-bunny," she said, smiling over her shoulder. "Almost there. We'll be out of the car in a minute."

"Is Auntie BB here?"

"Yes, my love. She's meeting us at the cabin."

Smiling back in delight, Violet repositioned the pale pink rabbit in her lap. Big floppy ears. Black button nose. Whiskers shorn short on one side—an experiment gone wrong with a pair of child-safe scissors. The stuffed animal had survived. Violet had spent the rest of the day in tears, worried her *friend* needed to go to the hospital.

"How's Lulu doing?"

"Good, Mommy, but her bum's sore."

"I can imagine," Theodora murmured, understanding the rabbit's complaint. Three nights stuck in a car. Three days spent in cramped motel rooms, mostly out of view. A few trips to the nearest grocery store and playgrounds. Not a lot of fun for bunnies and moms of three-year-olds, never mind three-year-olds. "Gonna get you both unbuckled soon."

"Okay." Rubbing Lulu's fake fur, Violet stuck her thumb in her month. Light brown eyes wide and curious, she looked out the window.

Nothing but thick shadows and miles of forest. No light up ahead, but that didn't mean anything.

Beatrice wouldn't announce her presence. She wouldn't flip on the outside lights even if the electricity still worked. Theodora sighed. Twenty years without a resident, Aunt Jean's cottage was nothing but a relic now. A log cabin set close to a river full of great childhood memories, replaced now by shadowed sorrows. The last place she'd felt safe, where she laughed and ran wild with her twin, a warm bastion standing between her and the other side of the family.

The dangerous one her father married into without understanding what it meant.

A fatal mistake. For him first, then for Anthony.

Her throat tightened at the thought.

Pushing through the fear, Theodora pointed the nose of the car up the lane. She didn't have proof Anthony was dead. Maybe her uncle had scared him off. Maybe he'd swallowed his pride and paid him to leave.

She clenched her teeth. A lovely bit of fiction, but no matter how many times she tried to convince herself her former boyfriend was on a beach in the Bahamas living the good life, she didn't believe it. The family didn't work that way. Once an insult was given—real or imagined—death came fast on its heels.

Navigating in the dark, she shoved all the *what-ifs* into the back of her mind. She didn't have time to rehash the past, or wonder why God saw fit to set her down inside a family who excelled at violence, not kindness. She'd asked those questions before and never gotten any answers. Nothing left to do now but pray her sister came with her this time, instead of staying mired in the dysfunction, doing things she didn't want to do, in the hopes of protecting Theodora's back.

Light from the headlights cutting a swath over a carpet of pine needles, Theodora followed the grooves worn in the dirt lane. The tires bumped along ruts. The Impala swayed side to side as crooked claws of untrimmed branches brushed against steel. To be expected. No one maintained the driveway anymore. No one paid attention to her aunt's place at all.

Neglect by design. The only safe house she and her sister used. One she prayed her uncle never learned existed.

Powering up the hill, she drove into the clearing at the top of the rise. A quick scan gave her the lay of the land. Overgrown thicket surrounded the A-frame. A compact SUV parked in front of what used to be the carport. Weathered by time, damaged by heavy snowfall in the winter, the roof had caved in, leaving the wooden uprights to stare down at the rubble piled between their concrete feet.

Heart hammering, she looked right and left, then back at the cottage. Log walls with light mortar layered between horizontal timbers notched at the corners. Sharply pitched roof with gaps between the decaying cedar shingles. A crumbling chimney pointed skyward. Once bright blue, now worn by weather, the front door stood sentry alongside windows that no longer opened, but kept the weather out.

A memory assaulted her.

The image surfaced like jetsam churned up by mental propellers. Two pairs of canary-yellow boots sitting on the porch. One set had belonged to her, the other to Beatrice. Identical footwear for twin girls who looked alike on the outside, but were anything but on the inside. Their aunt's idea, one she and Beatrice both fought. Identical, after all, didn't mean the same. Never had, never would. All the proof she required lay in the fact she'd run, escaping the darkness and the monsters inside it, while her twin stayed to fight.

Her burden to bear. She'd had a different battle on her hands.

Angling off to one side, Theodora rolled to a stop and put the Impala in park. An awful sense of dread slithered through her. She sat unmoving with the engine running, staring at the house, wondering if she'd made a mistake. She trusted her sister, but her uncle wasn't an idiot. He hadn't taken control of the Bratva, become a Pakhan in the Russian organized crime syndicate, by being a fool. With some skill, and a lot of luck, she'd managed to hide from him the last four years, but all good things came to an end...eventually.

The flashy SUV looked like something her sister would drive, but—

A tiny flame flared in the window next to the front door.

Gripping the steering wheel, Theodora exhaled in relief. No one but she and Beatrice knew the signal. A single candle burning in the window relayed the message: all clear, safe and secure.

Bowing her head, she closed her eyes, sent a silent thank you heavenward, and shut down the engine. Leaving the keys in the ignition, she smiled at Violet, then popped the handle and swung the door wide. Old hinges creaked in protest. Grabbing the backpack off the passenger seat, Theodora paid the complaint no mind.

The Impala might be ancient, but it had done its job and gotten her to Aunt Jean's in one piece. Provided a safe haven for her child while she outran the hunters. Made escape possible while leaving nothing but exhaust fumes in her wake.

Almost four years of the same.

Most would think she'd be accustomed to hiding by now—that somewhere along the way, covering her tracks would become as natural to her as breathing. Sad to say, but being someone else, answering to another's name, never got easier. The more she changed locations and jobs, the less familiar running became. Every time she rented a new apartment in a strange place, she mourned the fact her daughter would never have a regular life. Never know anything but running and hiding. A future without roots.

Slinging the backpack over one shoulder, Theodora opened the rear door and leaned in. Gorgeous light brown eyes met hers. She smiled at Violet. Her daughter grinned back, baby teeth flashing, not a care in the world, having no idea frequent address changes and cross-country trips weren't normal.

"Ready?" she asked, pressing the button to unclip the shoulder harness on the car seat. Eager to get out, Violet wiggled, little feet paddling as the prongs disengaged from the locking mechanism. "Hungry?"

"I want an apples, Mommy."

"What do you say?"

"Please."

With a nod, Theodora helped Violet climb out of her seat with one hand and set the backpack on the seat with the other. She unzipped the top and, yanking the canvas sides wide, peered inside. Pre-cut fresh fruit sat in small containers. Shoving the strawberries and pineapple aside, she unearthed the green apples and popped the top. Already up on her knees on the bench seat, Violet reached in, little fingers working to pull out a slice. Curling her hand around one, she grabbed Lulu by an ear and hopped forward.

Container in hand, pack settled on her back, she caught Violet mid-jump. Tucking her close, she pressed a flurry of kisses against the side of her neck. Her daughter giggled as she handed her the apple slices. As she settled Violet on her hip, Theodora turned toward the cabin.

"Hang on tight to Lulu, honey-bunny. Don't let her fall."

"I got her. She won't fall."

"Okay."

After pressing another kiss to her daughter's temple, she released a deep breath and moved toward the A-frame. Pine needles rustled underfoot. Tousled by a breeze, tree limbs creaked at the edge of clearing as the river rumbled in the distance. Less than a mile away. A favorite haunt of hers before her father died and the world turned upside down. A place she'd explored and felt comfortable when she was allowed to visit her aunt.

Eleven years old. The last time she'd felt safe.

Haunted by the past, Theodora ignored the chill in the air and kept walking, moving beneath scant moonlight toward the porch. Cast in shadow, the narrow bit of real estate occupied the entire front of the cabin, wooden planks twisted in places, dipping low in others. Her gaze tracked back to the candle on the windowsill. The flame danced behind warped glass, throwing light, drawing her in, reminding her of what it represented.

Refuge. Comfort. *Home.* Not a place, but a person. A sanctuary no matter the location. Beatrice was hers; Theodora was her sister's. Even so, she stayed sharp, took her time, looked over open terrain to the forest's edge, searching for trouble.

Old habits died hard.

Years of keeping her eyes and ears open, knowing when to move and when to stay put, had taught her well. Constant vigilance. *Things aren't always what they seem.* Interesting mantra. Second nature to a girl raised in uncertain circumstances, with people who couldn't be trusted.

Stepping onto the cracked concrete walk, Theodora hitched her daughter higher and dragged her attention from the forest. She looked behind her, then checked the south side of the property. Raised garden beds overgrown by weeds to her left. An old shed listing on the side near the edge of the clearing. A rusty lawn mower parked beside the skeletal remains of a small greenhouse. A clear expanse of undisturbed dirt around the house. No footprints. No recent tire tracks other than the SUV in the driveway.

No need for alarm.

Moss-covered treads groaned as she mounted the steps. Candlelight flickered through the window. She crossed the deck to the door. Wood planks squeaked. Pausing beneath the eaves of the sagging roofline, she listened a moment. All quiet. No movement inside. Not a surprise. Beatrice knew the drill. She wouldn't make a sound until Theodora stood inside, the door safely closed behind her.

Which made her move a little faster.

She hadn't seen her sister in years. Infrequent chats helped ease the loneliness, but never really satisfied. Nothing beat a tight hug, or sitting across a kitchen table while sharing a meal, a drink, and a laugh.

Excited by the idea she would get to do all three tonight, Theodora reached for the handle. Cold metal settled in her hand. The latch clicked. She pushed. The door swung open without making a sound. Putting her feet in gear, she crossed the threshold and—

"You're a difficult woman to find, pigeon," a man said, Russian accent slithering across open plan kitchen-living-dining rooms. "Nicoli had high hopes, but I was sure you wouldn't show."

She froze.

Fighting the urge to flee, Theodora glanced into the gloom. Her gaze landed on the last person she wanted to see, never mind encounter in a desolate cabin deep in the woods. The bottom fell out of her stomach. Her skin prickled in warning, making her quiver.

Markov shifted in his seat. The dingy kitchen chair he sat in creaked as he prepared to give chase.

She refused to give him the satisfaction.

Running would be necessary—eventually—but she needed to time it right. Strategy meant everything when dealing with Markov. Play her hand too soon, and she wouldn't get away. A solid plan, but as he stared at her, her resolve weakened. Another shiver worked its way loose.

He smiled.

Squaring her shoulders, she shifted Violet to her other side, keeping her body between him and her daughter, and looked him in the eye. Not much about him had changed in the time she'd been gone. Relaxed posture. Rapacious features set in sharp lines. Pale blue eyes hungry on her. Markov the Monster—a captain in the Bratva, her uncle's favorite thug, and her worst nightmare.

Putting on a brave face, she raised her chin. "What have you done to Bea?"

"Trixie will no longer be of any help to you."

The muscles bracketing her spine tensed. *Trixie.* Her sister's nickname. One given to her by the men inside the Bratva to celebrate her cleverness. The idiots considered it a compliment. Beatrice never had, disliking being labeled a trickster—the shrewd, brazen one, not the accomplished businesswoman. Never the savvy entrepreneur with a mind most CEOs would envy.

"Did you kill her?" she asked, dreading the answer. "Is she dead?"

"Not when I left her."

Fuck.

Shit.

*Fucking shit.*

Markov's lips tipped up at the corners. "Far as I know, she's in good hands."

*In good hands.*

Message received with no need for interpretation. She knew exactly what he meant. Beatrice was now at the mercy of a man who possessed none. Under her uncle's full control—contained, trapped, no doubt in a world of pain right now.

She wanted to close her eyes at the news, to scream in denial and charged out to find her sister. Her gaze stayed locked on Markov instead.

"If she's—"

"Your uncle decides her fate, *dorogoy*, not me," he said, calling her sweetheart in Russian, making her stomach twist.

Acid hit the back of her throat. She clenched her teeth to keep from throwing up.

A pleased look on his face, he turned a short piece

of half-carved branch in his hand. She didn't care about the stick. The knife in his other hand, however, caught and held her attention. Without a weapon, the guy was cruel. With one, he was downright sadistic. Rotating the dagger in his hand, he wiped the curved blade across the top of his thigh.

Steel *zinged* across the material of his suit pants.

"Come in and close the door, Theodora. We have much to discuss."

Holding Violet tighter, she shook her head. "I'm leaving."

"This you could do, but a warning before you decide. I have men stationed outside, ones you did not see upon entering. Do as I ask, and they will be left out of it. Fight and you will be returned to your uncle in a body bag after I am through with you." He shrugged, as though the outcome—her alive or dead —was all the same to him. "Four years, little dove. Four years spent chasing you. You've made a laughing-stock of him. The other Pakhan whisper behind his back, calling him weak for allowing your defiance. Your uncle has washed his hands of you and…"

He paused.

His focus cut to Violet. He trailed his gaze over her inky curls and brown skin.

She cupped her daughter's head, pressing her head beneath her chin, covering her ear with her palm, blocking the monster's view of her, protecting Violet the only way she knew how.

"You know Nicoli never wanted the child."

"I'm aware." The entire reason she'd found the courage to run before her uncle forced her into the clinic.

"He has given me permission to deal with you as I see fit. I have full authority here."

"What do you want?"

"What I have always wanted, *dorogoy*—you. On your knees. In my bed. Full access. The more you make it worth my while, the longer you and the girl live."

Shifting forward in the chair, he set his elbows on his bent knees, knife in hand, cold gaze on her. "Now, you have a decision to make. And a minute to make it."

Heart pounding in her chest, Theodora swallowed.

Markov raised a brow, waiting for her answer.

Death now, or months of torture followed by death later.

She knew it would come to this one day. If she was foolish enough to get caught.

Growing up in the shadow of the Bratva, she'd been made to understand early and often, had seen it done time and again. Betraying her uncle meant instant exile and certain death...even for a family member. Which meant Markov's offer left her no real choice at all.

The instant he grew bored, she and Violet were dead.

Better to try for freedom now than be trapped with no chance of escape later. A huge gamble, given she was outmanned and outgunned. Some things, however, couldn't be helped. She would never submit to Markov.

*Never.*

The word echoed through her, tolling a bell, insisting she be brave. The fierce need to protect her child pushed to the surface. Heart raging, she felt adrenaline hit her like rocket fuel. Theodora spun toward the open door. She sprinted across the porch and, holding Violet tight to her front, jumped off the edge.

Her feet slammed down on damp turf.

The container full of apple slices went flying.

Violet whimpered.

Markov laughed behind her.

The man leaning against the side of her car straightened.

Theodora veered left and, running flat out, reached the edge of the clearing.

"Mommy."

"Hold tight, baby. Hold tight," she rasped, legs firing like pistons, entering the forest at full tilt.

She knew the woods well. Spent hours playing amongst the trees as a child. Remembered every root, trail, and outcropping. If she made it to the bluff and the river's edge, she might have a chance of evading her uncle's men. If Markov and his thugs caught her before then, well...

She refused to think about it.

A shotgun racked behind her. Markov yelled for his men to run her to ground. Heavy footfalls crunched over uneven ground, echoing through the trees.

Theodora pushed harder, holding out hope even though she knew there wasn't any to be found. Her luck had just run out. Four years of defiance. Four years of hiding. Four years of believing she could have a better life. All of it for nothing, given she'd landed her here. In the woods with madmen, playing a game of cat and mouse she had very little chance of winning.

**4**

———

Standing on top of a cliff, Angela grappled with the need to throw up. Strong winds blustered across the narrow ledge. Nine feet deep, twenty feet long. A sliver of jagged rock that sliced into the black of night.

So little square footage.

So freaking high up.

Nothing but a splintered spine jutting off the north face of Mount Rainier, below fast-moving clouds, above certain death if she did what Sloan wanted and jumped into the toothy abyss.

Bile sloshed in the pit of her stomach. A bad taste entered her mouth.

She swallowed, killing the urge to back away from the five-thousand-foot drop.

The instinct was a good one. Any sane person would feel the same. Do the smart thing, say no way in hell, and demand to be taken back home—immediately. An understandable reaction to the reality of what stared her in the face. Problem was...

She wasn't normal anymore.

Not since waking up in Black Diamond's gymnasium changed beyond all recognition.

She'd known something was wrong for a while. The shimmy and shake, the tremor of physical disarray, hadn't been hiding. The changes started small—a whisper of intuition here, a spike of physical enhancement and sensory perception there. Continuous, tiny quakes. The opening of slim fissures deep inside her. She sensed each break, the slicing tears along with the tuck and draw of sutures as an invisible force stitched her back together. The slow knitting of two separate entities—human and dragon halves—to make a greater whole.

She hadn't understood it then. Couldn't say she did now, either.

Confusion arrived with the changes. Questions followed. How could the injection of a serum engineered in a laboratory cause such a massive shift in her cellular makeup? How had magic seeped into her blood and bones, shearing off huge chunks of her, only to replace it with something else? Something more. Something different. Something powerful. Would she ever become accustomed to and accept it— the monster who now owned one half of her whole?

Yes.

Questions. Tons of them.

No one, least of all her, expected her metamorphosis. In a single night, her world had tilted, been flipped on its edge and left to teeter. Neat and tidy no longer applied to her, so forget normal.

*Normal* was nothing but a memory. Command of her mind and body had been taken from her, stolen months ago by a madman with a syringe in a laboratory. One with sadistic tendencies and boundary issues, but...

*C'est la vie.*

Replaying her kidnapping, and the abuse she suffered at the hands of the Razorback pack, wouldn't serve her. The past had flown along with her choice in the matter. No changing course now. Nothing left to do but move forward. Become one with her dragon half. Trust that she'd be all right in the end.

A lofty goal. Super-healthy mindset.

Nothing but a bunch of psychobabble bullshit, given every time she tried to progress—move on and find level—life threw her another curveball, yanking her back into uncertainty.

Which left her standing on top of a cliff in the middle of the night, struggling to embrace her new normal for the umpteenth time in as many months. Rikar helped, providing a safe place for her to land. Each day, every night. Always supportive. Always loving. Forever playful. His understanding went a long way to soothing her wounded soul, giving back what had been taken from her, but...

He couldn't help her. Not now.

Angela understood why he'd opted out tonight. She might not like it—and neither did he—but Sloan was right. Having her mate cliff-side would make things worse, not better. Rikar wouldn't push her. The bond she shared with him would skew his objectivity. He'd balk the instant she became uncomfortable. Sloan would push back, assert his rights as her mentor (a role held in high esteem by Dragonkind, which meant his opinion superseded Rikar's when it came to her training), and force the issue.

Bad things would follow. Of the explosive variety.

The kind of chaos that stripped scales off dragons and woke mountains. And no one (other than Wick) wanted that kind of calamity. Wick might love the idea of volcanic ash clouds and lava flow, but none of the other Nightfury warriors did, which meant she needed to stop stalling. Avoiding the inevitable wasn't her style.

Still, jumping off a cliff seemed extreme. Even for the Sloan and the crazy-ass Metallics.

Staring at the lip of the ledge, Angela drew in a breath. She counted to twenty-five, then recited the numbers backward. Inside her head, of course. Sloan didn't need to know her knees quivered, threatening to buckle, or that—

"Ange."

She didn't need to look at him to know where Sloan stood. Radar up and running, her dragon half provided the details with uncanny exactitude. Information streamed into her head: accurate air temperature to the decimal point, precise measurement of wind gusts scoring over the mountainside, every star hiding behind thick cloud cover, the murder of crows nesting ten miles away in a cluster of pines.

Nothing escaped her perception. With magic frothing in her veins, she knew where each member of her dragon combat training team stood, perched, and flew.

"Ange," Sloan murmured again.

"Give me a second."

"Darlin'."

Bare feet crossed at the ankles, hands shoved into his jean pockets, Sloan shoved away from his lean against uneven rock wall behind her. Black eyes with a hint of green glowed against his umber skin. Beautiful combination. Tall. Dark. So handsome he possessed the power to take most girls' breath away. But not her. She loved him in her own way, but Rikar was her jam. Her be-all and end-all. The entire reason she opened her eyes each morning.

"What's the problem?" Sloan asked.

She threw him incredulous look. "Seriously?"

His lips twitched. "We went over this at home."

"You didn't tell me I'd have to jump off a cliff."

"Course not. Do I look dumb? You would've refused to come."

"Damn straight," she muttered, trying to ignore the sheer drop in front of her. Another gust buffeted her, making her shiver with unease. Her hands went cold. She flexed her fingers, trying to restart her circulation. "Why here?"

"Over five thousand feet to play with. Lots of room for you to get and stay airborne."

Crap.

He was making sense.

She resented the hell out of him for that right now, even though she knew he was right. She needed a launch pad—a high one, given her failed experiment off Black Diamond's roof. She hadn't been able propel herself skyward and ended up crash-landing in Mac's outdoor swimming pool. Not fun. Particularly since the instant she splashed down, water turned to ice, trapping one of her wings in what amounted to an iceberg. It had taken her half an hour (and a lot of swearing) to figure out how to use her magic to extricate herself from the situation.

"Ange, seriously...like a Band-Aid. Rip it the hell off."

"Easy for you to say. You know how to fly."

He huffed in amusement.

She sighed. Hell. Nothing for it. Being truthful was key. Sloan kept telling her that she needed to talk openly during dragon combat training. He reiterated the message on a regular basis. She'd never taken it to heart until now.

"Listen..."

She paused.

He raised a brow. "What?"

"I'm, ah...not a big fan of heights."

A snort sounded above her.

Angela looked up.

Hanging off the underside of the ledge a hundred feet above her head, bronze scales shimmering in the patchy light, Gage chuckled. "You're afraid of heights?"

She scowled at him. "Don't start."

Ignoring the warning, he grinned, baring huge fangs. "A dragon afraid of heights. Shit, Sloan...I can die happy. I've seen it all now."

"Swear to God, Gage," she said. "The second I figure this out, I'm kicking your ass."

"Looking forward to that." Shiny golden scales winking in weak moon glow, Nian popped his head above the jagged ridge. Eyes the color of multi-hued opals met hers. "Ice daggers at a hundred paces. Gage trapped inside a giant iceberg. You do that, I'll buy you whatever you want."

"Deal," she said, smiling at him.

Sloan frowned. "Rikar'll rip your horns off if you give her a gift."

"They'll grow back," Nian said, shrugging off the threat a second before static washed in, expanding inside her head.

Pain rapped against her temples. She winced, then closed her eyes, concentrating as her mind tunneled. Discomfort morphed into a hiss, then exploded outward, rampaging into tiny threads inside her head. Doing as Sloan taught her, Angela collected the spindles, merging individual strings into a whole. The cord whiplashed. She grabbed the tail end, wrapping it up and over, controlling the coil until it arrowed and sped off in one direction.

A link opened into mind-speak.

*"What's the hold-up?"* Haider asked, deep voice echoing inside her head. Moving like a missile, his silver scales flashed overhead. The smell of rain blew in. Dust billowed up. Small rocks rocketed down the mountainside. *"Thought we were good to go."*

*"Ange doesn't want to jump,"* Gage said, re-folding his wings. *"She's afraid of—"*

Angela growled. *"You always this much of a jerk?"*

*"Jump, Ange,"* Gage said, showing no sympathy. *"The longer you stall, the harder it'll become. Sloan, we talked about this. You're gonna have to—"*

*"I'm not throwing her over the edge, asshole,"* Sloan said, glaring up at Gage. *"She needs to do it herself. Otherwise, she'll always wonder...hesitate. Not a good start. You wanna explain that clusterfuck to Rikar?"*

Gage said something else.

Haider chimed in.

Angela ignored the budding argument. Let the boys squabble. She needed a moment, just a couple of seconds to get her affairs in order. Mind. Body. Spirit. She could do it. Collect her magic. Connect to her dragon half. Fly for the very first time. A lot to ask, given she'd only made the shift from human to dragon form at Black Diamond. Always with Rikar's help, but she refused to split hairs. Or dwell on that scary fact now.

Sloan wouldn't allow her to die.

Not on purpose, anyway, so...now or never.

Courage was a choice, not a feeling. She must make her stand tonight. No backing down. No more talking herself out of it. Rikar and the other Nightfuries were counting on her. She needed to start strong, conquer her fear, and fly in the face of the unknown.

Staring at a spot beyond the edge, she retreated

toward the rough stone wall behind her. Her shoulder blades collided with sheer cliff face. Nian met her gaze. She nodded. He tipped his chin and disappeared from view, giving her a clear shot into open air.

"Screw it," she whispered. "Gotta die sometime."

Palms pressed to cold rock, balanced on the balls of her feet, she pushed away from the wall. Her boot soles rasped over stone. Her heart went into overdrive, hammering the inside of her chest as she ramped into a run. Common sense screamed for her to stop. Duty and the need to know urged her on, propelling her toward the possibility of success.

Gaze riveted to the edge, she gauged the distance to free fall. Instinct took over, timing her vault into open air. Rapid footfalls punched through the quiet. The wind caught and held, snatching the sound away. Inhaling hard, she planted her foot on the edge and leapt, vaulting into the black. Pale stone flashed below her as Nian surged off the cliff face.

The argument died as the boys shut up.

Sloan mobilized behind her.

With a growl of approval, Gage took flight.

Ripped from the mountain by his claws, shale rained down as she left the safety of the ledge. A powerful updraft ripped at her clothes. Cold air blasted into her face. Exhilaration took hold as gravity let her fly before grabbing hold.

Suspended in midair, Angela prayed practice made perfect. She reached across the divide, hoping her dragon half allowed her to shift. Not a foregone conclusion. Transforming never came easy, but without Rikar to guide her, connecting to the beast living inside her became even more difficult. The link between her two halves wasn't fully integrated yet, and wouldn't be until she spent a considerable amount of time in dragon form.

Tonight wasn't about perfection. Here and now was about forging a strong bond, one that, if done right, would last a lifetime. Centuries, if she got lucky and didn't face-plant into the base of Mount Rainier.

Still in human form, she fell toward the base of the cliff.

She murmured to her beast, feeling it turn toward her.

*Come on, baby. Fly with me.*

Spiking sensation rushed down her spine. Arctic chill bubbled through the surface of her skin.

Her night vision sparked. A ripple of frost blew from her fingertips. Ice chips exploded from her spine. Damp air turned crisp as raindrops transformed into snowflakes. Thick flurries swirled in powerful wind gusts. Clear night air detonated into a full-blown winter storm, and—

*Presto-change-o.*

Her hands and feet turned to talons, her nails to razor-sharp claws. Ice-blue scales tipped with auburn fell like dominoes, wrapping her in armored dragon skin. Spiked tail lashing through the blizzard, Angela bared her fangs, snarling in delight as air filled the webbing of her winter-white wings. She laughed. A second later, she lost control, wings seesawing as gravity laughed right back, and she plummeted toward the rocks below.

**5**

---

Sloan cursed under his breath as Angela sprinted toward the edge. Staring at her in disbelief, he frowned. *Goddamn it.* She'd done it again, surprised him for the...shit, he didn't know. He'd lost track, along with a running tally, days ago. Which was a problem. Being off guard wasn't something he needed to be while protecting Rikar's mate.

He gritted his teeth.

Freaking female. So completely unpredictable.

He should be accustomed to her balls-to-the-wall attitude by now. He wanted to say he was a fast learner, but after less than a week as her mentor, Sloan feared he was wrong. He'd calculated the odds the instant he set her down on the narrow mountain ledge. Math was his favorite subject. He rarely miscalculated, and figured it would take another half an hour (minimum) to talk her into jumping.

Angela Keen. Bravest female he knew. Total pain in his ass.

Biting down on a curse, he watched her leap without looking. She sailed into open air. As she disappeared into the abyss, falling fast in human form, he sprinted toward the cliff. Vast panoramic views laid out in front of him. Thick forest in the distance. The snarl of a jagged mountain spine above him. Moonlight playing peekaboo between thick clouds as the scent of snow and pine combined, supercharging his senses.

His bare foot connected with the edge.

Reading the wind, eyes trained on the rocky expanse below, he leapt up and out. His gaze snagged on Angela. He witnessed her transform and spread her wings. Beautiful ice-blue scales tipped with auburn flashed in the gloom.

He grinned.

Nian whooped.

Gage grunted in approval.

"*Right on,*" Haider muttered, streaking like a silver bullet overhead.

Laughing, Angela angled into a turn. An updraft caught the webbing of her snow-white wings. Her velocity spiked. Her trajectory changed. Too much, too fast. Wind shear blew her sideways. One of her wingtips dipped, carving a path through unstable air. Contrails drew lines through the dark, jetting white behind her. She went topsy-turvy, then twisted into a nosedive. One wing folded, the other stretched wide, she tried to course-correct. Powerful gusts buffeted her, tossing her the other way, sending her into a death spiral.

"*Fuck,*" Gage growled.

Angela gasped. "*Shit.*"

Sloan shifted, moving from human to dragon form. Dark brown scales shimmering green and gold in the low light, he abandoned his original plan and put another into play. "*Nian, pull her out of it.*"

"*On it.*" Little more than a blurry streak, Nian rocketed beneath her.

A second before Angela collided with him, he opened his wings. Golden scales glimmered. Magic exploded in a multicolored shimmer around him. The blast pushed skyward. Wind blew straight up, creating a vertical tunnel. Caught in the vent, Angela stopped falling and started floating on a pocket of stabilized air.

"*Holy hell,*" she rasped, bobbing like a jellyfish in high current.

"*Open your wings, Ange,*" Sloan said, flying in above her. Wings spread wide, he mirrored Nian, creating a safe zone for Angela. "*Follow Nian's movements...the angle of his wings, tail and body position. Fly as we fly.*"

Held safe between Sloan and his brother-in-arms, Angela listened, stretching out, angling into each turn, soaring across open skies, above the treetops, becoming one with her dragon half.

Sloan watched it happen.

One moment, she fought the glide. The next, her ruffled scales settled, smoothing into aerodynamic arrows against her sides. Disjointed before, her spikes snaked into alignment along her spine. She flapped her wings, holding her own as he and Nian decreased the protective bubble around her.

She rotated into a slow flip. One way, then the other.

He and Nian moved in sync, following her lead across the dark sky. One below her, one above. A beautiful dance. Two males and the impossible—a she-dragon, the first of her kind in centuries—bonding in flight.

Sloan stayed quiet.

Nian said nothing.

Very different than a Dragonkind male's first flight.

Gentle, not jagged. Smooth, not violent. Settled and unhurried.

Without making a sound, Gage flew in alongside her. Haider set up shop on her other side, creating a makeshift fighting triangle, enjoying the gentle sway, absorbing the gift of watching Angela soar for the first time. Pure beauty, her two halves merging to create a whole, accompanied by the quiet hum of the forest and crisp northern winds.

Much smaller than her packmates, Angela was power tempered by grace, delicate lines touched by an elegance no male would ever manage. She ascended and dove, flipping and vaulting, testing her limits, becoming accustomed to her new form, sharing something beautiful with her packmates.

Deep in the wilderness, Sloan checked his sightlines. Mount Rainier behind him. Toothy ridges smoothing into sloping foothills to his right. Seattle a hundred miles to the north. Black Diamond a short forty-five-minute flight away. Clear, open skies. Crisp, fresh air. A fantastic night to fly, but...

Probably time to shut it down.

Angela was flying well on her own now. No need for support. No worries she'd fall out of the sky, so no need to push her training any further tonight.

Rikar was no doubt at home pacing a hole in the living room floor while Bastian watched, making sure his best friend adhered to protocol. Or, at very least, didn't do anything stupid—like challenge Mac to hand-to-hand combat.

The Nightfury warriors called the weekly bouts *friendly*. Sloan didn't agree, given the amount of blood that flowed from the warrior stupid enough to step into the ring with Mac. The male knew kung fu and wasn't shy when using his fists and feet to beat the shit out of people—a tremendous attribute when fighting the Razorback pack. Vicious and lethal was, after all, a combination welcome in war, but...shit. Mac was brutal. He'd gone toe to toe with the male once inside Black Diamond's sparing gym. Once ended up being enough. Broken bones hurt like a bitch when sitting in front of his computer digging up dirt on the enemy, so...

Decision made.

Hard pass on entering the ring again. One and done, an experience never to be repeated with Mac. Which left him free to fly all night if he wanted, but Rikar wouldn't wait that long. The Nightfury first-in-command would lose his mind if he didn't return Angela to Black Diamond soon. And since a smart male knew when to stop—time to cut the silent flight short and move on to the next thing...teaching Angela how to land.

*"Ange."*

*"Yeah."*

*"You good?"*

*"Feels awesome."* Wings undulating on a strong surge, she spiraled up toward the moon. *"Is it always like this?"*

Gage huffed. *"Usually, there's a lot more screaming."*

Nian laughed. *"And blood."*

*"Followed by dead Razorbacks and a sky full of dragon ash,"* Haider said, thumping Sloan with the side of his spiked tail.

The spikes along his spine rattled. Throwing an amused glance at his friend, Sloan grinned. *"Cabin fever, H?"*

Haider shrugged. *"Haven't gotten my claws in one of those assholes in over a week. Feeling the need for some action. Any news?"*

*"Lots of it."* Too much, actually. Sloan shook his head, thinking about all the projects he had on the go.

He would never admit it to Bastian or his brothers-in-arms, but he felt the pressure. The list of his responsibilities seemed endless. Being Angela's mentor. Finding a way to trap and contain Ivar while rescuing the females the Razorbacks had kidnapped and now held captive inside their lair before the Meridian realigned in four days and they ended up dead. The clusterfuck of Zidane and his death squad landing and putting down roots in Seattle. The coalition he was trying to build, one designed to change the power dynamic and oust the Archguard from Prague. With Rodin, leader of the Archguard, making moves, ill-advised ones, the future of Dragonkind hung in the balance, and...

Around his neck.

Attacking the tension, Sloan upped his wing speed. Taut muscles stretched, bringing some relief as he lined up and assessed his priorities.

*"Start talking, Sloan,"* Angela said, picking up on his unease. *"You keep forgetting, but you're not alone in this, man. Lay it out for us."*

He glanced at Angela.

She tipped her chin, encouraging him. Unaccustomed to sharing his thoughts with anyone, Sloan hesitated. She thumped him with the side of her tail, nailing him in the ribcage. Razor-sharp spikes nicked him. He huffed in discomfort, resisting the advice, but...

New to Dragonkind or not, she was right. She was wise. She knew him better than anyone. Enough to know staying silent always came back to bite him in the ass. He needed to learn to share. Flexing his talon, Sloan shook his head. He promised himself he'd do better. Become a better pack mate, let his brothers-in-arms in, but...man. He sucked at it. Had for years, remaining self-contained, part of the Nightfury pack, but separate somehow.

"*Give,*" Angela said.

Sloan cleared his throat. "*Meet's set with the Scottish pack.*"

"*When?*" Nian and Gage asked at the same time.

"*Three days. Ivy and her mate have pulled Cyprus on board,*" Sloan said, thanking the goddess for the green-eyed redhead mated to one of the Scottish warriors. She'd done all the legwork—convinced Tydrin, who in turn convinced his blood brother Cyprus (commander of the Scottish pack) to accept Bastian's call. "*Forge is uneasy, but is willing to roll with it.*"

Gage grunted. "*Hope's going to have her hands full keeping him even through that shit, but if we can get the Scottish pack on board—*"

"*We've got a chance at building a strong coalition,*" Sloan said, fighting to stay rooted in the facts, in the challenges and difficulties, and contain the hope of what the future might hold. Freedom. Equality. A shot at real change—a roundtable mentality where each pack's voice was heard instead of being snuffed out by the heavy hand of a dictatorship. "*The beginnings of one, anyway.*"

"*I'm working that angle too, Sloan,*" Haider murmured, somersaulting into a sideways flip, shifting positions with Gage. "*We've reached out to the other packs on our list. No callbacks yet, but—*"

"*It'll come,*" Nian said, sounding confident. A good thing, given no one knew the commanders of those Dragonkind packs better than Nian. Gage and Haider had traveled to Europe. Both understood the political landscape, but Nian had been one of the bastards.

Planted inside the inner sanctum. A member of the Archguard, an elite amongst the elite, a prince among warriors. The male possessed contacts not even Bastian (a warrior revered among Dragonkind) could tap. *"We were careful. We chose well. Two or three plus the Scots and the foundation will be set. Once done, we go after Rodin and the Archguard. Full force, no holds barred."*

His brothers-in-arms hummed in agreement.

Angela glanced at him out of the corner of her eye. *"Anything else bothering you?"*

*"The females."*

Gage growled. *"Nothing to be done until Azrad contacts me."*

*"You think he will?"* Arching up, Angela dove over the top of Gage's spine.

*"Male's smart. He'll find a way to get in touch. The instant he does, we move to block Ivar, intercept the females, and get Azrad and his warriors out of harm's way,"* Gage said, swiping at Angela with his paw. Rotating into a backflip, she avoided the strike and flicked the tips of her claws. Gage cursed as a snowball slammed into his face. *"Jesus, Ange."*

She laughed as Gage blinked snow from his eyes.

Sloan grinned. *"If he doesn't, we'll adjust...find a way to deal. In the meantime, we stay the course. Plan's set. We stick to it."*

*"One more thing,"* Angela said, flying on his left wingtip.

Intense hazel eyes met his as he tipped his chin. *"What?"*

*"The Razorbacks."*

*"Ange—"*

*"When do I get a crack at them?"* she asked with a low growl.

He glanced at Haider over the top of her horns.

His friend shook his head in warning. Sloan bit down on a curse. He hated to burst her bubble, but she had a long way to go before he let her anywhere near a battle...and the shitstorm brewing in Seattle.

He understood her drive. Hell, he approved of it. She needed to right the wrongs done to her. Make the Razorbacks pay for usurping her will while she ensured the other females Ivar had imprisoned made it out alive. Lofty goals. Ones Sloan shared. The bastards must be made to answer for their crimes.

Ivar had taken something precious from her, changed her in ways that could never be undone. Didn't matter how well she'd adjusted—or how much she loved her mate. The ends didn't justify the means. Happily-ever-after didn't make the way it started right. A female owned the right to choose. She had a say, a voice. Always. No arguing the point. Forcing one as strong as Angela to submit to something she didn't want was immoral, criminal, just plain cruel.

Sloan wanted to right that wrong just as much as Rikar. He'd grown close to Angela over the last few months. She'd become important to him, like the little sister he never thought he'd have.

"*Ange—*"

"*Seriously, Sloan—when?*"

"*Not for a while. You need to learn to conjure a cloaking spell before—*"

A sharp crack shattered the quiet. Rapid-fire staccato followed, echoing up from down range.

"*What the fuck?*" Gage snapped.

Haider's head jerked as he looked toward Black Diamond. "*Motherf—*"

"*Hellfire,*" Nian growled. "*That's close.*"

"*Shit,*" Sloan said, recognizing the sounds.

"*Gunshots,*" Angela said, gaze searching the

ground. Magic spiked, fogging the air with ice crystals as her sonar powered up. *"Less than ten miles from home."*

Instinct surged. Worry surfaced fast on his heels. *"Ange, don't even think about it. We don't get involved in human problems."*

*"Bullshit,"* she murmured, already ahead of the pack.

*"Fuck, she's fast,"* Gage said, awe in his voice.

With a curse, Sloan shot forward, attempting to stay on her tail, but... Goddess. Gage was right. She was fast, so quick, her velocity was spine-bending. Almost too much for him to handle. Fantastic to witness, but for the fact she was gone. Ignoring protocol, she blasted across the night sky, ice-blue scales flashing as more gunfire rang out, the cop in her frothing as she left her packmates behind.

Struggling to keep up, Sloan flew after her. He cursed under his breath as he lost sight of her. *"Rikar's going to kill me."*

*"Probably,"* Nian muttered back.

*"Say goodbye to your balls,"* Haider added, unhelpfully.

Gage chuckled, but hauled ass, moving like a rocket in Angela's wake, following nothing but a pale streak across the dark sky. Sloan bared his fangs. He couldn't wait to get his claws on her. The second he did, he'd throttle her. First things first, though. He needed to catch up before whatever fight she flew toward landed her in trouble.

## 6

Violet held tight to her chest, Theodora zigzagged between tree trunks. She knew Markov and his crew followed. Not too close. Not all that far away, either. She heard one calling to another, hushed voices echoing through the woods. City boys, each and every one. Something that would help her. Maybe even allow her to evade her uncle's thugs altogether.

High hopes.

Ones that moved toward a pipedream.

No matter what the challenge, Markov would never give up. Neither would any of his men. Too afraid to return to her uncle empty-handed, the pack would follow Markov's lead. Do anything and everything he required to avoid retribution.

Heavy footfalls sounded to her right, tracking her through the thicket. More drifted from her left. Lighter steps. More adept in the underbrush, not making as much noise as the other guy. No doubt someone more experienced at hunting prey—of the human variety.

Hearing the careful movement, she sliced between two massive tree trunks, veering away from whom she guessed was Markov. The ground dipped beneath her feet. She inhaled deep, fighting to draw more oxygen into her lungs. Rapid white puffs of expelled air rose in front of her, accompanying the raging beat of her heart, making her chest hurt and her throat burn.

She kept running. Being caught wasn't an option. She knew it. So did her sister. And yet they'd both managed to screw it up. Beatrice by thinking she could outsmart her uncle, and Theodora by trusting the intel her twin gathered was the truth.

Not her fault. As clever as Beatrice was, her uncle's IQ topped the scales. The fact he'd cracked the code, guessing their game, was just another hit in a long line of them. Unfair? Sure. Predictable? Absolutely. She should never have involved Beatrice. If she'd simply gone out on her own, her sister wouldn't be in danger right now. She would've remained insulated, working the legitimate side of her uncle's many businesses, instead of stuck on the illegal side trying to keep her finger on the pulse in order to ensure Theodora stayed free.

Now, Beatrice was screwed. No one lived long after betraying the Bratva.

Moving fast, but carefully, Theodora pushed the thought from her head. First things first. She couldn't help Beatrice if she didn't get away from Markov. Skirting a rocky outcropping, she continued down slope. She stayed low. She stayed silent. She stayed on target, using landmarks and her knowledge of the terrain to stay ahead of the thugs on her trail.

The thick layer of pine needles helped, cushioning her footfalls, dampening sound. Moving with precision, she took an indirect route toward the river. Keeping to the well-traveled hiking path would've been her first choice, but moonlight made that impossible. Light filtered through the branches, slithering like snakes through the valley. She avoided those patches and crept further away from the main trail. Thick tree branches with leafy canopies spread like wings above her head. Dense shadows aided her cause, keeping her hidden as she traversed the woods. No hesitation. Zero need to check her position or unearth a compass. She knew exactly where she was in the woodland.

Beatrice called the ability uncanny. Theodora didn't know why. She'd always just been this way—more comfortable surrounded by wilderness than concrete and skyscrapers. Just another way she and her twin differed. She liked cookouts and campfires. Beatrice enjoyed haute cuisine and candlelit dinners.

A branch snapped to her right.

Ducking around a boulder, Theodora stopped moving. Crouched deep in the shadows, back pressed against solid rock, she adjusted her hold on Violet. Her daughter took a breath. Knowing what that meant, she pressed her finger to Violet's mouth and breathed, "Quiet."

Spirited, but obedient when it mattered, Violet burrowed in, tucking her head beneath Theodora's chin. Dead leaves rustled. Hushed footfalls sounded, coming from the other side of the boulder. Fear tightened its hold. Desperation struck. Blood rushing in her ears, Theodora picked up a fist-sized rock to protect her child.

So close. Too close. Another few feet, and the guy would be right on top of her.

She had a decision to make—tuck her daughter under the narrow outcropping, under the lip of the stone behind her, and lead Markov away. Or make a break for it and hope, with enough zigzagging between tree trunks, she could continue to outrun them.

The hidden cave she planned to hide inside wasn't far away. Another quarter mile. One step up from the river's edge. No way Markov would find her hidey-hole. If she holed up inside it, after a day or two of searching, the Bratva would give up. The water bottles and snacks inside her backpack would see her through. Twenty-four hours—forty-eight tops—and she'd crawl out and find her way free. Hike north. Locate one of the small towns nestled at the base of the mountains. Use some of her cash and—

Gone.

She'd be *gone*. In the wind. Home free with nothing but—

"Here! I got her!" A snick of a gun cocking sounded at close range. "Don't move, bitch."

Baring her teeth, Theodora spun on the balls of her feet. She caught a flash of the gun barrel leveled at her a second before she raised her hand. Without hesitation, she hurled the rock at his head.

Stone cracked against bone. "Fuck!"

As he stumbled backward, she lunged forward. Arms curled around her daughter, she sprinted through the trees. Muzzle flash sparked through the darkness. Gunfire rang out from multiple directions. Bark above her head exploded. Wood chips hit the side of her head. She felt her skin split open.

As blood ran down her cheek, she dodged, one way, then the other, using the trunks as cover. More gunfire cracked through the quiet. She skittered down the slope, veering toward the bluff.

The river rumbled ahead of her. Men shouted behind her. A *pop, pop, pop* echoed through the trees.

Pain bit into her thigh, the back of her shoulder,

then ripped open her side. Her knees hit the turf, spilling her sideways. Pine needles scattered as she slid over the ground. Violet cried out. Wrapped around her daughter, Theodora collided spine-first with a tree trunk. Blood spilling from open wounds, she gasped as the enormity of her failure sank deep.

She'd failed—at everything. Failed to protect her daughter. Failed to protect her sister. Failed to protect herself. Now, she'd be made to pay the price, and so would they.

## 7

**B**lasting over the treetops, Sloan tracked Angela across the night sky. Ice-blue scales blurred up ahead, on full display without a cloaking spell to hide her. Many fledging warriors had difficulty with invisibility at first. Like landing, conjuring enough energy to hide from humans in dragon form never came easy.

Something Angela knew, which meant—

He was going to kill her. Strip her scales from her hide. Or at least scorch them a bit, given her total disregard for protocol.

A bonehead move. A dangerous one for all of Dragonkind. One Rikar would forgive her for, but Sloan refused to tolerate...or let slide. The mentor-apprentice relationship was an important one. He took it seriously. Angela needed to start doing the same. Otherwise, an already dangerous situation would go sideways in a hurry.

The sound of gunfire rippled, echoing up from the forest floor.

Angela swung into a fast turn. Hazel eyes aglow, she examined the ground. She circled wide, sweeping the area, no doubt trying to get a better look.

More gunshots.

Less than ten seconds away from intercepting her, he flexed his claws and fired up mind-speak. *"Ange—"*

*"Shit,"* she said. *"Sloan, we got a situation."*

*"Beyond the one where I rip your horns off?"*

She huffed. *"Shake it off."*

*"I'm gonna shake something, and it's gonna be—"*

*"Seriously, man—focus. I clock five, no—six...shooting at a woman down there."*

Rocketing in on her wingtip, Sloan wrapped her inside a cloaking spell. As she disappeared inside his web of invisibility, he glanced toward the ground and forgot about yanking the spikes from her spine (one by fucking one). Later would be soon enough to take her to task for her idiocy. Right now, he had a bigger problem on his hands.

Wings angled, he banked into a turn to get a better view. Six males, guns drawn, fanned out, ten feet between them. One female on the run, moving at a steady clip, using the forest as a shield, keeping the bastards at bay while she—

Bright light flashed up through the trees.

He jerked in mid-air, feeling as though he'd been plugged in the chest with a .357 Magnum.

*"Jesus,"* he muttered, trying to catch his breath.

Angela growled. *"Told you. We can't leave her, Sloan."*

*"Not gonna leave her, Ange."* No word of a lie. No way he could leave the female now that he'd gotten a glimpse of her. *"But you—"*

*"What's going on?"* Nian asked, rocketing out of the clouds.

Sloan didn't bother answering. *"Nian and Gage— with Angela. Watch her six, keep her airborne."*

*"Shit,"* Angela grumbled, sounding incensed.

*"Haider—with me."*

His brothers-in-arms all grunted, accepting his command.

Looking for the best insertion point, he assessed the situation. A woman sprinting through the forest, dodging thick trucks, leaping over down logs, skidding down the slope toward the river. Crazy enough in and of itself. Not something he saw every night, but more incredibly, the woman was high-energy. Powerful personified, plugged directly into the Meridian. Her connection to the electrostatic bands converged in her aura, flashing green, gold, yellow, pink, blue, and white through the darkness. A long-tailed streak against the forest floor, her light shone through the thick canopy into the sky.

Unable to dissect the array of color, he frowned. The blend of colors didn't make any sense. Most HE females had two, maybe three distinct hues in their aura. The female running for her life had six. Unusual. Confusing. Too much contradictory information coming from one source.

A male shouted, telling the others to bring her to ground.

Sloan's gut tightened. Logic fell away and instinct took over.

With a snarl, Sloan sliced between two huge pines. Treetops swayed. Thick branches creaked. Smaller ones snapped, blowing sky-high, pinging off his scales as he set down hard. His claws met dirt, carving up the turf as he slid sideways.

He uncloaked.

The male closest to him screamed.

Sloan flicked his tail. A gurgle sounded a second before the bastard's head hit the ground, rolling over raised tree roots. As the decapitated body collided with the ground, Sloan shifted into human form and conjured his clothes. Magic exploded through the forest. Pine needles blasted in all directions as he stomped his feet into his boots. Scales were safer, would give him added protection from flying bullets, but if he stayed in dragon form he couldn't move as swiftly through the forest as the situation required.

Safe was good, but right now, fast equaled better. If he didn't reach the female soon, she'd—

"Here! I got her!" a male yelled. "Don't move, bitch!"

He heard a thud, a curse, then a body hit the turf. A flurry of rapid footfalls came next.

Already running, Sloan tracked the abundance of her bioenergy. Feeling it spark over his skin, he moved to intercept the female racing toward him. The males hunting her could wait. He needed to become her shield. The second he had her in his grasp, Haider would move in and eliminate the threat, leaving nothing but bloody stumps behind.

More gunfire rang out.

Sloan heard her gasp. He saw her fall.

As she slid across dead leaves into the base of a tree, he realized two things at once. One, he'd failed to reach her in time. And two, she had a child cradled in her arms. The mystery of her aura disintegrated. Two auras close together, not one coming from a singular source.

The realization unleashed a wave of fury.

Rage burned through him, suffusing the air. The monster he kept contained burst from its cage. Baring his teeth, he roared. The forest responded, aligning its energy with his, coming alive under his direction. Thick, thorny vines shot from the surface of the earth. Tree limbs grew claws. Razored fingers reached out as the vines slithered like snakes across the ground, searching for prey.

*"Fuck."* A nasty growl followed by a hiss of pain.

Untangling a talon from the barbs of a vine rising to meet him, Haider put on the brakes. Wind billowed. Silver webbing stretched to the maximum, he heaved, flapping his wings, stopping his downward glide. Hanging like a ghoul over the treetops, he launched himself skyward, avoiding the snap of rambling brambles moving in for the kill.

Staying out of range, Haider made another pass. "Sloan—*reel it in, man. Can't land until you get control."*

Sloan ignored the male's pissed-off rumble. He was too far gone, so deep in the fog of war he didn't care if his friend landed. Unwise. A worse offense than the one Angela committed, but...

He didn't need any help.

With the woodland seething, his vines were on track, chasing the males out of the forest, into a clearing up range, slithering around and slicing the ones not fast enough in retreat.

Coming around the base of a thick oak, he slid to a stop beside the female. His night vision sharpened on her. His senses fired. He smelled the blood, understood the extent of her injuries by reading her weakening aura. Less bright, but still blinding, lifeblood leaked out of her while her child wailed.

The sound was both deafening and devastating.

*"Talmina,"* he murmured, calling the female "little one" in Dragonese, warning her of his proximity as he got close. "Hey—"

The child screamed.

His heart squeezed as he got his first look at her. A girl child, aura burning bright pink, blue, and white. Brown hair tumbling in fat ringlets. Smooth complexion, closer to his shade of umber than to her mother's fair skin. Jacket covered in blood. Small face screwed up in fright. Tears streaming down her face she cried, sobbing, "Mommy," as the female shuffled her around, desperate to keep her child from harm.

"Don't," the woman said, baring her teeth as she put her body between him and her daughter. "Don't."

"Easy," he murmured, hearing distant shouts of humans in full retreat. "You need help. You need—"

"Stay back!" She whipped her head around. Straight, dark hair flew, cascading around her head. Jade-green eyes collided with his.

Shock slammed through him.

He knew that face. Had seen it before inside the Luxmore Hotel when he visited, but...

Identical face. Same height and build. Different aura. Different way of holding herself. Different vibe as her bioenergy spiked, reacting to his presence, making his skin prickle. Not the same woman. A lookalike, though, right down to the beauty mark high on her left cheekbone.

"Name?" he said, growling at her.

"Don't—"

"Not gonna hurt you. Here to help."

"You're with..." Losing blood, weakening by the moment, she bit down on a groan. "Him."

"No. Heard the shots, came to investigate. My brothers and I chased the bastards away. Now..." Ignoring her attempts at retreat, he reached out and grabbed her ankle. She kicked out. He held firm and, with a gentle tug, drew her away from the tree. She hissed in warning. He ignored the attitude and, settling into a crouch at her side, yanked her coat open. Feather down puffed out as he searched for bullet wounds. He smelled the blood, but...shit. He couldn't see anything through the bulk and color of her jacket. "Name?"

"Theo," she rasped, losing her ability to fight. "Theodora."

"Violet," a small voice said.

"Sloan," he said, searching inside her jacket. Feeling wetness on the outside of her bulky sweater, he assessed her shoulder wound, then slid his hands down her back over her clothes. "Where else are you hit?"

"Thigh and side. I think...I think..." She trailed off, blinking as she struggled to focus. "It's bad. Side's the worst. I think—"

His fingers met bare skin. Energy zapped him, hitting him like a lightning strike. His dragon half responded, taking a closer look at the female. Finicky by nature, his beast tended to ignore humans—female or otherwise. Something about Theodora, however, grabbed his attention. Abundant energy notwithstanding, her spirit and beauty called to him, urging him to get closer.

"It hurts."

"Theo—"

"I'm cold," she whispered, shivering against him. "Really cold."

"Hold on, baby. Gonna take a closer look. See what's what before I move you, yeah?"

She nodded. "If I don't make it...if I don't—"

"Not gonna happen."

"Take Violet to Memphis Alexander. Lives in New York. Umbridge, Carter, Stern. In Manhattan."

"Is Memphis her sire?"

She shook her head. "Friend."

Searching over her sweater, he located the wet material above her waist. Bullet hole and torn flesh. A kidney shot, a nick to her renal artery. She was losing too much blood. So much fucking blood. He needed to stop the flow, and do it now, otherwise Theodora would die in his arms before he got anywhere near Black Diamond.

Shoving her sweater up, he pressed his hand over the wound. Blood slid between his fingers. The Meridian hummed. Her bioenergy surged. His dragon half snarled, then opened wide, drawing Theodora closer, curling around her, connecting his life force with hers.

Sloan blinked as his mind stilled. Rational thought disappeared, leaving him blank for a moment. Caught in the whirlwind, he felt the burn as the link solidified, then tunneled, drilling deep to unearth his magic.

The tether whiplashed. Powerful energy pulsed through him, then reversed course, flowing back toward Theodora.

She jolted in his arms.

Sloan bit down on a groan as he got his first taste of her. Perfect pitch. Exact frequency. Earthy. Rich. Abundant. His match in every way. The hum sank deep. The buzz lifted him up. Hand pressed to her wound, Sloan shook off the shock and applied steam, pressing, bending the stream, pushing healing energy from his palm into her skin.

"Theo," he murmured, urging her to link in and accept what he offered.

Her eyelashes fluttered. "What're you doing?"

"You feel it?"

"Yes."

"Take it, Theo. Let me feed you."

A second ticked past, then rolled into more.

"Theodora—"

"Is that you?"

"Yeah."

"You're so warm." With a sigh, she drifted into the stream, allowing him to feed her. "It's like the river. I'm floating."

He murmured, responding without words.

Her voice trailed off as the healing energy went to work.

Keeping pressure on the wound, he scooped her and the girl off the ground.

Theodora went limp against him. Violet whimpered in fear.

Sloan called to his vines. The horde changed course, leaving two males to escape unscathed. Within seconds, thick stalks slithered in to surround him. He murmured his wishes. Deadly vines with razor thorns coiled, creating a pedestal. The scent of peat moss and damp loam drifting, he stepped onto the platform. His plant, a monster fed by his magic and made for violence, lifted him skyward.

"*Haider.*" Tilting his head back, he searched the sky beyond the treetops. "*Coming to you.*"

"*You shifting?*"

"*No. I need to keep my hands on her. She'll bleed out if I don't. I need you to fly us home.*" Getting ready to be catapulted skyward, Sloan shoved his other hand under her jacket and beneath her sweater. His skin met hers. Powerful energy swirled. Theodora moaned. Sloan touched his mouth to her temple, strengthening the connection. "*Gage—call home. Put Myst on standby.*"

"*How bad is she?*" Gage asked.

Sloan tucked his mate and her child closer. "*Three bullet wounds. Losing blood.*"

"*Hellfire,*" Nian growled. "*Five minutes later, and she'd be dead.*"

Sloan clenched his teeth at the thought.

*"No time to lose."* Rocketing overhead, Angela pointed her horned head home. *"Let's move."*

She'd get no argument from him. The sooner Haider picked him up, the faster he'd be home, seeing to the health and wellbeing of Theodora and his new daughter.

Gaze on the line of whitecaps in the distance, Zidane banked right, flying fast over Sea-Tac. The smell of salt water and jet fuel mixed, tickling his senses. His sonar pinged, providing him a clear picture of the terrain. Nice, flat area. Tons of black tarmac, pinpricks of light glinting off painted yellow lines. Main terminals and airplane hangars fenced off from major roadways. Separate, but surrounded by human neighborhoods.

Too few trees, too many houses.

Way too many fucking humans. Far too much waste. The hallmark of a species who cared about no one but themselves

Cold air whipping off his wingtips, he bared his fangs. His nostrils flared, making his dark brown scales quiver as the scent of cooking oil and barbecue fumes burned over senses. He banked west, away from the hive of human activity toward the water.

Wind gusts blasted over the surface of the water, hitting him in the face. Squinting, he focused on the lighthouse on the shoreline opposite him. Mist and brine kicked up. The foul smell of humans cleared as he turned into a vicious updraft. Tips of his horns tingling, he recalibrated his radar. Topography came into sharper focus, guiding him through wispy clouds as he blasted out over the sound.

Maury Island to his right. Tacoma further down the coast to his left.

Clear night sky. Crisp spring air. Nothing better than a midnight flight through enemy territory after a productive night of reconnaissance.

The bubble of cold air pushed him farther south, closer to the bay, away from the flash of city lights.

Fine by him. Giving Seattle a wide berth for a week or two suited his purposes. He'd spent enough time in the Emerald City to get a handle on the terrain. He'd scouted north and south, east to west, over Puget Sound and into island communities, then made the trek out to the Cascade Mountain Range.

Almost as beautiful as his homeland, Washington had a lot to offer, a dazzling combination of land, sea, and sky, urban wasteland balanced by national parks, thick forest, and miles of coastline, inlets, and bays. Along with the good, however, always came the bad— a mix of the beauty Mother Nature provided and the awful destruction humans excelled at delivering.

The former, he always enjoyed. The latter, not so much.

Still, with the wind up and the coastline frothing, the night was ripe for flying. He wanted to stay out, take another tour around the area, but delaying any longer would be foolish. No matter how much he'd accomplished after landing in Seattle, more still needed to be done. His to-do list kept growing, becoming more onerous by the day. So many challenges. Too many tasks—even with all his warriors pitching in to make the new lair livable.

The renovations, however, would have to wait. The

second he landed outside his new home, he planned to retreat to his war room. Nailing down battle details came before installing drywall. He'd started a war. One he must win. Nothing less than abject brutality—death to all Nightfuries—would do.

Permission to take the bastards out had been granted. Signed, sealed, delivered by his sire over a week ago.

The papers—issued by the Archguard, granting him full authority—sat inside his new home, in the fireproof safe he'd installed the instant he closed on the property and picked up the keys. Not much to look at, the ramshackle mansion sat in south Tacoma, on a wooded lot in a bad part of town. Not a lot of land, a paltry five and half acres, but it was enough.

For now.

The time would come when it wouldn't be, but that was for later.

Right now, he had enough on his plate. *Xzinile*, the sanctioned assassination of the Nightfury pack, was serious business. A new twist for Zidane. He never took killing too seriously. He considered taking another's life to be more of a hobby, nothing more than a bit of fun to pass the time. But *Xzinile*? Hell. Even he'd sat up and paid attention when his sire made the announcement.

Putting a bull's-eye on Bastian's back, after all, counted as noteworthy. A triumph no one believed Rodin possessed enough power to pull off.

Well, the joke was on them, not him. Never him.

He was the chosen one. A prince among males. The warrior who would bring balance back to Dragonkind by punishing the Nightfuries for their crimes. Justice must be done. Bastian and his pack would pay for murdering Lothair in Seattle and ending Ferland's life in Prague.

The reminder hit Zidane somewhere foreign, in a place untraveled, opening a fissure inside him. Always the same. Never any different. Missing his comrades never got any easier. Ever-present sorrow cut so deep he wondered some afternoons, after waking in his bed, if his heart had been ripped out while he slept—and he bled from the gaping wound in his chest. Some days, he checked. Other afternoons brought fury to the surface so fast rage leaked from his pores.

Another reason to hate the Nightfuries.

He didn't want to feel the effects of losing males he valued. *Hovno*, he didn't want to *feel* anything. He wanted to stay focused. He needed to remain on task. He craved the nirvana killing Bastian and the Nightfuries would bring. The high from the kill would be unlike any drug on the market.

Zidane imagined bringing the Nightfury commander to ground all the time. The sound of the kill. The feel of hot blood pouring between his claws. The ash of dead dragons coating his scales. None of which would happen if he lost objectivity.

Excellent reasoning. Perfect logic.

Too bad anger kept clouding his judgment. His need for vengeance tested his control, urging him to skip important steps. Montgomery, his blood brother, saw his impatience. Yakapov, his first-in-command, kept warning him to check it. The others he'd chosen to join his kill squad never said anything, but Zidane knew his warriors watched him, waiting for his pot to boil over.

Drifting further down the coast, Zidane gritted his teeth. The sharp tips of his fangs bit into his lip. He eased the pressure, battling to hold on to his temper.

Much as he hated to admit it, Yakapov was right. He needed to find a way around his rage. Harnessing the fury, using it to further his pack's cause, would get him further, faster.

He possessed a plan. All he needed to do now was stick to it.

His future depended on the successful completion of his mission. Eliminating the Nightfury pack was his gateway to greater things. The instant he downed the last warrior, he'd earned the right to choose. To press his own agenda and get what he wanted above all else.

Freedom. A home far from the power corridors of Prague.

No more dealing with politics and the Archguard. No more walking on eggshells around his sire. Nothing but open skies and a new pack to call his own. So...

*Da.*

No question.

He must lock it down. Remain on task and in control. Allowing his grief to rule was a bad idea. No matter how much he missed his blood brother, and longed for the return of his best friend, both were gone. Nothing but ash, one scattered on Seattle wind, the other sitting in an urn on the mantel inside his kill squad's new home.

Revolving into a sideways flip, Zidane zigzagged over human houses nestled along the coastline. All quiet. Everyone tucked into bed, no doubt fast asleep.

Looking further south, he spotted the Port of Tacoma. Huge operation. The largest in Washington. Lots of different companies, warehouses, and buildings abutting channels and waterways spread like fingers flowing inland. Some outfits owned oil tankers, others ocean freighters hauling everything from consumer goods to natural resources. A five-minute flight from his new house. An ideal location, given his new business venture.

Connections in Russia had gotten him the shipping contracts. Strong-arming a private corporation had brought him the rest—the fleet of ocean freighters that would transport legitimate cargo, as well as not-so-legal cargo, from all over the world.

The Colombians had already been in touch. The Mexican cartels as well. The Bratva controlling the western seaboard would be next.

Lots of new friends to make. Tons of money to be made.

His mouth curved. No sense letting grass grow. He needed his network established (and smuggling routes set) before his sire attempted to call him home. The healthier his bank accounts, the greater chance he'd be able to move out from under Rodin's thumb.

His warriors were on board. None wanted to return to Europe after killing the Nightfuries, which meant as long as he stuck to the plan, things would—

Static attacked his temples.

Completing the connection, he opened a link into mind-speak.

*"Zidane."* Deep voice. Thick Russian accent. Pissed-off vibe.

Right on cue.

Like a punch to the throat, Yakapov's attitude never lost its edge or impact. Direct to the point of rudeness, he voiced his opinions. Sometimes he led with words. Other times with his claws, but whatever the method, he made his point, backing it up with the kind of viciousness most males worked hard to avoid.

Zidane huffed. *Kristus*, his friend was the best kind of brutal. Anyone who paid attention knew how the male felt just by looking at him. Or, say, by standing anywhere in his vicinity.

Flying over the water's edge, he glanced over his shoulder. Intense blue eyes shimmering with yellow flecks collided with his.

He bit down on a grin.

His friend's eyes narrowed. *"Don't know what's funny."*

*"If I said you, would you—"*

*"Slice you throat to dick?"* Bright yellow scales peppered with black and red flecks rattled as the male flexed huge talons. A warning. One Zidane heeded... most of the time. He and his first-in-command might be close, but there was only so much teasing the male would take. *"Probably, but since I'm about to fall out of the sky, I wouldn't be able to give it my best effort. You want, I'll rearrange your ugly mug later. After I've had some sleep. Now, we going home or do you plan to fly around all night?"*

Rounding out the fighting triangle, flying off his right wingtip, Hinz snorted in amusement.

Yakapov snarled at him.

Zidane powered through the need to laugh. Not a good idea, given Yakapov's current mood. The male, along with the entire kill squad, was suffering from serious sleep deprivation. Long days spent ass-deep in construction projects. Busier nights spent on recon and wreaking havoc in Seattle. Little time to relax. Hardly any to get a decent amount of shuteye. The combination had taken its toll, causing tempers to fray and Yakapov's grip on his more violent tendencies to slip.

Burning the candle at both ends and the middle was never fun. But the payoffs had been huge. Zidane's new lair might not be one hundred percent ready, but with all hands on deck, he and his warriors were making serious headway. All-new electrical wiring. All-new plumbing. New steel roof. Underground lair dug out along with the foundation set. Fixtures and flooring going in, furniture ready to be set in place.

The progress astounded him. Day by day, hour by hour, the hundred-and-twenty-year-old mansion came alive, becoming what he envisioned months ago, after seeing a picture of the neglected building online.

Instead of a nine-thousand-square-foot behemoth separated into apartments sometime in the seventies, he now lived inside the beginnings of a home. A real one. Something he'd never had in Prague. His sire's pleasure pavilion might be floor-to-ceiling luxury, full of plush furniture, expensive fixtures, and obedient servants, but it had never felt like home.

A crash pad, sure. A bed for him to get his bang on, no question. A place where he could put his feet up and relax, no way.

Even half finished, with holes in the walls and plaster dust in the air, the house on Easter Avenue surpassed his expectations, becoming more—

Hinz nudged him with his wingtip.

Bumped from a smooth glide, Zidane torqued into a flip, arcing over Yakapov's spiked spine. Yellow scales rattled in the blowback. His friend cursed under his breath. Zidane shook his head, marveling anew at the male's bad mood, then gave in. No sense poking an already ticked-off acid dragon. He'd end up being scalded in sensitive places.

With a sharp turn, he banked away from Commencement Bay and headed inland. *"Home, brothers. Time to rest."*

*"Thank Kristus,"* Yakapov muttered, sweeping across the sky in Zidane's wake.

Hinz chuckled. *"Any females in the mix?"*

*"Probably,"* Zidane said, upping his wing speed. *"I put Monty in charge of finding some."*

Yakapov hummed. *"Then we'll have a harem by the time we get home."*

*"Outstanding,"* Hinz said, eagerness in his voice.

No word of a lie.

Inviting his younger brother to join the kill squad had been a stroke of genius. Not only was Montgomery a mercenary, the best tracker in the business, he had great taste in females. He never messed around when it came to finding prime pieces of tail. Always young, early to late twenties. Always pretty, with adequate bioenergy. Always willing to fuck hard and often. Montgomery would no doubt have females lined up around the block by the time Zidane landed in front of Easter Avenue.

Hunger spiked, igniting a fire in his belly. Anticipation rumbled through him.

Rocketing over snaking city streets, Zidane headed into the wilds of south Tacoma. Victory came in all colors, shapes, and sizes. Killing Nightfuries represented one form of winning; keeping his warriors well rested, fed, and fucked was simply another.

He could let go. Enjoy a little R&R. Just for a couple of hours.

Tomorrow would be soon enough to set up his war room, sharpen his knives, and put phase two of his mission plan in motion. Bastian and the Nightfuries already had his attention. Ivar and the Razorbacks were next.

## 9

Flat on his back in an unfamiliar place, Azrad struggled to clear his mind. Lots of blur. Too much mental whirl. His body was so heavy, he felt the weight and pull of gravity dragging him under, drawing him down, messing with his ability to move.

And he needed to move. Now. Before whatever threatened him, attacked and tore him to pieces.

A guess. Nothing but speculation, but years spent in prison had taught him well. Mobility, the ability to adjust on the fly, meant holding the advantage. And keeping the upper hand equaled staying alive.

Swallowing past a bad case of dry mouth, he tried to open his eyes. His lids refused to open, sending him spinning inside his head. Abandoning the attempt to get visual clues, he worked to clear the cerebral tangle. Bead by bead, he sewed the broken string of his thoughts back together.

The haze began to lift.

His dragon half stirred, uncoiling deep inside him. Magic washed back into his veins. Sensory pathways ignited. His sonar pinged, a weak pulse, just enough to fed him some preliminary intel.

Dimmed lights. Soft, cushioned expanse underneath him; something softer curled along his left side.

Tingles ghosted down his spine. His fingertips twitched.

Eyes still closed, he strung more information together. Nothing hurting. All four limbs still attached. No major injuries detected. The drift of warm air against his skin. A quiet hum coming from somewhere close. Drawing a shallow breath, he felt his chest rise and fall and...

Something else registered too.

Perfume or—

No, not perfume. The bouquet was lighter, intoxicating, not overpowering—cherry blossoms combined with the warm scent of female.

Confusion burned through him.

"What the fuck," he muttered, hearing the words without feeling his mouth move.

He'd never slept the night through with a female. Never even considered bringing one home. He got what he needed in nightclubs and coffee shops, in bathroom stalls and back alleys, connecting with a female only when the need to feed forced him into her sphere. He was cautious. He was careful. He never made mistakes, which made what he sensed impossible.

He must've taken a hit to the head. A concussion would explain the sensory distortion. An excellent conclusion, 'cause no way was he feeling what his mind wanted him to believe.

"Fuck," he said, fighting to shake off physical lockdown.

His dragon half rallied.

As he sank back into his body, grounding himself in muscle and bone, his eyes opened and stayed that way. Blinking, he cleared his vision, only to stare up at a stark white surface. Hard, shiny, and smooth, the ceiling looked like molded plastic. Three grooves cut lengthwise through the expanse, soft light glowing from inside the furrows. The slashes provided visual interest while doing a bang-up job of illuminating the room. He stared at the lines a second, confused, alarmed, trying to figure out what the hell had happened.

Recall jogged his memory.

Azrad tensed a second before he looked down. His lips parted as wonder grabbed him by the balls. Fucking hell. Kasi, the gorgeous blond assigned to him. The female he'd chosen. One of five high-energy females imprisoned by Ivar and the Razorbacks for the purposes of breeding, the girl he planned to rescue, his companion for the next...

He frowned.

Shit, he didn't know how long.

Last time he'd been conscious, he'd had six days. *Six days* before the Meridian realigned, the *hungering* hit, and shit went from critical to out of control. *Six days* to figure out how to protect Kasi and the other women forced to do the Razorbacks' bidding. But after waking half-baked inside a room he'd yet to explore inside a secure facility Ivar put effort into ensuring stayed that way, the timeline could be anything. How long had he been asleep? How much time did the tranquilizer Hamersveld gave him take to wear off? A day? Two? Maybe even three?

He had no clue. Didn't know the date, time, or his location, never mind if the sun shone or night had fallen.

Exactly as Ivar intended.

The male might be twisted, but he wasn't stupid.

The leader of the Razorbacks, a pack he and his wing-mates infiltrated to help Bastian, made sure to protect his investment. Azrad felt the buzz all around him. The energy shield surrounding the underground bunker was a beast. Strong. Fortified. Alive with magic, powered by energy drawn straight from the earth's core.

Problematic enough. Add *Blakeite* to the mix, and doable became impossible.

Dragon senses roaming, he reached out with his mind. Magic fired in his veins, then slid through the apartment suite he'd been tossed inside. Not that he cared much about the space. He was more interested in what lay behind the walls, ceiling, and floors—a mineral of the kind and quality that might foil any attempt at escape. Closing his eyes, he concentrated on the search, looking for weaknesses in the structure.

He clenched his teeth.

None found.

The composition of the rock formation was solid, the denseness of the *Blakeite* a real game changer. Without the mineral present, he might be able to short-circuit the energy shield and unlock the fancy cage imprisoning him. With it, he was flying blind in dead air, no way of knowing which way was up.

No way of getting a message out.

*Blakeite* blocked a warrior's ability to connect through mind-speak and communicate with others of his kind. No magic passed through it. No signal escaped it. Which meant he must find another way to reach Gage and the Nightfury pack. Otherwise, he wouldn't get the backup he needed to break out of the subterranean bunker, spring his wingmates from their own apartment suites, and rescue all five females before the Meridian realigned.

Talk about a clusterfuck.

Lying still and silent, he chewed on the facts, wondering if Kilmar and Terranon were awake yet, listening to Kasi breathe, soothed by the warm weight of her against him. Brilliant bioenergy prickled over into his skin, nourishing him even though he hadn't tapped into the Meridian through her. But goddess... he wanted to. Wanted to know if she tasted as good as she smelled. Wanted to know if she'd been as amazing in real life as he imagined.

Saliva pooled in his mouth.

Unable to stop himself, Azrad breathed life into the connection, strengthening the flow, feeling it blossom and grow. He bit down on a groan. Fuck. *Fuck.* She felt amazing, her bioenergy so intoxicating he lifted his hand to touch her, but stopped at the last second. Fingers trembling, he held his palm an inch from her skin, tracing her shape from hip to shoulder.

He breathed deep, holding her in his lungs, and picked up a lock of her hair. Long, light blond strands, thick, heavy, soft to the touch. His gaze moved over her face. Pretty and relaxed in repose, cheek pressed to his chest, lips parted, eyes closed, curly eyelashes a shade darker than her hair. Small in stature, almost petite. Maybe five foot three to his six foot six. The muscles roping his abdomen tightened. Arousal undulated through him on a slow, incendiary roll. He thickened behind the fly of his army pants and—

"Shit," he whispered, shifting sideways to get out from under her.

He needed to move away. Slide out of bed and put a healthy distance between him and her—fast. Before he acted on instinct, did the unconscionable, and curled into her instead of away.

Not a good idea.

She'd been through enough. Too much. More than any female should be made to suffer, enduring goddess-knew-what at the hands of the Razorbacks. No way would he add to her pain. Not if he could help it. Which meant he needed to figure out how to circumvent Ivar's secure measures and get them both to safety before time ran out and the Meridian realigned, forcing the nightmare scenario—him taking her against her will when the *hungering* hit and he lost control.

## 10

Curled around Theodora in the center of Haider's talon, Sloan kept her tucked tight to his frame. Both hands pressed to the wound on her lower back, he mined her bioenergy. He smelled the blood, felt the wetness slip through his fingers as he battled to keep her stable in flight. She was unconscious, unresponsive, pale in the moonlight. Not good signs. Nor was the chill of her skin against the heat of his palms.

She was losing the battle. If he didn't do something fast, she would die in his arms.

Fear spiked before determination set in. Magic running hot, Sloan tunneled into her core energy, reaching for something intangible. Something he felt, but didn't understand. Insight came as he tapped into the stream. A grid formed inside his mind's eye as her aura pulsed green, gold, and white. He read the pause between each beat. Powerful energy. Soul-deep beauty. Glorious bright light. Awed by her, he mapped her mental pathways, capturing more ground, feeding her more healing energy.

Jerking in his arms, she shied, refusing to take

more. The connection wavered. Her vital signs mean-dered downward, dipping into dangerous territory.

With a muffled curse, he searched for another way in.

She blocked him, refusing to give way. Theodora was too strong-willed. Too fucking stubborn for her own good. Didn't matter that he'd already connected, that energy-fuse had already taken hold. The bond he now shared with her was still in its infancy. The link needed her acceptance to grow and thrive. Without it, his ability to nourish her the way she needed—to stop the blood flow and heal her from the inside out—was compromised, nowhere near as strong as it would be if she surrendered, allowing the bond to strengthen.

Frustration took hold.

Desperate to save her, Sloan dug deeper. Sifting through the threads, he pulled her strings, sequencing her DNA. He needed to understand what made her, how her energy dovetailed with his, in order to pro-vide what she needed. The spikes in her bioenergy helped him navigate. A pattern began to emerge, helping him understand.

Goddess, she was strong. Unbreakable in some ways, fragile in others. A contradiction. A rare puzzle. One he couldn't resist trying to solve, even as he bat-tled to pull her from the brink.

As she continued to fight him, Sloan waged war. He showed no mercy. He didn't care she was uncon-scious and didn't understand. Not his normal ap-proach. A female owned the right to choose. Always. The conviction was a hard and fast rule among Drag-onkind. One he'd never broken before, but...

Theodora was too important to allow stubborn-ness to win. He'd let her yell at him later, after she began to heal. After she landed on the road to recovery. After he saw pink return to her cheeks.

Asserting his will, Sloan tightened his grip on her. She flinched. He growled against her temple. The sound broke through, reaching some distant place inside her.

Attuned to her, he felt her subconscious shift. He snarled again, low in his throat. She drifted closer in the mental sphere, a breath away from connecting, almost accepting, but turned away at the last second, clinging to her autonomy.

An understandable reaction. Unconscious didn't mean weak...or compliant.

"Theo." Mouth moving against her temple, hands pressed to her wound, he pushed his voice deep into her head. Invading, marauding, breaking down barriers, he battered her will to resist. She needed the healing energy he offered or she wouldn't survive. He needed her to survive more than he wanted to fly in clear skies again. "Give over, *mazleiha*. Think of Violet. Think of your little girl. Accept me, baby. Reach out, grab hold, take what you need."

She mumbled something.

He kept talking to her, tone quiet and even, hammering mental walls built by her subconscious, the ones keeping him out. One moment fell into the next. Her guard weakened, then cracked under the pressure.

Energy exploded into the void.

He jerked as her essence slammed into him. His eyes drifted close. His dragon half purred and—

Fucking hell.

She tasted divine. Pure. Potent. Fresh and new, like budding leaves and dense forest dew.

Breathing deep, he drew her into his lungs.

The cracks in her mental walls widened.

Without mercy, he pressed his advantage, slipping through the fissures, forging new pathways, strengthening the connection he now shared with her. The Meridian rolled through the link. He welcomed its ferocity as white-hot energy infused his muscles and bones.

Theodora shifted against him. Her eyelashes flickered against his throat. "Wh-what...wh-wh-whaz—"

"Shh. It's all right," he murmured, feeling the connection gain speed and intensity as energy-fuse—the magical bond between mates—snaked into place.

Sloan groaned.

The Goddess of All Things must love him. Nothing else explained the burning beauty of Theodora. Her power humbled him. Her abundant energy shattered him, then pieced him back together, making him whole again. A powerful connection, a symbiotic union. Potent and impactful, a feeling the likes of which he'd hoped to experience in his lifetime, but never believed he would.

She wiggled against him.

"Relax." Nuzzling her temple, he smoothed away the last of her resistance. "Let it happen."

Mostly out of it, she tipped her chin up. Her mouth brushed then settled against his pulse point. She sighed, relaxing into him. "Warm. Good."

"Yeah, beautiful—it is."

Electrostatic current moving from jagged to smooth, the final thread settled into place. Wrapped in splendor, warmed by his female, Sloan exhaled long and slow as Theodora settled in, allowing him full access.

Gratitude streamed through him.

Heat bloomed behind his eyes.

Sloan locked down the emotion. No time to waste. Less time to analyze the miracle. He accepted the gift instead, thankful the goddess saw fit to provide a way for Dragonkind males to mate and do it for life.

She was beautiful in all ways. A blessing, given the perfection of their bond. An exact coupling. A perfect fit. No need to adjust the link or change the settings. Theodora matched and met him, vibrating at the same frequency, allowing him to take away her pain.

"My..." Deep in the stream, drunk on the healing energy he fed her, she slurred her words. "Wherz..."

"Safe, Theo," he said, knowing what she asked. Shifting forces for a second, he looked through the gaps between Haider's curved talons. In the grips of a sleeping spell, cocooned by a warm pocket of air, her daughter lay curled on her side in the center of his packmate's other paw, ringlets messy, eyes closed, breathing even and sure. "Violet's here. Your baby's safe."

"Who...whaz...again?"

His lips twitched as she garbled the question. "Sloan, remember?"

"Pretty eyes."

Eavesdropping on the exchange, Haider chuckled.

"Sloan," she said so softly he almost didn't hear her.

"Yeah, baby?"

"Thank you."

His chest tightened as satisfaction drilled him. "Pleasure's mine, *mazleiha*."

She hummed in response.

Overwhelmed by what she made him feel, he distracted himself by feeding her more, upping the dosage bit by bit. As he turned the dial, she sank beneath the cresting wave. The last of her tension faded.

Her hands unclenched, fingers relaxing as she accepted him fully. The moment she did, he cranked the link wide open, mainlining energy, bending it to his will, bathing her in a pool of white-hot energy.

Her breath caught on a ragged inhale, then evened out. Sluggish before, her heart picked up, ramping into a healthier rhythm.

Sloan wanted to crow in triumph as her blood pressure stabilized. He kept at her instead, nourishing her with his life force, stanching the flow of blood with his magic, beginning the process of knitting her back together, buying himself (and her) more time.

Glancing up between the curl of silver talons tipped by black claws, he nudged his friend with his boot. *"Haider—"*

*"Well done, man."*

*"Don't—"*

*"Never borne witness to the bond take hold before. Fuck, man—beautiful."*

Sloan bit down on a curse, stifling the need to hammer his friend. He hated the idea Haider had witnessed his moment with Theodora. The bonding of a male and female was special, a sacred ritual, a private meeting of minds, bodies, and souls. A memory meant to be cherished, not a moment to be witnessed by voyeuristic assholes who should know better than to watch, never mind mention it.

Haider knew better. So did every other Dragonkind warrior on the planet.

His brow furrowed, he glared up at Haider. *"H—"*

*"After watching that, I get it. I want it."* Mercury eyes alight, Haider swung into a tight turn. *"Can't wait to meet my mate now, Sloan. Can't wait for her to light me up as I make her mine. Fucking spectacular."*

Sloan opened his mouth to shut his friend up.

Jazzed, Haider kept talking. *"Might never happen. No guarantees in life, but after what you just did, how she reacted to you, the phenomenal blast of energy, I'm—"*

*"Done talking about this."*

*"—beginning the hunt,"* he said, ignoring the warning, too excited to read the signs. *"For real. No delay, cuz now I know how it's gonna be—"*

*"Shut up, Haider."*

He blinked. *"What?"*

*"Brother, you're gonna wanna shut your mouth before I shut it for you."*

Haider stared at him.

He glared back.

A moment later, understanding dawned. *"Shit, Sloan. Sorry, man. Privileged information, though..."*

Bracing for the next temper-fraying comment, Sloan gritted his teeth.

*"Don't know why. That was epic. We should broadcast that shit. Go wide with the information, instead of keeping it to ourselves,"* Haider said, head tilted, eyes narrowed, mind working. *"Teach about energy-fuse and the mating ritual. Put it online, make a video—"*

A video?

Sloan growled. *"No fucking way."*

*"Or whatever. Benefit the entire race, not just our pack. Dragonkind will thank us for it. We teach the ritual to other warriors, we'll build an even stronger coalition. Kick Rodin and the Archguard's ass all over Prague."*

The idea made Sloan pause. He toyed with the strategy. Rubbing his cheek against Theodora's, he ran down all the pros and cons. Sharing that kind of information didn't guarantee results, but it wouldn't hurt either. He needed all the ammunition he could get to bring other Dragonkind on board—to encourage the pack commanders he and Bastian targeted to cut ties with the Archguard and move toward a brighter future. One where every pack owned a seat at the table, every voice got heard, and each vote counted. Equal. Fair. Equitable. Not a dictatorship controlled by five dynastic families ruled by a single male, but a democracy enjoyed by all.

Heir to the High Chancellery, Bastian wanted no part in the Dragonkind aristocracy. Or the throne his sire had occupied before his death.

He wanted the system changed, and so did Sloan and his brothers-in-arms. Real change meant sacrifice, sure, but also giving his race a shot at a brighter future. A place where honor, skill, and commitment mattered more than birthplace, lineage, and the blood in a warrior's veins.

A lofty goal. An uncertain outcome. Which meant...

Sloan sighed. Hell. He had to give his friend credit. Only Haider could come up with a solid argument in the midst of an idiotic, rage-inducing conversation.

*"Bring it to the table and B."*

Haider grunted in agreement.

Keeping his hand pressed to his mate's wound, Sloan slid the other up her back until he found the one on her shoulder. He prodded the edges. Ragged, bleeding less, but still seeping. Not as serious as the wound under his palm, but more problematic. Unlike the shot that nearly took out her kidney, the hit to her shoulder wasn't a through-and-through. The bullet remained lodged inside her, right up against bone.

One eye on him, the other on the terrain ahead, Haider rolled into a smooth glide over the river leading into Black Diamond. Sliver scales shimmering in the moonlight, he tipped his chin. *"Those need to come out."*

*"You got a lock on the bullet?"*

Tingles swept over Sloan's skin as Haider went searching. As a Metallic, his biological make-up was unique. Heavy metal alloy merged with his dragon DNA, infusing his muscles and bones, tagging his magic, granting him the ability to control metal of all kinds.

*"Bullets...plural,"* Haider murmured after completing the scan. *"One fragmented on impact against her shoulder blade."*

*"The other?"*

*"Lodged in the back of her thigh."*

*"Can you pull them out—fragments included?"*

Haider nodded. *"Yeah, but brother..."*

*"What?"*

*"Brace. It's gonna hurt like a mother, and your mate's gonna react."*

*"Do it when we land."*

*"Inside the clinic?"* Banking hard, flying fast, Haider set up his approach to the waterfall.

*"The instant you touch down on the LZ."*

*"Sloan—"*

*"Don't argue."*

*"She's gonna lose more blood. Lots more."*

*"She's my mate. I know what I'm doing."*

*"Fuck,"* Haider growled. *"You're going subterranean, aren't you?"*

Sloan didn't answer. No need to waste the energy. He'd spent too much time talking already.

He was almost home. Less than thirty seconds from flying through the waterfall into the tunnel that led to the cavern that abutted the underground lair. Now wasn't the time to argue with his friend. He needed to concentrate, would require every thread of focus to see his female through.

She may have stabilized, but Theodora wasn't out of the woods yet. The damage she sustained was too severe, her bioenergy and vital signs too low. Which meant drastic measures must be taken. Otherwise, she'd slip away, and he'd lose her...before he got the chance to claim and make her his.

## 11

Wound tight, worried about Sloan, Angela flew over the forest in Gage's wake. Not her preferred wingmate. Not that he'd done anything wrong. He was a solid presence, a good guy ninety percent of the time. The ten percent, however—all the unknowns—jabbed at her. Questions kept popping up. Would Gage tell her if something was wrong, and her mentor was in trouble? Or would he do what he seemed determined to do now and continue to lead her home?

To Rikar. To safety. Far away from trouble and all those pesky little unknowns.

His silence wasn't helping. The information freeze upped the stakes, dragging her imagination into the equation. Breathing deep, she absorbed the chill in the air. Her frosty side sighed in satisfaction. The detective in her continued to evaluate, flipping through all the nasty possibilities.

Eyes narrowed, she drilled her wingmate with a look.

Not that he noticed.

On point, more than double her size in dragon

from, Gage blasted across the sky, charting a course toward Black Diamond, expecting her to follow without comment. She wrestled with the best way to approach him. The guy wasn't a lightweight. He was a warrior, one of the strongest, brutal in and out of dragon form. A man who took no prisoners. Once he made a decision, he stuck to it. Which left her two options—break radio silence and get slapped by his attitude or fall in line, adhere to pack protocol, and stay silent.

A tough decision.

Her fledgling warrior status didn't allow for a lot of leeway. In order to learn, she needed to pay attention, watch, wait, show some patience, not flap her gums. She might not be new to the Nightfury pack, but she was new to being a member of Dragonkind. She wanted to be a good teammate and make an even better impression. With everyone, not just Rikar and Sloan.

Wrestling with indecision, she kept her eyes glued to Gage's back. His bronze scales gleamed in the moonlight. Her pale blue ones glowed, throwing off iridescence as she did as instructed and stayed on his six. Close enough for her to be enveloped by the invisibility spell he conjured, keeping them both hidden from human eyes. Far enough away to avoid getting slashed in the face by the huge spikes tipping his tail. Covered by another's magic, instead of her own. Reliant on another. A new experience for her. One she didn't like or want to continue.

Rikar warned her the beginning would be rough. Angela thought she'd been prepared for the challenge, but after years of excelling as an investigator, being caught between somewhat able and nowhere near capable sucked.

Static blew into her head. Tingles attacked her temples as Gage opened a link into mind-speak. *"Ange —relax."*

Mired in frustration, she snapped, *"What?"*

*"I can hear your mind working all the way from here."*

She growled at him.

He huffed in amusement.

The urge to rip all his claws out rolled through her. *"Are we done with radio silence?"*

*"We're not in lockdown."*

*"Then why aren't you talking?"*

*"Didn't feel like it."*

*"Next time, Haider's my wingmate. He never shuts up,"* she said through clenched teeth.

*"Feeling neglected?"*

*"More like murderous."*

He chuckled. *"Why?"*

*"What happened back there was messed up. Now, instead of Sloan, I'm with you. We're flying home at breakneck speed, and Sloan— hit. My sonar's spotty. I can't pinpoint where he is, and Nian and Haider are MIA too."* Night vision sparking, she rocketed overtop of a clearing surrounded by giant oaks. Treetops swayed in her wake. New-growth leaves rustled, pushing the scent of sap into the air. *"You're not talking, so I'm thinking communication blackout is the way to go just in case there's trouble. You think, maybe given all that, it would've been good to have a quick chat and clue me in?"*

*"You worry too much."*

*"You need your horns ripped off."*

He grinned at her over his shoulder.

*"I'm feeling the serious, persistent need to gouge your eyes out."*

His grin turned into a smile.

She breathed deep, drawing cold air into her

lungs, and reached for calm. A good strategy. The guy pushed her buttons. The wrong ones, 'cause she wasn't lying. She wanted to maim him. Sinking her claws into him would feel good, relieve some of the stress, and, hopefully, dispel the anger threatening her sanity.

A new challenge for her. With her first shift, and new Dragonkind status, came volatility. More restlessness. More aggression. More violent tendencies. Just *more*. She'd never been particularly even-tempered, but now, with her dragon half beginning to integrate, she struggled to control the emotion. Oh, all the lovely pros and cons. Some perks to being a member of Dragonkind, some drawbacks.

Breaking formation, she swerved left and flew up on his wingtip. *"Is Sloan okay?"*

He nodded.

*"How do you know?"*

*"Nian's keeping me updated."*

*"He's with Haider?"*

*"Watching his six while Sloan deals with the female."*

*"And you're talking to him?"* She frowned, not understanding. Granted, she still had a lot to learn about Dragonkind and her new abilities. Her sonar wasn't as sharp as the other Nightfury warriors' yet. She misread her radar sometimes. Her inability to conjure a cloaking spell frustrated her more than it should, but she'd mastered mind-speak on day one. Or so she thought. Time to re-evaluate, given Gage was talking to Nian without her being able to hear. *"How?"*

*"Closed loop. Private conversation. Just like the one you and I are having now."*

*"But..."*

Seeing her confusion, Gage sighed. *"What the hell has Sloan been teaching you?"*

*"Tons,"* she said, hackles up, the need to defend her friend rising.

Sloan was an excellent mentor. Patient. Thorough. A no-bullshit kind of guy. No matter how many times she asked the same question, he explained, laying out the facts, providing what she needed to move on to the next lesson, letting her puzzle things out on her own when warranted. Just as any good teacher would.

Closing the knowledge gap, however, wasn't coming easy. The delay annoyed the hell out of her. She wanted to go quicker. She needed to learn faster, be more efficient in the classroom and the field. The fact she didn't know everything yet wasn't Sloan's fault. He'd had limited time with her, a few short days and nights, and still, he'd made a big impact. Proof positive rested in the fact she was airborne with her magic humming, sonar running, and night vision so sharp she saw the grooves on individual pine cones from a quarter mile away, so...

Screw Gage and his pissy attitude. No way would she allow him to belittle Sloan's efforts—and her progress.

*"You're an ass."*

Baring huge fangs, Gage laughed.

She scowled. *"Have you seen the dragon combat training manual? It's frigging huge. There's a lot to learn. I'm new, Gage. I'm not even supposed to exist. I didn't grow up inside a Dragonkind pack. Didn't attend Dragon High School or whatever the hell—"*

*"Dragon High School."* He snorted. Metallic flakes rose from his nostrils, flashing bright above his horns as he shook his head. *"Fuck, you're hilarious."*

She glared at him. *"I didn't have a father to learn the basics from before my first shift like you did, so it stands to reason my education is lacking. The things you learned in childhood...the stuff you take for granted...I never got. It's a lot all at once. It's——"*

"Overwhelming."

"Yeah." She exhaled a pent-up breath. A cloud of frost puffed from between her fangs, turning to snowflakes in the blowback. *"And you're an ass for blaming that on Sloan."*

*"Mentor, apprentice. Helluva connection. Mac and Forge share it. Now, you and Sloan,"* he said, staring at her, something she couldn't read working behind his eyes.

*"Gage——"*

*"Sloan's supposed to teach you this, but fuck protocol. We got less than three minutes before we hit the waterfall. Sloan needs to focus on his female, so I'm gonna guide you through that, but until then——listen up."*

Angela blinked. *"His female?"*

*"Looks like it."*

*"Awesome,"* she whispered, happy for her friend. *"So...closed loop. Explain."*

*"Fall back, Ange. I lead, you follow. Stay on my six."*

Somersaulting into a flip, she settled in his wake.

Gage banked hard, rocketing into a sharp turn. She followed, shadowing his movements. Thick forest thinned below her. Stubby brush and rocky terrain replaced huge sequoias and towering pines as the rush of fast-moving water broke through the quiet. Strong winds undulated across the plain, tousling the tops of long grass, trying to push her off course.

Wings spread wide, she sliced through the gusts, her gaze on the cliffs rising beyond the foothills. Angling up the sheer rock face, she rode the jagged spine, blasted across the top, then dove over the opposite edge. The smell of water hit her a second before she saw the inky surface of the river.

Contrails jetting off his wingtips, Gage settled into a fast glide over the water, slicing around the twists and turns. Wide and deep, the river rushed over rapids, slithering like a serpent through high cliffs and low banks. Branches creaked as massive trees rooted to both shorelines rocked. The waterfall rumbled up ahead. Mist landed on her scales, turned to ice, then blew off, cutting across the river like shrapnel.

Small icebergs surfaced in her wake, bobbing in the powerful current.

*"How close are we?"*

*"A minute and half out, so pay attention."*

*"I'm all ears,"* she said, needing a distraction to keep from thinking about the waterfall—and her first attempt at landing. Though *landing* didn't quite capture the meaning. For accuracy, she should probably put *crash* in front of landing. *"How did you talk to Nian without me knowing?"*

*"Mind-speak isn't an open line. You want to connect, you capture a warrior's energy signal, reach out with your mind, and knock on his mental door."*

*"I know that, but—"*

*"Doesn't have to be a group activity, Ange. Every Dragonkind male has a signature. One hundred percent unique to the warrior. You tapped into that signal and send out the call. Link up with only those you invite. No need for everybody to be in the know. You want a private convo, create one."*

*"I'll practice with Rikar."*

*"Good idea. You hit me up at home, and your mate'll rip my balls off."*

Her lips twitched. *"Might be fun to watch."*

*"So bloodthirsty. Keep that up, you'll end up being my favorite,"* he murmured, yanking her chain, razzing her like he would any other member of the team.

Felt good. As though she'd earned something important.

The waterfall rumbled up ahead. Mist billowed up from behind the treetops. More ice formed on her scales. Velocity tore the shards off, sending sharp chips flying toward a narrow stretch of beach below.

A gleam entered his eyes, Gage glanced at her over his shoulder. *"You ready?"*

*"No."*

*"You got forty-five seconds to get that way,"* he said, showing no mercy and zero understanding.

No surprise. The entire reason Sloan wanted Gage on her dragon combat training team. When push came to shove—like now—he wouldn't coddle her. He'd expect her to dig in and man the fuck up.

Flexing her red-tipped claws, Angela angled her wings. She blasted around the last corner. The waterfall came into view. Beautiful to look at, nowhere near as fun to approach, the cascade fell in a straight sheet, slamming into rocks and the river below. Three hundred feet of nerve-torquing perfection. Curling white-caps cutting through a curtain of dark blue water. A beast with teeth bared on a deafening roar.

Droplets gathered on her lashes. Angela blinked to clear her vision and, following Gage, set up her approach.

Now or never. No short cuts or way around it.

She took a deep breath, fighting to control her unease. Her reaction wasn't a weak one. She knew the odds and needed to prepare, steel her courage and lock down the fear. Simple flying. Straightforward course. Incredibly dangerous. She might land without problem. Probability, however, suggested the opposite.

Landing clean on the first try rarely happened. Fledging warriors never got it right. Most panicked, lost their cool, then their minds, somewhere on approach. Some even *died*, snapping their necks by flying into cliffs, drowning after crashing into lakes, rivers, and oceans, or her favorite—being skewered by huge trees after crash-landing in a forest. She knew all the stories. The guys loved to tease her about the pitfalls. Toss in the dragon combat manual Sloan gave her to read and...yeah. She understood all the ways beginners bought it when learning to land.

A shining example of TMI.

She didn't need that kind of information. Sometimes ignorance was bliss. Whoever put that manual together needed his head examined, or perhaps his claws yanked out. Not necessarily in that order, either. She'd settled for punching the idiot first—when and if she met him.

Night vision sparking, she leveled out. Thirty seconds away from entry. She inhaled deep and exhaled slow, settling her nerves. A nice try. One that didn't work. Uncertainty blurred the lines between bravery and self-preservation, dragging her back into fear of the unknown. If she didn't figure it out, she'd hit the back wall of the cavern at full speed, disintegrate into a messy pile of ash, and force Rikar to live without her.

The idea shook her.

Going wings vertical, Gage sliced through the waterfall, disappearing from view.

Focused on the raging wall of water, she went nine rounds inside her head, battling dread, burning with doubt, looking for a way out. She could abort on approach and refuse to land. Rikar would fly out to get her. No hesitation. No backlash or disappointed looks.

He always gave her what she needed, would accept whatever she decided, but...

Chickening out left a bad taste in her mouth. She wasn't a coward. Her mate deserved better from her. More than a half-assed effort. It didn't matter that she wasn't one hundred percent comfortable in dragon form yet. She knew enough, had spent an hour studying the diagrams before leaving the lair.

Reaching deep, she pulled it onto her mental screen.

Ten seconds away from the point of no return, she studied charts in her mind's eye. She had the basics down, knew how and when to angle her wings. What currents to ride and which to avoid. Hell, she was doing it now, using a strong updraft to regulate her speed and keep from entering the tunnel too fast.

A distinct possibility.

She'd learned some things about herself tonight. First and foremost—she was fast in dragon form. Really freaking *fast*. Sloan and the others struggled to keep up when she went supersonic. A good thing to know. A better one to exploit...some other time. Right now, she needed to slow down.

Her sonar pinged. A detailed map of the tunnel surfaced in her mind's eye.

Scales rattling, Angela tilted her wings, mimicking the angle of Gage's upon entry. Dragon senses dialed to maximum, she sliced through cold water. Wet chill wicked from her spikes. Snow swirled as she blew past the waterfall into the tunnel beyond.

Moonlight faded.

Total darkness descended.

Her night vision switched to infrared. Hazel light washed over dark granite as her eyes started to glow, allowing her to see through the black. Searching for problem spots, anticipating for the first turn, Angela took stock. Wide in some areas, narrow in others, the tunnel cut through solid rock. Jagged outcroppings in some places, narrow ledges worn smooth in others. The smell of must and moss combined with fresh water and fish. A hidden treasure formed by nature and aided by dragon claws. She saw the deep gouges in the stone as she flew past the altered sections of tunnel. No doubt Sloan's handiwork.

As an earth dragon, her friend preferred to be underground, the deeper the better, so...yeah. Her assumption wasn't a bad one. If digging needed to be done, Sloan would be the one to do it, and—

Light reached through the darkness. Soft at first, the glow intensified as she rounded another bend. The tunnel widened, propelling her into an enormous cavern. Illumination devoured the darkness. Her mind took a quick snapshot: three-quarters open air, one-quarter landing zone. Round lanterns bobbing like jellyfish against the domed ceiling. Three dragons— one gold, one silver, the other bronze—wings spread wide, setting down on the lip of the LZ.

*"Too fast!"* With a snarl, Gage transformed into human form. *"Slow down!"*

With a curse, Angela put on the brakes. Her wings stretched. Pain ripped over her shoulders. Her tail whiplashed, sending her into a downward spiral.

Haider shouted a warning.

Nian yelled at Sloan.

Baring his teeth, Gage sprinted across the LZ toward her.

Too little, too late. She was already spinning out of control.

Chest heaving, she thrashed in midair. Wind gusts blasted across the landing zone. The light globes blew sideways, flickering as she lost attitude. Revolving in spine-twisting circles, she slammed into the sharp edge of the platform. Rock shrieked against scales. Bone cracked. Agony seared her ribcage as rock ripped through the webbing on one of her wings, and she fell toward the aquifer below.

## 12

Sloan cursed as Angela lost control and slammed into the side of the LZ. The collision shook the cavern. Dust billowed toward the dome. Blown sideways in the rush, light globes rushed down the wall, butting up against sharp stone. Some deflated. Others flew back toward the ceiling as she flapped, fighting to sink her claws into solid rock.

He heard her gasp of pain as she failed to catch hold.

Her wingtip came around. Jagged stone bit. White webbing ripped. She cursed and, iridescent scales flashing in the gloom, fought to arrest her fall. For the second time in one night, she plummeted, torquing into an uncontrollable spin.

"Shit," Haider said, head turned toward Angela. Caught somewhere between full flight and landing, he hovered above the platform. Folding his wings, he set down fast. His back paws thumped against stone. "Sloan—"

"Put me down."

Haider uncurled his talon.

His boot soles met solid ground. Unable to release Theodora without severing the connection, he cradled her in his arms and sank to his knees. One hand pressed to her bare skin, he continued to feed her. The other he slammed flat against the floor. Cool to the touch. Rough against his palm. The perfect combination as he called on his magic. Wild and vibrant, the earth's vibration rose to greet him.

Strong current swirled in the center of his palm. With a hum, he entered the stream, tapped the untappable, and drew power straight from the earth's core. A dangerous move for other Dragonkind warriors. No less risky for him, but for one caveat: his earth dragon loved the burn.

Shielding Theodora from the brute force of earth energy, he pulled the potency into his veins. His muscles contracted. His fingertips flamed. His dragon half bared his fangs, drinking deep. Heat infused his muscles, then sank into his bones. Submerged in the stream, he manipulated the power, built the intensity, then let it go.

Supercharged by the planet, his magic tunneled through rock toward the aquifer below. Prehistoric seaweed woke, grew, then climbed, shooting from the surface of the pool at the base of the cliff.

Tracking her descent, he reached out with his mind. *"Shift, Angela."*

Wind swirled across the landing zone. Snow blew up from below as she transformed, moving from dragon to human form, trusting him without question. Pride moved through him. Thankfulness pushed it aside as one second ticked into another. Monitoring the plant's climb, Sloan listened as she continued falling, then heard her stop short.

Her hiss of pain echoed up from down below. "Motherfucker."

Gritting his teeth to keep from laughing, he controlled the weeds, wrapping the flat, thick ribbons around her, then murmured his wishes. The scent of wet vegetation drifted up. Slithering like headless snakes, seaweed curled over the lip of the LZ and across the platform.

"Unreal." On one knee, peering over at the edge, Gage pushed to his feet.

Slimy green tips curled like cobra heads, swiveling toward him.

Gage froze mid-retreat.

"Steady," Sloan murmured, controlling the monster he'd created, pulling Angela up from the depths.

"Wicked, Sloan." No movement from behind him as Haider, already in human form, stood off to one side, holding the girl child in his arms. "You should do that shit more often."

"You should visit the greenhouse," Nian said, keeping the beat-to-shit Honda sitting in the middle of LZ between him and the vicious coil of twisting plant life. "I nearly got eaten in there by...something. Never seen anything like it."

Sloan's lips twitched. "A Yateveo."

Dark brows raised in surprise, Gage glanced his way. "A what?"

"Man-eating tree."

"Isn't that a myth?" Nian asked, taking a giant step back as seaweed curled over top of the front bumper and inched toward his boot.

"You tangled with it." Controlling the speed of Angela's rise, Sloan returned his mouth to Theodora's temple. The angry hum of earth energy downgraded. He switched the streams, drifting away from the more volatile current to re-engage with the Meridian. The buzz in his veins moved from brutal to calming and smooth. He turned the valve, widening the stream, feeding her more healing energy. "Real enough for you?"

"Hellfire," Nian muttered. "What else you got in there?"

A lot of things. All nasty. All lethal. All part of the botany experiments he conducted when not planted inside the Hub.

His packmates thought he never did anything other than monitor computer systems and hack through firewalls. On the contrary. He might not spend as much time as he wanted to inside the green-house, but he never went more than two days without saying hello to his collection—or what Angela liked to call his pets. Like all things beloved, the Yateveo re-quired attention. Lots of it. Otherwise, the antisocial creature would forget the manners Sloan taught her, spill out into the corridor, and eat everything that moved.

Affection for her rolled through him. His mouth curved up at the corners.

Seeing his expression, Nian shook his head. "Forget I asked. I really don't want to know."

"Probably a good call," Gage said as Angela came into view.

Tangled up in thick, tentacle-like ribbons, covered in slime, she exhaled on a curse as his monster dragged her onto the LZ.

Nian snorted in amusement.

Lips twitching, Haider shook his head.

"You okay?" Gage asked, grinning like an idiot.

"Drop her," Sloan said, gaze raking her, searching for injuries. Nasty bruise on her cheekbone. Superfi-cial scrape marring her jaw. Arm and elbow tucked tight to her ribcage. No broken bones or serious gashes. Nothing that wouldn't heal without Rikar's help. "You'll live."

"Terrific." She grunted as ribbons of seaweed dropped her five feet from where he sat. With a wince, she rolled from her back onto her knees. Face contorted in disgust, she stared at her hands, then flicked her fingers. Slime hit the cavern floor with a splat. "Ugh. Revolting."

He smiled. "You're welcome."

She rolled her eyes, then returned her attention to him. Sitting back on her heels, she ran her gaze over Theodora. "How's she doing?"

"Better. Holding steady. She's deep in the stream."

"You're feeding her?" Her lips parted as wonder flickered across her face. "She's yours?"

Sloan held her gaze, but didn't answer. As his apprentice, she shared a special bond with him. One that allowed her to read him.

"You found her, Sloan," she said softly, pleasure shining in her hazel eyes. "Pleased for you, brother. So freaking—"

"All right," Gage said, pissy tone shattering the moment. "We gonna have a love-in or go inside? My mate's waiting. I need to give her another of the orgasms she likes so much."

"Jesus," Nian muttered.

"Uncool," Haider grumbled, throwing a dirty look at his best friend. "Not all of us have mates, you know."

Gage fielded the complaint with a shrug. "Get on that, man. Nothing like it the world."

"Fucking hell." Cupping the back of Violet's small head, Haider tucked the sleeping child into his shoulder and strode toward the back of the landing zone.

Footfalls echoed through the enormous cavern.

Sloan's monster retreated, slithering back into the abyss as Haider murmured to his own beast, one only a silver dragon could create. As volatile as Sloan's pets, the energy shield that protected Black Diamond, keeping it hidden from human and enemy Dragonkind alike, had a mind of its own. The thing loved Haider, doting on its maker, but despised everybody else, often lashing out with its multi-tailed lightning whip when he and his packmates crossed the threshold...and that was on a good night. Sometimes, the bad-tempered beast refused to allow Nightfury warriors entry at all. Something Sloan both lamented and adored about his friend's creation.

Magic undulating like a heat wave around him, Haider whispered to the beast. The energy shield hummed, welcoming its master home, opening the portal without the usual hissy fit. The wall holding up the back of the cavern went from solid stone to wavy blur. Dust motes played in the drift of musty air as the archway appeared, granting entrance into the underground lair.

"I'm gonna have Myst take a look at Violet. Confirm she's all right." Poised on the threshold, mercury eyes shimmering, Haider looked over his shoulder. "You coming, Sloan? Or are you taking your mate deeper underground?"

He debated a moment, instinct warring with practicality. His dragon half wanted to tunnel through solid rock and build a burrow for Theodora. Keep her safe. Keep her close. Keep her comfortable while she finished healing. Waking up curled around her in a private place, with his hands on her skin and his face in her hair, instead of inside a lair crawling with his brothers and their mates, would give him the time he needed to explain her new situation.

Primal need urged him to do it. But logic prevailed, pushing him away from compulsion. Creating a nest for his female would feel good, but it wouldn't be wise. Theodora might still be healing from her wounds, but the energy he shared with her had done its job, pulling her out of danger. She no longer needed the extra boost of energy burrowing would give him. Which meant taking her into the lair, laying her in a comfortable bed inside a normal room, was the better play.

Theodora didn't know it yet, but the instant he touched her, the life she knew had ceased to exist. He'd claimed with her in the way of his kind. She'd accepted and grabbed hold of the connection. Once energy-fuse took hold, the bond was irrevocable, tying minds, hearts and souls together. Fair or not, in less than an hour, her circumstances had changed. She now lived inside a Dragonkind pack.

The shift in situation would be difficult for Theodora to understand at first. It always was when a new female entered the lair. But he'd paid attention, watching his brothers with their chosen females. His job as Theodora's mate was important, but not that complicated. He must see to her care, ensure she had everything she needed to be comfortable, and convince her to stay. Pretty straight forward, so...

Much as the idea inspired him, burrowing was out.

Boots thumping on stone, Nian walked around the beat-up Honda. "Sloan?"

"Good to go," he said, his mind on the greenhouse and the bed he'd moved into the middle of his jungle.

Energized by the idea of waking up with her there, he wrapped Theodora up and pushed to his feet. Her brow furrowed as he walked across the LZ. Her bioenergy spiked. He murmured, using his voice to soothe her.

As she settled back into a deep sleep, he released a long breath. "The earth energy boosted my connection with her. She's healing faster than expected. I'm bringing her inside."

"Good call." Auburn hair full of goo, short strands sticking up at odd angles, Angela pushed to her feet with a grunt of pain. "Violet's gonna want her mom when the sleeping spell wears off."

"Right," he said, thinking he now had two females to win over.

A pint-sized, ringlet-haired one, and the green-eyed beauty he carried over the threshold in his arms.

**13**

Holding his breath, Azrad slipped his arm out from underneath Kasi. Dead weight against his shoulder. Curvy body nestled into his side. A gorgeous face, eyes closed, thick lashes on display, turned his way. The total package in human form. The kind of female he'd imagined for months every time he climbed into bed alone each day, struggling to find sleep.

After seeing Gage with his mate—how the warrior handled her, his gentleness, his attentiveness along with his drive to protect her—Azrad couldn't stop thinking about what he'd witnessed. The way Samantha reacted to her male in the clearing intrigued him, providing an endless source of fascination.

A smart male would let it go. A diligent one would purge the memory from his mind.

Inching away from Kasi, he tried to do both. Recall kicked him in the teeth, forcing him to replay the encounter inside his head. Focus keen, he devoured the details, feeding a beast already raging out of control. Logic kept insisting he smother the flames. Do the hard thing. Choke on the smoke and return to baseline. Nice and normal. The best course of action, all things considered.

Like a fool, he stoked the internal fire instead, needing to believe, dreaming the dream as the idea of claiming a mate of his own picked up a shovel, dug a hole, and took root. Like always. Havoc arrived right on time, messing with his mental grid, opening a fissure to a hidden place inside him. Deep yearning spilled out, forcing him to imagine his life with his dream girl in it.

Undaunted, hope picked up the gauntlet, asking dangerous questions. How would she react when he finally found her? What would she say when she saw him? Who would she be—the perfect mix of tough and tender, like he dreamed, or something else entirely?

Azrad bit down on a curse. Pointless speculation. And yet he tortured himself anyway, going round after round, beating himself up with the possibilities. Nothing but pleasant fiction. Or so he'd thought...

Until three minutes ago.

The second he woke with Kasi in his arms, he understood the true meaning of trouble. Even without talking to her, he recognized her for what she was—his Achilles heel.

Gaze riveted to her face, he reached for the side of the mattress. His fingers found the edge. Azrad pulled. He glided into a smooth, sideways shift.

The light grey duvet cover rustled beneath him.

Kasi muttered in her sleep, sounding unhappy, making him want to embrace the insanity, roll back into bed, and curl around her like well-fed cat.

He kept moving, shoving a fat pillow into her arms, replacing his warmth with soft cotton and feather down. She frowned her disapproval. He breathed out in relief as she accepted the substitute and settled back in, breathing even and sure, no indication he'd disturbed her sleep.

Thank fuck. His first big break. One he needed just as desperately as a way out.

Any more of *that* kind of closeness would lead to other things. Things he wanted, but didn't need. Things that must be murdered before his beast got the better of him, and he ended up in even more trouble. He frowned at the lamp sitting on the bedside table. Shit. *More trouble.* Was that even possible? Seemed unlikely, given he was already in over his head, screwed in ways he didn't understand...and really didn't like.

Staring down the barrel of a loaded shotgun would be easier than being trapped inside a swanky apartment with Kasi as a companion. Alone, he would've been all right. With her, he struggled to concentrate. Unfortunate under the circumstances. A little clarity would go a long way, given the situation—and the fact he was the only one to blame.

He'd put himself inside the room, gone undercover to impress his blood brother and right Ivar's wrong. He'd planned the mission and carried it out, preparing to land right where he sat now—in the middle of a fucking mess.

With a soft growl, he dragged his attention from Kasi and sat up. Swinging his feet over the edge, he gripped the mattress with both hands and set his bare feet flat on the floor. Head bowed, he stared at the area rug. Muted colors, busy pattern, soft underfoot. The feel of the short threads grounded him.

His focus narrowed. The last of the drug faded. Dragon half wide awake, magic thickened in his veins, heating the space around him.

Without moving, he sent his senses roaming. Large, open floor plan. Warm air. Faint buzz coming from across the room. He sent his sonar exploring, mapping the space, filling in the blanks without looking. A grid opened inside his mind, giving him an impression of his prison. Matte white walls and ceilings with rounded corners composed of molded plastic. No seams in the structure. No plaster to break through or flaws in the design. Though he sensed the ragged rock edges beyond the cosmetic perfection…along with all the *Blakeite*.

Reaching out with his mind, he probed the mineral, following the thick veins, looking for weaknesses. He clenched his teeth as the rock reacted to his probe, vibrating in warning. A hum began inside his head. His sonar winked out. The map he held in his mind's eye flickered, then disappeared, leaving him without a clear image. Zero information gathered. No weaknesses for him to exploit. Just miles of impenetrable *Blakeite* threading through compact granite.

"Shit," he growled softly, knowing he'd never get a signal through the tangled threads of a mineral designed to suppress his magic. Which meant…

He couldn't use mind-speak to call for help.

Worry sank deep.

Azrad pushed to his feet. The bed creaked.

With a sigh, Kasi shifted across the duvet. He glanced over his shoulder and, muscles tense, feet rooted to the rug, afraid he'd woken her. Relief streamed through him when she stayed in la-la-land, hugging his pillow closer. The instant she curled into the warm spot left by his body heat, he scanned the room, searching for imperfections. He didn't need much, a crack, a forgotten detail, a minor chink in the apartment's armor. Something, anything, no matter how small, to use against the madman who'd designed the underground complex.

Turning full circle, Azrad scanned the space again. He noticed the cameras his second go around. Tiny pinpoint lenses the size of spider eyes, mounted in every corner, installed to capture every angle and invade the privacy of whoever occupied the suite. A twenty-four-hour feed, no doubt sent directly to Ivar's personal computer.

Azrad bared his teeth.

The fucking sicko. After months spent undercover inside the Razorback pack, nothing should surprise him about Ivar anymore. The cameras, however, threw him off course. The bastard was smart and methodical, a skilled scientist who loved manipulating variables and analyzing the results, but a voyeur? Azrad frowned. He hadn't read that on him. The eyes watching him, however, didn't lie. Ivar planned to record his warriors—and the females assigned to each—during the realignment. More data for his experiment. Living proof to add to his pie charts, bar graphs, and statistical analysis. Maximum humiliation delivered inside a luxury suite built for one purpose—to obliterate a female's right to choose and take control of her womb.

The breeding program. A sick invention created by an even sicker mind.

Acid sloshed in the pit of his stomach, rising to touch the back of his throat. Swallowing the bad taste in his mouth, Azrad left Kasi to sleep and stepped off the rug. He pretended to be relaxed for the cameras. In reality, he scanned every surface, leaving nothing untouched, walked beneath the archway. His bare soles met heated floors. His gaze met haute luxury as he stopped beside the kitchen island and looked around.

Nothing but the best. Rich wood cabinetry. An ocean of white quartz countertops. High-end stainless-steel appliances. A pair of high-brow, low-backed stools sat beneath the lip of the island. Beyond them lay the living room, kitted out with a television mounted to the wall and a teak entertainment unit stretching from floor to ceiling and wall to wall.

Lots of shelves. Most held books. A single section housed a record player and high-end speakers. Vinyl records stood on edge above and below it. Looked like a decent-sized collection. Nowhere near as large as his own—not many were—but as he stepped around the long, deep-seated sectional, the need to explore hit him. He wanted to slide the records out, one by one, and see what kind of music lay hidden inside the paper sleeves. An excellent distraction. Just as Ivar intended, so instead of assuaging his curiosity, Azrad turned and studied the space again.

A side table beside the couch. Another colorful area rug large enough to span the entire room. No armchairs. No throw pillows. No fussy artwork hanging on the smooth walls.

Clean lines. A cozy setup. A lovers' paradise full of comfortable furniture, fancy-ass décor, and...more spider-eye cameras than he cared to count. The fuckers were everywhere, all over the bedroom, kitchen, and living room, but—

His eyes narrowed on two doors in the room.

The first he ignored. He didn't need to examine it. With nothing but a glance, he understood its function. Thick vault door. Complicated locking mechanism comprised of three individual combination locks. No way to break through the reinforced steel without the full force of his magic. No way to unlock it from the inside. Ivar was kicking it old school, using the tried and true to keep Azrad contained.

Which left door number two.

Footfalls quiet, he moved toward it and grabbed the handle. Cool metal settled against his palm. The quiet hiss of hinges sounded as he pushed the heavy wood panel open. He stepped over the threshold. Motion sensors activated. The lights came on, making black and white tiles gleam. Huge shower stall surrounded by glass walls to his right. Freestanding soaker tub to his left. Whitewashed wooden vanity with double sinks tricked out with brushed nickel hardware and a pair of antique mirrors. Separate room for the toilet with a pocket door.

Taking it in without really seeing it, Azrad continued his assessment. He exhaled in relief. No cameras in the bathroom. A space shrouded in privacy. Triumph rolled through him. It wasn't much, hardly anything at all, but—

A whisper of air ghosted across the back of his neck.

Steel flashed in one of the mirrors, reflecting movement behind him.

With a curse, he spun around to face Kasi. Blue eyes flashing with fury, she lunged at him with a butcher knife. Blade held high, she slashed at his chest, aiming for his heart. Azrad jumped back, avoiding the downward arch, drawing her further into the room. Each breath coming hard, she attacked again. Bare feet sliding across ceramic, he blocked her thrust and turned his hand. Fingers wrapped around her wrist, he pushed her arm out of the side and twisted, not enough to hurt her, just enough to force her to drop the knife.

Her fingers started to open. The blade wavered in her hand. "No."

"Kasi."

"No."

Refusing to apply more pressure, he held steady. "Let it go, *kazlita*."

"Fuck you!" Desperate to hold on to the weapon, she surged forward, then back, trying to break his hold. "Fuck you! Fuck you! *Fuck you!*"

"I'm not going to hurt you," he said, voice soft, gaze boring into hers. "I would never do that."

Chest heaving, she hissed at him.

"I'm Azrad."

"Like I care. Like you're not like all the rest. Like you're..." Her voice broke.

His heart broke with it as tears filled her eyes. "I'm not like them. I swear, Kasi. I won't hurt you."

Baring her teeth, she tried to stab him again. The tip of the blade nicked the back of his hand. Stepping into her, he yanked the knife from her grasp. As he tossed it into one of the sinks, she screamed, the sound so rage-filled he flinched. His grip on her loosened. Bleeding emotion, aura flashing bright with fury, Kasi attacked, pummeling him with her fists, kicking him with her feet, aiming for his most sensitive spots.

An excellent strategy if used against a less skilled opponent, but he knew all her dirty tricks. He was a warrior, born and bred, a vicious predator designed by nature and nurtured by a harsh prison. He didn't just fight, he brawled, destroying his enemies without conscience or mercy. Problem was...

Kasi wasn't his enemy. She was a female in pain, so traumatized by the Razorbacks and what she'd endured she couldn't stop. Azrad understood her reaction. He'd swum in those perilous depths most of his life and knew the damage sinking into a place like that could do. She needed an outlet, a way to purge the emotion...and somewhere safe to direct it.

He gave her one, welcoming her fury, becoming a willing target, allowing her what no one else would survive.

Focus steady on her, he moved in concert, but kept her inside the bathroom, away from watchful eyes. She lunged at him again and again, trying to reach the knife on the countertop. He turned each punch aside with gentle hands, shifting left, moving right, channeling her rage even as he sought a way to soothe it.

As she unraveled, he talked to her, voice low, saying things while saying nothing at all.

She sobbed each time she landed a blow, one after another until her strength waned and her arms gave out. Tears running down her cheeks, she backed away. He followed her retreat, staying close without invading her space, herding her toward the shower stall.

"Easy, Kasi."

She bumped into the door, then scuttled sideways along the wall. "I can't...I can't..."

"I know, but I can. Let me help you," he said, holding his hands out.

She veered left to get around him. He stepped right, blocking her path. Kasi raised twin fists. He kept his open and out to the side, hemming her between him and the large glass enclosure, Azrad murmured his wishes. Magic sparked, curling down his spine. Water came on, cascading from two rainfall showerheads, splattering across tiny black and white tiles.

He adjusted the temperature with his mind. "Right now, I'm gonna lead and you're gonna listen."

"No," she whispered.

"I know it's not fair. I know you don't trust me, but I'm telling you that you can." He flicked his fingers. The glass door opened. "Step inside, Kasi. Water's just right."

She shook her head.

"Yes, *kazlita*," he said, calling her *fierce one* in Dragonese. "Get in."

Breath hitching, bottom lip trembling, she stared at him.

He held her gaze, then tipped his chin. Fully clothed, shaking like a leaf, she stepped into the shower. Following her inside, he closed the door behind him and stood close without crowding her, using the rush of the water to muffle his voice from those controlling the cameras. He debated a second. Should he be honest and lay out the situation or shield her from it?

Excellent question. No clear answer.

Instinct urged him to protect her by softening the blow. Respect for her strength warned him to go the other way. Kasi might be frightened, but she wasn't weak. She wouldn't like it. No female would, which might lead to another round of one-sided combat, but...

She deserved the truth. All of it. Down to the last detail.

Water hitting him between his shoulder blades, Azrad slicked his hair back and started talking. He started out fast, feeling awkward, discomfort making his throat tight and his chest burn. Standing in wet jeans and a soaked t-shirt, he forced himself to continue, telling her things he'd never shared with anyone. He told her about Prague. He shared about Dragonkind, the Archguard, and the murder of his sire, along with his desire to join the Nightfury pack.

He explained the breeding program, the reasons behind her capture, then laid out his mission.

Arms curled against her chest, she drew a shaky breath. "You're undercover? You've been searching for us?"

"For months. Along with Kilmar and Terranon."

"Your friends?"

"Yeah."

"They're here too?"

He nodded.

"Do you know who they chose?"

"Kilmar's with the Asian female and—"

"Her name's Riku."

"Terranon chose the black girl."

"Mirabel," she whispered, pain in her light blue eyes.

"They're safe, Kasi. My warriors won't hurt them. The other females...the two with the Razorbacks...I have no way of knowing—"

"God help me." Bowing her head, she pressed her palms against her forehead. She stayed that way, curled in on herself, aura dimmed by sorrow. One second ticked into ten. Her hands dropped. Her chin came up. She wiped away another round of tears, then squared her shoulders and took a deep breath. "What else do I need to know?"

The bleakness in her expression tightened his chest. Her strength of spirit, the steel in her words, earned his respect.

Hiding nothing, he ran down every detail—his history, his imprisonment inside Tazenmed, how he'd escaped and made his way to Seattle. She remained silent as he showed her the brand on his forearm, burned into him by Rodin on his seventh birthday. The scar—a series of numbers signifying his status as a slave in the Archguard's underground fight club—marred more than just his skin. The mark seared his very soul.

As he talked, Kasi calmed, listening as he laid himself bare, telling her about being forced to fight for his life as a child and his hellish existence inside the prison he'd been sent to before his first shift into dragon form. He left nothing out.

She stood under the water, quiet, focused, absorbed.

"So…" he murmured, blinking water droplets from his eyes. "That's it."

Looking shell-shocked, Kasi stared at him. "That's a lot."

"Yeah."

"We're a real pair, aren't we?"

Throat still tight, he swallowed. "Seems like it."

"Okay, so…" she whispered, raking wet hair out of her eyes. "What next?"

"If I'm gonna get us out of here, I'll need your help."

"How much time do we have?"

"Three days, five hours, and fifty-four minutes."

"That's really precise."

"You see the clock on the bathroom counter?" he asked, pointing over his shoulder. "It's ticking down, like a—"

"Bomb."

"Exactly."

White teeth worrying her bottom lip, she frowned. "You got a plan?"

"A good one," he said, going over the details inside his head. He didn't need much, just—

"Lay it out for me, Azrad."

"I need to find a weak point in one of the wall

joints. If I can find a crack—a small hole or unfinished edge—Scandal will be able to slip through and climb to the surface. If we can get her topside and clear of the *Blakeite* blocking my magic, I'll use her like an antenna, call for help, and get the backup we need to break out of here."

"Scandal?"

"Scandela, my spider," he said, touching the tattoo on the side of his neck. The moment his fingers brushed her, Scandela woke. The ink on his skin shifted. His spider moved from 3D image to living creature in an instant. He turned his hand, palm up. The weave of red arachnid skin flashed as Scandela leapt from his throat onto the tips of his fingers. "She's with me everywhere I go."

Lips parted, Kasi leaned in to get a better look. "She's beautiful. Venomous?"

"Deadliest in the world."

"Cool."

"You like spiders?"

"Before...you know, before all this..." Her voice cracked. She cleared her throat. "Before I got taken, I..."

"Yeah?"

"Late bloomer. Work during the day, evenings and weekends at school," she said, making no sense. Azrad didn't ask her to explain. He waited instead, watching her head tilt as she studied Scandela. "I'm doing my Ph.D. in entomology, with a heavy lean toward—"

"Arachnids." His mouth curved. A spider lover. A girl after his own heart.

"I was planning a trip overseas. Maybe to Southeast Asia. Lots of spiders there."

"I've got a great collection at home."

"Live?"

He pretended to be offended. "Of course. Wanna see it after we get out of here?"

Wariness entered her eyes.

"It's not going anywhere," he said, disappointed but not surprised. Setting Scandela on his shoulder, he studied Kasi from under his lashes. More relaxed, less afraid of him, but absolutely no trust. A natural reaction, given what she'd been through and her current situation. If he wanted to get to know her, draw her closer, he'd need to put in the effort. "How about we play the visit by ear?"

She nodded.

"You with me on the escape plan?"

Her chin jerked up. "I'm with you."

"The second we step out of the bathroom, we'll have eyes on us, Kasi. I don't know whether the apartment is mic'd, so watch what you say."

"Got it," she said, reaching out to turn off the shower. "We need to start searching. The instant we find a crack, Scandal can get to work."

His thoughts exactly.

Now, all he needed to do was pray his plan worked and the cavalry arrived before the clock ran down and he lost his mind.

**14**

---

The loud thump outside his door woke him.

Tangled up with his mate in the middle of his bed, Sloan grumbled as the noise drew him out of a deep sleep. Tucked tight against him, ass to his groin, back snug against his front, wearing nothing but a racy pair of panties, Theodora didn't move. She was dead to the world, deep in the stream, taking every bit of healing energy he fed her.

Half-asleep, he slid his hand across her bare belly, then up to curl over her waist. Enthralled by her softness, he stroked the pad of his thumb across her skin. A barely there touch, just enough to heighten the hum and his contentment. Goddess, he loved being wrapped up in her, adored everything about it—her scent on his skin, the vibrancy of her bioenergy, the way she fit in his arms along with how she snuggled in, seeking maximum contact in sleep.

A fantastic trait for a female.

Not something he'd pushed, a right Theodora had claimed the instant he came near her. He'd expected the closeness, needing three points of contact—lower back, nape, and temple—to provide what she needed to heal. What he'd gotten instead surprised him.

Trying to be respectful, he hadn't undressed her. Three-quarters unconscious, one-quarter frantic, she'd taken off her own clothes while he watched, partly shocked, mostly amused.

The image of her rolling around in his bed wasn't one he would forget. He could still see her—dark hair rippling as she wrestled her shirt and bra off, muttering incoherently, kicking her shoes halfway across the arboretum before attacking her jeans. He'd helped with the last, tugging her feet free of denim cuffs before settling beside her. She'd done the rest, pressing up against him, tucking her face into his throat, not just wanting him close, but *CLOSE!*

His mouth curved. Such a fond memory, one he'd cherish forever. Almost as much as the moment he lived now with her asleep in his arms.

He kissed the back of her shoulder, thanking her for the gift.

With a mutter, she shifted in sleep, twisting on the sheets. He loosened his hold. She turned in his embrace, ending up where she started, breasts pressed to his chest, head tucked beneath his chin, bent knee hooked over his hip, long, soft hair falling across his skin.

Heaven.

Down to his marrow, straight to his heart, soul-soothing contentment.

An odd feeling. One years of solitude and grief wanted him to fight. Self-imposed isolation was, after all, a hobby of his. A bad habit his brothers-in-arms worked hard to cure him of all the time. He'd spent years alone, and the rest keeping himself apart. Always around his Nightfury brothers, never quite part of the pack. Self-protection by design—walls up and knives out. The strategy, however, was no match for his mate.

In less than an hour, Theodora had knocked down his shields, blown past his hard limits, and obliterated his boundaries, finding the soft place deep inside him. Which meant...

He'd be an idiot to fight what she made him feel.

He wouldn't win. His mate refused to allow him physical and emotional distance, giving him no place to hide. Knot by knot, she unraveled the messy tangle inside him, helping him relax—truly let go—for the first time in over a decade. A miracle in many ways, a feat accomplished with no effort on her part. She'd taken him by storm, usurping his will, replacing it with her own. No need for her to talk him around to her way of thinking. The connection he now shared with her did all the work. Now, his dragon half followed where she led, allowing his mate to undo him without even trying.

A rumble started deep in his chest. Quiet on the inhale. Low growl on the exhale. A sound he'd never made before, and...

Shit.

*Fuck.*

He was purring. Freaking *purring.* So deep under Theodora's spell, his beast broke the surface while he rested in human form, forcing the low growl from his throat.

Sloan huffed. Unbelievable, yet somehow true. The power of energy-fuse and mate-to-mate connection showcased to maximum effect. Another gift, one the goddess saw fit to bestow, and he needed to work hard not to screw it up.

Dipping his chin, Sloan buried his nose in her hair.

His mouth brushed over her temple. Theodora sighed as the gentle touch drew energy across her skin. The threads tying him to her—and her to him—curled inward and multiplied, growing more resilient as the bond deepened. Heat flowed through him, nourishing her, caressing him from the inside out. Manipulating the stream, he mined her bioenergy, monitoring her vital signs and the healing process.

The Meridian surged. The channel widened, gaining in speed and intensity.

Gentling the stream to protect his female from the burn, Sloan controlled the flow and tapped into her life force.

Strong vibration. Steady heartbeat. Each breath coming easy and sure. Her wounds weren't yet one hundred percent healed, but his mate was out of danger, well on the way to being on her feet again come midafternoon.

With a hum, he drew his knee up and nestled his thigh between hers. One hand cupping her bottom, the other flat on her back, he nestled deeper, breathing in the sweetness of elderberries, and slid back toward sleep.

Another thud outside his door. One bang sounded, then another.

He cracked one eye open, wondering if Bastian would mind if he strangled whoever hammered on his door. A distinct possibility. His commander might enjoy killing enemy warriors, but didn't condone his own maiming one another.

Frowning, Sloan slid up onto his elbow.

Theodora mumbled in her sleep.

"It's nothing, *mazleiha*," he murmured, calling her *sweetheart* in Dragonese. Dipping his head, he kissed the hinge of her jaw. "Go back to sleep."

The crease between her brows smoothed out. A moment later, she relaxed, cheek resting on his forearm, legs still tangled with his.

The knock came again, more insistent this time.

His eyes narrowed, he glared through the gloom, through the collection of tree trunks between his bed and the door. An unconventional spot to choose for sleeping quarters. Most Dragonkind warriors slept in regular rooms surrounded by normal things. Not him. As an earth dragon, he required more than the regular fare. Daimler—the Nightfury pack's go-to guy—had helped him get it, providing the plans for the greenhouse. Sloan had done the rest, building the large glass and steel structure before filling it with his favorite plants.

His private space. Small when compared to Black Diamond's main arboretum, but his little patch of heaven was just as engaging. The garden under glass showcased a cornucopia of plants. He knew each by name. Outside his computer lab, the conservatory was his favorite place in the world. He spent an hour or two each afternoon roaming the rough pathways and serpentine garden trails, visiting the different sections, ensuring his garden thrived. Eleven thousand square feet of wonder. Nature's beauty on display, pulled from every corner of the globe. Some specimens humankind grew on a regular basis, but others, like the *Yateveo*, no one outside him (and a few others) knew existed.

Fed by earth magic and artificial sunlight, the greenhouse kept him sane, smoothing out his rough edges, providing the forestlike environment his dragon half required to stay even-tempered and strong. A boon, given the activity and frenetic energy inside the Nightfury lair.

Any member of the pack could visit the main arboretum. The huge glass enclosure wasn't, and would never be, off-limits. He liked that his brothers-in-arms and their females visited his sanctuary. Tania, Mac's mate, spent a lot of time walking the garden paths, exploring the vast conservatory, discovering his waterfalls, relaxing in his Zen garden and the tropical jungles he created. Sometimes, she even worked alongside him and Daimler in the vegetable patch, picking fresh produce to put on Black Diamond's table.

His bedroom, however, was off-limits. No one who wanted to remain healthy entered his private domain.

Which explained the knocking—now pounding— on his door. Whoever stood outside refused to enter, just in case he got pissy.

With a growl, he fired up mind-speak. *"What?"*

*"Know you're busy, Sloan, but—"*

A loud wail raged through the connection.

Sniffling and hitched breathes followed a second before Violet started crying again.

The sharp edge of urgency hit him. *Violet.* His mate's daughter sounded more than a little upset. She'd passed inconsolable, sobbing so hard she struggled to draw full breaths. He heard Angela whisper to her, trying to soothe a little girl who wanted her mother, refusing to accept anyone else.

Her distress jackhammered through him. Flipping the covers over his mate to keep her warm, Sloan slid away from her, moving slow, being careful not to disturb her. *"I'm coming. Stay there, I'm coming."*

Angela huffed. *"Been trying for five minutes, man. Can't get in. Your watchdogs won't let me open the door."*

With a snort, Sloan rolled out of bed. Compact dirt

met the soles of his feet. Tall ferns behind his head-board swayed. *"Watchdogs?"*

*"The monsters you call your friends."*

On the move, he checked to make sure Theodora slept on, then rounded the end of his bed. *Monsters.* She was referring to his vines and...really, he had to give it to her. The brutal razor vines were savage. Powered by his magic, ready to be called on at a moment's notice, the plants lived in his mind. He controlled them. He nurtured them. He called on *the horde* whenever he needed, enjoying the carnage each snaking limb left in its wake. They came in handy at other times too, like now, covering every inch of the greenhouse, walls, ceiling, and parts of the floor, enhancing the jungle-scape his magical side enjoyed.

More crying. The sound of little-girl sobs and hard, hitching breaths.

*"She wants her mom, Sloan."*

*"She'll settle for me. Theo's still out of it,"* he said, conjuring loose-fitting pajama pants. Walking through the leafy vegetation surrounding his favorite reading chair, he jogged between two tall elm trees. *"How long's she been crying?"*

*"I don't know. Not long, but—"*

*"Five and a half minutes,"* Rikar said, making his presence known.

Sloan's lips twitched. *"Keeping track."*

Rikar growled. *"Not used to hearing little girls cry, man. Discovering I don't like it much. Fucking heart-wrenching."*

He couldn't disagree. The sound of Violet's sobs were soul-destroying, tying him in knots, unleashing the need to shield, protect, and keep her from harm.

Dipping beneath a low-hanging branch, five feet from the entrance, Sloan murmured a command.

Leaves rustled. Thorns rasped against steel. Razor vines released the handles, then slithered away, allowing him access to the double doors. He flicked his fingers. One of the steel-framed, triple-paned panels swung inward on well-oiled hinges.

His mind took a snapshot. Angela standing in the corridor connecting his greenhouse to the main arboretum with a crying Violet in her arms. Rikar standing behind his mate with a helpless look on his face. Which naturally made him appear as though he wanted to rip someone's head off.

Stopping on the threshold, Sloan raised his hands. "Give her to me."

Big, light brown eyes full of tears landed on him. Chest hitching, nose running, bottom lip trembling, Violet blinked when he met her gaze.

"Zone," she said, reaching for him. "Zone."

"Hey, darlin'." Taking her from Angela, he swung her into his arms. She settled like a gift against him, snuggling in, reminding him of what he'd lost, but the universe now sought to give him back—a child of his own. "Having a hard time?"

"I want M-Mommy. I want my m-mommy."

"I know, Vivy," he murmured, tucking her close, cradling her slight weight, holding her like a sire would his daughter. "Let's go see her, yeah?"

A tear quivered on her chin.

Cupping her small head, Sloan wiped it away with the pad of his thumb. "It's all right, baby. It's all good now."

She sniffled. Her bottom lip trembled. Deciding to trust him, she set her cheek against his shoulder and settled in.

Another moment to cherish.

"Good, Vivy," he said, then tipped his chin at the pair outside his door. "Later."

Angela blinked, astonishment on her face. "That's it?"

"What else would there be?"

Rikar snorted in amusement.

Her eyes narrowed. "We've been trying to settle her down, like, *forever*. Nothing Myst tried worked. Nothing Hope tried worked. Nothing *I* tried worked. Sliver-tongued Haider couldn't even distract her. How did you do that?"

"Magic touch," Rikar said, grinning at him.

Sloan didn't bother to answer. He slammed the door in their faces instead.

Laughing, Rikar hammered the glass once with the side of his fist. A sign all was clear, all was good, and he'd handle Angela.

Turning his back on their shadows coming through from the other side of the door, Sloan retraced his steps through the woodland. As he walked, he murmured to Violet. Twirling a ringlet around her tiny finger, she hugged her stuffed rabbit, stuck her thumb in her mouth, and listened to his voice. The hitch in her breath disappeared. Her tears dried up. A hush gathered, following him through the foliage, across the greenhouse to the edge of the bed.

Restless without him, Theodora frowned in her sleep, shifting around on the sheets.

Violet popped her thumb out of her mouth. "She's sweeping."

"Yeah," he said, needing to return to his mate. "Mommy's tired. We're gonna need to be real quiet. You think you can do that, Vivy?"

Tipping her head back, she considered him a moment. "Okay, Zone."

"Thanks, darlin'" he said, loving the way she bungled his name.

"We going to sweep too?"

"Are you tired?"

"I don't want to sweep in my car chair anymore. It hurts my bum."

"You been doing that a lot?" he asked, knowing he shouldn't prompt her. She was a little girl, three, maybe four years old. Pumping her for information wasn't right. He crossed a line by doing it, but...

He needed to understand what happened in those woods...and what kind of trouble his mate had found. The assholes chasing her hadn't been messing around. They'd been heavily armed and well trained. His first guess: an experienced crew versed in the kind of wet work he and his brothers engaged in with the Razorbacks all the time. Which meant Theodora had landed in the middle of some serious shit. The kind that got her shot three times.

*Three fucking times.*

A wrong duty required him to right.

He'd start small by finding the two males who'd escaped his vines, extract the information he needed, then deliver retribution. The bigger game would come when he learned who employed them. He didn't care the bastards were human. He planned to gut every last one of the assholes, and those connected to them. No hesitation. No mercy. Nothing less than total annihilation would do.

His mate had nearly bled out in his arms. If he hadn't taken Angela out flying, if she'd stayed close instead of taking off on him, if he'd arrived five minutes later, Theodora would be dead.

*If.*

*If.*

*If.*

All the *could've-beens* plagued him. Such a close call. One that would never be repeated. He'd nearly lost his mate without ever having met her. He could be holding a dead child in his arms, instead of a living, breathing, beautiful one.

His chest tightened.

Rage, always close to his surface, welled inside him.

The sound of thumb sucking stopped as Violet froze.

Sloan tipped his chin down. Big brown eyes collided with his.

Drawing a breath, he locked the wrath away without killing it. He'd draw from the well another time. Right now, he needed to focus, give his mate what she needed, and Violet what she wanted. Forcing himself to move, he slid into bed. The mattress dipped. Silk sheets rustled. Eyes closed, still fast asleep, Theodora threw her arm out, reaching toward him and her daughter.

Violet wiggled.

Sloan set her down. The little girl burrowed into her mother, secure in the fact she was welcome. His heart thumped harder. His throat tightened as he took in the beauty. A family for him to care for and love. Two females in need of rescue and him.

A gift given to *him*...and no one else.

Adjusting the covers, he settled flat on his back, then reached out and hauled Violet and Theodora into his side. The little girl giggled. Her mother curled closer, wrapping her arm over his chest, throwing her thigh over one of his before setting her head on his shoulder, welcoming him in a different way. All without waking up, which left him free to ask questions he shouldn't be asking, and Violet all the time in the world to answer.

**15**

—————

S nug beneath the weight of warm blankets, Theodora woke to the sound of rustling and little-girl chatter. The second she lived with every day. The first didn't make a whole lot of sense.

Her place in New York had never sounded anything other than what it was—a one-bedroom apartment facing a busy street that saw more traffic than most four-lane highways. Her neighborhood specialized in barking dogs and honking horns, not gentle breezes and the scent of freshly cut grass.

Feeling thickheaded and wan, she stayed still and listened, taking stock, trying to wake up. Her brain chugged along, delivering information in drips and dribbles. Not unusual for her. She never jumped out of bed in the morning. The snooze button was her friend, which left her setting her alarm half an hour earlier than she needed to get up each day. Violet, however, started the day wired. She chattered to her stuffed animals, played at planning rescue missions to save elephants while telling stories and singing songs from the seventies and eighties. One hundred percent Theodora's fault. She never listened to anything but the classics. So, Violet didn't either.

Another soft breeze washed through.

Her mind cleared a little, allowing her to identify the sound. Rustling leaves along with the soft creak of branches. The ripples came in surround sound—from everywhere, as though she lay in Central Park beneath the trees instead of a bed. Soft sheets against her skin, a comfortable pillow beneath her head, forest sounds all around.

The data coming at her didn't compute. Particularly since she never took Violet there. Public parks made her skin crawl. She never felt safe outdoors anymore. A true shame, given her affinity for nature.

In the golden years, before her uncle took control of her life, she'd never wanted to come inside. Later, after he had, she'd braved his wrath by folding the glass doors fronting her studio wide open—breathing in the fresh air, throwing clay, making pottery, surrounded by homemade glazes, sculpting tools, and the kilns that fired her creations, bringing each one to life.

The last four years had changed things—and her —in innumerable ways. She rarely went outside anymore. Instead of settling in the country and calling a small town home, she hid in big cities. Safety in numbers. Nothing but another faceless human in a sea of them, camouflaged by inattentiveness, lost inside an urban landscape gone stale with apathy.

A good strategy, all things considered. The best one she knew. The Bratva had outposts everywhere, and her uncle used his connections.

Determined to drag her home, he'd spread her picture far and wide. Beatrice kept her apprised of his efforts. Paranoia did the rest, insisting Theodora change her name and location every few months.

She'd spent almost a year in New York, though. Her longest stint anywhere in the four years she'd been on the run.

Rubbing her eyes, Theodora mashed her lashes together. A shame she'd had to pull up stakes. She might not enjoy city life, but she'd liked being Olivia Cartwright. Straight, staid, boring old Olivia excelled at her job, liked her boss before Umbridge took over, and made her tiny apartment into a home. She'd done what most everyone did—her very best to get through the day unscathed.

Still groggy, she raked her hair out of her face and rolled from her side to her back. Dizziness disoriented her before discomfort intruded. Trouble spots acted up, making her aware of the soreness. Eyes closed, she compiled a list of her body's complaints: tightness across her lower back. Left leg stiff. Tired muscles, scratchy throat, and tender shoulder.

Nothing too serious, simple aches and pains, but she needed to get up, get moving, and face the day... the way she always did. Never any deviation in her routine. Wake up. Marshal her enthusiasm. Corral her beautiful, energetic three-year-old daughter. Stay positive in the face of what felt like overwhelming odds. Work through whatever problems came her way. Smile, be polite, hide the fact she was a member of the walking wounded and, most days, wanted to kick rude people in the shins. Never ask for help. Keep her guard up, the boundaries clearly drawn, and all the sightlines covered.

A lonely existence. A necessary evil, given her psychopath of an uncle.

With a sigh, she shoved the covers aside. Humid air washed over her bare legs. Theodora froze. A second later, her eyes popped open. She looked down and nearly jumped out of her skin. Not her regular pajama pants. Not her usual top, either. She always wore loose drawstring bottoms with a camisole.

Alarm spun through her as she stared at the huge t-shirt. Man-sized, probably a triple XL, and the soft, washed-so-many-times-black-faded-to-grey fabric declared someone's love of the Cincinnati Bengals.

Fear hit her with a shot of adrenaline.

Planting her palm on the mattress, she pushed upright. Another round of dizziness hit. Blinking, she steadied the mental slosh, then looked around. Not her pajamas, but someone else's. Not her room, but someone else's. Not her own bed, someone else's. A king-sized one planted in the center of what looked like a greenhouse.

One with greenery so thick with leafy vines she couldn't see any glass.

Shadows hinted at sunlight, but none shone through, leaving the cathedral-like space shrouded in shadows. And the trees... God, the *trees*. Huge elms, maples and red oaks, canopies spread wide, reached toward the peaked ceiling, making her feel as though she sat deep in a forest. Dimmed, oversized hurricane lamps hung from the steel center beam holding up the roof, spilling soft illumination, dappling over tangled vines and outstretched tree limbs.

"Shit." Heart galloping, she spun on her knees, moving across the silk sheets. The view became even more confusing.

A true jungle-scape with gigantic ferns and other leafy plants grew around the bed. The butterflies, though, threw her. She stared at the collection of colorful wings opening and closing on top of the headboard a second, then turned the other way. The butterflies took flight, finding new resting places as she searched for the bed's owner.

She was alone.

The smattering of mismatched furniture around the space told another story. Someone lived here. The ugly olive-green armchair with a ratty ottoman looked well used. A standing lamp with a ripped shade stood behind the chair, alongside a stack of books with cracked spines, suggesting whoever owned it spent a lot of time with his ass planted in the atrocious-looking thing. The beat-up antique table, with more books and a laptop sitting on top, rounded out the décor along with the bedframe—a low-slung, gorgeous piece made of black walnut. A work of art with a wide slab step surrounding the mattress, gorgeous woodgrain, and—

"Zone?"

She snapped her head toward the sound of Violet's voice, searching the shadows beneath the trees.

"Yeah, darlin'?"

The deep voice with a hint of Texas tugged at her memory. Pleasure curled through her. Fear shoved it aside, making the fine hairs on her nape stand on end. Violet's voice drifted through the quiet again. As was her way, she chattered, asking question after question, the last one about thorns. The man answered with gentle patience.

"Goddamn it!" Theodora said, kicking away the covers.

Ears trained on the conversation, she jumped off the bed and, missing the wide step, landed on the dirt floor. Sore muscles protested. Theodora ignored the discomfort and scrambled around the foot of the bed.

Ferns rasped against her thighs. Shoving the leafy fronds aside, she stepped through the jungle and followed the voices into the trees.

Dense shadows began to lighten. Arched glass doors, folded back and opened wide, appeared out of the gloom.

Feet moving double time, she shot over the threshold into a short corridor and ran toward another set of doors. Lights made to look like torches flicked on, leading her through, showcasing the vaulted brick ceiling and stone walls.

"These are yummy. I bet the spider likes them. I just said hello to him. He didn't answer, cuz he can't talk," her daughter said with her usual exuberance. "Do you think he has a house?"

"The spider?" the guy asked, sounding amused.

"Do you have any sticks? I could build him one. He would like that. A warm place to sweep."

"Well—"

"Do you want some? I already ate, like, a thousand."

The guy chuckled. "So many?"

Frantic to reach her child, Theodora burst through the door at the other end of the hall. Bright lights blinded her. The floor shifted from compact dirt to smooth tile. Seeing spots, she blinked as her bare feet slid across ceramic and—

"Watch out!"

Unable to stop, she slammed into the end of a table.

"Fuck," the guy growled as she grunted in pain.

Rocked by the contact, the plants sitting on the tabletop swayed. She whirled around, stumbling backward. Her mind took a snapshot. Another greenhouse with a peaked roof, but blacked-out glass. Row after row of rectangular tables topped by long wooden boxes. Plants *everywhere*, leafy vegetation of every size, shape, and color. Powerful lights, strung in straight lines above each table row, fed the indoor garden artificial sunlight.

Scanning the space, she hunted for her daughter.

"Easy," he said, beautiful baritone pitched low. "Violet's safe. You're good. Take a breath, *mazleiha*."

Chest heaving, she spun toward the owner of the voice. Her eyes swept over him and locked on. Hidden by a tall hedge, he met her gaze through a break in the leaves. His intensity captured her attention. The warmth in his eyes arrested her panic. Her mind stilled. A weird sense of calm moved through her, allowing her to take a breath as fear vanished, leaving her nothing to do but stare at him.

Dark brown eyes riveted to her, he held her steady.

Swallowing past her sore throat, she opened her mouth to ask him to return her daughter. Her voice stalled as he stepped out from behind the hedgerow, overwhelming her from ten feet away. Dear God in heaven. He was beautiful, stunningly impactful, with strong, masculine features that tilted toward the exotic. Black hair clipped short. High cheekbones in a gorgeous face. His muscular physique hit all the high notes, making her want to reach out and touch him... just to see if he was real.

Astonishment pushed her off balance. Intense attraction encouraged the fall, tangling her up in his strings. Lips parted, mind blank, she gaped at him.

"Theo," he growled, eyes shimmering an odd greenish gold.

She jerked as his baritone yanked on mental threads. Reality returned as her memory spun back into place. Recall sharpened, throwing down images like playing cards inside her mind. The old cabin. The nasty glint in Markov's eyes. Running through the woods. The sound of gunshots and the pain that followed. Her terror for her child and...this man.

"Sloan," she whispered, unable to shelve her surprise.

"You remember."

"I thought I dreamed you."

One corner of his mouth tipped up. "Real as ever, *mazleiha*."

"But that's... I mean..." Picking through shards of memory, she tried to put the pieces back together. "I remember running. I remember gunfire. I remember pain and you, but beyond that, I'm... It's just blank."

He shrugged. "You were out of it."

"Out of it?" she said, frowning at him. "I must've been a shade shy of comatose to have missed landing here."

"What's wrong with here?"

"It's a crazy-ass jungle." One that smelled like strawberries, looked like heaven, and, for some reason, felt just right.

Which meant she needed to fill in the blanks. Right now. Before things went from bad to worse, and she ended up running for her life again.

"Where am I?"

"Black Diamond, my home."

Theodora shook her head. She didn't understand. None of what she remembered—or he said—made sense. She'd been injured. He should've taken her to a hospital, not hunkered down with her inside his home. She might be missing pieces of the puzzle, but nothing erased the facts. She'd felt the force of the bullets strike. Gritted her teeth as agony clawed through her. Accepted her fate as blood rolled down her back. A warm, wet trickle. The sapping of her strength. The beginning of the end.

Or, at least, it should've been.

Tilting her head to one side, she slid her hand under the neck of her t-shirt and over her shoulder. Nothing but smooth skin. Her brow furrowed. She shifted focus, pressing against her lower back. She prodded with her fingertips. A tender spot, but no gaping wounds, stitches, or bandages.

What in the hell?

She hadn't imagined the attack. She wasn't crazy. No way she should be standing in a strange place staring at a strange guy while listening to her daughter sing Sheryl Crow's "All I Wanna Do" (repeating the chorus over and over) from somewhere inside the hedgerow when she shouldn't be *standing* at all.

The mother in her insisted she check on her child. She needed to ensure her daughter was okay, though the singing pretty much cinched it. Violet always sang when happy. Mostly rock songs, a preference that got her into trouble during her time in daycare, but... whatever. Theodora had no interest in forcing her child to sing nursery rhymes instead of Guns N' Roses and Bon Jovi. Her child, her decision. To hell with the naysayers of the world.

Ignoring the fact, she wore nothing but a t-shirt, Theodora crossed her arms over her chest and glared at Sloan. "What happened?"

"Theo—"

Violet stopped singing Crow's anthem and started belting out "Gimme All Your Lovin'" by ZZ Top.

Sloan grinned.

Momentarily dazzled by his beauty, Theodora blinked. Tingles attacked her in interesting places. A second (or ten) passed before she wrestled her body away from the dark side and dragged it back to the good side of the Force.

"Seriously, Sloan—what's going on? How did I make it out of there in one piece? How am I even standing—"

"Does your daughter nap?"

Thrown by the swift subject change, she scowled. "What?"

"Violet, does she—"

"Mommy!" her daughter screeched, coming out from the end of hedgerow carrying Lulu by one ear along with a small wicker basket. "You woked up!"

Heat hit the back of her eyes. Tears threatened.

Without thinking, Theodora ran straight for her child. Sloan stepped out of the way, helping her avoid colliding with him. The side of her shoulder brushed his chest. He grunted. She didn't slow and, bare soles slapping across tile, snatched her daughter from the floor. Warm weight settled in her arms. Her breath hitched as she buried her face in Violet's ringlets and hugged her tight.

Wicker creaked in protest. The sweet scent of fruit drifted up.

"Mommy, my rappaberries!" Wiggling in her arms, Violet yanked the basket sideways to protect her haul. The stuffed rabbit flew out of her little hand. "Lulu!"

With a quickness that defied logic, Sloan intervened, catching the pink ball of fluff before it hit the ground.

Violet gasped. Her arm shot out. Gaze locked on Sloan, she made a grasping motion with her fingers. "Mine, Zone. Gimme my bunny."

"It's Sloan, honey-bunny. Remember the sound the letter S and L make together? Sss...sss... Sssah-le-own... Sloan." Holding her daughter close, Theodora kissed the crown of her head. Soft curls against her lips. The sweetness of her little girl in her arms. God must really love her. He'd given her the world when he gave her Violet, then helped keep her safe.

Focused on Lulu, Violet reached for her companion as Sloan stopped beside her. "She's mine."

"What do you say?" he asked, holding her gaze.

Violet's mouth twisted sideways in disgruntlement.

Refusing to intervene unless she needed to, Theodora stayed quiet, waiting her daughter out, wanting to see how Sloan reacted to a stubborn three-year-old.

"Vivy," he murmured, tone firm.

"Please."

He nodded and held out Lulu. "Well done, darlin'."

Snatching her bunny from his hand, Violet pressed the fluffy pink head beneath her chin. Small fingers ruffled over fake fur before turning to rub the tip of one of the rabbit's ears. "I want down, Mommy. We're gonna eat pancakes."

She blinked. "Pancakes?"

"Mr. Goldtooth's gonna make me some."

Her brows popped up. "Who?"

"Daimler," Sloan said with a chuckle. "Black Diamond's chef and all-around caretaker. He makes awesome pancakes."

"Okay," she said, unable to shake off the feeling of un-reality. Everything felt as though she'd stepped out of the normal world and crossed into another. Setting her daughter down, she waited until Violet was steady on her feet before letting her go. "Are we doing that now?"

Sloan opened his mouth to answer.

Violet got there first. "Mommy?"

"Yes, honey-bunny?"

"What happened to your pants? You can't eat pancakes without pants."

A vague memory poked at Theodora. The sense she'd kicked off her shoes and yanked off her jeans flittered through her mind.

A wicked gleam in his eyes, Sloan chuckled.

She glared at him, guessing the loss of her pants (and the gaining of the t-shirt) was one hundred percent his fault.

"I'll find you some," he said, grinning at her. "Pick a few more raspberries before I get back, will you, Vivy? They'll go good with maple syrup and pancakes."

"Okay, Zone. I'll nick you some more," Violet said, dragging Lulu behind her as, basket swinging, she entered the hedgerow.

The second Violet was out of earshot, Theodora spun toward the gorgeous man who was great with kids. "You and I need to talk."

"Later."

"I had a backpack with me," she said, the urgency in her voice a rare slip of emotion.

She'd spent a lifetime deflecting. And practice made perfect. Giving anything away meant providing her uncle with ammunition, the kind of information he never hesitated to exploit. Always a bad idea. Understanding his tactics, being on guard every minute of the day, had taught her well. Her reflects were sharp...normally. But Sloan wasn't normal. Something about him said *other*. He seemed more perceptive, was definitely more intense, and she understood without knowing why she wasn't hiding anything from him.

A problem, given what lay inside her pack. The

bag contained her lifeline. All she needed to ensure her safety and, by extension, her child's.

Struggling to control the heave of emotion, she looked him square in the eye. "Did you see where it went? Did you pick it up?"

Speculation shuttered his expression. The outer rims of his irises contracted, making his eyes look green instead of black-brown. Her breath snagged as she picked up the shift. Weird. Such a strange shimmer. Nowhere near normal.

*Other.*

But...

Quick as a lightning strike, the glimmer disappeared. Green and gold returned to dark brown. A trick of the mind? After everything she'd been through, was she now seeing things? A distinct possibility, given all the weirdness. Maybe the stress was getting to her. Maybe she'd lost her mind. Or maybe the shifting light inside the greenhouse played tricks on her.

Holding her gaze, Sloan quirked a brow.

Theodora wanted to squirm. She raised her chin instead, refusing to shy away from his intensity. Showing weakness to a man who possessed none was the kiss of death, so instead of looking away, she stared back, reading him in ways she shouldn't be able to as an odd buzz droned in her veins.

Barely there, soft, almost silent, the vibration drew realization to the surface.

Somehow, someway, she was attuned to him—his mood, his thoughts, his intention. Everything about him screamed dangerous—the power of his body, the directness of his gaze, the lethal vibe he wore like a second skin—but as awareness rose, instinct spiked.

Logic took a back seat in the barrage, making her aware she wasn't afraid of him.

He wasn't a threat to her. Not now. Not ever.

The idea settled her. She drew a fortifying breath. "You have it, don't you?"

"I do."

"I'd like it back."

One corner of his mouth tipped up.

Unease curled in the pit of her stomach. "I need you to give it back, Sloan."

"Now?"

She nodded.

"Why?"

"None of your business."

"You're smart, Theo. You gotta know we're already well past that," he said.

"What do you mean?"

"Point of no return, *mazleiha*. Just one of the many things we're gonna talk about later. But right now, your girl wants pancakes, I'm hungry, and you'll want to shower before you put pants on," he said, then turned and walked away, leaving her wondering how he knew she wanted nothing more than a hot shower, knowing she shouldn't care.

Curiosity was a dangerous animal. Tempt it too many times, and a person got bitten. But as she watched him go, long strides steady, footfalls rapping across tile, a pang rolled through her. Her chest tightened with regret. He really was top-to-toe spectacular. Kind to her. Gentle with her daughter. A straight talker with a gorgeous voice, strong will, and magnetic presence. The kind of man most women would beg, borrow, and steal to land and keep, but understanding he wouldn't hurt her didn't mean he was safe.

No way she could trust him.

She'd been burned before when the stakes weren't nearly as high. She learned the hard way then, and remembered the lesson now. She needed to figure out where she'd landed, decide where she was headed, and move on to the next place. The sooner she retrieved her backpack, the faster she got on the road, the safer she and her daughter would be.

**16**

The sound of rainfall floated beneath the trees, tapping against the leafy undersides of wide-spread canopies. Boots planted in the dirt at the foot of his bed, Sloan listened to the soft echo of voices merge with the splash. An enchanting little-girl giggle. Her mother's amused response. Fucking beautiful. A sound that had never been heard inside his greenhouse. One he'd never imagined possible...until today.

Until Theodora showed up and split his narrow world wide open.

Nice and neat wasn't so tidy anymore.

Dragon senses attuned, he heard the dial turn. The click echoed inside his head. The sprinkle of rainfall rolled into the rushing cascade as Theodora experimented with multiple jets inside his shower.

She murmured in wonder.

Violet cheered.

His mouth curved.

He liked that setting too, often stood inside the glass shower stall in the back corner of his space and let the waterfall wash his tension away. Hidden in the depths of the greenhouse, his private bath's décor embodied rainforest and screamed world-class spa. Surrounded by trees. Wrapped in the protective curl of his climbing razor-vines. A five-minute walk from the buzzing hive of the Nightfury lair, yet a world away. A sanctuary for him to return to after a hard night of fighting.

A place he'd never thought to share with anyone.

Drawing a deep breath, he closed his eyes. Sound frothed over the rim of the indoor forest, flowing into his bedroom. The rushing waterfall. The splash of bodies under the cascade. The tapping of feet against marble tile and clapping glee of tiny hands playing in the water. His mate's laughter. More beauty. Something he didn't deserve, given he'd already crossed one line and planned to do it again.

Some wrongs, however, couldn't be avoided.

His need to protect Theodora was too strong. He couldn't deny the drive to see her worry-free and safe. Which meant...

No way in hell was he going to wait to find out who'd tried to kill her and why.

After his chat with Violet, Sloan didn't know much. He'd learned a few things, tidbits of little-girl life. Scraps of information, like: frogs lived in the ditch near her apartment, the daycare lady hated singing, and the neighbor across the hall picked his nose and ate it (which, according to Violet, was *gross*), and how often she played hopscotch, avoiding the many sidewalk cracks on her way to the corner every day. A corner at which Theodora made her look both ways *twice* before crossing. Quite an imposition for Violet.

His lips twitched.

He didn't have any experience with children, but man, she was cute, a fiery ball of exuberance in all her talkative three-year-old glory. She'd told him all kinds of things, all of which he found fascinating, but didn't need to know. The information he wanted, Violet didn't have. A credit to Theodora. Despite the uncertainty of her situation, she'd shielded her child, providing a pocket of safety for Violet, leaving her not only untouched by violence, but also unaware of the danger.

Something to celebrate. But a circumstance to lament as well.

Violet's ignorance left him in the dark, a place he didn't want to be when it came to his mate. He needed to know who threatened her, sooner rather than later.

Sloan wasn't stupid. He might have her now, but Theodora didn't plan on sticking around. His mate would run the first chance he gave her.

He frowned. Maybe that was for the best. Despite energy-fuse and his attraction to her, he knew she deserved better than him. He should do the right thing—the kind, unselfish thing—and leave her unclaimed. He could solve her problems, keep her safe, without making her his, but...

Sloan shook his head as pain spiraled deep. Shit. The thought of letting her go gutted him, shredding him from the inside out, making his dragon half snarl in disagreement. Too bad he understood what his beast refused to acknowledge: he had history. An ugly one that included a dead female.

"Fuck," he muttered, trying to navigate the swamp inside his head. Deep bog. Lots of muck. Way too many monsters lurking in mental shadows.

Logic insisted that Theodora didn't need the upheaval he'd bring into her life. His dragon half stood firm, winding him so tight primal need infected him like a virus, making him sick with the desire to claim what his beast believed belonged to him.

Sloan gritted his teeth. Goddess forgive him, but he wanted Theodora with a desperation that bordered on obsessive. But more, he needed to help her in the way of his kind, as a male would his female. No rhyme. Zero reason. All instinct. Brutal in its intensity as he remembered her fear in the forest, how she'd begged, so desperate she'd trusted a stranger with the safety of her child. For that alone, the bastards who hunted her would pay. With their fucking lives.

But first, he needed the information she refused to give him.

Theodora didn't give away much, but he read the desperation in her muscles and bones. She wore her past like a piece of clothing...in plain view. The abuse she'd suffered was written on her face and in the way she moved. The echo of it haunted her eyes. No outward marks, nothing but smooth skin, but he saw the scars beneath the beauty—a hurt buried so deep dread and doubt oozed from her pores, informing every move she made.

He might not yet understand all she'd endured—or who scared her—but he understood pain, had suffered so much of it his soul rose to greet the ache in hers, allowing him to see beneath her surface. He yearned to soothe her ragged edges. He longed to be her soft place to land. He wanted her trust. A tall order, given what he read in her bioenergy. Then again, he didn't need everything all at once. Still...

*Her trust.*

*Fuck.*

He knew he was asking a lot. Maybe too much. His mate didn't trust him. Theodora didn't trust anyone. Her focus was singular—keep running, stay hidden, protect her child at all costs. Which meant she would never tell him. He needed leverage. The kind that informed, but also provided the opportunity for his mate to heal.

Staring into the forest, Sloan shook his head. He hated to do it, but a male on a mission didn't shy away from the uncomfortable. Underhanded or not, he used every weapon in his arsenal. He might abhor the methods, but Sloan refused to give Theodora the rope to hang herself. Protecting her and Violet had become his reason, his end-all and be-all, which left him no choice. He needed to dig in without her permission, unearth what he didn't know and she didn't want to tell him. Begin the difficult process of unraveling the tangle inside her head and put her on the path to recovery.

With a soft curse, Sloan frowned at the collections of ferns surrounding his bed. Green fronds bobbed in the gentle breeze, shedding no light on the situation. The taut muscles bracketing his spine grew tighter. Magic pooled in his palms. Razor vines uncoiled, slithering around tree trucks and across the peaked ceiling, reacting to the volatile hiss in his veins.

Sloan pressed his chin to his chest. The knots sitting between his shoulder blades pulled. Discomfort raked its claws down his spine. Violet's voice drifted; she was voicing her disappointment about the lack of bubbles. His lips curled as Theodora answered, asking her daughter to be grateful for what she had, not disappointed by what she didn't.

The sound of her voice reached through the trees, soothing him from two hundred yards away. His tension downgraded from brutal twist to nagging burn.

Exhaling in relief, Sloan glanced at his watch. Black on black metal, military grade, high performance, one of his favorites. Pressing the side button, he turned the exterior dial. An hour before he needed to be inside the Hub. A mere sixty minutes until he discovered whether his plan had hit the mark or if he was shooting blind and way off target. No time like the present to invade Theodora's privacy.

Boot soles silent on compact dirt, he skirted the end of his bed and fired up mind-speak. Static flooded his senses as the connection unspooled.

His commander caught hold of the spiraling threads. *"Yeah?"*

*"T-Minus sixty-one and a half minutes."*

*"You ready?"*

*"All set. You?"*

*"No idea what we're gonna find, but it needs to be done. I'm tired of the bullshit."*

*"Everyone is, B."*

*"Should've done it years ago."*

*"Hindsight, man—always twenty-twenty,"* Sloan said, unwilling to let his commander shoulder the blame. Remaining apart, moving to America and out of Dragonkind circles, had been a pack decision, one Bastian spearheaded to get out from under the Archguard, but every Nightfury owned a vote. Sloan had cast his. So had his brothers-in-arms. None had hesitated to follow Bastian into unexplored territory. Seattle, no matter the trouble that arrived with Ivar and the Razorbacks, had given his pack a chance to start fresh, to become a family, instead of a band of misfits. *"Can't go back. Gotta—"*

*"Go forward. Yeah, brother, I know."* Bastian sighed, sounding pissed off. *"How is she?"*

*"Crazy gorgeous."*

B laughed. *"HEs usually are, but not what I meant, Sloan."*

*"She's mine, B. Goddess, unbelievable. The connection's strong, so fucking strong, she healed up tight in a matter of*

*hours,"* he said, stopping in front of table serving as his desk. Rare butterflies took flight, fluttering around him before flying off to find a quieter perch. *"But now, Theo's putting the pieces together. She's reading me, knows I'm not what I seem, and I'm having trouble hiding."*

*"So don't. Open wide, brother. Let her feel you. Give it to her straight. She's gonna know eventually. Might as well make it now."*

*"Easy for you to say,"* Sloan said, feeling the itch between his shoulder blades return. *"You got your mate in your bed."*

Revealing himself so completely gave him a bad case of indigestion. He lived in the shadows and existed on the outskirts. He never stepped into the light unless forced. His brothers-in-arms didn't like it, but after what he'd been through, trusting others seemed too big a leap to take. He stood on the precipice most nights, feet balanced on the narrow ledge, doubts circling. Should he? Or shouldn't he? He always wrestled with the answer. Sometimes, he won and his demons lost. Other times, like now, his past got the better of him.

He'd made mistakes. Serious ones. Ones that ended lives.

He didn't know Theodora well yet, but the bond he shared with her brought perspective into sharp focus. Now, he rode the razor's edge. He could turn away, dig up the intel he needed, then let her go. It wasn't too late, but...

What would that say about him?

Being conflicted was one thing; allowing fear to rule was another.

For some reason, the Goddess of All Things had intervened, placing his mate in his path. Her timing sucked—per usual—what with the war between the

Nightfury pack and Rodin coming, but as much as Sloan wanted to deny the truth, he couldn't.

He acted the part of a lone male well, but that was a lie. The instant he'd touched Theodora, need blew through his guard, exposing what he refused to acknowledge. He wanted what the mated Nightfury warriors possessed—someone to call his own. A female who loved him as much as he did her. No negotiating the depth of the emotion. Just straight-up acceptance with a healthy dose of devotion.

He already felt that for Theodora, already needed her in ways that boggled his mind. And yet the volatility of his nature continued to kick up mental debris. He'd failed one female and lost his newborn son. Despite the cosmic bond, was claiming Theodora the smart thing to do?

Yet another ball-busting question.

*"Sloan—"*

*"I got shit in my past."*

*"I know that, man. Doesn't mean you don't deserve her and the happiness she'll bring you."*

*"Might be she's better off without me."*

*"The connection's been made, Sloan. Can't undo it. She'll suffer without you now. You let fear guide you, you'll fuck it up and Theodora doesn't get what she needs. And that little girl, man, hate to say it, but she goes without the sire she deserves. You ready to land that blow?"*

Sloan clenched his teeth. *"Hardball."*

*"I'll play as rough as you need to make you see reason,"* B said, amusement in his tone.

*"Myst saw you in dragon form within minutes of meeting you. No buildup, just in her face with the fact Dragonkind exists. Theo's already planning to run. I'm gonna hafta finesse the hell out of revealing my dragon half to her, otherwise—"*

*"Talk to Forge. He did something similar with Hope."*

Sloan frowned. *"Seriously?"*

*"His mate wasn't brought into the fold in the usual way."*

*"By what—scaring the absolute shit out of her?"*

Bastian huffed as the barb struck. *"You need me to come over there and kick your ass?"*

*"Maybe."*

*"I'll rearrange your scales later. Right now, gotta go. Daimler's thumping on my frontal cortex."*

Shit. That didn't take long. Violet's breakfast order was already making the rounds.

Sloan sighed. *"Pancakes."*

*"What?"*

*"Never mind. See you in the kitchen."*

*"Bringing your new family?"*

*"Fuck off."*

Bastian laughed.

Sloan severed the connection and dragged his mind back to the matter at hand—finding the leverage he needed to protect his mate.

He picked up a stack of papers off the tabletop, tossed the pile out of the way, then murmured his wishes. His vines obeyed, unraveling overhead, revealing the treasure entwined in their embrace. He glanced up as the backpack came down. Canvas rasped against sharp thorns as the horde set the bag beside his laptop.

Listening to the splash coming from the shower, he glared at the black canvas pack. He hesitated a moment, then flipped the flap back and unzipped the bag. The top sagged open, unveiling the contents: small plastic containers sealed tight with chopped fruit sitting on top. Two boxes of unopened granola bars. A couple of bottles of water. Three coloring books and a large package of markers. Two zip-up hoodies, one large, the other small.

Finished with the main compartment, Sloan rummaged around in the interior pockets. He found and pulled out a wallet. With a flick, he undid the clasp and looked inside. Leather wallet with a designer label. A total of four hundred and thirty-three dollars inside. No ID, credit cards, or receipts of any kind. No memberships to big-box stores. Nothing with her name on it. Not a single thing that would tell him where she'd been or planned to go next.

Frowning, he shook his head. A ghost. His female was a fucking *ghost*.

He glanced in the direction of the forest. She was still in the shower, still unaware he'd invaded her privacy. Sloan returned his attention to the backpack. All of a sudden, he didn't feel quite so bad. Whatever he expected to find inside his mate's pack, *nothing* wasn't it. Theodora had been adamant, desperate, determined to get her hands on the bag. She wanted—no, *needed*—whatever lay inside it. Could be the cash, but instinct told him to dig deeper, look harder, uncover whatever she hid and didn't want anyone to find.

He checked the inside pockets again, then rifled through the outside ones. He unearthed two plain metal rings. One held a house key. The other looked like it might unlock a storage unit. Interesting in and of itself, but not the whole story.

Rotating the empty bag in his hands, he ran his fingers along the seams, inside and out. His skin snagged on a rough patch. He turned the pack inside out and—

Sloan hummed, discovering the imperfection in the padding lining the back.

He tugged on the tiny tear. Nearly perfect, so small

he almost missed it. Handsewn stitches began to unravel. Careful not to rip the material, Sloan pulled the seam open a little at a time. He stuck his fingers inside the opening. Papers rustled. Plastic crinkled. Leather rasped against canvas as he drew Theodora's cache from its hidey-hole.

"Clever girl," he said. "Well done, *mazleiha*."

He knew it was crazy to want to praise her for the deception, but couldn't help himself. She had all she needed to stay hidden from whoever hunted her. Six excellent fake identities, complete with birth certificates, driver's licenses, and Social Security numbers. No passports, but...

Whoever made the kits did topnotch work, almost as good as the guy Sloan used when the females inside the lair needed paperwork to move out of their old life in the human world.

Paper-clipping the fake IDs back together, he set them beside his laptop and opened the leather sheath. Two birth certificates slid out—one for Theodora Jean Romanov, the other for Violet Beatrice Romanov. No sire listed on Violet's papers. An Ezekiel Romanov listed on his mate's. Unlike with the others piled alongside the driver's licenses, Sloan knew without looking too hard these two birth certificates were government issue and authentic.

Good to know. Theodora could've lied about her name when he found her in the forest. The fact she hadn't pleased him more than it should've under the circumstances, but...whatever. She'd been on the run, injured, desperate to protect Violet in the face of overwhelming violence, and still, on some level, she'd trusted him enough to be honest.

A small thing. Hardly worth noting. It felt like a gift anyway.

After slipping the real certificates back inside the protective envelope, he went after the letters, unfolding each one. Type written. Professional looking. Glowing references from past employers. All someone would need to show a potential boss or HR department in order to land a new job. Each one with a different company name, logo, and address listed, but the same phone number.

The contact information of an ally? Someone Theodora paid to back up her references when a potential employer called? Or someone she trusted with her life?

All good questions. Ones he wanted answered.

Letters in hand, Sloan flipped his laptop open. Typing one-handed, he brought his supercomputer online. He connected to the network, dropped the open letters in a pile on the table, and brought up a search window. The AI that protected his system went to work as he fed the beast, plugging in Theodora's aliases and her sire's name, along with the phone number.

His system would provide any and all intel, tracking the names she'd used in the past, comparing her picture to millions of DMV records, unearthing job history, finding rental agreements, and any property owned for each alias...along with anything else of note. An unfair advantage, one his mate would never come close to counteracting. As an elite hacker, he was just that good. No one knew he existed, and no one ever would. His mate didn't stand a chance.

She'd be angry when she found out. After talking to Bastian, Sloan didn't care. Sometime during the conversation, he'd made his decision. He would be doing more than just keeping her safe.

"I'll be making her mine," he whispered, driving

the truth of it into his mind, muscles, and bones. The heart of him answered, settling into acceptance. Theodora belonged with him. He belonged with her. No sense fighting it. *"Mine."*

His dragon half bared his teeth in triumph.

Rolling his shoulders, Sloan worked out the kinks as the shower cut off. The sound of the waterfall died. Hushed voices drifted beneath the trees. Terry cloth rasped over skin as Theodora dried off.

Focused on the movement, one eye on the woods, Sloan returned her cache to its hidey-hole. He ran his knuckles against the broken seam. Magic did the rest, sewing the tear closed, erasing all physical proof of his incursion into her space.

He smiled. *Clever, clever, Theodora.* He adored her resourcefulness. He loved her resilience. He responded to the toughness of her stance, the look in her eyes, as she confronted him, telling him without words she wasn't afraid of him, demanding the return of her possessions.

She thought she could continue to go it alone. His mate was about to find out she was wrong.

She'd just gained a powerful ally, a warrior who would stop at nothing to keep her safe. No more running and hiding for his female. She had him to shield her now. He would make it right. He would see her happy and carefree, but...

"First things first," he muttered, listening to the pair dress in the clothes he conjured while neither was looking.

He needed to collect his females and get to breakfast. The sooner he ate pancakes with his girls, the quicker he'd figure out the best way forward. Winning Theodora wasn't going to be easy. She was too strong-willed, too independent—too fucking frightened—to take anything he did at face value. Without knowing it, in the way of mates and the Dragonkind world, she'd use energy-fuse against him—dig deep, burrow in, fortify the connection by trying to force his hand.

*Perfect.* A welcome strategy.

The more Theodora dug, the closer she'd come, and the sooner he'd get what he wanted—her acceptance as he set her down soft and loved her hard in the middle of his bed.

Shadows flickered as Theodora wound her way through the indoor forest. Lightning bugs flashed in near-dark, lighting her way along the twisting path. Leaves rustled above her head. She glanced sideways at a red maple, its wide trunk with a slash scarring the bark on one side. An old wound, but a fresh landmark for her, one she'd seen on the way in. Another minute, maybe two, and she'd be back where she started—standing in the middle of Sloan's bedroom.

An intimidating thought.

Her body, however, forgot to read the memo, fizzing with excitement the closer she came to a man she didn't trust, shouldn't want, but was attracted to all the same. Her reaction to Sloan baffled her, sending her in dangerous directions. Final destination? Complete disaster. She might not be a rocket scientist, but it didn't take one to know she was in serious trouble. The kind that got a girl laid, pregnant, and left to figure things out on her own.

Flexing her hand, Theodora gave her daughter a gentle squeeze. Oblivious to her mother's mental turmoil, Violet tipped her head back and grinned. Wet ringlets bobbed around her face. Theodora's heart caught as she smiled back. Her baby. So beautiful, precious beyond words, but her beauty didn't negate the facts. Theodora had been abandoned, betrayed, and forced to make her own way in the world, under the most extreme conditions. No support, dangerous family ties, a frayed lifeline thrown to her every once in a while by her sister.

Screwed, alone, and desperate with a baby to protect. Been there, done that, no need for her to pull on the frigging t-shirt. She already wore the label, battling to stay as far ahead of her uncle as she could every day. Which meant...

She had no excuse. She knew the dangers, had survived the unhealthy ambitions of powerful men and come out the loser. No one needed to tell her where the path to Sloan led. She understood, possessed real-world knowledge and carried the scars to prove it. And yet here she was, walking to her doom, jazzed by the prospect of seeing him again.

As though she hadn't just tangled with him half an hour ago.

Such a dangerous tango, one Theodora didn't want to dance. She moved to the beat anyway, unable to stop from stepping onto the floor with him. Sloan practically dared her to every time she met his gaze, freeing her to fight back for the first time in years. The zip in her veins didn't lie. She came alive in his presence, returning to the girl she'd once been, but had left behind. The strong, vibrant woman unafraid to share her opinion. The one who laughed often, loved hard, and showed it.

The phantom of a life well lived. Nothing but a

memory—until she'd woken up in a stranger's bed and clashed with its owner.

She sighed. "There is something seriously wrong with me."

"What, Mommy?"

"Nothing, honey-bunny," she said, smiling at Violet. "Time for pancakes."

"Pancakes!"

Misdirection one hundred percent successful.

Her daughter didn't need to know what occupied her mind. Hell, Theodora didn't even want to know, and she *owned* her brain. Well, at least usually. The usual, however, seemed to have abandoned her along with the ability to tell good from bad, safe from dangerous, and idiotic from smart.

Case in point? The fact she was still here.

She'd showered, for goodness' sake, dressed in clothes provided by a man she should've put in her rearview mirror the second she woke up.

Biting the inside of her lip, she fingered the toggle on the hoodie she'd zipped up less than five minutes ago. A deep hunter green. Her favorite color. Soft, comfortable, expensive, and as warm as the sweatpants she'd pulled on in the shadowy confines of a bathroom that belonged in a fashion magazine. Or inside the high-class, overpriced spa she'd frequented in her old life.

Beauty all around. There was no shortage of money inside Sloan's home.

The realization made her nervous. Money meant power. And men with power liked control. They also liked to win—at all costs. Which left her wondering what to do about Sloan.

As the question surfaced, more rose, attaching like train cars pulled by a locomotive going way too fast.

She chased the caboose a moment, struggling to understand her attraction to him. He was beautiful to look at, sure, but that wasn't it. In all her misadventures, she'd never met anyone like him. He spoke to her without speaking. He drew her interest in ways that couldn't be healthy. The mystery of him surrounded her. She couldn't touch it, but sensed what he concealed. So many secrets hidden in the depths of his eyes. Dark. Deep. Dangerous. He was a puzzle waiting to be solved, and...

Theodora pursed her lips. Nothing about him made sense. He was a moving target—solid one moment, gone the next, like a mirage in blistering desert heat. An enigma in some ways, knowable in others.

The dichotomy tilled the fertile corners of her mind, putting her need to know into overdrive. Curiosity encouraged her to get closer. Unwise or not, she wanted to listen, lean in instead of away, and solve the mystery he presented.

The kiss of death for someone like her.

She needed to keep her interest in him under wraps. Learning the hard way came with a few perks. The moment she gave in, Theodora knew she'd be done. Cooked. A couple of pieces of burned toast smoldering alongside the perfection on his plate.

His face.

His voice.

His body.

Dear God. *Perfection.* Utter beauty. He was soul-wrecking devastation for a girl with a hard shell, but a soft heart. Dangerous on every level, and yet the temptation of him taunted her, urging her to go the distance, to rip away the ribbons and bows to see what lay underneath—to discover what made Sloan. Was he shallow, like so many others? Or did he possess unmatched depths, the kind instinct told her lay beneath his surface?

Risky questions. Curiosity wasn't a luxury she could afford.

A man like Sloan could do real damage if she let down her guard. He'd burrow into her heart, make a home, encourage her to relax, trust, and...just be. Be who she wanted. The woman she was born to be, instead of the one her uncle had forced her to become.

Ducking beneath a low-hanging branch, Theodora hesitated a half a beat. She should turn around, take the safe route, avoid Sloan, and find another way out of Black Diamond. The best strategy, all things considered, but...her bag. She couldn't leave it behind, so instead of running, she kept walking.

Cork-lined sandals smacked the bottoms of her bare feet. Violet hop-skipped, jumping over raised roots, jarring Theodora with each tug on her arm, saying without words she wanted to go faster.

Probably not a bad idea.

Lingering in strange places never ended well for Theodora. She preferred to move fast when in public, narrowing the window of vulnerability. Here, though, in the shade of trees that should need sunlight to survive, but somehow grew tall without it, she refused to hurry. She drifted through the forest, moving at Violet's pace instead of urging her daughter to move at her own. Watching a butterfly float by, she relaxed little by little, letting nature do what it always did—stitch the tattered corners of her soul back together.

God, it had been so long. Years since she'd leaned into relaxation instead of away.

Breathing out, Theodora immersed herself in the feeling. Long-held tension resisted a moment, then let go, releasing her one taut finger at a time. The starburst of stress powered down, allowing a gentler buzz to take its place. She followed the curve, connected to the hum, hunting for the source.

Her temples tingled. A click echoed, unleashing a swirl of sensation. The soft hiss ghosted through her veins, drawing out the bad, replacing it with good.

"*Theo*," Sloan said, sounding surprised. "*You connected.*"

She frowned, then looked around, searching for him in the shadows. Prickles tapped down her spine. She heard him again, a soft murmur, a touch of awe, but none of it sounded in her ear. His voice came from inside her head.

She stopped mid-step.

Happily hopping along with Lulu, Violet didn't notice. She tugged her mother's hand, pulling Theodora forward. She kept her feet moving as her mind whirled, trying to make sense of the impossible.

She shouldn't be able to feel him, but she could.

He shouldn't be able to do what he was doing, but he was.

Her connection to him corkscrewed, dragging her deeper. An image flashed in her mind's eye, quickly there, just as quickly gone. But she saw enough to know where Sloan stood—twenty feet beyond the forest's edge, boots planted in the dirt, leaning his hip against the table, arms crossed, gaze intent, waiting for her and Violet to emerge.

She couldn't see him yet, shouldn't be able to hear him either, but she sensed him, the pull so powerful perception shifted, allowing her to see without seeing.

Tingles spread like wildfire, rampaging over the nape of her neck. A shiver shook her. Her heart picked up a beat, throbbing hard against her breastbone. Theodora swallowed. What she sensed was alarming, but also...somehow...enthralling. Her awareness of him crossed boundaries best left unexplored. She didn't understand it. All she could do was *feel*. Align with his heartbeat. Absorb his intensity. Stand in a space filled with desire and be eclipsed as he made his presence—and what he wanted—known without words.

Dear God in heaven. Her. Sloan wanted *her*. Despite the damage. In the face of her pain. All his rampaging pieces collided with shattered remnants of hers, reassembling the broken bits, filling in the cracks, smoothing out the rough edges until all she experienced was him.

The invasion should've scared her, shut her down and sent her running for cover. And yet she didn't make any effort to stem the flow. She allowed the strange tide to pull her farther from shore into deeper water, toward him.

Her feet kept moving. Her mind kept searching as she walked beneath the trees, looking for order in chaos. It wasn't natural. She didn't feel normal. She felt *better*, as though the thick curtain shrouding her had been ripped away. Insight took its place, leaving a sharpness of mind she didn't understand, but knew changed everything.

"Shit." Not good. Nowhere near good.

"Mommy." Bouncing along beside her, Violet yanked on her hand. Theodora glanced down. Head tilted back, Lulu clutched close, her daughter looked up at her with big eyes. "You said the S-word."

"Sorry, honey-bunny. I'm just—"

"There you are."

The deep voice curled around her. Residual vibration shimmied inside her head, making her skin prickle.

Theodora jolted. Her head snapped up. Dark eyes full of heat, Sloan met her gaze. Her belly fluttered. Desire, thick, raw, and rich, ran ragged over her senses. Theodora quivered. Sloan's nostrils flared. A growl rumbled from deep in his chest. Goosebumps spiked across her skin. She froze. Violet hopped, bumping into her side, dragging her out of her body back into her mind.

As her brain reasserted control, two things became apparent. One, she'd left the cover and security the forest provided. And two, Sloan looked like he wanted to eat her for breakfast. No need to read his thoughts or interpret his growl. The expression on his face said more than she needed it to, making her wonder what he'd do if she ended the day alone with him.

The thought banged around inside her head, knocking self-preservation loose. Goddamn it. She'd already decided—no more hot-guy complication. *Pointe finale.* Discussion over. The end.

She hadn't driven halfway across the country to get laid. She didn't want a lover. Black Diamond was nothing more than a way station, a place for her to get her bearings and figure out her next move, not a place she planned to stay. Sloan might intrigue her, but he didn't factor in her future. She made a list of rules while on the run. One, no more mind games. Two, no more guys. Three, absolutely no getting caught up in situations she couldn't control.

*No. Just no.* No to whatever power ended up being the greatest.

Drawing a fortifying breath, she sent Sloan a warning look.

He grinned at her.

Sensitive areas—places that hadn't seen any action in years—tingled. Theodora sucked in another breath.

Holy hell, her libido needed to get with the program and decide it didn't want Sloan. Now. Before he caught on and chose to push—

"*Mazleiha.*"

His voice vibrated through her. She twitched like a tuning fork.

Gaze riveted to her, Sloan pushed away from the side of the table.

"Zone, guess what?" Letting go of her hand, Violet bounced on her toes, then pulled loose and skipped over to him. "We had a waterfall."

"You did?" He held Theodora's gaze, talking to her with his eyes, delivering a silent message she understood (but didn't want to), then dipped his chin and looked at her daughter. The steely determination in his eyes softened. "Was it fun?"

Head tilted way back, Violet nodded. "I splashed in there."

"That's good, Vivy." Crouching, he came down to Violet's level. Eye to eye with her, he flicked the tip of one of Lulu's long ears. Dark skin against fluffy pink fur...enchanting, enthralling, something Theodora didn't need to see. His actions, the gentle way he spoke to her daughter, said too much, all of it good. "Lulu didn't get wet."

"She doesn't like water. Except in the basement machine."

"Your apartment building."

"It's stinky down there."

"Well, then, good thing you're with me, Vivy. It's not stinky here," he murmured, tapping the tip of her nose.

Violet giggled.

Sloan smiled. "Give Mommy and me a minute, will you, darlin'?"

Reacting to his tone, Violet scrunched her face up. She leaned in, going for quiet, ending up being loud. "Are you going to have the *talk*?"

"The talk?"

"Mommy likes to give talks," Violet told him with great authority.

A sparkle in his eyes, Sloan glanced Theodora's way.

Heat bloomed in her face. She couldn't help it. It didn't matter that Violet didn't mean what Sloan thought she meant. She wasn't wrong. She possessed firsthand knowledge of Theodora's tactics. Violet didn't enjoy her *talks*, or timeouts, for that matter. She wouldn't either if she happened to be a three-year-old being disciplined by her mother.

She cleared her throat. "Violet—"

"Yeah, darlin'," Sloan murmured, doing his best to keep a straight face. "Me and your mommy are gonna have a talk."

Curly hair flying, Violet half turned and looked over her shoulder. "Good luck with that."

Hearing words she often said parroted back to her, Theodora closed her eyes and muttered, "Please, God, deliver me. I'll do anything—"

Sloan snorted, then got his amusement under control. "Vivy—you wanna go jump on the bed?"

Little-kid brain enraptured by the idea, Violet snapped her attention back to Sloan. Mouth half open, she stared at him as though he was a gift from the gods. "Really?"

"Yeah." Sloan flicked his fingers toward the bed. "Go for it."

Violet pivoted so fast dust swirled around her sandals. Holding her rabbit by one ear, she closed the distance to her target in record time. Arms and legs pumping, she climbed over the wide step of the wood frame and, with a maniacal shriek, hurtled her little body into the middle of a pile of messy sheets.

Sloan chuckled.

Theodora cursed under her breath, knowing she'd lost her shield...and all hope of avoiding Sloan.

Pushing to his feet, dark eyes intent, he strode in her direction.

Raising both hands to keep him at bay, Theodora backed up. "Don't."

"Don't what?"

"Toy with me."

"I would never do that, Theo," he said, the spark in his eyes moving from playful to serious in a flash. "You're too important."

"I don't understand."

"I know you don't. Doesn't make it any less true."

Closing the distance fast, he strode toward her.

She retreated, making calculations. Half a second to shift course and change direction. Less than that to start running. Maybe five before he caught her. No way could she outrun him. She would never make it to the bed before him. Sloan would cut her off long before she reached Violet. He was too strong, much bigger than her, way faster, which made her reaction to him curious.

Everything about him screamed *aggressor*. But Theodora didn't react as though he was one. She wasn't frightened by his tactics. Or the fact he herded her backward, moving her farther away from a too-curious-for-her-own-good little girl.

Intuition fired like pistons, ramping up her ability to read him. He had no intention of hurting her. He wanted her undivided attention, along with a little privacy. Nothing less, not a whole lot more. Just enough separation to keep Violet from overhearing and Theodora from being distracted.

"Sloan."

"I'm not gonna hurt you, baby."

"I know that," she said, unable to believe she said it out loud, never mind accepted the assurance as God's honest truth. Not after all she'd been through. "But—"

"Violet's good. I'm not. I need a few minutes, *mazleiha*. A little one-on-one time with you, that's all. Swear."

The undertone in his voice rocked her. She recognized what it held—low-lying desperation. Shocking, coming from a man like him.

Theodora knew violent people. She recognized unsafe ones on sight. Years spent around dangerous men had fine-tuned her skills. None ever asked for what they wanted...or in Sloan's case, needed. Powerful people took without giving back, without regret or regard for another's feelings.

Sloan was dangerous, no question. She'd clocked his volatility, understood his strength, knew he'd be lethal when the situation warranted, but he wasn't a threat to her. She was safe with him. The truth rested in his eyes as he herded her toward the edge of the forest—carefully. So very carefully, doing his best not to scare her.

Pressing her palms toward him, she slowed to a stop beneath the outstretched arms of a huge oak. "Listen—"

"Just a few minutes."

"Sloan, slow down."

Flexing his hands, he stopped a foot away.

Gaze locked to his, she swallowed. He twitched, leaning toward her as though pulled by some invisible force. Reacting on instinct, unable to stop herself, she reached out, shuffled forward, and—

Laid her hands, palms flat, on his chest.

He shuddered.

She drew a shaky breath. "What's happening?"

With a low growl, Sloan bridged the gap. She jumped as he wrapped his arms around her. One hand went low to the hollow of her lower back. The other skated up her spine, threading through the ends of her dark hair. His chin dipped. Stubble rasped over her temple. Deep in his embrace, pressed tight against him, she shuddered, fighting the pleasure as he cupped the nape of her neck. His skin brushed against hers. Heat poured from his palm. He hummed, the sound low, full of satisfaction when she settled in, arms trapped between her chest and his, allowing him to hold her.

Each of her breaths came out jagged.

"Calm, baby. Settle," he murmured, pressing a gentle kiss to her temple. "I've waited a lifetime for this. I wanna hold you while we talk. Get a few things straight, put your worries to rest. Nothing more right now."

She swallowed. "And later?"

"Later will be later. You'll decide, and we'll see."

"What's going on?" she asked, doing her best not to freak out. A losing battle. She was already past the point of no return, back to thinking nothing made sense. A circular argument that led nowhere, given her reaction to Sloan. Being in his arms felt good. Talking with him while being tucked against him felt right, safe, and...*necessary*. As though she'd been waiting for him her entire life. "I shouldn't be able to... It doesn't make sense. I don't know you. This isn't normal."

"You connected with me earlier. It wasn't me who reached out, Theo. You did that, wanting to feel me. I would've let it lie, waited until you knew before diving that deep, but you're mine. You're strong. The bond's already unbreakable.

"Fuck, so quick, Theo. Our connection is unbelievable," he said, giving her a squeeze. "I know you've been running awhile. I know you're scared. I know you're confused by what I make you feel. I get why. I wanna go gentle, but feel I gotta give you fair warning. I fight for what I want and don't stop until I get it."

"And what?" Pulled apart, ripped wide open by his certainty, she struggled to bring her mind back online. She inhaled deep, but... God. There wasn't enough oxygen. She couldn't breathe. Couldn't think. All she could was react, fight in her corner, and try to back him off. "You've decided you want me? You don't even know me."

"I know you."

"You don't. You have zero idea what's happened, what I'm up against. How hard I've worked to—"

"Tell me."

She shook her head.

"All of it, Theo, every detail. I'll clear you a path. I'll make it right, keep you and Vivy safe. I am, and always will be, your safe place to land."

"This is nuts. All kinds of..." *Crazy*. Start-to-finish *certifiable*. What he offered defied all the laws of logic.

And yet she believed him. Zero proof offered. Little common sense in sight. She was running on instinct, and the strong sense she should give him the benefit of the doubt. A hard thing to accept. Trusting people always ended in disaster. Self-reliance, going it alone, served her better. "It's too sudden, Sloan."

"Sudden," he said, the menace in his soft tone

telling. He raised his head. The intensity in his eyes did her in, making her breathless all over again. "*Sudden* happened in the woods, Theodora. It happened when I held you, when I healed you, when you stripped down without my asking, pressed up tight, skin to skin, giving yourself to me before I decided to take. But now, the decision's made, so you're gonna hafta suck it up, get on board, and tell me what I need to know to keep you safe. Cuz a female like you is worth having, and I'm not gonna stop until you understand where I am is the best place for you to be."

Halfway through his speech, her mouth fell open. "It's like you're speaking in, I don't know, hieroglyphics or something."

Humor sparked in his dark eyes. "Theo."

"It's not funny! How can you not see this is whacked? Totally freaking *whacked*," she said, not finding anything about the situation amusing. He could laugh all he wanted. She refused to play. "All you said...and there was a lot of it, way too much to unpack with Violet jumping on the bed, singing..." She listened a second. Hell. "Hysteria" by Def Leppard. Fitting, given her current level of upheaval. "Jesus. Unreal. Right on topic."

"Baby—"

"No. Nope. Do not *baby* me, Sloan. Seriously, I'm not kidding. I don't even know what to do with any of what you just said."

"Decide quick. You got thirty seconds to process it before I take your mouth. After I get my taste, we're gonna grab Vivy and go eat pancakes."

*Take her mouth?*

Was he insane? They were talking, trying to get things straight, not...

Her eyes narrowed. No way in hell she would allow him to kiss her. "You are not going to—"

"Fuck it," he growled. "Five seconds, long enough."

Tightening his grip on her nape, he lowered his head and invaded her mouth. His heat hit her. The feel of him destroyed her. Desire somersaulted through her veins. Willpower spun out of reach. Playing catch-up, she battled to hold the line, but... Dear lord. He tasted fantastic. So freaking good. Better than anything she'd ever—

"Want more?"

The low snarl obliterated good sense.

Her mind went on hiatus. "Yes."

He slanted his head, deepening the kiss, dragging her under. So hard. So fast. So beautiful. Everything she'd never known, and once, a long time ago, dreamed of having.

Right. Wrong. Neither mattered anymore. All she wanted was him.

Unable to stop herself, Theodora sank into sensation, opened her mouth wider, and welcomed him in. One hand clutching his shoulder, she cupped the back of his head. Making a rough sound, Sloan wrapped her tighter against him, taking what he wanted, giving more in return.

Pleasure spiked. Delight picked her up. One second, she floated. The next, she sank beneath the waves, happy to drown in the raging current he folded around her. It was uncontrolled bliss and unstoppable yearning, all at once, raging into desperate passion. Nothing but the burning need to get closer. Theodora knew if she let him in, there'd be no going back. She wasn't wrong, but he felt so right she left caution behind, shoved her hand beneath his shirt, spread her fingers wide, touching as much of him as she could, and kissed him back.

He groaned.

She became the aggressor, pushing him against a tree trunk, tangling her tongue with his, drinking directly from the source to get what she needed—more of Sloan and the ambrosia he fed her.

## 18

Knocked off his moorings, Sloan struggled to get his bearings. He knew he was on his feet. He felt it each time one of his boots connected with the floor. Stumbling a bit, he battled through the mental haze. Muscle memory made him glance at his watch. The matte face stared back, seconds hand ticking, passing numbers on its way to meeting twelve.

The movement grounded him. He frowned at the time, having no memory of how he'd made it into the hallway. A total wipeout. Yet he still tasted her on his tongue. Still vibrated—skin tingling, mind burning, fingers twitching—from the force of her intensity.

Goddamn, his female could kiss.

Holding Theodora had been heaven. Kissing her kicked his ass.

The instant his mouth touched hers, his mind had fogged. The second her bioenergy flared, he'd gotten scorched. Rubbed raw. Stripped down and laid bare, reduced to rubble as he plugged into the Meridian and tapped into the stream. He didn't remember much after connecting. Theodora laid waste to his control, turning him inside out as she fed him straight from the source, filling him so full, so fast, his brain short-circuited.

The reality of her floored him. The power she possessed shocked him. He'd never met a female like her. Never come close to touching one, either. She was a force of nature. Glorious. Addictive. Bold. His mate took what she needed, putting her stamp on him in the process.

How she'd slipped past his guard was a mystery. He never lost control, and rarely ever powered down. His dragon half refused to let him, keeping him plugged in twenty-four hours a day, ensuring the earth's energy always hummed in his veins. The extra infusion meant he needed to feed less often than other Dragonkind males. But his connection to the planet had nothing on Theodora. In the span of seconds, his mate broke the energy barrier, shutting down his senses, stealing his ability to think.

His beast loved it, accepting Theodora without reservation.

Sloan possessed more caution. The cosmic bond between mates was powerful, an elemental, healing force in the right hands, but destructive in the wrong ones.

He'd heard the stories more than once. Too much hunger. A warrior who lacked control. A female drained dry, killed as one of his kind tapped in, drank too deep, absorbed her core energy instead of nibbling around the edges. An honorable male never took a feeding that far. Mistakes, however, had been known to happen when males got lost in the stream. The curse of his kind. The Goddess of All Things' fault. Some said she'd severed Dragonkind's connection to the Meridian in a fit of jealous rage. Others thought she'd gotten bored and decided to experiment—toss humans and dragons together for the fun of it, make his species' survival dependent on a weaker race, just to see what happened.

Sloan didn't care either way. Only one thing mattered to him now—his ability to connect safely with his mate.

Without knowing it, she'd accepted his ties while he got caught up in her strings. The bond was steady, complete, and unbreakable. Which meant...Theodora's welfare was his responsibility. He initiated the link to the Meridian through her. He controlled the flow of energy. Her continued good health required him to fine-tune energy-fuse, turn up the volume when warranted, turn it down when necessary. If he didn't—or lost his mind whenever he touched her so he couldn't—Theodora would end up hurt.

She'd suffer catastrophic damage in the form of organ failure. He'd lose his every-loving mind the second he hurt her, so he needed to pull his shit together. Take control of her. Get control of himself.

One big problem with the plan. Theodora didn't understand the rules. She'd blown him wide open with a burst so powerful he forgot to resist, forgot he needed to monitor the flow, which explained the messy scramble inside his head.

His baseline was all messed up. His memory wasn't far behind.

He didn't remember breaking the kiss, or letting Theodora go. He had no recollection of collecting Violet or exiting the greenhouse. But he must've at some point. Otherwise, he wouldn't be holding Theodora's hand, walking down a hall with a shit-ton of honey-colored doors in a complete fucking daze.

Blinking, he battled to clear the mental blur.

Arms arched over her head, Violet pirouetted

across the floor. Pink sandals tapping out a rhythm across dark hardwood, she danced to her own beat, chatting with Lulu, oblivious to adults moving in stunned silence in her wake.

White walls came into focus. Twelve-foot ceilings with recessed lights registered. His spine realigned. The fog cleared, allowing him to see the paintings hanging on the walls.

He was in the aboveground lair. A minute or two away from entering the kitchen.

Voices drifted from that direction. The smell of sweet dough and maple syrup rolled up the corridor. Sloan took a deep breath and, absorbing the excess energy buzzing in his veins, settled back into his body.

He glanced sideways.

Still in a daze, unsteady on her feet, Theodora drifted into him. Her shoulder bumped the side of his arm.

He firmed his grip on her hand. "Are you all right?"

She blinked. Her head turned his way a second before she tilted her chin and looked up. Unfocused green eyes met his.

He laced his fingers through hers. "*Mazleiha?*"

"Holy crap," she said, sounding as astounded as he felt. "That was...had to be...illegal."

He snorted. "All you."

"My fault?"

"Yeah. I think I may have lost some brain cells back there."

Theodora huffed before she shook her head. He caught a glimpse of humor in her eyes before she pressed her face into the side of his shoulder. She laughed, the soft sound full of disbelief.

Sloan understood her reaction. He was accustomed to energy feedings. His mate was not. She had no reference point, no way of knowing what she shared with him flew in the face of physics, surpassing normal limits.

"Once again, I'm stymied," she said, words coming slow.

"Why?"

"I thought you were crazy, going on about bonds and connections. Now, after what just happened, I have no idea what to do with you."

Sloan almost said, "Whatever you want," but stopped himself. She was already on overload, in need of time, no doubt some space too, in order to come to terms with the conundrum he presented. So instead of talking, he stayed silent. Forehead pressed to his arm, she walked with him. Unable to resist, he untangled their fingers and wrapped his arm around her. A gentle tug brought her closer, right up against him. A snug fit. Just what the doctor ordered. Complete absorption with the female pressed along his side.

He expected her to resist, pull away, maybe even tell him to stop. Theodora didn't do either. With a soft exhale, she relaxed into the intimacy, fitting her curvy body to his hard one. Wedged under his arm, hip pressed to his, she hooked her thumb through one of his belt loops and swayed to his beat, following where he led.

"Okay," she said, watching Violet pirouette into a lopsided spin.

"Okay, what?"

"The connection. I think, maybe, you need to—"

"Don't deny you feel it."

"After that kiss, I'd be an idiot to try," she said, sounding less dazed and more confused. "Just a hunch, but I have a feeling I need to know about that before I tell you anything about me."

"Would that make you feel safer?"

"I don't know. I can't remember what it means to feel safe. I'm not sure I've ever really known."

Her admission cranked him tight. A rough sound left his throat. "Who's after you?"

"Tell me about the connection."

Sloan stared at her a moment, then nodded. Being honest was the least he could do. Made sense she'd want to know. Theodora wasn't one to follow blindly. She needed assurances, ones he could give her, except...

Being honest, sharing the truth of Dragonkind too soon, might send her into a tailspin. He sensed she'd been through a lot, more than most people could handle. He frowned. Maybe telling her now wasn't a good idea. Maybe he needed to hook her deep first, wait until the bond transformed into love, acceptance, and—

"Sloan."

He glanced down as she jostled him.

She gave him a warning look. "Don't lie to me. I already know there's something different about you. Stalling to keep from scaring me won't work. I'm already freaked out. I'm asking 'cause I need to know— for me, sure, but more for Violet. Nothing bad touches her, Sloan. *Nothing*. I've worked hard to make sure of it, so it doesn't matter that I feel safe with you. It's not about me. It's never been about me. It's all about her. You get me?"

"I get you," he said, tone low and tight. He couldn't help the way he sounded, couldn't keep the emotion from bleeding into his voice. Theodora's love for her child touched him in places so deep devotion for her poured out. "You're a really good mom."

"I know. Now, start talking."

"You'll keep an open mind?"

"I'm holding on to you despite the freakiness, aren't I?"

He nodded, then did as she asked and started talking. "Dragonkind."

"What's that?"

"Me. I'm Dragonkind, Theo." Nerves getting the better of him, he cleared his throat. "A different species than you. Half human, half dragon, a magic wielder able to shift forms at will."

Shock registered on her face. Her mouth opened, then closed. She stopped walking. Feet rooted to the floor, she stared up at him as though waiting for him to grow a second head. "A shifter? Like in one of those books?"

Pivoting to face her, he slid his hands across her shoulders, then up to cup both sides of her neck. The chaotic beat of her heart registered. With a murmur of understanding, he caressed her, drawing gentle circles on her skin.

"Not fictional, Theo, *real*."

"But..." Her brow furrowed as she tried to wrap her brain around a truth most humans would never know. "How is that possible?"

"Humans like to think they're the ultimate apex predator, the one sitting at the top of the food chain, but—"

"We're not?"

"Not even close. There are lots of things humankind can't explain. Most of it our doing," he said, watching her absorb the truth. She shook her head.

He hit her with more honesty. "Think back. Remember what happened in the forest?"

"I was running, trying to get to the river, away from..." She flinched, refusing to say the names of the men who'd chased her out loud. "Gunshots. I was bleeding. In pain. I remember the pain, then you. I was alone, then all of a sudden, you were there."

"What happened when I touched you?"

"It went away."

"What went away?"

"The pain. It went away, and I wasn't scared anymore." Tears filled her eyes. She blinked them away. "Your eyes. I remember your eyes, Sloan."

"What about them?"

"They were glowing green. Gold, too."

"Yeah," he said, resting his forehead against hers. "The instant I touched you, energy-fuse took hold— the bond we now share snapped into place. I was able to connect and feed you from the source that nourishes my kind. Directly from the electrostatic bands ringing the planet."

"And that healed me?"

"I healed you. Spent hours closing your wounds, making sure you were all right."

"The skin-to-skin thing. Did I really strip down?"

"Rolled around in the middle of my bed. Took off all your clothes. Latched on to me the second I got close."

"God," she said, red blooming on her cheeks.

"Don't be embarrassed." Stroking his thumb over her cheekbone, he chased the blush across her skin. "Your needing me like that? Most beautiful thing I've ever seen."

"I want to crawl into a hole and never come out."

He chuckled. "What you feel, the thrum in your

veins, the hum in the back of your mind, it's me. It's you. It's us connecting. The cosmic bond between mates. So your need to be close to me, for me to need that too—totally natural."

"That's..."

He quirked a brow. "Impossible?"

"Weird."

"For you, maybe, but not for me. I've been waiting for you all my life. Most Dragonkind males never meet or claim their mates, but I'm one of the lucky ones. I get to—"

A door opened down the hall. The sound of claws clicked over hardwood.

Violet shrieked in delight. "A puppy! Mommy, Zone, look! A puppy!"

Frowning, Sloan broke eye contact with his female and looked toward Violet. Smooth blue scales flashed beneath the dimmed halogens. Half in the room, half in the hallway, Exshaw, Mac's wren, bared his fangs. Yellow eyes with vertical pupils locked on the little girl standing six feet away.

Hands clasped together in glee, Violet hopped toward the miniature dragon. "Oh, look-it. He's so cute!"

"Shit," a deep voice said from inside the room with the now-open door.

Letting Theodora go, Sloan shoved her behind him. "Exshaw, move back."

The wren snarled.

Violet froze so fast Lulu swung out in front of her.

Mac growled. The low warning joined the sound of rustling, drifting over the threshold into the hallway. "Motherfuck."

"Exshaw, get back here," Tania said, tone sharp, trying to help her mate. "Exshaw, seriously. Don't make me come out there and—"

"Give me a second, honey," Mac said, thump echoing as he rolled out of bed.

Exshaw shifted closer to Violet.

Sloan got ready to move. Magic hissed through his veins. The air in the corridor went from comfortable to blistering. Razor vines grew around his feet, cracking through wooden floorboards, ready to be deployed as he stared down Mac's wren. He didn't know Exshaw well. What little he did know about miniature dragons, however, told him Violet was in serious peril.

Wrens possessed no human DNA...and zero conscience. Exshaw's subset of Dragonkind was all animal, total instinct, lethal inclinations and volatile temperament packed into six and a half feet of apex predator with razor-sharp, dual-clawed front talons, all of it driven by a nasty attitude.

Exshaw took another step toward Violet.

Afraid sudden movement would cause the wren to attack, Sloan did the only thing he could. He bared his teeth and snarled in warning. Bright yellow eyes sliced in his direction. The wren's head moved sideways like a serpent getting ready to strike. His jaw shimmied, rattling serrated teeth as Exshaw issued a warning of his own, making it clear he had Violet in his sights and didn't plan on backing down.

**19**
___

Terror seized Theodora, wringing her dry as she watched the dragon dip his head beneath the doorjamb and move toward her daughter. Smooth blue scales clicked in the quiet. A double row of serrated teeth flashed. Twisted horns rose above slanted eyes with vertical pupils.

Nothing about the thing said friendly.

Sloan had called it Exshaw. Theodora didn't give a shit about its name. It was dangerous, a wild animal loose in a normal-looking corridor, inside a supposedly safe house. Hooked claws scraped against the floor. The scent of salt water rose as the dragon's nostrils flared. Her heart quivered and her mind screamed as she stood frozen and watched Violet smile at the beast. Oblivious to the tension, ignorant of the danger, she didn't understand Exshaw planned to eat her.

Adrenaline hit Theodora like rocket fuel.

Shock evaporated.

She jerked and, eyes on her daughter, pushed through the deep freeze locking her muscles, forcing her legs to move. The rambling vines slithering around Sloan rose in front of her. Hearing the blood rush in her ears, she jumped over the jumble, hop-scotching between the stems, attempting to skirt around him.

His arm shot out, blocking her path. "Stop."

"Sloan," she whispered, her fear so stark she could barely breathe.

"Let Mac get him under control."

Disbelief slashed through her. She shook her head and, swallowing past a bad case of dry mouth, succeeded in getting her voice to work. "Violet, honey-bunny, come here. Right now, baby. Come here."

Light brown eyes full of confusion, Violet looked her way.

The wren hissed.

"Don't move, Vivy," Sloan said, contradicting Theodora, making her want to kill him.

"Okay, Zone, but he's just a puppy." Too excited to do what Sloan instructed, Violet wiggled in place. "Don't worry, puppy. You're safe. I won't hurt you."

Reacting to her voice, Exshaw lowered his head. The blade riding his spine gleamed, snaking into alignment. Lethal-looking spikes rose like daggers on his blue scales, forming a thick collar around his throat.

"Oh my God," Theodora whispered in horror. "Sloan."

"Wait."

Exshaw tilted his head one way, then the other. Spikes vibrated like a rattlesnake's tail.

Theodora sucked in a breath. A tremor shook her. She shuddered, trying to do as Sloan asked. Every instinct she owned urged her to snatch Violet away from the danger. One that include fangs and claws, horns and scales.

Dear God. *Dragons*.

Sloan had tried to tell her. He'd explained energy-fuse, his species, and the magic. Feeling him, connected to him, she thought she'd understood...until now. Until Exshaw. But she didn't understand. Not really. The situation was unreal. Everything about the dragon left her staring down the barrel of a thinning reality. An unknowable one.

She wanted to discount it, but couldn't, so she stared instead, taking in the beast threatening her daughter, trying to trust Sloan and accept the truth. She wasn't imagining things. The instant she met Sloan, she'd stepped out of her world and into his, where the impossible existed and her child faced dangers Theodora couldn't outrun.

The cuff around Exshaw's throat undulated. A tinkling sound drifted.

"Oh, that's pretty. You've got a singing necklace," Violet said, chatting with the dragon as though she did it every day.

"Exshaw, stand down." Boots thumping on hardwood, a tall, dark-haired guy crossed the threshold. The scowl on his face was so fierce, he looked like he wanted to kill someone. "I mean it, bubba. Back off."

Exshaw hissed at him.

The guy growled back.

Sloan shifted, moving forward. The vines followed, slithering like a nest of snakes behind him.

The dragon took a quick step forward. His tail whipped around to curl around Violet. With a tug, he reeled her in, drawing her across the floor to rest between his front paws. Words whistled between the sharp points of his teeth. "Mine...*mine-mine-mine-mine-mine.*"

Theodora's mouth fell open.

The guy's eyes narrowed. "Not gonna say it again."

*"Mine-mine-mine-mine-mine."*

"She's not a toy, Exshaw. You don't get to keep her."

"Hi," Violet chirped, staring up at Exshaw.

Yellow eyes flashing, he tipped his snout down to look at her.

She raised her hand and stuck her rabbit in his face. "This is Lulu, and I'm Violet."

Exshaw snorted. Fine mist that smelled like brine rose from his nostrils. "Lupy-lupy-lu. Vi-vi. Vi-vi."

The guy sighed, then threw a perturbed look at Sloan. "You gotta give him a break. Wrens have their own language. He's still learning English."

"Looks like your daughter made a new friend, baby," Sloan said, dark eyes full of amusement.

Hysteria bubbled up. Locking her knees to keep her legs from buckling, Theodora glared at him. "No offense, but I'd rather she made one who won't eat her."

"He's not going to eat her," the guy said. He met her gaze. The glow in his aquamarine-colored eyes powered down, moving from intense to a soft glimmer. "See you found her, Sloan."

"Yeah."

"Happy for you, man."

Sloan tipped his chin. "Thanks, brother."

"Hello," she said, interrupting the moment of male bonding. "Mother in distress. I'm still here."

The guy grinned at her. "I'm Mac."

"Theo. Can I have my daughter back?"

"Too soon to tell." Hands planted on his hips, Mac looked from the wren to Violet then back again. "But if she starts walking, he'll follow."

"Terrific," she mumbled, not at all excited by the news.

As if on cue, her daughter patted Exshaw's leg and,

hopping out from between his paws, continued pirouetting down the hall. She chattered to him. Exshaw swung his head around, then followed, prowling along behind her like a sedate dog.

"Dear God in heaven."

"Relax, Theo. It's all good."

"Easy for you to say. You're used to all the dragon stuff."

With a chuckle, Sloan flicked his fingers. The writhing vines retreated, slithering around her feet, disappearing behind broken floorboards as he reached out and grabbed her hand. With a slight tug, and he drew her forward, towing her toward Mac. "Isn't Exshaw banned from the kitchen after what happened the last time?"

Mac shrugged. "Daimler'll have to suck it up."

"We're having pancakes," Violet informed Exshaw. "Mr. Goldtooth said so."

Exshaw answered with a low chirp.

Sloan smiled at her over his shoulder.

Mac laughed.

Accepting her daughter was no longer in danger, Theodora frowned as the sense of the unreal struck again. "I think you all might be certifiable."

"Stick around," Mac said, a wicked gleam in his eyes. "You meet the other girls, you'll understand the true meaning of crazy."

"I heard that," a woman said, opening a door further down the hall.

"You were supposed to."

"Venom, new mission. Kick Mac's ass."

"That's always the mission, Evie, but you know...I live to serve," a new guy said, disembodied voice drifting out the door as a stunning woman with inky, shoulder-length curls and smooth sienna skin exited the room.

Focused on Mac, Evie narrowed her dark eyes. "You know Tania's gonna take my side."

"I totally am!" a woman Theodora couldn't see yelled from somewhere inside Mac's room.

"Motherfuck," he muttered, throwing Sloan a long-suffering look. "Bionic ears. My mate hears everything."

"I totally do!"

Lips twitching, Mac shook his head.

Theodora snorted in amusement.

The black woman's gaze cut to her. A smile started to form on her face. An instant later, the welcome she saw there died, and Evie froze, staring at Theodora in horror. "You."

The hoarse whisper made dread rise.

Her stomach cramped as she saw the shock in the other woman's eyes.

Sucking in a breath, Theodora shook her head, reacting as she always did when faced with the wreckage her family left in its wake. She wanted to run. She needed to hide. She prayed the vines came back, dragged her into the hole, and buried her under the house.

Sloan squeezed her hand, asking without words for an explanation.

Snared by the pain in Evie's eyes, she couldn't look at him. "It's not me. I swear, whatever happened, it wasn't me."

Evie recoiled at the sound of her voice.

"Goddamn it, Evie—breathe," the huge blond man behind her said, wrapping his arms around her from behind.

And Theodora wanted to die.

It had been years—*years*—since anyone recognized her. Not *her*, precisely, but the replica of her. The woman with whom she'd shared a womb. Her twin. People often mistook Theodora for her sister until they got to know her. She and Beatrice might look alike, but that was where the similarities ended. Same bone structure, different mannerisms. Same eye color, different interests. Same voice, different ways of moving through the world.

Not that it mattered now. The look on Evie's face told Theodora all she needed to know. Haunted. Humiliated. Reliving something in her past she preferred to forget. Somewhere along the line, the woman had rubbed up against the Bratva. As always, for Evie and everyone else who met Theodora's uncle, the experience hadn't been good one.

## 20

E xercising extreme control, Azrad stared at his bare feet and flexed his hands. Open and closed. Deep breaths in, long exhales out. Trashing the apartment, ripping shit off the walls, wouldn't help. Neither would scaring the hell out of Kasi.

She didn't need his aggression, or the reality check witnessing the volatile edge of his temper would cause. She was already living a nightmare, had already faced so much real-world stress, it was a wonder she'd only cracked, not broken. A testament to her strength. Something he admired about her—then again, there wasn't much not to like about the female.

Her forthright pragmatism was one of them. The fact she continued to keep it together—hadn't lost control since he explained things in the shower—was another.

Taking another deep breath, he scraped his hands over the top of his head. Trimmed in precise lines, the strands of his mohawk brushed against his palms. A familiar motion, just what he needed to settle his mind. Frowning at kitchen cabinets, he laced his fingers against the back of his skull. Elbows out, he pulled. His chin touched the middle of his clavicle. Taut muscles stretched. Pain twisted down his spine. The burst of unpleasant sensation grounded him even more, downgrading his rage, permitting him to focus.

He ran through the parameters again. Locked inside an apartment suite deep underground. Magic and his ability to link in and use mind-speak blocked. Room sealed up tight. No cracks in the walls that he could find, so...

Good luck getting Kasi, Scandela, or himself out. The place was a fucking tomb.

Azrad clenched his teeth. Clever, clever Ivar. Any other time, Azrad would've applauded the male for his brilliance, but not right now. Not while shut inside a confined space with a female he respected (liked, enjoyed, wanted...take your pick), and would be forced to hurt if he didn't find a way out before the Meridian realigned and *the hungering* took over.

"Fuck." Releasing the stretch, he raised his chin.

He couldn't give up. Not yet. Not ever. Surrender had never been part of his make-up. The myriad skills housed in his arsenal didn't include quitting. He must keep looking. The Razorback commander might be smart, but he wasn't infallible. Ivar made mistakes. All Azrad needed to do was find the weakness, expose the soft underbelly of the underground complex, then go in for the kill.

Dropping his hands, he took another turn around the kitchen. Bare feet moving across warm tile, he trailed his fingertips along the underside of the cupboards. No change in texture or material from countertop to backsplash to cabinets. One solid piece from floor to ceiling, backed by magic-blocking *Blakeite* and miles of solid rock. He re-checked behind the fridge. No waterline. No power cable or outlet. Everything in the suite was powered by battery and wireless connection. Which meant no seams for Scandela to slip through. Nothing for him to latch on to, pull apart, or—

"Azrad?"

He closed his eyes as her melodic voice came to him. Hungry for any part of her, he tucked the sound into his memory banks, hoarding it like treasure, holding some small part of her close. Completely wrong. One hundred percent creepy, but he couldn't help himself. Everything about Kasi appealed to him. His dragon half, the territorial bastard, had already decided he wanted to keep her.

"Azrad?" she called, a little louder.

"Yeah?"

"Can you come here for a minute?"

A bad idea. Being too close to her might break him.

Rolling his shoulders to combat the tension, Azrad went to her anyway.

As he rounded the kitchen island, he caught a glimpse of her through the archway. Back to him, crouched beside the bed, she focused on something in the corner. Instinct prickled through him. His heart rate picked up. Holy shit. She'd found something. A small break in the hard shell of the apartment, perhaps. Something he could use, maybe.

Upping his pace, he strode under the archway and walked up behind her. She tensed. Her head snapped around. Eyes the color of sapphires struck him with the force of a fist. Battling hard, Azrad suppressed a flinch and took a step back, giving her plenty of breathing room.

"Shit," she said, unclenching her fists. "Sorry."

"Ain't no big thing."

Kasi blinked. "Isn't that from a song? Are you quoting lyrics from The Radiants?"

"The 1960s. Excellent decade."

A smile tugged at the corners of her mouth. "Why? That when you were born?"

"No," he said, relaxing as she did.

"How much earlier? You look thirty, tops."

"Dragonkind doesn't age the way humans do."

"Not gonna tell me, huh?"

He shrugged. "We get out of here, I'll tell you anything you want."

"My reward for keeping my shit together?"

"Something like that."

She stared at him a second.

"Stop trying to figure me out, Kasi. I'm not that interesting."

"Now that's a lie." Pushing to her feet, she turned to face him. "You're the most complicated guy I've ever met."

Azrad frowned. What the hell did that mean? Was it good she found him complicated? He longed to ask, but killed the inclination. Wanting to know what she thought of him was a terrible idea. How she viewed him didn't matter. How much he wanted her, however, did.

He needed to be cautious. Maintaining a safe distance was essential. For his peace of mind, sure, but also for her continued wellbeing. He wasn't an angel. Interpersonal relationships weren't his forte. Intimacy and fables about happily-ever-afters bought a male nothing but in trouble. He avoided messy emotional entanglements, taking what he needed from a female, feeding fast before leaving the flavor of his week behind.

Out of sight, out of mind. He never went back for seconds.

Kasi didn't deserve to become a casualty in the long line of devastation he'd left in his wake. He held no attachments and only called two males friend—Kilmar and Terranon. Warriors he trusted without hesitation or condition, but this—whatever the fuck with Kasi—needed to stop. She pushed him off balance, made him yearn for something more than brotherhood, fighting, and revenge.

*Complicated.*

She wasn't wrong about that, or the fact he was out of his depth. Her continued attempts to get to know him would only spotlight his inadequacies. He'd given her as much honesty as she required, enough for her to accept the situation and help instead of hinder his escape plans. Anything more, and he risked crossing lines best left unapproached.

Refusing to show weakness, he held her gaze. "What did you find?"

Her eyes narrowed.

Crossing his arms over his chest, he raised a brow.

She rolled her eyes. "Tough nut to crack. Should've known you're a hardass."

"Remember that," he murmured, fighting the strange urge to laugh. Kidnapped, abused, now trapped with the threat of *the hungering* hanging over her head—and still she managed to keep her sense of humor. "Now, what—"

"Look," she whispered, glancing over her shoulder.

Shifting to his left, Azrad shuffled to get around her in the space between the bedframe and the wall.

Kasi moved before he got to her. Planting her knee on the mattress, she climbed onto the bed, settling on her knees, giving him plenty of room to get past her. Focused on the corner she indicated, he missed it when she reached out. Her hand curled around his. The electrifying pulse of her bioenergy lit him up, burning over his palm, sinking into veins, opening a floodgate of sensation.

She sucked in a quick breath, but held firm, refusing to let go of his hand when he tried to shake free.

"Shit," he rasped, twitching as she tugged him closer to her perch. Pivoting away from the corner, he turned to face her. "Kasi."

"Just hear me out, okay?" she asked softly. So fucking softly he forgot to object. He looked at her instead, getting lost in the fierce blue of her eyes. "I have to say it cuz I know you won't."

"What?"

"I want you to know I won't blame you if this goes bad. *The hungering*, if we don't... If it happens, I won't fight you. I hate where we are or what we're facing, but I think it would be better all the way around if we find a way to...to..."

"*Kazlita*—"

"—work together and get past it."

"That's not what I want, Kasi. You deserve so much better from me...from any male you allow to touch you."

"I'm glad you believe that, Azrad, but whatever happens, it won't be your fault. Won't be mine either. After our talk, I've been thinking on it. You don't want to be here any more than I do, but we're in this together, and for the time that we are, we've got to have each other's backs."

She paused to take a breath, and no doubt reset her courage. "I've spent the last few months without a lifeline, in fear and desperation, and I know it seems strange, but being here with you, despite what's coming, I'm not scared. For the first time in months, I'm not afraid of who or what's going to come through my door. And that's got a lot to do with you, so whatever happens, it won't be your fault. I don't want you to blame yourself."

Absolution in the form of permission. The bravery she showed tore him apart, then turned and put him back together.

"Kasi."

Her breath hitched.

"Honey."

Bowing her head, she shuffled closer to the edge of the bed. Her knees touched the fronts of his thighs as she grasped his hand with both of hers. "You need to promise me, Azrad. I'm not sure I'll get through if you don't."

He made a rough sound, then raised his free hand. Fingers poised above the nape of her neck, he hovered an inch away, torn between wanting to comfort her and preserving his sanity. He shouldn't allow the intimacy. He should do the smart thing, shake her loose and back away. He waffled a moment too long. Compulsion won out, making him palm the side of her throat. With a murmur, he stroked the underside of her jaw, then dipped his chin. His mouth touched the top of her head.

"Promise me."

"Okay," he whispered into her hair. "It's gonna be okay. Don't give up, honey. I'll find us a way out."

She nodded.

He gave her hand a firm squeeze. "Let me have a look at what you found. Might be something, yeah?"

"Yeah," she said, but didn't let him go.

He waited.

She pressed her thumbs into the palm of his hand.

The Meridian hummed. The electrostatic bands powered up, opening a link. Energy flickered, curling through her to feed him from the source. Pleasure knifed through him. Like a fool, he sank into the blade, sharpening his edges on the beautiful burn. Kasi whispered his name. Immersed in the stream, he murmured back, but drank deep, keeping the draw light, tasting her for the first time, enchanted by her generosity.

How long he stayed connected, Azrad didn't know. He floated instead, letting the current take him, bobbing in the ebb and flow until his dragon half told him to stop.

Withdrawing with slow precision, he flexed his hand against her nape, lifted his mouth from her crown, and disconnected.

Silence expanded. Relaxation took hold, drowning him in warm comfort.

"I know about energy feedings," Kasi said on a deep inhale, breaking the spell, ripping him from the cocoon she created. "Never felt it like that, so gentle, before."

"Don't."

"What?"

"Tempt me."

"Too late, I think. I felt you take from me," she said, not sounding upset, but intrigued. "Is that something you need often?"

A growl rumbled from deep in his chest. "Kasi—"

"I mean, is it something that would help boost the signal when Scandal gets up there?"

"Probably."

"All right. Good to know. Now I'll be prepared for it."

Son of a bitch. She was killing him.

"No more talking."

"But—"

"Give me five minutes of silence. You think you can do that?"

She huffed, sounding amused. "I think I can manage."

"You haven't so far."

"Shut up."

With a curse, Azrad let her go of her hand and, in favor of self-preservation, spun toward the corner she'd been investigating without looking at her. Following her example, he dropped to his haunches next to the nightstand.

"To the right."

"Quiet."

Kasi, of course, didn't listen. "Do you—"

"I see it," he said, running his fingertip along to the floor beside the table leg. Rough edges rasped against his skin. "Fucking hell."

"Enough?"

"Perfect," he murmured, pushing on the splinter, widening the gap as he called on Scandela the same way he always did—with love and affection. *Scandal... time to go to work, my beautiful girl.*

Responding to his voice, the red spider inked into his skin came alive. She clicked a welcome. He clicked back, talking to her as she crawled across his throat. She knew what he wanted. Eyes searching, eight legs moving, she leapt from his shoulder to the floor. Blood-red skin against stark white plastic provided an interesting color contrast as she used the setae on her front legs to explore the fissure.

Tight space. Too small for her to disappear inside in her current size.

"*Split,*" he murmured to her, watching her hunt for a way in.

Scandela obeyed without hesitation, multiplying her number in the blink of an eye. One large spider became a hundred small ones. The army of tiny red arachnids swarmed around the slice in the floor. As he watched the last of her disappear inside the hole, Azrad smiled. A day, maybe two, before she reached the surface, a day or two before he knew whether his plan would work, but Scandela had just given him and Kasi a fighting chance. Something to be grateful for, but nowhere close to the consideration and respect she deserved.

## 21

Leaning against the bar inside The Lucky Dog, Zidane scanned the crowd. Lots of humans milling around for a Wednesday night. Amazing how many bikers came out of the woodwork, continuing to cross the threshold well after midnight. Dressed in leather vests with patches, faded jeans, and motorcycle boots, the rabble of humankind screamed rough. Lots of facial hair and tattoos. Lots of attitude and cigarette smoke in the air. Lots of beer being drunk and shots being shot.

Tough crowd. So different from the refined establishments he frequented in Prague.

Right up his alley tonight.

Harley pipes fired up outside. The roar of multiple bikes rolled through the open front door, into the travesty the regulars considered a watering hole.

Out in the middle of nowhere, The Lucky Dog wasn't much to look at. *Hristos*, there was shit on every available surface. Old license plates nailed to the low timber beam ceiling. Tons of mismatched frames with black-and-white pictures from fifty years ago on the walls. Old signs with weird sayings. Faded flags with bullet holes in the fabric. With a bunch of grimy wooden tables gouged by knives and blackened by fire scattered around.

The only new things in the fire hazard pretending to be a building were a couple of TVs mounted across from the long bar.

Looked terrible. Smelled even worse.

One corner of mouth tipped up. His new haunt was straight-up vile, but for some reason, he loved it.

Setting his empty on the scarred bar top, Zidane glanced toward the pool tables. Three sat in a large alcove under a sloping roofline. Plenty of room to maneuver between the trio, less chance of a fight breaking out given all the elbow room. A good call. The first smart decision whoever managed the establishment had made. But also a shame. Watching humans fight was always fun, and despite his mission tonight, Zidane hoped he got to witnesses one.

So did Yakapov.

He could tell by the way his first-in-command watched the humans at the next table. Hinz nudged him, drawing the male's attention back to the game. Yakapov nodded and stepped up to take his turn. Head and shoulders above the rest of the crowd, Zidane's attention drifted over his warriors.

Pride washed through him. He'd chosen well. The males he now commanded never failed to impress.

Camped out in the back corner around the last pool table, Montgomery and Warsaw leaned against the wall, eyes on the TV, watching a ball game while Yakapov and Hinz played. Achan, Strecklin, and Lynhurst kicked back at one of the tables, relaxed, beers in hand, yakking with the newcomers.

Zidane's focus shifted to the males he'd only just met.

Four Razorbacks, all young, all inexperienced, all

here at Ivar's behest. Zidane had to give it to the bastard. The leader of the Razorback pack kept his word, sending the warriors he'd promised into Zidane's den. Though—he pursed his lips—given the quality of the males, maybe Ivar hadn't taken the request seriously.

Fine by Zidane.

He hadn't expected his rival to send him real warriors. Ivar wasn't that stupid. Not that Zidane cared. Their inexperience worked in his favor. He didn't need fighters from the Razorback stable to fight in the war he started. His warriors were lethal enough to take down Bastian without adding firepower to his crew. What he needed from the Ivar's lackeys was access—to everything. To Ivar, sure, but mostly to every scrap of the intel the bastard refused to share.

Something Zidane would get tonight. And the whole reason he'd invited his "new warriors" in for a drink, allowing the males to get to know him and the kill squad he put together.

A whiff of perfume drifted into his space.

He glanced sideways as a female stepped up to the bar. Shoulder brushing his arm, she set a tray down, caught the bartender's eye, and yelled her order. Pretty brown eyes met his before she asked, "You need another?"

"Another round for my friends," he said, pointing to his bottle of Notch Session Pil toward his warriors.

"Third pool table?"

He nodded.

"Sure thing, sugar." Fake lashes with too much mascara flicked up and down as she gave him the once-over. "New here?"

"Just arrived."

"Nice addition to the scenery."

Enjoying her boldness, he assessed her. Short

skirt, skimpy top, showing lots of skin. A waitress working her tail off for tips in high heels. Attractive enough. Adequate bioenergy. Not too picky. Perfect for what he had in mind.

Setting his forearm on the bar, he leaned into her, giving her all of his attention. Her pupils dilated as she parted her lips, body language saying she wanted him. Moving further into her space, he dipped his head and put his mouth to her ear.

She shivered.

"Feeling like a rough ride, *dorogoy*," he murmured, calling her sweetheart in Russian. "You up for one?"

"You fuck as good as you look?"

His mouth curved. "You'll have to play to find out."

"I'm on break in a few." Picking up a tray loaded down with beer bottles and shot glasses, she looked toward the double doors at the back of the bar. Both stood wide open, giving him a view into a courtyard surrounded by a chain-link fence. "Meet me out back."

Drawing his fingertip along the back of her bare arm, he nodded.

Goosebumps rose where he touched her. "Shit, sugar. Got a feeling you're gonna be worth my while."

She had no idea.

The night's mission off to a good start, he glanced at Yakapov.

Bent over the table to line up a shot, the warrior's pale gaze met his. He tipped his chin, then straightened and said something to Montgomery. His brother moved, taking the cue and his place in the game as Yakapov motioned to one of the Razorbacks—the leader of the group.

The strongest male. The one with the most sway

over the others. The warrior with enough arrogance to believe he could hold his own against Zidane.

A false perception. One the Razorback would learn all too soon.

Coming out of the break room, the waitress walked, hips swaying, attention on Zidane over her shoulder, down the hallway toward the outdoor patio.

Zidane pushed away from the bar. The Razorback he'd chosen met him halfway across the room. Hazel eyes rimmed by black set in a handsome face. Good build, strong presence. Right intensity, wrong kind of training. Zidane assessed him a moment. The kid had potential, maybe enough to keep him around for a while.

Stepping into the male, Zidane palmed his shoulder. "Blakmor, *da*?"

"Yeah, Zidane."

"You hungry?"

The male's gaze shifted from Zidane to the female striding out the back door. "She yours?"

"For a while."

"You good with sharing?"

"Good way to get to know one another, don't you think?"

Desire fired in the younger male's eyes.

"Let's go."

Boots crunching on discarded peanut shells, Zidane treated him to an affectionate slap on the back, then turned and led the way outside. Human males shuffled out of his way. He barely noticed, refused to allow the distraction. The next ten minutes would be the difference between success and failure.

Such a thin margin for error.

He needed to thread the needle, do it just right, or Ivar would find out and Zidane would be back where he started—nowhere, hunting for a way to infiltrate the Razorback pack.

Pace steady, he crossed the threshold. The soles of her high heels rasped against stone pavers as the female turned to greet him. Her breath stalled in her throat. Gaze full of speculation, she looked from him to Blakmor, then back again.

Surprise lit her brown eyes. She raised a brow. "Two for the price of one?"

"You game?" he asked, asking for permission even though he didn't mean it. She would be doing what he wanted her to do—distracting Blakmor long enough for Zidane to get what he needed.

Her head tilted as she considered. Her attention moved from him to Blakmor again. Her bioenergy flared. "Sure. Why not? Could use the stress relief, but—"

"Name?"

"Stacey."

"You take him first, Stacey," Zidane said, making the Razorback think he was all about getting the male what he needed. "I want to watch you suck him off. You'll get what you need from me after you take care of him."

Blakmor shifted, broadcasting his eagerness.

Stacey smiled. Stilettos clicking across stone, she approached Blakmor. Grabbing her by the nape, the male pulled her in, then kissed her, tasting her as she reached for his belt. Quick hands unbuckled and unzipped him. The Razorback groaned as her hand slid inside to cup him.

Circling behind the pair, Zidane watched her break the kiss and kneel in front of Blakmor. Her mouth found him. Fisting his hand in her long, dark hair, Blakmor took control and thrust forward, making her swallow him to the root. He grunted. She sucked hard, being a team player as the male pulled out.

The smell of her arousal rose.

With a snarl, the Razorback upped the pace.

Energy spinning in a web in open air, Zidane waited until the male was close, so deep in the stream he lost sight of his surroundings. Eyes closed, blinded by sexual need, Blakmor tipped his chin up. Humming her pleasure, Stacey became more demanding, opened wider, taking him to the back of her throat.

"Beautiful," Blakmor rasped.

Zidane smiled. Ready. The male was so fucking *ready*. So deep in the stream he couldn't protect himself.

Approaching the Razorback from behind, he made his move. Feet planted, dragon half rising, he grabbed the back of Blakmor's head. The warrior jerked. Stacey moaned. Zidane didn't hesitate. Pressing the pads of his thumbs to the base of the male's skull, he unleashed a magic-driven brute-force attack. Heat burrowed through skin and bone. A grid flashed onto his mental screen.

The Razorback arched.

His eyes narrowed, Zidane held steady. Holding the kid upright, he mapped the neural network of the brain. He hunted less than a moment before he found what he needed—the cosmic connection used by the Razorbacks to communicate with one another. A distinct series of numbers, the main line of communication. Gritting his teeth, he copied the link, drawing the information from deep inside the male's head.

Blakmor growled.

Easing his grip, Zidane flexed his hands, soothing Blakmor with a warm wave of magic. Careful and sure, he withdrew his tentacles one at a time, repairing neural pathways, tampering with Blakmor's memory. After leaving no trace of his part in the encounter behind, he made sure Blakmor was steady on his feet, then let him go and backed away.

He could've killed the male with nothing but a sharp twist of his hands. Reducing Blakmor to a messy pile of ash on cracked concrete, however, wasn't part of the plan. The Razorback would eventually report back to his leader. When he did, Zidane didn't want Ivar to guess what he'd done. So, *da*. No sense killing the kid and destroying the advantage.

Zidane had gotten what he wanted. Now he possessed what he needed to undermine Ivar—a link into mind-speak. Nothing left for him to do but tune in and listen while his rival issued orders to his warriors, then string together important intel. All without the bastard knowing Zidane held the keys to the castle, and Ivar now sat on cusp of losing control of the Razorback pack.

## 22

Fingers playing in Rikar's hair, Angela lay beneath him in their bed and kissed him back. His taste—phenomenal. The chill in his hands—fantastic. His scent—out-of-this-world amazing. She loved everything about her mate, even when he pissed her off.

Like he had five minutes ago, when he yanked the laptop out of her hands and set it sailing. It bounced then skittered across the bedside table.

Uncool.

But he felt magnificent in her arms, so she went with the change of plans and attacked him before he got a chance to take control. A bad habit of his—another thing, if she was being honest, she adored about the man in her arms.

Planting her foot in the sheets, she pushed up and flipped him over. He landed on his back. She settled astride with him deep inside her. He growled his approval. She smiled and continued to ride, giving him a show, taking what she wanted while he got what he deserved—unbelievable amounts of pleasure.

"After we finish, I want my computer back."

"You can have whatever the fuck you want, you finish me off in the next five minutes."

A challenge. One she accepted with wholehearted determination.

Her man had stamina. And shitloads of staying power. Rikar proved it all the time, fucking her before they settled down to sleep for the day. Waking her up with a gentle loving each and every afternoon.

Smoothing her hand over his chest, Angela put the hammer down, undulating on top of him, wrecking his control as he watched her.

"Fuuuuuck."

"You earned it, gorgeous. Take it."

"I'm close, angel. Touch yourself for me."

He didn't need to ask her twice. She got off on what Rikar did to her in bed. Or, well...she just plain got off. The second he began working her, she lost control, like now, while she did as she was told, riding him hard and fast.

"Rikar," she breathed, spine arched, bliss coiling deep in her belly.

"Go, angel."

"Rikar!"

He squeezed her hips. "Go, Angela."

At his guttural command, she went...*spectacularly*. He groaned beneath her, wrapping his arms around her as, breathing hard, she came down. Sprawled across his chest, breasts pressed into his skin, she sighed. Running his hand up her back, he purred, the sound so full of contentment that her mouth curved.

"Always an incredible fuck. Blow my mind every single time."

Aaaaand...

A meeting of the minds. Great ones always thought alike.

She laughed, then raised her head, folded her forearms on his chest, and set her chin on top of the stack. Her gaze met then clashed with his. He quirked a brow, asking without words for her to explain.

Angela knew what he meant. She wasn't good at hiding how she felt—or anything, for that matter—from him. With a sigh, she pursed her lips, twisting them to one side.

"Spill, angel."

"I wasn't ignoring you."

"No?"

"I've got something on my mind. I'm running some intel on Sloan's system. I needed to check to see if—"

"Sloan know you're doing that?"

"Not yet."

"So, like I said—spill."

"Hard to explain."

"Try."

Great. Lovely. Just terrific.

How to explain? Especially when she didn't know what she was looking for. She figured she'd have a little more time to get her thoughts in order. Time to ask Sloan for help. Time to hack into the databases she needed to solve the mystery. She liked to go it alone, thrived on the chase, but the concern in Rikar's eyes stopped her cold. Keeping things from him never ended well. Talking out problems with him worked better, so...

She needed to stop stalling and share. Otherwise, she'd never unravel the messy tangle inside her head.

"It's kind of a jumbled mess," she said, staring at him without really seeing him.

"It have anything to do with why you broke protocol and left the lair without backup?"

She sighed. Of course, Rikar understood. As her

mate and a Dragonkind male, he had full access to her mental cortex. Not that he invaded her privacy without permission—he was more respectful than that—but he could read her, often cherry-picking topics right off the front of her brain.

"I don't really know what's driving it. I'm not sure what's bothering me about her."

"Who?"

"Sasha Cooper. The woman I met while I was out. You know, the one who studies bats."

"The wildlife ecologist. Lives on Walton Street."

Angela nodded, not needing to explain. She'd told Rikar all about her meeting with Sasha the night she got in trouble for slipping out on her own. "I see the loose thread in the fabric of her, but each time I try to pull it, it disappears. It's like I've got a mental block that won't let me see her clearly. She—"

"Rubs you the wrong way."

"Not exactly. She was cool, Rikar. Lovely, friendly, real in a way that was genuine, not fake, but..."

With a quick shift, he sat up. Leaning back against the headboard, he caressed her sides, traced the curve of her hips before resting his hands on the outsides of her thighs. "But?"

"Her scent."

"What about it?"

"I didn't notice it then," she said, struggling to puzzle it out. "But since my shift, since my dragon half came on board, memories of the night the Razorbacks took me are surfacing."

"Baby," he said, no doubt worried about her state of mind, concerned she was reliving the nightmare. The one she endured the night she'd been raped.

"It's not that." Though she didn't enjoy talking about it. "It's still fuzzy. I couldn't remember before, but now I'm getting flashes. It's like my dragon is collecting the shattered pieces of my memory and fitting them back together. I remember being in a clinic of some kind. I remember the feel of needles and the cold of the serum being injected. But more, I remember what it smelled like in there. And Sasha—she carries a hint of that scent."

"Christ." Big hands flexing on her hips, he shifted closer, putting her nose to nose with him. "Dissect that, angel. Break it down. Think about what I smell like. Is it something similar? Could it be the scent of a Dragonkind male?"

She blinked as his question unlocked another memory. Pink eyes. Thick red stubble. The sharp angle of a chiseled cheekbone. Stomach acid clawed up the back of her throat. Swallowing the burn, she rasped, "Ivar. You're thinking it might've been Ivar."

"He's a scientist. The breeding program is his pet project. He created the serum, Angela. I know that asshole. He's hands-on when it comes to his experiments. No way in hell he'd allow anyone else to inject the HE females he's been kidnapping."

"Shit."

"The fucker," he growled at the same time.

"But that means—"

"Sasha might be his. If she smells like him, there's a good chance he's been visiting her."

She sucked in a quick breath. "She might be his weak spot. Apply enough pressure, and we'll force his hand."

"Was the scent on her strong?"

She nodded.

"Then he was there recently...or he visits her often. Either way—"

"We need to talk to Bastian."

"Yeah, and I need to get my nose on Sasha Cooper. You may not know what Ivar smells like, but I do." He slid to the side of the bed with her in his lap. "Quick shower. Then breakfast, angel. After that, pack meeting where we'll fill everyone in and make a plan. Sound good?"

Sounded better than good.

The scenario sounded perfect if it landed her anywhere near the Razorback commander. She'd get to hammer Ivar with Rikar and the boys backing her up. Get to take back what had been stolen from her, before she took her revenge.

## 23

Focus rivetted on his female, Sloan tugged on her hand, drawing her closer. Magic up and running, he mined her bioenergy. Theodora's vitals blipped onto his mental screen. He felt the throb of her pulse, listened to her heart hammer and her breathing accelerate as she stared at Evelyn.

Pain streamed from her into him, so much anguish he flinched as her aura contracted, dimming her light. Not understanding, he reached out to her with his mind. Her silent scream of denial came through the link as the Meridian crested on a rolling wave. The surge burned through his veins. Desperate to soothe his mate, he gentled the stream, looping it over, then under before sharing it with his female. A warm, gentle wave.

Theodora shivered as the current moved from him into her. Her hands twitched in his, beginning to tremble as she continued to stare at Evelyn, her emotions bouncing all over the place.

His sonar pinged. Perception narrowed. He turned his hand, threading his fingers through hers, then raised the other.

Gaze locked on Venom's mate, Theo drifted toward

him but didn't acknowledge his presence at her side. She was deep in her own head, ensnared by horrors he couldn't see, but felt with every breath he took. Primal instinct rose. His senses sharpened. The dial turned, giving him a more accurate read as he sorted through the chaotic twist of emotion.

Shame. Sorrow. Dismay. And equal amounts of panic.

His hand touched down.

Theodora jerked as he cupped her cheek, and yet she didn't take her eyes from Evelyn. "Theo, look at me."

"No." Low and guttural, the denial rasped in her throat. His heart twisted. Pain made manifest in a single word. Goddess help him, so much trauma. His mate was suffering, and he didn't know why. "Swear. Wasn't me. Not me."

Venom murmured, trying to soothe his own mate.

"Talk to me, Theo," Sloan said, stroking her bottom lip, wanting her attention, needing—

"Evie, my love. It isn't her." Voice soft, blond head bent, Venom hugged Evelyn from behind, whispering the assurance in her ear. "She looks like Trixie, but it isn't her. Different energy signature, different color aura. Not the same female, *jalâyla.*"

Evelyn drew a shaky breath. "But...how... She looked just like her."

Sloan looked over his mate's head. "Mac."

"She's covered. We'll watch her," Mac said, grabbing Tania's hand, drawing her out of his room. "Though the second Violet makes it to Daimler, we'll lose her. He adores females. Give him a miniature one to care for, and he'll go overboard...lose his frickin' mind."

The door clicked closed.

Tania gave him a concerned look.

Sloan shook his head, urging the pair along, needing all his concentration to cut through the tension and give his mate some relief.

With a nod, Mac strode after Exshaw and Violet, taking Tania with him.

"Venom."

"Come in." Ruby-red eyes shimmering, Venom walked backward, taking Evelyn with him, retreating into his bedroom. "We'll talk it out. See what's what."

Good. A solid plan.

Not that Theo agreed.

Absorbing the soothing energy he fed her, she came back to herself, resisting as he walked her toward the open door. Sloan grimaced. He hated to do it. He wanted to give her a little more time before diving into her past—before making her face whatever frightened her. But the universe didn't always align with what a male requested. His mate was stuck in the past. Suffering in silence when she didn't need to...not with him.

She was hurting. Seeing it, feeling it, he refused to skirt the issue and allow her to hide. He might be new to her, but as his mate, she needed to learn—and do it fast. He wasn't a male who avoided confrontation, so instead of ceding to her silent plea, Sloan wrapped her up and pulled her forward, carrying her over the threshold toward what he knew she believed was her doom.

~

Digging her heels in, Theodora tried to back-pedal. She didn't want to go into the door Sloan walked her toward...or have any part of what would happen once inside the room.

A coward's way out. A chickenshit way to react. She hated it, but couldn't stop old patterns from rising.

She was a runner, had always been a runner, finding an escape hatch when necessary, using physical distance and frequent absences from her uncle's house to stay away from the dangerous men in his employ. When that didn't work, when she wasn't fast enough, she curled inward, disappearing inside her mind. Her safe space, one that looked a lot like the pottery studio she'd set up before being forced to flee.

A defense mechanism learned in childhood. A crutch she kept trying to throw away, but old habits died hard.

Sloan didn't seem to care about her inclinations. He slammed right through the barricades she'd erected to protect herself.

Effective. Annoying. A total alpha-male move.

Wrapping his arms around her, he grasped her wrists and crossed her arms over her chest. Chest pressed tight to her spine, he lifted her feet off the floor, telling her without words her running days were done. He wanted her to face it, wanted to know what frightened her so much. Wanted her to talk to him, share her past, lay it all on the line. Probably for the best, but as he carried her forward, panic set in. Her lungs seized, making it difficult to breathe.

"Deep breaths, *mazleiha*. In then out."

"I w-want to"—she shuddered as another ragged breath sawed out—"k-k-kill you right now."

"That's the spirit."

"God," she wheezed, chest rising and falling way too fast. "I h-haven't had one of t-these in f-forever."

"A panic attack?"

She nodded. The room spun. Her skin heated. Perspiration misted her skin as Sloan ignored her wishes and carried her into an enormous library. Two stories high, so many built-in bookshelves, a narrow walkway separated the lower and upper levels. A king-sized bed sat in the center of the space below a colorful fresco painted on the ceiling.

"Those happen often?"

"Not anymore." Staring at a fixed point, she focused on a tall shelf, trying to keep her head from spinning. A red section of thick spines, followed by a row of yellow ones. Sucking in a lungful of anemic air, she moved on to the blue books. The smell of old parchment lingered in the air along with a hint of wood smoke. "Not since I l-left."

"How long ago?"

"Four years."

"So..." he said, putting the pieces together as he pulled the truth out of her. Why she let him, Theodora didn't know. Something about his voice, about the gentle way he spoke to her, along with the warm current trickling down her spine, smoothed out the panic, allowing her to share things with him she refused to talk about with anyone else. "Before Violet was born."

Her emotions heaved. Tears filled her eyes. Two spilled over her bottom lashes. "He wanted me to get rid of her. He tried to make me get rid of her."

"Who, baby?"

"My uncle," she rasped. "He made the appointment at the clinic. Bea found out. Anthony refused to help. Said it was for the best. Told me to go, but I couldn't. I *couldn't*. I wanted her. From the moment I took the test, I wanted her. So, I left everything and ran. I ran, Sloan. I ran as far and as fast I could, but—"

"Theo."

"No one says no to him, Sloan. *No one*. He's hooked in. He's got police and powerful politicians in his pocket." On a roll, split wide open by the pain, she broke. The truth poured out. Against her will, she kept talking, spilling her secrets, unable to contain the fear anymore. "I knew he'd hunt me down. I knew he'd drag me back, take his revenge, make an example of me by killing my little girl, so what was I to do? Huh? Tell me...what was I supposed to do?"

A low growl sounded in her ear. "Who's your uncle, baby? What's his name?"

Her throat clogged.

She shook her head, refusing to say it out loud. The asshole had controlled so much of her life. God. She was twenty-nine years old, an adult capable of making her own decisions and living with the consequences. But the iron hand she'd lived and suffered under had a long reach. Her uncle had taken control of her and Beatrice the moment they laid their father in the ground, and never let go.

She'd been forced to live in his house, under his rule, most of her life. Told what to wear, what to eat, when to come and go. Heavy chains to carry, a hard burden to unload. She'd succeeded—barely—gaining some separation when she opened her studio.

Her twin had done the rest, going to work for their uncle, diverting his attention from Theodora. A measure so self-sacrificing Theodora suffered under a mountain of guilt for leaving Beatrice to deal with the monster alone.

Sloan jostled her a little. "Theo—tell me his name."

A tremor shook her. More tears spilled over her lashes.

"Nicoli Antonov," Evie said, her voice whisper-thin. "I never met him. He had Markov shadow me, but Venom—he did some checking—now, I know for a fact Trixie pulls his strings."

The blond guy snarled. "Never should've let you talk me out of going after the bastard, Evie. He left marks on you. Should've finished him then and there. Shouldn't have—"

"You know this asshole?" Sloan asked, sounding as though he wanted to rip someone's head off.

"I know him. I know your mate's sister too. Real piece of work. Got a file three inches thick."

"I wanna see it."

"No problem, brother."

Exhausted by what she'd admitted, Theodora sagged into Sloan...until the words registered. Her brain came back online. Wiping tears from her cheeks, she replayed the conversation. "Wait...what? What did you just say?"

"I'm so sorry, Theo. I know you don't know me, and after what just happened, how I reacted to you." Evie paused and took a step forward, bringing Venom with her. "I'm Evelyn, mated to Venom."

"Hello. I'd say nice to meet you, but I'm not sure it is."

Sloan chuckled.

Venom's lips twitched. "Yeah. Pretty intense, but you should know Evie's got firsthand knowledge. She knows exactly what Trixie's capable of—"

"Her name is Beatrice, or Bea," Theo said sharply. "She doesn't like to be called Trixie."

"Go easy, Ven," Evelyn whispered, the concern in her eyes telling.

He inhaled, then exhaled, long and slow, no doubt searching for patience. "Hate to tell you this, Theo. I can see that you're hurting, and I don't want to pile on, but your sister is not who you think she is. She's neck-deep in the Bratva's West Coast operations."

"She works for him, sure, but only on the legitimate side of his business," she said, denying what he insinuated. "She doesn't—"

"She does, Theo." Pointing his thumb over his shoulder, Venom gestured to the floor-to-ceiling shelves crammed full of books behind him. "I've got the pictures to prove it."

Theodora shook her head. Her sister was ambitious, sure, a woman with a sharp mind and the instincts of a shark when it came to business ventures, but she wasn't a thug. She would never have allowed herself to be pulled into their uncle's dirty dealings. *Never.*

"*Mazleiha.*" Letting go of her wrists, Sloan turned her in his arms. "How long since you last saw her?"

She swallowed. "Four years, but I've talked to her."

"On the phone?"

"Yes."

"Any video calls?"

"No. Too dangerous. We were both afraid computer networks would be monitored. We always use burners. Short conversations. Just a quick check-in every three or four months. But Sloan, what you're thinking can't be true." Laying her hands flat on his chest, she leaned in. "She's the one who helped me get out. She—"

"The reason you came home?" he asked, hitting the nail on the head. The one she feared might get hammered into the top of her sister's coffin. "When did you last talk to her? Did she call you? Is that why you were in the woods last night?"

She clenched her teeth. "You're wrong. What

you're thinking—it's wrong. Bea's in as much danger as I am. Markov told me so at Aunt Jean's cabin."

"The bastard was there? Fifteen miles from Black Diamond?" Venom asked.

Reacting to the fury in his tone, Theodora flinched.

"Ven," Evelyn said, tone sharp with warning. "Did you not hear me tell you to go easy?"

"Sorry, gorgeous, but I've wanted to kill him for a while."

Ignoring the byplay, Theodora returned her attention to Sloan. "I need to talk to her. I need my bag. I've got to—"

"No."

"Sloan—"

"You don't talk to her, you don't see her until I look at Ven's intel, hack into some systems, and make sure it's safe."

She opened her mouth to protest.

"You trust me?"

"Unfair," she whispered, knowing she did.

Her certainty qualified as crazy. Completely insane, but in a ridiculously short amount of time, he'd wormed his way under her guard. She had nothing to go on but the way he made her feel and the deep-seated belief Sloan would have her back, keep her safe, no matter what.

"You trust me." A statement of fact. No room for argument, wipe it clean off the table. "So, here's how it's gonna go, Theo. You don't lie to me. You don't run from me. You don't do any stupid shit, like steal a car and crash it into trees on some maniac mission to save your sister."

Crash into trees? Her brows popped up. What in the hell was he talking about?

"You wait for me to make it safe," he said. "I'll find out what's going on and be honest with you about it. If Beatrice is in danger, I'll get her out. And you will give me the time needed to do that. You get me?"

She bristled, disliking his bossiness. "Do I have a choice not to 'get you'?"

"No."

"Terrific," she mumbled as uncertainty took root. More emotional upheaval. But ignoring Sloan's warning wouldn't be smart. Dipping her chin, she pressed her forehead into his chest.

He murmured in understanding.

Theodora released a shaky breath and tucked away her tears. No more crying. Falling apart never helped. She needed to be able to think. She must remain objective. A tall order, given Sloan's suspicions. None of what he said was untrue.

Still, context mattered. He didn't know her uncle. He'd never met her sister, and yet Venom's accusation Beatrice wasn't whom Theodora believed shook her foundation. The guy didn't seem like the sort of person who lied. His directness struck like barbs. Toss in Evelyn's initial reaction to meeting her, and no question: something bad involving Beatrice had gone down—might still be going down, given the Bratva and her uncle's depravity.

Which left her between a rock and a hard place. As much as she hated waiting for answers, she needed the protection Sloan provided. Otherwise, she'd end up right back where she started, under her uncle's thumb.

Double jeopardy.

Second time around.

Worse odds than four years ago, with her daughter's life once again on the line.

**24**

---

Standing next to his mate at the kitchen island, Sloan listened to the low roll of conversation drift under the archway. The whole Nightfury contingent was present and accounted for, chowing down on Daimler's pancakes in the dining room. Perception expanded, giving him the lay of the land without looking.

Utensils clicked against fine china. The sweet scent of syrup hung in the air. Wick growled in disagreement. Venom told him to shut up. Violet giggled as Mac teased her, saying something about the butterflies on the front of her long-sleeved tee. Sloan heard the other Nightfury warriors and their mates talking about the meeting to come, one he hoped provided the ammunition needed to oust the Archguard from its perch once and for all.

His mind, however, stayed on Theodora. She was quiet. Deep in her head. Mired in dark thoughts. In need of space from the rest of the pack.

He'd given it to her, asking Daimler to set them up at the island instead of with the others. He glanced at the Numbai pouring perfect silver-dollar pancakes onto the hot griddle across the kitchen. The male sang an upbeat tune, spatula swaying, motion keeping time with words, thrilled to have the entire Nightfury pack all together for the first meal of the day.

Sloan shoveled another bite into his mouth. He hummed as he chewed. Canadian maple syrup, fresh raspberries, and homemade pancakes cooked to perfection. The breakfast of champions, though he noticed Theodora wasn't enjoying it nearly as much as him.

Wrapping his arm around her waist, he moved closer.

The tines of her fork jabbing, she massacred her stack of pancakes instead of eating it. He shifted, pressing his hip into hers. She leaned his way, accepting his support, telling him she liked him in her space, while frowning at her breakfast.

Sloan tapped his fork against hers. "Gonna be all right?"

"Yeah, I'm just..." She pursed her lips, then sighed. "I've got a lot on my mind."

Understandable. Theodora had been thrown one curveball after another. The most recent of which, the possibility her sister was an active member of the Russian mafia. "Don't think too hard, *mazleiha*. You're safe here. Violet is too. No one will find you at Black Diamond. Relax, if you can. I've got the rest well in hand."

She swiveled to meet his gaze, green eyes full of worry.

"Tell me."

She bit her bottom lip. "This a part of the energy-fuse thing—cherry-picking thoughts off the front of my brain?"

"Nice perk, don't you think?"

Amusement wiped the anxiety from her expression. A second later, it returned. Her aura dimmed as doubt crept in, tinging her magnificence with grey. His chest tightened. Rage slipped its leash as he watched her struggle to come to grips with her new reality.

Connected to him, sensing the incendiary burn of temper, she tensed.

Sloan locked his fury down, refusing to fuel the tumult of emotion she already labored under with his own. Theodora needed soft and stable. Not an angry male with a loose grip on his control. No matter how much he disliked her turmoil—or how much he wanted to rip her uncle to shreds—providing her with clear skies and smooth sailing would serve him better right now.

Avenging her would come later. After he filled in the branches of her crooked family tree, unearthed all the roots, and understood the importance of each one.

Taking a calming breath, he gave her a gentle squeeze, encouraging her to voice what he already knew bothered her.

She stared at him, something working behind her eyes. Coming to some sort of conclusion, she nodded. "Okay. Here I go."

"Make the leap, baby."

"Right now, I'm worried about everything—Bea, my uncle, Violet...you and being here, in a strange place, with strange, dragony-type people."

His lips twitched. *Dragony-type people*? Fuck, she was cute.

A crease between her brows, she stabbed her pancake again. "But mostly, I'm worried about the next step. I'm not good at being idle, Sloan. I'm used to being on the move. I don't know what to do with myself while you're off doing whatever it is you do."

"What did you do before?"

"Before I escaped?"

He nodded.

"I owned a pottery studio. Threw my own clay. Made and sold my own stuff."

"Online?"

"No, just in store."

"That's gonna change," he said, an idea sparking to life.

His female wasn't accustomed to sitting around. She'd been under too much stress for far too long. Her repertoire for dealing with new situations didn't included relaxation. She possessed too much restless energy—the unhealthy kind. Given time, he'd drain that out of her, bring her back to baseline and, eventually, herself. For now, she needed something to do, a task to keep her mind from racing and the worry at bay.

"I want you to talk to Daimler after breakfast, Theo. Make a list of everything you need to set up a studio here. I mean *everything*. Don't be shy. No skimping. Only the best equipment. I'll sort the rest."

Her lips parted. "Really?"

"Absolutely." His breath caught as hope sparked in her eyes. Needing to please her, he went full bore, thinking on the fly. "I'll build you a website. Get an online store rolling when you're ready. Anonymous. Safe. No blowback from your family. It'll be yours, one hundred percent—"

"Seriously?" she asked. The light in her aura shifted. Grey pushed out. Green, gold, and white moved in, beaming so bright she nearly blinded him. His heart pounded as she reacted, wonder overtaking worry, despair morphing into excitement.

"All yours, Theo. A business you control and run any way you want."

"You're going to make me cry again."

"Happy tears?"

Hand fisted in his t-shirt, she nodded.

"Those I'll accept anytime, anyplace." He tucked a thick lock of dark hair behind her ear. "Get on that, baby. No delay. Daimler'll get whatever you need."

Theodora swiveled in her seat. Ass sliding across leather, she hooked the back of his leg with her calf and pulled him between her thighs. Arousal rose hard. The muscles roping his abdomen clenched. He dropped his fork and shoved his plate away. Fine china rasped across marble, banging into glass. The pitcher fell over, spilling maple syrup across the countertop.

Daimler gasped in outrage.

Sloan didn't notice. He was too absorbed in Theodora, in thrall to his female as she gripped the back of his head, hauled him down to her level, and kissed him. No preamble. No gentle exploration. She demanded. He gave without hesitation. The incredible taste of her dragged him to the edge. With nowhere else to go, he went over. The second her lips touched his, everything but her ceased to exist.

His surroundings dropped away. The voices died down. He became deaf, blind, and mute, transported to a place he'd never been before.

Miles away from the here and now, Sloan palmed her ass and picked her up. A quick pivot, and he set her on the lip of the countertop. Tugging him closer, she wrapped him up. Welcoming him. Accepting him. Feeding a need he'd had for years without having the right outlet.

He had it now. All of her attention. All of her passion. The gorgeous spark of her in his arms. A gift males of his kind dreamed of every night—and all day long—but rarely found.

Reveling in the burn, uncaring where he stood, he kissed her back. Her nails scraped over the short strands of his hair. Pleasure buzzed through him. Magic sparked along his spine. The air heated, enveloping them in a cocoon driven by desire.

Getting zapped, Theodora purred and pushed in, tightened the connection. One leg wrapped around the back of his thigh, the other around his hip, she shifted, rubbing her heat against his erection.

Sloan groaned.

"God," she whispered, lips brushing his, kissing him soft and slow, killing him with her sweetness. "Better and better. You just keep getting better and better."

"Theo."

"Please be real."

"Baby—"

"Please be real."

"I'm real, *mazleiha*."

"I won't survive it if you turn out not to be real."

With a hum, he kissed her again. Taking his fill. Reveling in the taste and feel of her.

"Know she's new to you, buddy, but rein it in," Venom said from somewhere close. "You spilled the maple syrup. Capital offense. Daimler's about to lose his shit."

Arms wrapped tight around him, Theodora stilled, then opened her eyes. Lips still touching his, she blinked a couple of times, then muttered, "Crap."

Snug between her thighs, chest pressed to her breasts, he smiled against her mouth. "Out of control."

Drawing away, she frowned. "Who—me?"

"You keep initiating."

Her frown turned into a scowl. "Well, you keep…"

"What?"

"Short-circuiting my hormones…or something."

Angela laughed behind him.

"Hot and heavy," Rikar said, dropping two plates in the sink. "Way it should be, but tick-tock, Sloan. We got a meeting to make."

Pale green eyes shimmering, Bastian strode beneath the archway. One arm wrapped around Myst, the other cradling his newborn son, he nailed Sloan with an intense look before his gaze swept through the kitchen, landing on each warrior under his command. "Ten minutes, boys. Do what you gotta do, then get your asses to the Hub. Ange, you too. Time to see what the Scottish pack has to say."

Violet skipped into the kitchen. Giving her mother a huge grin, she skirted Wick and went straight to Daimler.

As Theodora smiled back at her daughter, Forge snarled. The low sound slithered across the kitchen. Tension ratcheted up. Heavy muscles shuffled as the Nightfury warriors reacted to the aggression. Sloan waited for the explosion, ready to intercede if Forge lost control. It would be understandable if the lethal male decided to let loose. No one would blame him after what happened in Scotland half a century ago. He'd almost been killed. His sire and brothers hadn't been as lucky.

Unsanctioned assassinations. The murders of Forge's blood kin. Orchestrated by Rodin beneath the Archguard's nose. A strategy designed for a single purpose—to keep Forge's sire from moving to strip the bastard of his power. A secret Rodin wanted to keep buried twenty feet under, never to be unearthed.

A smart plan, all things considered.

Rodin might be a psychopath, but he wasn't an idiot. The leader of the Archguard had played his hand well, slapping the Nightfury pack with *Xzinile* (sanctioned assassination rubberstamped by the Archguard), setting Zidane and a kill squad on their tails for refusing to hand Forge over for the murder of Rodin's second-born son.

A trumped-up charge. Didn't matter Forge hadn't touched the male. Or that Angela pulled the trigger, putting two bullets in Lothair's brain. One hundred percent justified after what the bastard did to her. Still...

The situation was a clusterfuck. One Bastian needed to navigate with care.

No one knew whether Cyprus, current commander of the Scottish pack, had been in on the kill. Had he facilitated the murder of Forge's family by welcoming Rodin in? Was he a power-hungry asshole or just a warrior caught in the middle of a bad situation? Good questions. No way of getting answers without talking to him, given intel was thin, practically anemic, when it came to the Scottish pack.

Which made Forge's reaction understandable. And put the rest of the Nightfuries on edge.

"Forge." Holding G.M., the Scot's seven-month-old son, Hope stepped into the fray and broke the silence. "Honey..."

Purple gaze aglow, Forge switched focus to his mate. Flames flickered over his shoulders, washing the white cabinets in purple glow. Hope stood firm, unflinching in the face of his ferocity, meeting his fury with a strength of her own. The Scot cursed, doused the fire, and, without a backward glance, walked out of the kitchen.

"Shit," Bastian said under his breath.

"I got him." Hope set G.M. in J.J.'s outstretched arms, spun toward the exit, and hurried after her male.

"Don't worry about him, B." Towing Tania behind him, Mac trailed after his best friend and mentor. "He'll be good. Keep his mouth shut, listen in, but stay out of sight until his former pack shares what they got, and we know where we stand."

Bastian nodded.

Sloan drew a cleansing breath.

The rest of the Nightfuries filed out, the mated warriors with their females, the single ones alone.

"This meeting," Theodora said, watching the warriors go. "It's important."

"Very. If the Scottish pack has what I think they do, it'll change everything."

"For the better?"

"Yeah."

"Then go. Get ready. Violet and I'll be fine here."

Caressing the outsides of her thighs, he studied her. She seemed settled and calm for the moment. Dipping his head, he gave her a kiss. "Come see me in the Hub after the meeting. Daimler will show you the way."

She nodded.

"Get on to making that list, Theo."

"You're very bossy, Sloan."

"Just wait till I get you in bed."

She wiggled in her seat.

He grinned, then let her go and stepped away. "Be good, Vivy."

"Okay, Zone," Violet said, now standing on a chair beside the stove, distracted as Daimler helped her pour pancake batter onto the hot griddle.

Skirting the end of the island, Sloan prowled out

of the kitchen. Boots thumping across hardwood, he entered the corridor and made his way to the elevators.

As he walked, his mind realigned. His priorities shuffled. He pushed Theodora into the background. Out of sight—never completely out of mind, but claiming his mate didn't mean he could allow his other duties to slide. He needed to stay sharp. For her. For him. For the warriors counting on him.

The future of the Nightfury pack hung in the balance. No way would he let his brothers down.

## 25

Rikar at her back, Angela exited the elevator and stepped into the underground lair. Seven stories beneath Black Diamond proper. Same diamond-shaped foyer in front of her. Same pungent scent of pine drifting in from the corridor. Same scarred, whitewashed stone staring her in the face.

The usual setup. Nothing, however, was normal about her current situation.

She'd sat in on meetings with the guys before—given her stint as a homicide detective for SPD, Bastian liked to get her take on things—but today was different. Her inclusion in the meeting counted as special, drawing a hard line between old and new. Hard stop to her old life as a human. Clear start to her new one as the first female born into Dragonkind in centuries.

Elevated status within the pack. Ridiculous amounts of pressure.

*Born into Dragonkind.*

She huffed, recognizing the irony. She hadn't been *born* into anything. She'd been dragged kicking and screaming. Had she been given a choice, Angela wasn't sure what she would've chosen: to remain one hundred percent human, but on the periphery of Nightfury pack missions. Or asked to be injected with the serum (had she known about it first) and embraced the magic along with the shift in her DNA.

Half dragon, half human.

She'd never thought much about it, never believed anything about Rikar was strange. He was who he was—charismatic, lethal, beautiful in all ways. She'd embraced his ways, become a part of his world, left her own behind, the moment he pulled her from danger, but...

A big divide lay between being his mate and becoming a Dragonkind warrior. Right now, her packmates called her a fledging (the label given to untrained Dragonkind). She felt like an infant with zero coordination and even less confidence. Her newly minted status as a she-dragon might be cool, but truth was...

She didn't know what the hell she was doing.

All she wanted was to fit in, do well, and make her mate, along with the other members of the pack, proud. Which, in her mind, meant being included...in everything. Being denied the green light to go on missions made her feel like a weakling. Like a failure. Like she couldn't be trusted to get it right.

Sloan kept asking her to be patient.

Rikar urged her to slow down.

Her she-dragon tugged her the other way. The beast was impatient, aggressive, and surly. A fun companion, a magic-wielding juggernaut she welcomed with open arms, but for one thing: the added dimensions of her personality were hard to slow down. Her dragon half wanted to go hard, do it fast, protocol and caution be damned.

The wrong approach with Sloan. Nowhere near the right one with Bastian, given the intel she and Rikar planned to share at the meeting.

"Don't get your hopes up," Rikar said, footfalls sounding behind her.

His deep voice ghosted through the quiet. Shivers of pleasure prickled down her spine. Glancing over her shoulder, she met his ice-blue eyes. "You've got no pull?"

He shook his head.

"You're sure?"

"Not when it comes to this, angel. Once we relay the information, Bastian'll weigh in, but as your mentor, Sloan has final say."

She gritted her teeth. Dragon combat training along with all the rules it entailed were a pain in her ass.

Not that she didn't think she needed the instruction. She did—a lot of it. Her crash-landing into the side of the LZ proved it.

Rikar enjoyed teasing her about her near-miss and almost-drowning. All the guys did, but Angela didn't find anything funny. Landing well would've ensured she moved on to the next lesson, the one that would teach her how to cast invisibility spells, in and out of dragon form. She needed to master the skill—sooner than soon. Otherwise, she'd remain sidelined, stuck at Black Diamond while the boys flew out on the next mission.

A mission she knew would include Sasha Cooper.

Her intel. It should be her mission.

"I hate this," she grumbled, moving down the wide corridor. Twelve-foot ceilings slanted down to meet polished concrete floors. Embedded in the sea of grey, round lights threw bright, V-shaped splashes up the walls, acting like a runway. Two doors stood up ahead, near the end of the hallway. Sliding glass ones fronted the medical clinic. The other was a gateway into Sloan's computer lab. "It sucks, Rikar."

"Mac felt the same way. Par for the course for a warrior new to Dragonkind." He grabbed her hand. She laced her fingers through his, hanging on tight, allowing him to ground her. "You gotta get used to your new body in dragon form, let the magic mesh, graft onto your heart, mind, and soul. It takes time. You can't rush it. When you and your dragon half are ready, it'll happen."

Not liking the message, but knowing he was right, Angela dropped the subject, turned a right, and walked into Sloan's domain...and now, in a lot of ways, hers too. She spent tons of time in the Hub, helping Sloan hack into all kinds of databases. Without looking, she veered away from the cherry wood conference table with twenty rolling leather chairs. Her gaze settled on the six screens mounted above a beat-up desk. Angela shook her head. Every time she looked at Sloan's set up, she wanted to pull out a flamethrower and torch the entire thing, 'cause man...

The long desk looked like someone had attacked it with a hatchet. And it wasn't even the worst part. A huge, ugly chair sat in front of the stretch of scarred wood, bright purple leather worn white in spots, frayed seams popping, metal base rusted, looking sad next to her expensive leather one.

Angela stared at the monstrosity a second. She stutter-stepped, pausing just inside the door. Sloan's chair was an eyesore, a total travesty gumming up the works in a sleek, high-tech space. She envisioned soaking the thing in lighter fluid and lighting a match every time she entered the Hub.

Lovely fantasy, but she didn't dare. Sloan would lose his mind. Her mentor loved his chair more than anyone should, given its condition.

Dragging her gaze away, Angela nodded to the males in the room. The whole gang was here. Gage, Haider, and Nian milled around by the snack bar Daimler had set up. Venom, Wick, Mac, and Forge stood with shoulders propped against the back wall. Bastian sat at the head of the table, big boots planted on top, legs outstretched, ankles crossed, watching Sloan carry a big screen in from the storage area at the back of the room.

"Ange." Sloan set the TV down on the table. "Fire up the program."

With a nod, she skirted the train wreck he called a chair and claimed her own. She swiveled toward the desk, pulled her wireless keyboard closer, and started typing. Six screens came alive, each with a different background, all images that captured forest and mountain views. She entered the multiple passwords needed to access the system. The supercomputer came alive. Jumping screens, she moved through each step the way Sloan taught her, then glanced over her shoulder.

The monitor Sloan stood beside powered on. An image of the table—and Bastian—appeared on screen.

Pride in his eyes, her mentor nodded at her.

She smiled back, needing his approval without understanding why. Could be she needed to know he valued her. Could be she liked knowing he trusted her. Could be anything or nothing. But the fact he was proud of her struck some place deep, helping wipe away the idea she might be inadequate.

"Right." Taking his feet off the table, Bastian let his

boots hit the floor. The thump rolled through the Hub as he wheeled his chair back from the table. "We've got a few minutes. Anyone got anything to share before the meeting starts?"

Angela glanced at her mate. Arms crossed over his chest, Rikar nodded. She opened her mouth to start the conversation about Sasha.

"Tania's pregnant," Mac said, cutting her off at the knees.

"What the fuck?" Mouth half-full of croissant, Gage stared at Mac. "How's that possible?"

Forge grunted, sounding as though he was trying not to laugh. "About time you said something, Irish. Her scent's begun tae change. Wouldn't have been long before the pack picked up on it."

Mac sighed. "I know."

"Seriously," Gage said, sounding scandalized. "What the fuck?"

Nian echoed his shock. "The Meridian hasn't realigned."

"How far along is she?" Haider asked, mercury eyes full of speculation. The most cerebral of the Metallics, the male never missed an opportunity to pull a mystery apart.

Ignoring Haider's question, Venom threw out one of his own. "You're sure? Absolutely positive she's pregnant?"

"Motherfuck," Mac said, glaring at Venom. "I wanna talk about this about as much as I want a lobotomy."

"Don't care," Wick said, sticking to the usual two words. Though Angela had heard him use three... when he was feeling chatty. "Explain."

Angela huffed. Guess Wick *was* feeling chatty.

Mac blew out a breath. "I shouldn't have said anything."

Golden eyes narrowed, Wick pushed off the wall. "Explain."

Faced with a fuck-you in the form of a lethal male no one in their right mind wanted to fight, Mac gave in...ungracefully. "I know Dragonkind males aren't fertile outside a realignment, but Tania and I got talking about it a couple of months ago, trying to decide whether I would lock down when the Meridian realigned, or if we should go for it."

Rounding the table, the Metallics sat down, settling in the chairs across from Bastian.

The Nightfury commander shifted in his own. "You wanted to lock down."

"Tania vetoed that quick." A chagrined look on his face, Mac transferred his attention to B. "Myst was already pregnant. Tania and Myst are best friends. My mate wants your son and mine to be close in age, grow up together. You know the drill."

"I do," B said, planting his forearms on the tabletop. "Still doesn't explain how you got her pregnant outside the window."

Mac shrugged. "No fucking clue. Tania decided. I gave in, thinking I'd have the two months before the Meridian realigned to get used to the idea. Four weeks later, she pees on a stick, and I find out I'm going to be a father."

Another round of shock. More silence. The quiet lengthened, stretched, and stirred, becoming uncomfortable

"Water dragon mojo. The only explanation," Angela said, breaking through the astonishment, gaze locked on her ex-partner at the SPD, a guy she considered her big brother. Two years working side by side, sixteen-hour days spent in his company, had forged a serious friendship. From the beginning, she and Mac had been tangled up in each other's strings. "Congrats, Mac. Happy for you, man."

The corners of his mouth tipped up. His eyes warmed, making his aquamarine irises shimmer. "Thanks, Ange, but...water dragon shit aside, I can't be *that* different."

"You are. I've known it from the beginning." Stacking his arms on the back of her chair, Rikar leaned in, giving it his weight. Springs creaked. Leather squeaked. Her mate didn't notice. Ice-blue eyes trained on Mac, Rikar studied him for a moment. "So little is known about your subset of Dragonkind. Shit. We all thought water dragons were a myth until we got a load of you. Stands to reason you'd be different when it comes to siring offspring too."

"Could be you're only fertile with your mate," Sloan said. "Might explain why there are so few of you around. Maybe you need energy-fuse. Maybe you need to bond with a female before you can procreate."

Expression shifting from confused to fierce, Mac scowled. "I was done talking about this before. Now I'm *really* done talking about it."

"Me too," Venom muttered, tossing the pastry he held aside. Shedding crumbs, the blueberry muffin bounced across the table, then rolled off the opposite edge. "Talking about Mac procreating... I've lost my appetite."

Wick snorted.

Forge grinned.

The Metallics laughed.

"Christ," Rikar said, smiling down at Angela.

She took the bull by the horns, bringing the conversation back to her topic. "If we're done with that, I've got something. We still got time?"

"Nine minutes." Kicking the discarded muffin out the door into the hallway, Sloan sat in his ugly-ass chair. White stitching popped against purple leather as the thing groaned, objecting to the ongoing abuse.

Everyone waited, watching to see if the victim would give up the fight and dump Sloan onto the floor.

When it didn't, Bastian said, "Shoot, Ange."

She took a deep breath. No time like the present. No sense avoiding what she couldn't control. She didn't want to share. Would've preferred to keep her experience under wraps, but her packmates needed to know, required all the information to understand what she faced.

Flexing her fingers, Angela leaned back in her chair and began to share: about the night she'd been taken by the Razorbacks, about her forays into Seattle on her own, laying down what she knew about Ivar and his connection to Sasha Copper.

## 26

Ass planted in his favorite chair, Sloan set his forearms on the tops of his thighs and listened to his apprentice talk. He focused on her face, catalogued her distress, and picked up on her pain. The need to hit something clawed through him. His chest tightened as Angela paused, then kept going, refusing to shy away from the truth.

She laid out the facts instead. The details of her kidnapping. Her runs into the city after he and the other Nightfury warriors left the lair for the night. The intel she'd found during the course of her investigation, along with what she and Rikar suspected about some female living in a quiet neighborhood.

Unbelievably courageous. Balls-to-the-walls honest. Incredibly difficult for anyone to do, but even more so for a female sitting in a room full of males, lethal ones. Ones who skewed toward unpredictability and a willingness to eliminate problems the old-fashioned way—by slitting people's throats.

As she went over a painful memory, her voice cracked.

Rikar crouched beside her chair. A muscle flexed along her jaw. The Nightfury first-in-command palmed her shoulder, offering his mate emotional support the only way he knew how—through proximity and touch.

Swallowing past the knot clogging his throat, Sloan made twin fists, forcing himself to stay seated. Fucking hell. He wanted to do more than hit someone. He wanted to get his claws on Ivar, tear the bastard limb from limb, then go back and do it again.

He'd known a few of the details, the bones of Angela's story, but not all of it. Not everything. Not even close.

Bearing witness to her pain made it real. Rage bubbled over his already sharp edges, threatening to undo him. As her mentor, the desire to avenge her burned through him. As her friend, his heart broke for her. Aaaand...around and around he went, trying to contain the fury, only to have it well up and spill over again.

He clenched his teeth.

Angela glanced his way, hazel eyes steady on him, heart solid with Rikar at her side. Spirit not only intact, but unbreakable. Sloan had already respected her, but in this moment, his pride in her grew.

Goddess, he was proud of her. So goddamn *proud*. And yet...

The longer she talked, the more Sloan wanted to kick her ass. For being so stubborn. For being so smart. For inching out onto a dangerous limb and going it alone. He would've gone with her if she'd asked, would've watched her back while she followed her investigative nose. He might not have been her mentor then—or responsible for her like he was now after her first shift— but he'd always been her friend. And she knew the rules.

No one left the lair without backup. *No one.* Male.

Female. Didn't matter. Pack protocol existed for a reason.

Venom had broken the rule once and ended up paying the price. He might still have the burn marks to prove it. A painful lesson. Bastian hadn't fooled around. He'd conveyed his displeasure with a swiftness that no warrior would mistake. No dummy, Venom received the message loud and clear. So had everyone else: fall in line or get your ass kicked by a male who controlled lightning and never hesitated to strike.

Angela stopped talking.

Silence descended.

"Fuck," Gage muttered after a while.

"Hellfire," Nian growled, shifting in his seat.

Haider flexed his fingers, then made twin fists against the tabletop. "B—tell me we're flying out tonight. I need to kill something."

"You're shitting me," Mac said, stomping around the table. The grip on his temper slipped as he moved. Water droplets collected, rising in waves around his shoulders. The smell of brine blew into the room, making the fine hairs on Sloan's nape stand on end. "Tell me you're shitting me, Ange. You went out alone?"

"Mac—"

"Little sister." With a growl, Mac yanked her out of the chair. Rikar bristled. Water dragon calling the shots, Mac ignored the threat, pulled her close, and wrapped his arms around her. "You didn't tell me."

Agony underpinned his tone. The same kind Sloan felt in his gut and down to his bones.

"You didn't fucking tell me."

"Mac..." Hugging him back, Angela fisted her hands in his t-shirt. Mist shrouded the pair, collecting in the strands of her short auburn hair. "It was done. No undoing it. Knowing all of what happened would've sent you off the deep end."

"I'm about to go there now. Motherfuck." Closing his eyes, he took a deep breath. Wet froth swirled, then evaporated as he regained control. "You went out alone. *Alone.* I don't know whether to keep hugging you, or shake you until your teeth rattle."

The rest of the Nightfuries grumbled, echoing the sentiment.

Angela pushed her best friend away. "I know I didn't go about it the right way. Believe me when I say I'm fully aware. Rikar made it clear real quick, in ways I'm not sure I want repeated. But guys…"

She trailed off, sensing the vicious vibe in the room. Swallowing, she glanced Sloan's way, looking for help.

He scowled at her.

Amusement sparked in her eyes. She shook her head, then returned her attention to soothing the violent tempers about to explode all over the room. "I might have gone about it the wrong way, but seriously —you can't argue with the results. We've got a lead, a really good one."

"First off," Venom said, pushing away from the wall. "I wanna know what Rikar did to make you think twice about doing it again."

Bastian grinned.

Arms crossed over his chest, Wick glared at his best friend.

Lips twitching, Sloan turned his attention to his boots.

"What?" Ruby-red eyes searching, Venom looked around. "Total chickenshit pricks. Don't tell me I'm the only one who's curious. Seems like information every male should have when dealing with his mate. Might come in handy when Evie—"

"Shut up, Ven," Angela said.

Rikar snorted. "Already telling Ven off. You get in the swing of things fast, angel."

His brothers-in-arms chuckled. All except Wick, who continued to look as though he wanted fry Venom with a fireball.

Angela sighed. Sitting back in her chair, she speared Bastian with an intense look. "We done with this crap? Can we get back on track now?"

B's lips twitched. "Sure."

She drew a deep breath to control her temper. Redheads. Always a crapshoot. It must keep Rikar on his toes, wondering which way his mate would lean when faced with the unknown—calm, smooth, and sensible...or hell on wheels the second she let loose.

"Okay," she said. "What I want to know is how we're going to handle the Sasha situation."

"You've spent time with her. How do you think we should handle it?" Bastian asked.

"I want in on this one, B."

"Ange," Sloan said in warning.

"My lead, my mission."

"Doesn't work that way, and you know it. You're not ready. You won't be able to fly out on missions until you can cloak."

"So teach me."

"I will, but conjuring an invisibility spell isn't like learning to fly...or land. Cloaking isn't a skill you learn, Ange, it's one your dragon half grants. Your magic will have limitations until she comes fully on board."

"How long?"

"Took me three weeks. Frustrating as hell, but nothing I tried worked. Couldn't force it," Mac said, coming to Sloan's rescue by backing him up. "My dragon half decided when and where. I had no say."

"Crap. Three weeks." Disappointment written all over her face, she raked her hands through her hair. "Way too long."

"What's the rush?" B asked, stretching his legs out under the table.

"We can't sit on this intel. We need to decide what to do, then do it fast, but…" Her brow furrowed. "I'll say now, I don't want her kidnapped. We do that, Bastian, and we're no better than the Razorbacks."

"We're at war," Sloan said, turning his chair toward her. Leather groaned. Old springs creaked. He made a mental note to get the WD-40 out after the meeting. "None of us want to put a female in the middle, but if Sasha's who you think she is, taking her may be the only way to stop Ivar. We know what the serum he created did to you. Now we need to find out what's in it, and whether the shift from human female to she-dragon can be duplicated. Only way to do that is to bring the asshole to heel."

"She's a nice girl, Sloan. Completely oblivious."

Chair springs hissed as Haider planted his elbows on the table. "How do you know?"

"If she knew about Dragonkind, if Ivar shared who he is, do you really think she'd be living in a little A-frame on Walton Street? Going to work every day, coming home with mud on her piece of crap Jeep every evening?"

Another round of grumbling. Which meant Angela not only aimed true, but hit the bull's-eye.

"No, she wouldn't. Sasha would be halfway around the world by now, running for her life," Angela said, holding firm against the collection of strong personalities, making him even prouder of her. "So, we need to find another way. You know I've got skills the Razorbacks won't expect and can't anticipate. The last week of training has proven I'm unaffected by sunlight. I'm good to fly during the day, so that's what I'll do. Fly out while the Razorbacks are grounded. Do some more scouting. Gather more intel and—"

Rikar snarled. "Fuck no."

"Not on your own," Bastian said at the same time. "You're done doing that shit."

"You got that right," Sloan said, asserting his rights as her mentor. "No more going out alone, Ange. You try it, I'll do more than rattle your teeth. I'll take a strip off your hide."

Nose out of joint, she glared at him.

His computer chimed. Sloan spun toward his terminal. Saved by the bell. Time to get the show on the road, and the Scottish pack up on screen.

Grabbing his wireless keyboard off his desk, Sloan shoved out of his chair and crossed the room. "B— who's on screen?"

"You, Rikar, and I. The rest of you spread out. I'll talk to Cyprus, but need you all to listen, pick up anything I miss. And Forge..." Drilling the male with his pale green gaze, Bastian said, "Keep your shit tight, yeah?"

The Scot nodded. He and Mac moved to the opposite side of the table, setting up shop next to the Metallics, Venom, and Wick. Angela stayed where she sat, swiveling to face the monitors, getting ready to record the video chat as Rikar joined Sloan and Bastian at the end of the table.

The computer chirped again.

Sloan slid his keyboard across the table. Adjusting the screen, he placed the curved thirty-two-inch monitor closer to Bastian. The best way to keep the Scottish pack's eyes off the setup inside the Hub. No one needed to know the ins and out of his private domain. The most Cyprus would get was a view of the sitting area Angela had insisted he set up in the rear of the room. Daimler, of course, got involved and went overboard—per freaking usual—dragging in two long couches, four low, wide-backed armchairs, and the snack bar, then accessorized with side tables, fluffy blankets, and an army of throw pillows, but...whatever. Sloan didn't care about the invasion. Just as long as the Numbai left his system untouched, Daimler could do whatever he wanted.

"You good?" Rikar asked Angela.

"Yeah, handsome. Go."

He nodded, pushed up from his crouch, and rounded the table, electing to set up shop behind Bastian.

Flicking the black toggle, Sloan uncovered the monitor's camera. He adjusted the angle of the screen, framing the shot, making sure B sat center stage. A couple of keystrokes brought his AI on line. He watched code scroll across the wall-mounted monitors across the room, ensured his system was secure, then opened a video chat window.

A clear image appeared on screen. A pretty redhead with green eyes came into view. Background blurred behind her, aura glowing like a starburst around her, she tipped her chin.

"Ivy," he murmured.

"Good to see you, Sloan," she replied from her command center deep in the wilds of the Scottish Highlands. Rotating the pen nestled between her fingers, she clicked the top with her thumb. *Snick-click. Snick-click.* The sound, like everything else about her, came through loud and clear. "Ready to rock and roll?"

"Whenever you are." One hand planted on the tabletop, he pushed away from the monitor, expanding her view. Green eyes widened as she got a load of Bastian sitting at the head of the table. Sloan tilted his head toward his commander. "Bastian—no need to tell you who he is."

Ivy clicked the top of her pen again. "Nope."

Sloan hitched his thumb, indicating the big male standing with arms crossed behind him. "That's Rikar, XO of the Nightfury pack."

The blur behind her swirled.

Ivy pressed a button.

As the area behind her cleared, she pushed sideways. A huge male with nearly colorless eyes pushed away from the credenza behind her. Moving like a predator, he approached the screen, taking up the space Ivy vacated. Sloan took him in, analyzing everything about him. Intense vibe. Crackling energy. Powerful magic. All conveyed via monitor from thousands of miles away.

"Cyprus, commander of the Scottish pack," the warrior rumbled in his thick brogue. His pale violet gaze moved from Sloan to Rikar, then back to Bastian. He flicked his hand out, indicating two other males. "My blood brothers—Tydrin and Vyroth."

Sloan's gaze landed on the first male. He blinked in surprise. The warrior with dark hair and purple eyes looked so much like Forge he was almost an exact replica.

Frowning, he stared at Tydrin a second, then shifted focus to the Scottish commander's other brother—and did a double take. Holy hell. Twins, rare among Dragonkind. The warrior looked exactly like Cyprus. Same face. Same build. Same kind of lethal intensity. Only one difference—the eyes. Cyprus's were so pale a purple his irises looked colorless. One of Vyroth's carried the identical hue, but the other fired with a bright electric blue.

"Well met," Vyroth said, rolling his chair alongside Ivy.

Planting his hand on the backrest, Tydrin shoved his brother sideways, away from his mate, then settled in, arms crossed, hip pressed against the side of her chair. Ivy rolled her eyes. Battling to stay upright, Vyroth cursed. Wheels squeezing underneath him, the male grabbed the desk edge, coming to an abrupt halt before he slammed into Cyprus.

Vyroth scowled at his brother.

Tydrin ignored him.

Unfazed by his brothers, Cyprus planted his hand on the desktop. Attention on Bastian, he leaned in. "Good tae meet you, Bastian. Heard lots about you."

Leaning back in his chair, B raised a brow. "None of it good, I hope."

Cyprus smiled. "Depends who you talk tae. I've always thought Rodin and his ilk are a waste of space. Total gasbags. Crooked as the day is long. After Vyroth's visit tae Prague, I now know it tae be true."

"You've been to Prague?" Sloan asked.

Mismatched eyes went from shimmering to glowing, broadcasting his upset. "I was chasing a rumor. Landed on radar. Ended up imprisoned for two months for my trouble. Nearly starved tae fucking death. Zidane and his sire are tae blame."

Bastian leaned forward in his chair. "Can you prove it?"

"Not yet, but the intel we're finding suggests Rodin's neck-deep in it. Montgomery, the male who downed me, has close ties tae Zidane. The kind that tell me the two are blood kin. He disappeared after I escaped and returned to attack his lair. Been searching for him ever since, but the arsehole's smoke. Nowhere in Europe. Which means—"

"He might be here with Zidane," B said, growling low in his throat.

Cyprus nodded. "Best guess, but...aye. You see him, get word tae me. We'll make the trip. Vyroth and I—shite, my entire pack—want a crack at the bastard."

Bastian nodded. "Description?"

"Venomous dragon, vibrant green scales. Black horns and claws," Vyroth said, sounding pissed off. "A deep scar bisecting his right eyebrow."

"Got it," B said.

Unloading his bulk into a chair, Cyprus laid his cards on the table. "Pack commanders are talking, Bastian. I've heard the rumors and know what you want tae do—dismantle the Archguard, install a system of government in which all packs are equal and everybody gets a vote. I've also heard about the Archguard's play tae stop you—*Xzinile* for your pack. Bullshite move. Donnae know about you, but that added tae the other, and I'm thinking it's time tae get off our arses. With Zidane leading the kill squad, Rodin's less insulated in Prague, more vulnerable. Perfect time tae take him out."

Excitement shivered through Sloan. *Pack commanders are talking.* Goddess, such good news. He'd been working for weeks, tapping into cyberspace, running his algorithms, sending messages into the ether, trying to get something going. No answers back, no engagement before Ivy contacted him, but his efforts hadn't gone unnoticed.

Keeping his expression neutral, he stared at the Scottish commander, giving none of his elation away, but...*goddamn*. Pack commanders were talking.

"Could be," Bastian replied, cagey and noncommittal, bursting Sloan's bubble. "I've got some questions for you first."

"Ask, lad. Got nothing tae hide."

"Your uncle and his sons."

"Fuck," Cyprus growled. "I knew this was going tae come up. I hate talking about it. Still hurts like hell..." Emotion burning in his eyes, Cyprus trailed off.

Patient as always, Bastian waited.

Feet planted at the opposite end of the table, Forge rolled his shoulders, but managed to stay quiet and off camera.

The Scottish commander cleared his throat. "I miss him. So fucking much. My cousins, too. I hate knowing my sire had a hand in it. Bloody hell. He invited the kill squad in, hid the rogues on our land, and watched while Uncle Leonid, Conn, Droztan, and Forge got torn apart. He laughed about it—my bastard sire *laughed* about it when I confronted him. He watched it go down from his perch on the cliffs and didn't lift a talon tae help. I know other packs think I murdered my kin tae take control of the pack. Letting them believe that shite has served us well, keeping rogue warriors away and our territory secure, but—"

"I'm thinking they've got it wrong," Bastian murmured.

Cyprus snarled, fighting for control. "I would never. My sire was mentally unstable. So unbalanced, Uncle Leonid stepped in and raised me and my blood brothers. He shielded us when needed, gave us harsh lessons when earned. He was sire tae us all. No way in hell would I have gone against him. I loved him too much."

"We all did," Vyroth said, sounding pained.

"Cy killed our sire," Tydrin said. "He avenged Uncle Leonid and our cousins the second he learned the truth...long before we voted him in as pack commander. He's carried the burden alone for years. Didn't tell anyone until a couple of months ago."

"Hell," Sloan muttered.

"Every fucking day," Cyprus said, a muscle flexing in his jaw.

Forge cracked his knuckles. The snap ricocheted through the quiet.

Bastian looked at his warrior. "Your decision, brother."

With a nod, Forge hesitated a moment, then moved. Heavy footfalls silent against polished concrete, he walked the length of the table. Purple gaze glowing with high emotion, he turned the corner and looked straight into the camera. "Lads."

The Scots froze.

Three mouths fell open.

Ivy murmured, then reached out and grabbed her mate's hand.

Cyprus closed his eyes, his relief so stark, Sloan felt it a continent away.

"Holy Christ," Tydrin rasped, tears welling in his eyes.

"Thank the goddess. Thank the goddess." Bowing his head, Vyroth gripped the edge of the desk. "I heard the rumors. Went tae Prague to get the truth. Couldn't find any...couldn't..." His voice wobbled.

"Cousin," Cyprus whispered, opening his eyes, confusion plain to see on his face. "Where've you been all these years? Why did you not come home?"

Forge stayed silent, no doubt trying to figure out what to say.

"You thought we killed him. You thought I—"

"I had no memory of the attack, Cy. I woke up in a bog, buried up tae my eyeballs in muck, completely blank. I was grieving, a week out of my first shift, scared shitless. I assumed the worst. That's on me, lad. You, me, Ty, and V'll have a conversation about it and catch up later. Sloan and Ivy'll set it up," Forge said, his voice thick with emotion. "For now, we need tae concentrate on building a coalition that'll put Dragonkind on a healthier path, aye?"

"Aye," all three Scottish males said at the same time.

"But I'll say now, just tae be clear...so bloody glad tae have you back, Forge," Cyprus said. "So bloody glad."

Forge grunted.

Pushing out of his chair, Bastian stood and gave Forge a slap on the back. The male rocked forward with the force of the love tap. Cyprus huffed. Forge scowled, then retreated, joining Rikar behind his commander.

Question answered to his satisfaction, Bastian said, "Right. Time to lay it out. We've been busy. We've got proof Rodin led the kill squad that assassinated Leonid and your cousins. The evidence is thin. We'd have to put Forge's mate in front of an Archguard tribunal, which—"

Forge growled.

"—none of us want to do," Bastian said, ignoring the interruption. "Not sure we'd win even if we did. *Xzinile*'s pretty much closed that door. But Sloan and the Metallics have been reaching out to other pack commanders. I didn't know until you told us those efforts haven't been wasted, and I'm encouraged by the fact there's chatter. Maybe if we team up—"

"Others will come out of the woodwork and jump on board," Cyprus said, a gleam of excitement in his eyes. "The dominos will fall, and we'll change things for good. For the better."

"That's what I'm thinking." Crossing his arms over his chest, B rocked back onto his heels, then rolled forward again. "I might have Zidane in my backyard... for now. Until I kill him or his sire recalls him to Prague. I've got my finger on the pulse, but I'm a world away, Cyprus. And I have no plans to return. If we want to go after the Archguard, Rodin's gotta be the first domino to fall."

Nian snarled, viciousness out in full force.

Sloan understood his packmate's reaction. As a former member of the Archguard, Nian had grown up watching Rodin manipulate the system. He'd chafed under the weight of the high counsel's rule, had sat at the table after his sire's death, been forced to look Rodin in the eye and bear witness to all the nasty power plays and dirty dealings. He knew where the bodies were buried. The male wanted Rodin dead just as much, if not more, than the rest of the Nightfury pack.

"Agreed," Cyprus said, dragging Sloan's attention back to the conversation. "Rodin goes down, the others will scramble. Added to what you've got, I may have what we need tae knock the fool off his perch, ruin his chances of becoming high chancellor tae our kind once and for all."

Bastian raised a brow. "What do you have?"

"I would've sent it sooner, but I needed tae talk tae you first. Wanted tae look you in the eye, be sure you're the male everyone says you are. No offense."

"None taken."

"Ivy," Cyprus said, "send the files."

Letting go of Tydrin's hand, Ivy grabbed her keyboard. "Sloan...I've got over fifty video files. Give me a minute or two to compress them. Get ready, though—they're gonna take a while to download. You got a secure portal you prefer?"

"Yeah." Accessing the program he needed, Sloan opened a link and entered his address. "Sent."

Eyes on a different screen, Ivy hummed in response.

"Look at the first three videos, Bastian," Tydrin said, watching his mate's fingers fly over the keyboard. "Those will be of particular interest tae you."

B nodded.

"Good." Rapping his knuckles against wood, Cyprus pushed out of his seat. "After you look at those, we'll talk again, firm up our strategy. But I've got tae fly now. Got rogues in need of killing and not a lot of night left tae see it done."

One corner of Bastian's mouth tipped up. "Later."

"Later," the Scots echoed a second before the screen went dark, leaving the Nightfuries smiling at each and Sloan waiting for incriminating evidence against Rodin to land in his inbox.

## 27

Kneeling on the floor beside the couch in Black Diamond's living room, Theodora watched her daughter fight sleep. Always the same battle. Violet never wanted to miss anything, so no matter how tired, she tried to stay awake.

With a murmur, Theodora adjusted the blanket. Sleepy light brown eyes opened and closed. Tucking the soft fleece around her daughter, she rubbed her back, helping her lose the war on sleep.

"I'm not sweepy, Mommy."

"I know, honey-bunny, but Lulu is," Theodora whispered, sweeping the riot of ringlets away from Violet's face. "She needs her rest. Close your eyes, so she can close hers too."

Curled on her side in the middle of the sectional, Violet clutched her stuffed rabbit closer. Seconds ticked by. Theodora kept rubbing her back. Exhaustion and the crackle of a well-laid fire did the rest, tugging Violet over the line. With a sigh, she gave up the fight. It was a dirty trick to pull Lulu into the fray, but it never failed. Whatever Lulu needed, Violet worked hard to give. As she drifted into a deep sleep, relaxing beneath her hand, J.J. snorted behind them.

Theodora glanced over her shoulder.

Sky-blue eyes in a beautiful face surrounded by pin-straight, black hair met hers. "You play dirty."

"Mothers always do when trying get three-year-olds to nap."

"No doubt," J.J. said, bright pink marker poised above one of the coloring books Daimler unearthed half an hour ago.

A welcome distraction, one that kept Violet out of the kitchen while he and the other women cleaned up and put the leftovers away. A real family affair: lots of chatter, tons of laughter, everybody pitching in to make quick work of a kitchen reduced to disarray. With so many hands already at work, Theodora and J.J. had retreated, settling down to color with Violet on the coffee table in front of the fire. Myst joined the party a minute later, sitting in one of the deep armchairs to breastfeed her four-day-old son.

Yeah, a real family affair. So normal. Completely natural. Contained inside a lair inhabited by Dragonkind.

The realization jackhammered through Theodora. Her throat tightened. God. Who would've thought she'd find what she needed here—the safety, the security, the acceptance—in a place bound by magic, ruled by dragons, with a man who handled her with care and looked at her as though she hung the stars in his sky?

A dream come true. Weird to think of it that way.

Spinning toward the coffee table, Theodora picked up a marker. She fiddled with the cap a moment, then pulled off the top. Coloring was good. Coloring was *great*. The mindless activity would allow her to avoid thinking about Sloan, what meeting him meant, along with the last four years, while she—

"You need to let it go."

Turquoise tip hovering above paper, Theodora frowned at a butterfly wing, trying to decide where to start. "What?"

"The past," J.J. said, voice so quiet Theodora almost didn't hear her. "I know from experience that's a hard one, but Theo, trust me...you stay in the past, the future won't unfold the way you want. Accept whatever happened before you met Sloan happened for a reason, let it go, and move on to the good stuff."

Sage advice. Difficult to follow for a girl who spent all her time looking over her shoulder, waiting for the past to catch up.

"How did you meet Wick?" she asked, sensing a story.

Done feeding her son, Myst chuckled. "Oh, boy."

Blue eyes twinkling, J.J. smiled at her. "Long story short?"

"Sure."

"He broke me out of prison."

Theodora blinked.

J.J. went on, "I was doing a dime for first-degree manslaughter. Wick didn't think that was fair. Still says I didn't do anything wrong when I took out my abusive ex-boyfriend for beating the crap out of me on a regular basis, then threatening to kill my sister and me after I left him."

"She lured him into a parking garage," Myst said. "Put two slugs in him...center mass."

"Wick's got the crime scene photos," J.J. said, bizarrely. "He'd frame and put them up on the wall if I let him."

"I might be on his side on that one, J.J." Holding her sleeping son in her arms, Myst stood up, then sat back down, sitting cross-legged in the chair. "He beat the crap out of another woman, put her in the hospital, two days before you shot him. Almost killed her. Brain damage. She'll never be the same."

"Still…" J.J. murmured, guilt seeping into her tone.

Expression set in fierce lines, Myst shook her head. "Don't do that, girl. I'm sorry you were put in that position, sorry you were the one who had to do it, hate that you've got those images in your head, but Wick's right. The jerk needed to be put down. Follow your own advice and don't go back there."

J.J. sighed. "See what I mean, Theo? The past is hard to get over, but—"

"You killed a man to protect yourself and your sister, and honestly, in my opinion, that's noble." Frowning at the tip of her marker, Theodora shook her head, then looked back at J.J. "I don't care what the law says; it's one hundred percent justified. But you have no idea how many people my family has hurt. I knew things, J.J. *I knew things.* Things that could've hurt my uncle. Stuff the police could've used to take him down long before I got pregnant with Violet and he threatened me. But he's powerful, connected in all the right places, and I got scared. I ran instead of staying to fight. How many people have been killed in the past four years? How many lives ruined? How many might have been saved if I'd just—"

A low curse rippled across the room. Heavy footfalls shook the floor. The glass-topped coffee table vibrated under her marker. Violet stirred on the couch, then resettled.

Theodora looked up from the coloring book.

Dark eyes edged by glimmering green and gold, Sloan slowed his roll. Angry footsteps quieted. Thick file folder tucked under his arm, he stopped five feet away and glared at her. "That's crap, *mazleiha.* All of what you just said—total crap. Your uncle's business, your sister's bullshit...none of it is your fault."

Surprise wiped her mind clean. On her knees beside the coffee table, she stared up at him, unblinking. A second later, his words registered. "What do you mean, my sister's bullshit?"

"Uh-oh," J.J. whispered.

"Watch out," Myst mumbled, gaze bouncing between Theodora and Sloan.

Brushing aside the wayward comments, Theodora popped to her feet and set her hands on her hips. Sloan's eyes narrowed. An instant later, he moved. Unbelievably quick, so fast Theodora didn't have any hope of avoiding him. She jolted when he picked her up. A quick flip, and he tossed her over his shoulder. Air exited her lungs on a puff as she went head down and ass up. Carrying her like she weighed nothing, he pivoted and headed for the exit.

"Sloan!" she hissed, locking down the urge to shriek like a banshee. She didn't, after all, want to wake Violet, but—

"J.J.," he said, ignoring her rising fury. "You got Vivy?"

"No worries, Sloan. I'll watch her while you, uh—" Myst snickered.

"—do whatever it is you need to do," J.J. said, turning traitor after giving such good advice.

"Sloan!" she snapped through clenched teeth.

"Quiet, Theo. You'll wake Vivy," he said, so calmly she wanted nothing more in that moment than to kill him. "I'm gonna fuck you long and hard. More than once. Work out the kinks, so when we talk afterward, all the crap in your head will be long gone."

"You...you..." she sputtered, trying to find her voice through the shock.

Good God, the audacity. The sheer arrogance of him. If he thought for one second she would allow him to make love to her after acting like a Neanderthal, then...

Then...

Well then...

Taking its cue from her mouth, her brain sputtered, misfiling her objection as he carried her out of the living room, across the kitchen, into the corridor, ass in the air, head hanging down, with the stupid file folder under his arm.

**28**

The private elevator came to a smooth stop. Shiny steel doors opened, spitting Sloan into a wide, well-lit corridor. He headed to his bedroom, Theodora over his shoulder squirming in protest. Hooking his arm over the backs of her thighs, he strode toward the double doors at the end of the hall.

She growled at him.

He palmed her ass, then turned his head and nipped the curve of her hip. She squeaked, then squirmed for different reasons. His mate wasn't trying to get away. She might be playing at pissed off, but Theodora wanted him. He smelled her heat, could almost taste her wetness on his tongue. Longing spiraled deep as he imagined her naked in his arms. His dragon half rumbled, impatient, needy, unhappy with his pace. Appeasing his beast, Sloan nudged the hem of her sweatshirt up and found what he needed—a strip of smooth skin between her waistband and t-shirt. He raked the edge of his teeth over the tender area.

Theodora quivered. Her toes curled. He upped the

stakes, trailing his fingers over the crease high on the back of her thigh. A sensitive spot. More wiggling. With a grin, he stroked the inside of her thigh.

Fisting her hands in the back of his shirt, she cursed, but went with instinct and spread her legs a little, giving him greater access.

Teeth against her skin, the taste of her in his mouth, Sloan kept walking, carrying her to his bed, pace steady, gait smooth, ensuring he didn't jar her. No sense ruining his fun...or the moment. He needed her tuned in, on board with his plan, not distracted by her temper. Though, Goddess knew, he enjoyed her attitude. She lit him up when she got feisty, making primal instinct sing and arousal soar. The memory of her standing strong, facing him down in the living room, worked for him...in a big way.

He liked the way she dished it out, unafraid to go head to head with him. The Goddess of All Things understood what she was doing. The power of energy-fuse knew no bounds. He and his mate were so well matched, the perfection of her shocked him.

A female with Theodora's clever mind and boundless strength would never allow him walk to all over her. Her personality dovetailed with his, complementing him in ways he hadn't believed possible until meeting her. He'd never been an easy male. Not by a long shot. His presence, the force of his nature alone, frightened most females. Not his mate. She stood strong in all the right ways.

Too bad the soul-deep connection he shared with her didn't prevent her head from being fucked up.

Following the seam, Sloan stroked her through the fabric of her jogging pants. She kicked her heels up. Her hips rocked on his shoulder. He hummed against her skin as she gasped, the sound of her pleasure cranking him tighter. A more cautious male would stop and think, pump the brakes and slow the hell down. But after overhearing her conversation with J.J. —after seeing the expression on her face and witnessing the extent of her guilt—he refused to give her any breathing room. Theodora didn't need any more time to think. She would only dig herself into a deeper hole.

His mate needed to be yanked off the idiotic path her brain kept traveling. A risky proposition, given the attitude she'd just thrown his way. Theodora had a temper, one that fired quick and burned bright. He wanted to be patient and understanding. His compassion for her knew no bounds, but given the extent of her pain, talking the problem through with her wouldn't work. Not right now.

She'd spent years building her emotional stronghold, then taken to hiding inside it. Those walls were high and thick, the top wrapped with razor wire. She was little more than sharp edges and open wounds, and had been for over a decade. No way he'd be able to blast through all that history without using some sleight of hand. Which meant...

He must dig deeper. Play dirty. Use physical intimacy to draw her closer and strengthen the ties that already bound her to him. By laying her down, he'd get what he wanted—her beneath him while he reassembled the broken pieces and put her back together. Being skin to skin with him would shake the foundation of her stronghold, open her heart, and clear her mind. Well, at least, after he muddled it with soul-scorching pleasure.

His mate deserved the release. She'd been through

so much, lots of changes in a short amount of time. So much past trauma to wade through, too little time to process it while she'd been on the run.

He understood her need for denial. Staying inside her fortress, turning away from the chaos around her, kept her safe. She refused to believe the worst about Beatrice. Her sister had been her lifeline, the person Theodora counted on for years.

Much as he hated to push her, he refused to allow her to shoulder the blame for someone else's actions, for the decisions made by a demented crime boss bent on the destruction of others.

Sloan frowned. Might be he was overstating it a bit, but her uncle hadn't gone into the business of loansharking, drug peddling, prostitution, and gunrunning for the good of humankind. He'd done it for money. He'd done it for power. The bastard enjoyed hurting others. She'd had no part in any of the twisted shit her uncle pulled...with the help of her goddamn sister.

He'd read the file Venom left on his desk after the meeting. Flipped through the pictures, too, then gone on his system and dug up a few details on his own while waiting for Ivy's files to download. His brother-in-arms was right, but three inches missed the mark. The accordion folder he carried under his arm surpassed four on its way to hitting five inches thick.

"Sloan."

"A minute, *mazleiha*. Almost there."

"You need to—"

He stroked her again.

She cursed through her moan. "I'm about to lose my mind."

"Told you I'd work the kinks out," he said, letting his magic roll.

The double doors opened on his command. The scent of wildflowers and damp soil spilled out. He drew a deep breath, relaxing into the hum of the healthy ecosystem inside his private domain.

Stepping off polished concrete, Sloan crossed the threshold. His boot soles crushed rose petals fallen from the iron trestle he'd installed above the doors. A sweet, fragrant scent, almost as beautiful as his female's. The forest greeted him. Tree limbs swayed above his head. Ferns and flowers whispered in welcome. The soil beneath his feet sighed, connecting with his earth dragon, absorbing his energy even as it fed him its own.

Gripping the waistband of his jeans, Theodora lifted her head and looked around. "I thought this was a greenhouse."

"It is."

"But...it's underground."

"Yeah," he said, tweaking her clit with his thumb.

She made a strangled sound. Another quiver of pleasure. Fighting her reaction, she reached for a distraction. "How does anything grow? There's no sunlight. No artificial UV lamps."

His nipped her again.

"No way any plants should be able to live," she said, clinging to her train of thought.

Nice try. An excellent subject, one guaranteed to shift his focus any other time, when he didn't have his hand snug against an unbelievably sweet part of her.

"I'm an earth dragon, Theo."

"And that means?"

"Later."

"What?"

"I'll explain later."

Walking out of the circle of trees that surrounded

his bed, Sloan tossed the thick file toward the antique table. It landed with a thump. Stacks of books swayed. He stopped next to the bed and, with a gentle hop, tossed Theodora into the middle. He took a second to admire her there, then followed her down.

His knees hit the mattress. His hands went to her pants. Curling his fingers in the ribbed waistband, he tugged, dragging soft cotton down her legs, stripping her lower half. The scent of her arousal strengthened. His attention trailed over her. A sexy pair of lace panties. Pale pink against soft skin and curvy hips, framing her to perfection.

Jade-green eyes met his. "Sloan—"

"I already told you what's gonna happen. We'll talk...after."

Gaze riveted to his face, she licked her bottom lip.

He watched the tip of her tongue flick over rosy flesh. The muscles roping his abdomen tightened. Wild grew wilder as he planted one hand in the bed and, hovering over her, cupped her jaw with the other. Tracing her lower lip, he stroked his thumb through the wet trail she'd left, giving her a chance to protest, to tell him no before he kissed her and their passion took flight.

Holding her gaze, he toyed with the toggle a second, then unzipped her hoodie. "Take it off."

Panting now, she obeyed, drawing her arms out of the sleeves, leaving her in nothing but a t-shirt and underwear.

Keeping his touch light, he trailed his fingers over her jaw, down her throat, between her breasts, drawing a line down the center of her body. Hand flat against her belly, he absorbed her shivers, felt the racing thump of her heartbeat reach up to meet him through her womb. "What'chu want, Theo?"

She bit her lip, worrying it with her teeth. "You. I want you, but…"

"Tell me."

As she trembled beneath him, her aura flared. Nervous energy sparked around her. "Sloan, it's been a while. A really long time."

A low rumble left his chest as understanding struck. "I won't be able go gentle, baby. Not the first time. Got the scent of you in my nose. Got a fire for you in my belly."

Her throat worked as she swallowed. "I don't want gentle…the first time."

Excitement thrummed through him. Magic rose to his surface. His gaze began to shimmer, bathing her in a warm glow. Dipping his head, he licked over her bottom lip, following the trail she left with her tongue. The decadence of her hit him. Incendiary need bubbled up, scorching him, making bliss burn brighter.

Mouth hovering over hers, he teased her with the promise of a kiss, but didn't give it. "You'll take it how I wanna give it."

"Yes." Drawn in by his gentle touch, she parted her lips, inviting full possession, graceful hands restless, moving over his shoulders, along his jaw, through the short strands of his hair.

He hummed in appreciation.

Theodora drew one knee up and opened wide, letting it fall to one side. He settled deeper into her, erection pressed to her core.

"Goddess. Brilliant. You're a fucking dream."

Breathing harder now, she whispered his name.

Unable to hold back any longer, he took her mouth. She moaned and undulated beneath him. Tongues tangled. Hands sought and found skin. His energy threaded through hers, connecting her to him and him to her as touch and taste whirlpooled into stunning need.

*Goddamn.*

His mate was beyond incredible. So brutally intense. Unlike any female he'd ever touched. Sloan groaned as the beauty of her burned through him. So long. He'd waited so long for her, to find the right one. The only one who could connect with his dragon half and soothe the warrior within.

The past fell away. He forgot the sorrow and expunged the rage.

Made for him.

Meant for him.

His female in every way but one. A circumstance he was about to change.

Under her spell, deep in the flow, Sloan slipped his hand under pink lace, down, then *in*. Her hips bucked as he found her. Hot and wet, her slickness coated his fingers, encouraging him to take her farther. He played in her heat, advance and retreat, destination assured as he kissed her, swallowing her whimpers, feeling her bend her knees, spread wider, asking him for more.

Hard. Deep. Without mercy.

He gave her what she wanted, receiving what he needed in return. She arched. Rasping breaths left her chest. Lifting his head, he let her mouth go, planted his forearm beside her, and glanced down to watch his hand work. Her t-shirt bunched beneath her breasts, her hips rose and fell, driving to his rhythm as she closed her eyes, tipped her head back, and accepted his will.

Fuck. She was gorgeous, greedy as she reached for the orgasm he planned to give her. Unabashed in her passion, she moved faster, demanding more. He took her close to climax, then backed off, only to drive her to the edge again. And again. Waiting for her to beg.

Hands grasping at him, she groaned. Her nails scraped over the nape of his neck. The reins on his control slipped.

Planting his knees in the bed, he tore the scrap of lace down her legs, then grasped the backs of her knees and spread her even wider. Her scent in his nostrils, the sight of her burned into his brain, he rolled in between her thighs, set his mouth on her, and licked between her slick folds.

"Shit! Sloan, honey. Ohmigod..."

He growled as she trailed off, fighting for breath. Whipping her into a frenzy, he took what he wanted, and... Fucking hell. She was delicious. He was starving, and she tasted so good he showed no mercy. He devoured her, pushing her to the brink, eating his fill, feeling her twist beneath him.

"Slow... God, Sloan. You need to slow dow—"

With snarl, Sloan increased the pace. He wasn't gentle. He held her down and sucked hard, licked deep, reveling as she tightened around him.

Listening to her, feeling her come apart underneath him, he brought his fingers into play. Showing no mercy, he returned to her clit. Adding the pump of his fingers, he drove her to the edge, held her suspended in time, made her beg for the pleasure. The second she surrendered, he nipped gently and sent her flying.

Theodora moaned as she came, pulsing against his tongue.

Eating everything she gave him, Sloan licked her one more time. He kissed her mound, then rose above her, taking her in, looking his fill, memorizing the beauty of her. Half-naked. Eyes closed. Breasts rising and falling fast. Rosy, soft skin under his hands. Long, dark hair in disarray, surrounding her face, spread all over his pillow.

The taste of her like a decadent treat on his tongue, he called on his magic. The scent of rain and new growth swirled. With a murmur, he discarded his clothes. Kneeling naked beneath the spread of her thighs, he yanked her t-shirt over her head. Racy bra, same color as her discarded underwear. A feast for his senses. Even better as he flicked open the front and cupped her breasts.

Her eyes cracked open.

"God," she breathed, gaze trailing over him. "You're beautiful."

"I'm only gonna get better," he said. "I'm gonna show you now, Theo."

"You better."

"Brace, baby. Hard and fast now. Gentle later."

"Please."

Grasping her hips, he sat back on his heels and dragged her ass up his thighs. Notching his erection against her, he murmured, "Knees up. Spread for me, Theo."

Ass balanced on the tops of his thighs, she didn't hesitate.

Straightening one of her legs, he pressed her calf to his collarbone and pushed the other open even wider. Need in her eyes, she tilted for him. His hands flexed on her. She quivered. He pushed his erection against her core. Her slickness welcomed him. His nostrils flared. Fucking hell. A tight fit. Such gorgeous heat. She was going to have trouble taking all of him, but instead of stopping, he kept his word and showed no mercy, thrusting forward, pushing in, watching her eyes widen and her lips part.

Surprise left in her throat on a rasp. "Uuuh…"

Sloan drove deeper, feeling her stretch around him.

"Sloan," she said, struggling to accommodate him.

"You feel beautiful." Undone by her, focused on their connection, he stroked her clit each time he nudged deeper, making it easier for her. She made a wild sound. He kept at her, sinking deep, making her take him. "So fucking beautiful."

Buried to the root inside her, he circled his hips, allowing her to adjust. He counted to three, then withdrew and thrust forward. Doing as he promised, he took her hard and fast. She moaned each time he filled her. Over and over. Again and again. Giving him beauty, showing him perfection, driving him higher as desire rampaged out of control.

With a soft groan, she reached for him.

Consumed by her, he folded forward, glorying in the feel of her as she tucked her knees to his sides and moved with him. Becoming more and more demanding, Theodora offered her mouth.

Driving deep, teetering on the edge, he kissed her, hot and wet as he rode her the way he wanted. Holding him close, she raked her nails over his back. Tiny pricks of pain scrambled his molecules. Pleasure heightened. He forged deeper. Took more. Moved faster.

Her body rippled around him.

He tore his mouth from hers. "Feel it, Theo. Let go, baby."

"Sloan." A soft sob turned desperate plea.

"Again, *mazleiha*. Give me that beauty."

Her head jerked back. A low whimper left her. Coming apart in his arms, she clenched around him. Tearing a hoarse cry from his throat, she dragged him to the edge, then threw him over. Ripped apart, too rattled to think, he exploded from the here and now into paradise, a place so rare, so astounding, Sloan knew his life had just started, and nothing would ever be the same.

## 29

Blood still rushing in her ears, Theodora lay sprawled on top of Sloan, face tucked into his throat, hair all over the place, desperately trying to catch her breath while he caressed her with gentle hands.

She sighed as she settled back into the room a little at a time, allowing the sound of rustling leaves and his callused hands to ground her while her mind drifted.

Total mental haze. Complete body drain. All those pesky worries down for the count.

The first time around, his version of rough destroyed her. How she survived with her brain intact, she didn't know. The second go, however, his gentle version of lovemaking fried her circuitry, leaving her a limp, brainless mess.

Circumstances from which she was still recovering. A reasonable response, because...good Lord. He was an amazing lover. Out-of-this-world good, so far outside her experience she wondered at her bad luck.

She'd lived in Seattle for years. Owned a shop, walked around downtown, camped on and hiked most of the mountain trails—and never once crossed his path. Years spent without him. Days, weeks, and months without ever experiencing anything close to the peace he brought her.

*Years, for the love of Christmas.*

Such a huge waste. One she lamented as she lay sated in his arms, marveling at the mind-boggling beauty of him.

Had the stars aligned then, so much would be different now. Most of it good, only one thing bad. If she'd met Sloan sooner, she would've avoided the chaos and pain, but wouldn't have Violet, or any of the joy her daughter gave her.

Tears stung the corners of her eyes.

"Thinking too much, *mazleiha*," Sloan murmured. "Do I need to fuck you again?"

"Probably." Trying to get herself under control, she inhaled deep and exhaled slow. Her breath hitched. Big hands moving on her back, Sloan tried to soothe her as she fought to bring herself back in bounds. "Though, given the state I'm in, I'm not sure I'd survive it right now."

"Baby—"

"I know it's stupid," she said, keeping her head pressed beneath his chin.

She wanted to stay hidden, just for a little while longer. Something had happened in the last hour. Something important. Something so dangerous she couldn't begin to process it. Didn't even know where to start.

Amid all the pleasure, the walls she'd built to protect herself had cracked. With every stroke of Sloan's hand, the fissures widened, leaving her exposed, without the usual defenses. He stripped each one away, forcing her to confront what she didn't want to face.

The vulnerability staggered her.

Her heart reacted to the brutal onslaught, hurting like it never had before as memories she'd kept buried broke free and rose to the surface. Anger and sadness spilled over her emotional dam, flooding her with recriminations. She seesawed between the two, battling to stay even, trying to repair walls that had never once failed her.

Until now. With Sloan.

"It's really stupid. I've ignored it for years. All I wanted was to get out, be free, be my own person, and do my own thing. Hard to do when you're an identical twin. Everyone thinks it's so great, sweet, and super cute. Two little girls in dresses. Two girls who are expected to act the same because they look the same. Problem is, Bea and I are so different, it's like night and day. Doesn't seem to matter. When people look at us, they don't see individuals, they see a matched set," she said, the pressure rising, swelling, threatening to choke her. "I tried to take her with me. I wanted Bea to pack a bag and run with me."

"She refused to go."

"She wanted to stay. Said it would be better. If she stayed behind, she'd be able to smooth over my leaving with Nicoli. Distract him. Keep her finger on the pulse until Violet was born. She protected me, Sloan, so...I just..."

"Venom's not wrong about her, Theo."

"I hear you say it, but she's my sister. I don't want to believe it's true, but I trust you. It's so weird I don't know what to do with it, but I feel the bond we share. It's all around me, in everything I touch and taste. And

I know, deep down in a place I can't deny, you would never lie to me."

Heavy muscles flexed as Sloan surrounded her with his arms and sat up, taking her with him. She settled astride him. He shifted backward, pressing his shoulder blades to the headboard. And still she hid, feeling scared and small and powerless. The same way she had all her life when dealing with her family. A pawn in her uncle's game.

Cupping the nape of her neck, he urged her without words to look at him. Arms wrapped around him, she fought the gentle tug and kept her face tucked against his throat.

Sloan didn't force her to lift her head. Sensing what she needed, he allowed her to remain right where she was—in his arms, pressed to his chest, rooted in him. "Keep it coming, beautiful. Tell me everything."

"It's all jumbled up inside my head," she said, trying to understand it, not knowing how. "I'm in the weeds, praying you're wrong, drowning in the possibility you might be right. I'm remembering things. Little things, details hardly worth noticing, but they keep popping up, bobbing around, bumping into each other. Something Bea said. Something she did. The way she looked at and spoke to my uncle. Not just with respect—everyone gives him that if they want to continue breathing—but with reverence. A kind of hero worship that has always made me uncomfortable."

"Shit, baby."

"Yeah," she whispered, allowing the truth to spill out. "I'm scared of what's in that file, Sloan. I know it's the one Venom told you about. I know it's probably full of bad stuff. I hate it, but I know it.

"I want to stay here with you, in this moment, in the beauty of what we just shared, but I just...I don't know...keep drifting back to the phone call. To the panic in her voice. To the terror in her tone when she thought Nicoli had found me."

Tweaked by the memory, she re-examined everything. Things that happened in her childhood, growing up with Beatrice before their father died, the shift in their lives afterward. Conversations with her twin bobbed to the surface, those she'd had with her in the last four years along with the most recent one.

It was hard to know what to think. Beatrice was a great actor, and an even better liar—a skill that allowed her to pull the wool over their uncle's eyes for years. And the entire reason Theodora had been able to escape. Her sister provided the window, the small slice of time needed to pack a bag, get in her car and out of the city. She'd hidden at Aunt Jean's cabin for a couple of days. Just long enough for Beatrice to deliver the fake IDs.

It had happened fast, so fast she wondered how her sister pulled it off—and whether she'd planned it in advance.

Until Venom's accusation, the thought Beatrice might've wanted her gone for her own reasons never crossed Theodora's mind. She'd been so grateful for Beatrice's quick thinking she never questioned the motive behind it. Or the fact her twin hadn't seemed upset to see her go.

She frowned and eased back. Bottom cradled by his thighs, she gave Sloan what he wanted—eye contact. Seeing her distress, he cupped her face in his big hands. The pads of his thumbs stroked over her cheeks, wiping the tears away.

"It's messed up."

"I know," he murmured.

"I'm worried I'm remembering things wrong, that all the little things that have never added up are nothing but coincidences, and I'm being disloyal for thinking the worst, but..."

She paused and set her hands flat on his chest. She felt like a traitor for asking, but she needed to know. To say it out loud. Give a face and name to her suspicion before she put it to bed once and for all. "I have to wonder...with the way my sister is...do you think it was all an act? Do you think something happened, and she was forced to trick me into coming home?"

Such an awful accusation.

Another one she didn't want to believe.

Her uncle was a savage who pretended to be civilized. Hiding his criminal activity behind legitimate enterprises, he spread his wealth around, using money to make inroads. An unrelenting predator, he supported worthy causes—charities, food banks, boys and girls clubs—helping communities thrive. His favorite place to exert his influence, however, was in the political sphere. Powerful politicians fascinated him. He donated to political campaigns, glad-handing with the big boys until he became one, a grand puppet master with charisma and benevolence to spare.

A lovely façade. Theodora had seen behind the curtain and knew what kind of ugliness his generosity disguised.

Beatrice, on the other hand, loved people. Social by nature, she organized charity balls and community events. She liked fancy parties and flashy crowds almost as much as she enjoyed taking their money to help support those in need.

Something about all her efforts, though, rang hollow. She had always been a little too desperate to please. Still, Theodora found it difficult to believe Beatrice had gone from belle of the ball to pirate in four years.

"Maybe she's in trouble," she said, still hoping despite all Sloan had said. "Markov failed to bring me in. If Beatrice is mixed up in that, my uncle will make an example of her. Blood is blood. Through thick and thin, we're supposed to stick together, but family or not, my uncle doesn't let mistakes go unpunished."

Sloan shook his head. "I know you don't want to believe Beatrice is—"

"She could be in trouble."

"I need you to look at the file."

She wrinkled her nose.

"Knowing is better than not knowing."

"Never been my motto."

His amusement filled the air, warming her from the inside out. "You wanna get to the truth, you need to murder your motto and adopt mine."

"Probably."

"No question about it." Fingers in her hair, he gathered the strands at the nape of her neck before drawing the thick mass over one of her shoulders. The ends tickled the tip of her bare breast. Brushing the curls away, he cupped her, traced over the curve of her with his thumb, then returned his gaze to her face. "You gonna be brave for me?"

Her brow furrowed.

"Be brave for me, *mazleiha*."

Seeing the understanding in his eyes, there was little else she could do but say, "Okay."

"That's my girl," he said, but didn't move, continuing to hold her safe. "It's gonna be all right."

She swallowed, struggling to believe him. "It's never been all right."

"You've got me now."

"Yeah." Thank God. *Thank God.* Outside her daughter, he was the best thing to ever happen to her. "I've got you now."

Her acceptance made his mouth curve. He palmed her hips and lifted. Knowing what he wanted, she dismounted, settling on her knees beside him.

He flicked his fingers.

A shirt appeared in his hand.

Her brows popped up as her mouth fell open.

Sloan grinned, but didn't explain. He'd already had the Dragonkind conversation with her. She knew about his magic, understood most of what he could do, even though she'd never seen it, but...wow. Seeing him in action trumped listening to him talk about it.

Gathering the material in his hands, he slipped the soft cotton tee over her head. As she shoved her arms through, he leaned in for a kiss. Theodora didn't deny him. She loved the taste of him, but enjoyed his easy affection more. He made her feel beautiful and wanted, valued and important, a person worth knowing, instead of one destined to live her life on the sidelines.

"Give me a sec," he said, then nipped her bottom lip before pulling away. "Be right back."

Theo nodded and watched him go. It was hard not to do. Comfortable in his skin, he didn't bother getting dressed and strode across his fabulous forest room. Muscles rippling, back, ass, and long legs on display. Places already made sensitive by his touch tingled. She wiggled, struggling to control her reaction as he grabbed the file folder off the table and turned back toward her.

Her breath caught. Wild became a little wilder as he crossed the room, giving her a show.

"Hold that thought, Theo," he said, tossing the accordion file on the bed. "We'll come back to it later."

A little breathless, more than a little hot and bothered, she dragged her attention from his body to his face. "What?"

"File first. We'll fuck again later."

"For the love of Christmas," she muttered. "You're blunt."

"Had you twice. Gonna have you again. No sense being any other way."

True. Though his words combined with the rumble of his voice weren't doing her any favors...or helping her cool off. "You want me to concentrate, stop talking to me like that."

He laughed. "Feeling the need to attack?"

"Feeling the need to return the favor and put my mouth on you."

Heat sparked in his eyes. His nostrils flared. One of his knees hit the bed, then the other. Hooking her around the waist, Sloan hauled her across the mattress, moving her where he wanted her. She ended up sitting cross-legged between his thighs, her back against his chest, his strong arms loose around her, day-old stubble scraping her skin as he set his chin on top of her shoulder.

"I'll give you that play, Theo—later. Right now, stop stalling and open it."

"Right." Staring at the file like it was a snake about to strike, she shifted against him, turning until she sat sideways in his lap. She reached out and dragged the folder closer. Fiddling with the frayed end, Theodora took a deep breath, wrenched the tie free, and flipped the top open. "Here goes nothing."

Sloan gave her a squeeze.

She started digging. Stacks of papers came out of

the first, second, and third compartments. Surveillance reports. Real estate property evaluations. Financial documents and bank statements. Two sets of books—one for all her uncle's legal dealings, the other an accounting of his shadow businesses. Not complete records, but enough for her to understand the structure along with the ebb and flow. Lots of money changing hands. Some of it so dirty Theodora wondered how her uncle kept it under wraps.

Reaching into the last compartment, she pulled out a file full of photographs. All of Beatrice in various situations. Business meetings. Cocktail parties and charity events. Holding court at the Luxmore, a hotel owned by their uncle. One of her exiting the back seat of a car at night on the docks, in a huddle with a man Theodora knew meant bad news. She'd seen him before with her uncle; he had connections to Columbian and Mexican drug cartels.

The last picture, though, put the nail in Beatrice's coffin. It was taken through a window. Beatrice having sex with Markov.

Disbelief and anger collided. Betrayal sliced deep. Bile touched the back of Theodora's throat. Swallowing the burn, she tossed the photo aside. "How did you get all this?"

"Venom went to Mac. He recommended a human PI."

"Private investigator?"

"Yeah. He did some surveillance and took the pictures. The rest...what you see there," he said, pointing to a bunch of confidential financial information, "that's me."

"You hacked in?"

He nodded.

She shuffled some papers around. Her heart

throbbed, making her chest hurt, the pain more than just physical. "Bea's doing more than running his legitimate businesses."

"He's dragged her deep. Shits me to say it, but she's really good at what she does. No way he'd have gotten so big, this successful, without her. Beatrice could be CEO at a Fortune 500 company and run another as a side hustle. She's that good."

"But she's chosen to stay with him."

"Family and misplaced loyalty, baby. The ties that bind."

"Do you think we can get her out?"

"I don't know."

"I need to talk to her."

"No," he growled. "You are no longer part of that world. You and Vivy are now in mine."

"Honey," she whispered, loving the fact he not only thought of Violet, but included her. "I need to talk to my sister. Not on your computer. Not on the phone. Face to face."

His gaze bored into hers, dragon half sparking, temper rising fast and furious.

His expression changed. Theodora saw his anger, but more...she felt his concern for her as her connection with him boomeranged. The tether tightened, allowing her to read him. His thoughts washed into her head. A wave of emotion hit her. Wonder picked her up and swung her around. God. He was extraordinary. His spirit and strength of will so abundant, so incredible, she struggled to absorb it all.

The urge to buckle beneath the pressure—and let him have his way—assaulted her. Feeling his confidence surge through her, she gathered her own, holding the line, refusing to back down.

A revelation. A welcome one.

She had a choice, possessed the strength of mind to weigh her options. She didn't need to bend to another's will. She could decide for herself and move forward, instead of retreating into a place she no longer wanted to go.

Squaring her shoulders, she raised her chin.

His eyes narrowed.

She held her ground.

"Fuck. You're not going to let this go, are you?"

"No. She's my sister. I know what she's doing is screwed up, but I love her. If there's a chance I can pull her out, make her see reason, I have to try." Tossing a stack of documents aside, she cupped his jaw. "I have a choice in this, and so do you. Make it safe for me, Sloan. I have to walk back into that world, but I don't want to do it alone."

"Theo—"

"Make it safe for me, honey. Help me set a meeting with my sister. Protect me while I walk into that vipers' nest and put the past behind me."

"You don't fight fair."

"No other way to deal with you."

He huffed. "Give me a day or two. I'll set it up. I'll keep you safe. You never have to go it alone again."

Tears filled her eyes. Throat so tight she couldn't talk, she thought, *Thank you.*

Gathering the mental threads, Sloan wrapped his arms around her. "You're welcome, *mazleiha.*"

Heartfelt words, ones she felt deep down in places that had never seen the light of day. The fissures inside her widened. Her wall crumbled, tumbling into a messy pile around her.

Cracked wide open, she burrowed in, taking the comfort Sloan offered, giving him all of her in return. He could've fought her. He could've blocked her path and made it impossible for her to find her way. Instead, he provided what she needed—a lifeline, a pathway, a safe place to land.

An extraordinary gift given by a beautiful man.

Now, all she needed to do was pray Beatrice wasn't in too deep and listened to reason when they sat down face to face.

Sprawled in the corner of the couch with his feet planted on the coffee table, Azrad stared at the TV, unseeing, with no understanding of what the hell he was watching. Aware of nothing but the female sitting cross-legged on the middle cushion, a bowl of popcorn in her lap, muttering things like "Who does that?" and "Ridiculous" and "Dumber than a stump," aiming a "Don't you think?" his way every so often, adding to a running commentary about a stupid story full of idiot characters.

Turning his head, Azrad stared at her. He was fascinated, completely taken by Kasi—how she sounded, the way she looked, what she said, and her fierce opinion about a movie that, in the grand scheme, didn't mean a fucking thing.

He'd never sat with a female like this before. Never relaxed with one, been so casual while he shared her space. Never watched her react while she manically munched on snack food that tasted like straw.

Something exploded on screen.

With a grumble, Kasi shook her head. She tossed more popcorn in her mouth.

He continued staring at her.

"What?" Glancing at him out of the corner of her eye, she pointed to the bowl then dug out another handful. "Want some?"

"I'm good," he said, knowing not to make the same mistake twice. He'd already miscalculated and tried it the first time she offered. No sense compounding his mistake. He enjoyed a good meal, but didn't eat anything that didn't fuel his body. When he cooked, he did it right, making nutritious choices, preferring to give his body what it needed, not waste time filling it with what it didn't.

Humans would call him a health nut. After years of deprivation and scarcity inside Tazenmed, Azrad called it smart decision making.

"Azrad."

"Yeah."

"You're staring."

Shifting in his seat, he looked away. Another explosion on the TV. Humans riding around doing fake "death-defying" shit on motorcycles. More popcorn munching.

"Something you want to know?" she asked around a mouthful.

Azrad fought the need to squirm. He should ignore the question. Let her go back to watching the movie. A smart decision, yet even as he decided the way to go, he opened his mouth and said, "I don't know how to do this."

"What do you mean?"

"Have a normal conversation while sitting around doing normal shit."

Her hand stilled inside the bowl.

He tensed, but remained perfectly still, as she looked his way.

"Must've been hard," she murmured. "I mean, our

prisons are terrible places, but a Dragonkind one? I can guess, but I bet I'd still be way off base."

Softly said words. A gentle inquiry. Not invasive or nosy, but concerned and caring. A combination he wasn't accustomed to getting from anyone, never mind a female who should be frightened of him. Instead, Kasi sat beside him on a couch, unworried, relaxed, taking jabs at the movie as though she felt safe sitting with him beside her.

*Him.* A vicious male with a terrible track record. In a Razorback bunker deep underground.

Like everything about her, the realization floored him. But worse, her understanding gave him permission to start talking, to tell her the truth, to repay her trust by giving her some of his in return.

"In the beginning, it was bad. Really bad," he said, feeling uncomfortable in his own skin. Sharing his past with her rubbed him the wrong way. And yet he didn't shut up. His story spilled out despite his knowing he should stop it. "I learned fast. Killed everyone they sent after me. Carved out my territory and protected it. When the Archguard realized they were losing too many warriors to my claws, they left me alone."

"How big a territory?"

"Two-hundred and fifty square miles."

"Wow."

He grinned at her. "Gonna do it, might as well do it right."

"Good attitude to have, but still...must've been really lonely in there."

He shrugged, pretending she hadn't hit the nail on the head. Dragonkind was a social species. Males of his kind lived in packs, in tight-knit communities build on mutual respect, love, and loyalty. Singling a warrior out, leaving him alone for too long, did terrible things to a male's mind.

Tazenmed always took its chunk of flesh, and he hadn't been immune. He escaped, sure, but hadn't done it unscathed.

"Got a whole lot better, much easier, after I met K.K. and T."

"Your friends?"

"My brothers."

"Family without being blood."

"Pack. Strong warriors, strong bonds. The cornerstone of Dragonkind."

Looking pensive, Kasi frowned. "I've got a brother."

"Yeah."

"Ten years younger than I am. He'll be fifteen soon. When we get out of here, I need to go and get him."

"What about your parents?"

"My mom died when he was born. Some kind of blood infection," she said, voice shaky. "My dad's a piece of shit. Hit my mom. Hit me when I got in between, trying to protect her from him. Pretty much everything I make goes to my brother. Keeps him in boarding school, far from my father."

"What's his name?"

"Kingdom."

"Cool name."

She smiled. "Isn't it, though? Not sure where my mom picked it up, but she made the nurses file the paperwork before she died. Made sure my dad couldn't change it."

"Smart."

"My mom was awesome," she whispered.

Sounded like it. Sounded like Kasi might be just

like her: a strong female in a bad situation, one who knew what she wanted and fought for those she loved.

Holding her gaze, Azrad nodded, wishing he'd been so lucky. He'd never met his sire. Hadn't known his older brother growing up. Hadn't benefited from having Bastian to protect him, never mind—

Power rippled through his veins.

Clicking followed as Scandela dialed in, re-establishing her connection. His sonar contorted, coming back online so fast pain slammed into his temples. Azrad jerked as awareness expanded, widening perception. His mental screen flicked on. Images formed in his mind's eye. The forest beyond the cement factory. The gravel road snaking up to the front door. The silo Scandela swarmed over before reassembling from many spiders into one. She blinked, her eight eyes giving him a panoramic view.

Azrad narrowed his focus and...holy fuck. He had a signal, a weak one, but beggars couldn't be choosers. He needed to use what little he possessed to get a message out. A concise one, given the instability of his magic. A minute, maybe two. Not very long, but time enough to communicate his location. Information Gage could grab and hold on to—a signal for the Nightfury pack to detect and track.

Relief rolled through him. Heart hammering, hope rising, he turned toward Kasi. Meeting her gaze, he bared his teeth in triumph.

Startled, she stared at him a second. "Shit."

"Kasi, I've got a—"

"Shut up," she said, tossing her popcorn aside. The bowl slammed down on the coffee table, wobbling as she planted her knees in the cushion and swung his way. Eyes glued to his, she grabbed his face with both hands. Shocked, he stared at her. She studied him, then threw her leg over his thighs. He flinched as she settled astride him and wrapped her arms around the back of his head. "Hug me back, Azrad."

"What the hell?"

"Hug. Me. Back," she said, her mouth against his ear. "The cameras. Your eyes are starting to glow. If they see, they'll know your magic's back."

Turning his head, he tucked his face into her throat. "Fuck."

"What do you need?"

"You to stay right where you are," he murmured, holding on to her. "I need to feed, Kasi. Boost the signal by combining my energy with yours. Try to get the SOS out."

"Do it."

"Be sure, *kazlita*, cuz once I connect, I won't be able to—"

Her aura flashed. Bright blue light poured into the air around her. White-hot energy eclipsed him, making him groan against her skin.

"Go, Azrad."

He didn't argue. Tapping in fast, he mined her bioenergy. The heavy throb of her heartbeat registered. He heard the blood rushing in her veins. Each of her quick inhalations and fast exhales slid onto his mental grid. A snick sounded inside his head. The Meridian rose with a hiss, curling up like the head of a cobra. Abundant and glorious, the wave struck and took him under, shoving him into to the stream.

Her hands clenched in his hair, Kasi quivered.

He murmured, reassuring her, drinking deep, accepting the bounty she offered. His dragon half realigned. Magic tumbled in the surging tide, gaining power, boosting the signal as he used Scandela like an antenna, stretching his abilities to send out the call.

## 31

Data pad in hand, Sloan watched the elevator door slide shut. Green gaze steady on him, Theodora treated him to a finger wave. His lips twitched. He shook his head. So freaking cute. No one held a candle to his mate. She was beautiful always, but more so now that she'd settled back into her skin, letting go instead of holding on to the stress. Nothing hidden—open, honest, much more relaxed after their talk. After he made love to her a third time. After she re-dressed, kissed him softly, told him good luck and...

Set him up right for the night.

Reading his mood, she grinned a second before metal met metal, enclosing her inside the elevator. He murmured. Huge magnets went to work, sending the cage and Theodora up toward her daughter and Daimler. He listened to the hum a moment, then turned and opened the door to the stairwell. A spring in his step, he started down, leaving the greenhouse level to move deeper into the underground lair.

Focused on the screen he held, Sloan jogged down the first flight of stairs and swung around a landing. A path he traveled every evening. Though he wouldn't be spending any time in the Hub tonight.

Bastian had made the call. All the Nightfury warriors answered.

Ready to roll out of the lair, his brothers-in-arms were already gathered in the corridor outside the LZ. Sloan sensed the collective buzz of high-octane energy. The lethal vibe spiraled up from below. He rolled his shoulders, battling to control his reaction as eagerness prickled through him. It didn't work. Nothing much did when his dragon half caught the scent and wanted the hunt.

Sloan breathed in, using the technique Mac had taught him. Deep inhale. Hold to the count of four, long exhale. The method usually worked like a charm, evening out his volatile tendencies. No joy tonight. He was too excited, so amped up by the incredible energy Theodora fed him he could hardly contain it.

A lovely problem to have. A privilege every Dragonkind male would kill to possess, but one that presented real problems for him right now. He needed to get a handle on it, quick. Otherwise, his dragon would tip the scales, drag aggression to his surface, and unleash hell. A welcome occurrence most nights. Killing Razorbacks required brutality, the kind his earth dragon enjoyed delivering. Tonight, however, necessitated pulling out a different skill set.

Bastian wanted finesse.

Rikar called for patience. Less death, more subtlety.

Too jazzed to hop on board with the plan, Sloan just wanted to rip shit apart. Though he might settle for getting out of the lair. His beast wouldn't like it, but...whatever. After overseeing Angela's training all week, he needed to stretch his wings. Streak across open skies. Let his freak fly without the safety of his apprentice weighing heavy on his mind.

Selfish, maybe, but he needed the break.

He'd already informed Angela, grounding her for the night. B and Rikar backed him up, which, of course, made her all kinds of unhappy.

"Rikar's problem," he muttered, scrolling through the information on his screen.

His apprentice needed to learn some patience. Cooling her heels while the pack flew out for the night would teach her some. At least, he hoped. One never knew with Angela, but it wasn't as though he'd left her nothing to do. He'd laid out the lesson plan over a week ago, giving her plenty of distractions to pick from—workouts in the gym, practicing how to sharpen her claws, learning how to cast a few of the easier spells. All of which would get her closer to what she wanted, but hadn't yet managed—complete amalgamation, the merging of her two halves, she-dragon and human sides working together to become an unbreakable whole.

The regular song and dance.

Normal for a fledgling member of Dragonkind. But completely new territory for him. As much as she longed to be, Angela wasn't an ordinary fledgling. She was female. A she-dragon. A veritable unknown in his world. She hated he kept pointing out the indisputable, but facts didn't lie. Dragonkind hadn't see anything like her in centuries. With a male, Sloan knew what to expect, how to operate and proceed. With Angela, normal got turned inside out and backward, becoming a guessing game, so it stood to reason there'd be some hiccups along the way.

Which left her gnashing her teeth, and the rest of

the Nightfuries playing duck and cover when things didn't go her way.

Again...

"Rikar's fucking problem."

Locating the data stream he wanted, Sloan slowed his pace on the stairs. He tapped on the screen. His AI went to work, opening files, feeding him details, helping him understand Theodora's past. Four years of running laid out in chronological order, the activity of her aliases tucked into neat columns. Information at his fingertips, he paused on the last step.

His brow furrowed. Wow. She'd been busy, refusing to let grass grow under her feet, moving every three or four months. New address. New job in a different industry each time she changed direction. Fingers scrolling, he moved through her employment history. Fast food joints. Big-box retailers. An art gallery. A library. Two museums, one in a small town, the other in Washington, D.C. She'd been a bean counter at a transportation company, a moderator at a summer camp, and part of a gardening crew at a horticultural center.

Small towns. Big cities. She'd zigzagged all over the country. Seemingly random. No rhyme or reason to her movements, which left little chance of tracking her.

Smart as all freaking hell.

Still, his heart broke for her as he continued to scroll. Dates, states, and jobs—the list went on and on. So many different places, so many new faces, never able to put down any roots. Difficult for anyone, but for a single mother on the run trying to protect her child? His throat tightened. The fear—the constant checking over her shoulder—must've been devastating. No wonder Theodora didn't know how to relax.

Practice made perfect. And his mate had more than enough to spare.

The last place she landed before returning to Seattle caught his attention. Location—New York City. Alias—Olivia Cartwright. Job—executive assistant at a well-heeled law firm. Time frame—five days shy of nine months. The longest she'd stayed anywhere. Her decision made a certain amount of sense. People got lost in the Big Apple, making it an excellent place to hide.

"Well done, *mazleiha*."

He'd already told her, but...goddess. Seeing the proof of her cleverness on screen, he could barely contain how proud she made him.

Putting his feet back in gear, Sloan stepped off the last tread. Footfalls thudding in the confined space, he murmured a command. The electronic keypad installed next to the steel jamb lit up. He entered the code with his mind, turned the handle, and pulled the door open. Hinges hissed. The heavy panel swung wide. Without breaking stride, he walked over the threshold, turned right into the corridor, and—

"About frigging time," Venom snapped at him.

Wick grunted, agreeing with his wingmate.

Eyeballing Venom, he raised a brow. "How long you been waiting—two minutes?"

"Two minutes is too long." Arms crossed, feet planted in the middle of the hall, looking like he'd swallowed something sour, Venom glared at him. "Need to fly, man."

Sloan tipped his chin, a nonverbal apology. Not that he owed Venom one. But given the video files the Scottish pack had sent—and the screwed-up shit each one contained—pack mentality teetered on the edge, threatening to boil over.

"I needed to check something," he said, raking his gaze through warriors standing in the hallway outside the medical clinic. All tense. All angry and impatient. Not a happy face among the bunch.

"You send it?" Bastian asked, shoulders flat against the wall.

Sloan nodded. "To the pack commanders on our list—yeah. Gonna see how that plays out, how those males respond, before I send that shit wide."

Gage grunted.

Opalescent eyes shimmering with violence, Nian bared his teeth.

"Good call," Haider said. "Though I'm not a big fan of anyone seeing it."

"A necessary evil, H," Rikar said, palming the male's shoulder. "The others need to see what Zidane did to you, Gage and Nian in Prague...under Rodin's roof, with the bastard's blessing."

Nothing but the truth.

Bastian needed tangible proof of Rodin and the Archguard's treachery. Of the corruption and how deep it went. The video evidence Cyprus shared was irrefutable. No one who saw it would be able to remain on the sidelines.

Sloan knew it firsthand. After watching the footage with Bastian and Rikar, he was still suffering the side effects. Images he wanted to—but couldn't—forget kept popping into his head. Zidane was unhinged, a sadist of unparalleled perfidy. All of Dragonkind's worst attributes rolled into a single male. Toss in a sire who encouraged his son's sick hobby, and...

Sloan's lip curled in disgust. Bile rolled up his throat. He should've sat that meeting out. Had he been smart, he would've cued up the files and walked away.

He didn't need to see Zidane's savagery to believe it. Instead, he'd hit download, then play, rolling the videos the Scots told Bastian they needed to watch first.

Now, he couldn't stop seeing it. The kill room and his brothers-in-arms' pain as each one battled to stay alive. The pleasure Zidane took in the brutality. The grunts of agony and snarls of pain, the promises of retaliation. The blood running in rivulets across the cement floor toward the drain, metal stained red by the life force of different warriors over many years.

Every time he closed his eyes, he saw Gage, Haider, and Nian strapped to a vertical metal grille charged by electrical current. The Metallics had held the line, refusing to surrender, denying Zidane what he wanted—information about Bastian and the Nightfury pack. The other males in videos taken inside the torture chamber hadn't fared half as well. Each one had screamed and begged, telling Zidane whatever he wanted to know as the Archguard prince took each apart piece by piece until death came, ending their suffering.

"Fuck," Sloan said as rage grabbed hold. The vicious onslaught rampaged through his pores, heating the air around him.

Bastian pushed away from the wall. "Sloan—"

"Fuck!" he barked, trying to contain the emotion. Reacting to his outrage, earth magic pulsed from his palms. The tablet he held went flying.

Wick ducked.

Venom hopped sideways.

The data pad smashed into the wall. The screen exploded. Shattered glass, metal, and plastic rained down, debris landing in messy starbursts around his packmates' feet.

Moving to intercept him, Forge held his hands out to the sides. "Lock it down, laddie."

Sloan flexed his fingers as barbs of energy swirled up his arms. "I don't know where to put it."

Aquamarine eyes steady on him, Mac exhaled long and hard. "None of us do, man."

"We're good, brother," Gage murmured, ready to lock Sloan down if his earth dragon powered up and he did more than throw his hardware around. "Working through some shit together as Metallics. We've got each other. We'll get through to the other side."

Haider and Nian grunted in agreement.

Struggling for control, Sloan concentrated on breathing.

"We'll get him, man." Rikar stepped away from the wall and palmed Sloan's shoulder. "One way or another, Zidane and Rodin will go down, but we've got to play it smart. Working with the Scottish pack is the first step. The next comes tonight. You cool enough to fly out, or do I need to open the vault and lock you down?"

Sloan shook his head.

Rikar's eyes narrowed. "Be sure. Can't have you flying out maverick."

"Won't happen." A guttural denial. One dragged from deep inside his chest. Sloan drew another calming breath. "I'm solid."

"Good," Bastian said. "So, here's how tonight's going to play out. We've got Razorbacks, the kill squad, and mercenaries in the air, so we fly in two groups. Sloan, Wick, Mac, Forge, and Venom will head to the Luxmore, see what they can find on Antonov, the Bratva, and Theo's sister. The rest of us will get a line on Sasha Cooper and—"

"Shit," Gage said, jerking away from the wall. He pressed the heels of his palms to his forehead. With a groan, he doubled over, then went down on one knee. A faraway look entered his eyes. One second ticked into more before he blinked and refocused. "I got him."

Rikar frowned. "Who?"

"Azrad."

"Where?" Sloan asked.

Fingers fisted in his hair, Gage shook his head. "He's in trouble. Trapped."

Bastian took two quick strides, hauled Gage to his feet, and stepped in close. "Where, Gage?"

"Don't know. I'm... It's unclear. No words are coming through." Bronze gaze aglow, Gage paused to retune his sonar. "He's not giving me a location, just a blip to follow. Listen..."

Static tapped on Sloan's temples.

Opening a line into mind-speak, he captured the signal Gage broadcast. A series of beeps and clicks echoed inside his head. One fast, two slow. Two fast, one slow. Three fast, five slow. The rhythmic beat repeated and sank deep. His earth dragon rose, building topography around the signal, laying down a grid. His mind's eye expanded the view. Landscape started to take shape and form, moving from forests and hills to cliffs and mountains, then zeroed in on a cluster of buildings.

Sloan framed the image. His dragon half did the rest, providing the flight plan. "Got it. I know where he is, B."

"Everybody move. Follow Sloan," B barked. "We need to get airborne."

Already on the move, Sloan ran past his brothers-in-arms. Boot soles slamming on polished concrete, he snarled at the spell protecting Black Diamond. Obstinate and bad-tempered, the monster pushed back, refusing to obey. He narrowed his eyes. The nasty thing needed to have an attitude adjustment. Or better yet, have its brain rewired.

Pulling energy from the bedrock beneath his feet, Sloan hammered the shield again. Magic exploded up the corridor. Staring out at him from the magical abyss, the monster roared, but held firm, shaking the lair's foundation. Electricity whined. Glass doors rattled. Dust billowed up, slamming into twelve-foot ceilings.

Sloan bared his teeth and blasted it again. The powerful protection spell buckled under the pressure. The invisible door cracked open an inch. He shoved at the portal with his mind. The wall dead-ending the corridor moved from solid stone to wavy blur. An archway appeared, opening into the LZ.

Musty air blew in. The scent of pine cleaner moved out.

The sound of pounding footfalls behind him, Sloan sprinted out of the corridor into the cave. Halfway across the LZ, he shifted from human to dragon form. Razor-sharp claws gouging granite, he launched himself off the edge of the platform. Dark brown scales speckled gold and green flashed beneath the light globes. Air caught the webbing of his wings. Surging upward, Sloan blasted out of the cavern into the tunnel. Night vision pinpoint sharp, he navigated the tight turns and sliced through the waterfall.

Cold water splashed across his scales.

Locked on to the signal, Sloan shook off the droplets and banked south. He didn't have time to waste. Azrad had none to lose. Bastian's blood brother had finally managed to get his pack a message. He needed help fast. Sloan planned to give it to him. He must reach the male and his friends...and do it without setting off any alarms.

A simple strategy, with a tiny margin for error. Slipping beneath enemy radar was never easy. Pulling the warriors out before Ivar realized what Azrad had done would be almost impossible.

All hell could break loose, and the high-energy females Azrad wanted to protect might end up dead, instead of rescued.

## 32

Ahead of the pack, Sloan descended like a wraith through heavy cloud cover. Humid air streamed over his scales. The smell of new growth, old leaves, and pond scum kicked up. Treetops swayed beneath him. Nothing but thick woodland for miles. A smattering of pinpoint lights clustered along the banks of a small lake. Hunting cabins, most likely. A bunch of weekend warriors gathered around firepits telling stories about the catch of the day.

Ignoring the human activity, he banked east, then flew further south. The first raindrops hit, splattering across his shoulders. Thunder rumbled in the distance. Lightning cracked jagged across the sky, beckoning him toward the eye of the storm.

Any other night, he would've played in the bluster. Gone head to head with Mother Nature. Sliced through angry clouds and enjoyed the light show. Absorbed the energy and returned home happy in the afterglow.

Happy, however, wasn't in the cards tonight.

Dialed into the signal Azrad sent, wings spread wide, he blasted above the forest. Dense foliage. Narrow, snaking streams and thick underbrush. No signs of the building he held in his mind's eye yet, but it was coming fast and furious. A hop, skip, and a horn-torquing flight away. Less than ten miles until he hit the mark, which gave him mere minutes to inform his brothers-in-arms of the problem he detected up ahead.

His sonar pinged.

He fine-tuned his ground-penetrating radar. Scales rattling in the wind, Sloan cast his net. Magic rushed out in front him, blanketed the ground, then sank under the top soil. Holding the ends, he pulled on the threads, dragging information up from the depths of the earth, uncovering all her secrets.

Details streamed onto his grid. The hazy image he held in his head sharpened.

A human factory. Abandoned for years. Long forgotten by whoever owned it. Nothing around it for miles.

He tweaked his radar. More data came back.

Using every bit of intel he unearthed, he built a 3D model of the complex inside his head. With a mental flick, he spun the image around, looking at it from all angles. One main large structure built from concrete, five smaller outbuildings. Two large silos. Several different entrances and exits. A bunch of pipes sticking out of the flat roof. But what truly interested him lay beneath it—deep underground.

Narrowing his focus, Sloan examined the subterranean structure. Contained and compartmentalized. Small by Dragonkind standards. Three stories below-ground. Accessed by a single shaft containing stairs carved into the solid bedrock. One long corridor granting access to what looked like six large pods. Ten heat signatures. Two to a room, leaving the last pod empty.

Bingo. He'd hit the jackpot, unearthing the Razorback facility.

With a low snarl, Sloan opened a link into mindspeak. He pushed the plans through the connection, downloading the information straight into his packmates' heads. His brothers-in-arms cursed. Sloan tightened his control over the link, drilling the details into each of their brains.

"*Christ,*" Rikar growled.

Venom hissed. "*Goddamn it, Sloan. A little warning next time.*"

Sloan ignored the complaint. "*Everybody got it?*"

Low grumbles rippled through the group.

Sloan scanned the horizon. Despite the temple-piercing pain, everyone had picked up the floor plan.

"*Also...*" he said, trailing off to sift through more data points.

"*What?*" Gage asked, sounding pissed off. Nothing unusual there. He always sounded like he wanted to rip someone's head off.

Recalibrating his radar, Sloan looked at the information again. Different data points, same results. He bit down on a curse. "*Slight hiccup.*"

Flying off his right wingtip, Rikar adjusted his speed. "*What are we looking at?*"

"*Blakeite. Rich deposit. The shit's everywhere.*" More than a slight hiccup. Might make for a serious complication, given the amount of the mineral Sloan sensed underground.

Forge growled. "*What the hell is Blakeite?*"

"*Is it dangerous?*" Mac asked.

"*To you—yes,*" Sloan said, probing the deposit, testing the mineral density. Solid, deep, and wide, the vein ran for miles. No weakness he could see. No fissures in the *Blakeite* surrounding around the underground facility. *"To me—remains to be seen."*

*"Fuck,"* Bastian said. *"We need another plan."*

*"No,"* Sloan said. *"I should be able to dig through it."*

At least, theoretically.

*Blakeite* blocked Dragonkind's ability to wield magic, but that didn't mean it would affect him the same way. As an earth dragon, he enjoyed perks others of his kind didn't. Chief among his gifts was the ability plug in and siphon power straight from the electrostatic bands ringing the planet. He never took much. Tapping into the stream directly was dangerous, but the extra draw should provide what he needed to burrow through without the *Blakeite* shutting him down.

Again, great in theory. Not so hot if he got down there and discovered the premise was wrong while elbow-deep in the stuff. Still, the idea intrigued him.

Flexing his talons, Sloan listened to his claws click. *"I'm good to go."*

*"Fucking Ivar,"* Wick said, saying what everybody was thinking.

Venom grunted. *"Needs his head split in two."*

Sloan bared his fangs. *Fucking Ivar*, indeed. The Razorback commander had chosen well. The site he'd locked Azrad and the others inside was diabolical. A masterpiece of engineering—all natural, no need to build walls or truck in what Mother Nature had already provided. A secure location guaranteed to give even the most powerful males trouble. No wonder Azrad couldn't break out. Given the level of ground saturation, Sloan was surprised the warrior managed to get a signal out at all.

*"Be sure, Sloan,"* Bastian said.

"*Can't be sure until I get down there and take a look.*" Reading the landscape, Sloan tilted his head. His horns tingled. More information registered on his radar. "*You sensing what I am? We've got rogues in the area.*"

"*Razorback sentries,*" Rikar said, white scales flashing in the gloom. "*You see any guard posts on the ground?*"

"*Not yet.*"

"*I sense the bastards.*" Tucking his wings, B rotated into a flip over Sloan's spine.

A risky proposition, one made even more dangerous as the trio of venomous pods full of flammable liquid hanging from the tip of his scorpion-like tail swayed, then spun, threatening to explode.

"*Watch it,*" Sloan said, locking each bomb back into place.

Grinning, his commander thumped him with his tail. Midnight-blue scales rattled against his dark brown ones. Sloan frowned. Bastian ignored the warning, powered up his magic, then let it roll. Electricity crackled around him. The air thinned. Water droplets evaporated. Green eyes narrowed, he mined the enemy's unique energy signatures, dissecting each male's skill set from nine miles away.

A neat trick. One Bastian excelled at without breaking a sweat.

"*Six strong, two full fighting triangles deep in the weeds. Three males scattered to the north, three others to the south. Five hundred yards between each one,*" Bastian said. "*Three fire dragons, one acid, one venomous, the last exhales Scald.*"

"*Nothing's ever easy.*" Dark purple scales blending with stormy skies, Forge glanced at his wingmate. "*Divide and conquer.*"

*"Split into teams."* Water dragon out in full force, rain tumbled in Mac's wake as he rocketed overtop of Sloan. *"Kill the six before—"*

*"Any manage to send Ivar an SOS,"* Venom said, finishing the thought. *"The instant he knows, more rogues'll fly out. We'll be—"*

*"Fucked,"* Wick growled, keeping his commentary short and sweet, per usual.

Velocity supersonic, Sloan blasted over the treetops. Big oaks swayed. White pines creaked, tossing sharp needles and dead branches into the air. Dodging the debris, his brothers-in-arms cursed. He kept flying, looking for a clearing, and another way in. Doing the expected—entering a building via the front door—was never his favorite way to fly. He preferred to hedge his bets, create a second entrance and exit, instead of relying on just one.

The forest began to thin.

He blew past another mile marker. Six down, four to go. The next one, though, counted as the most important. The second he broke through the three-mile marker, the Razorback sentries would register his presence and sound the alarm.

Which meant he needed to slow his roll. Right now, before he gave away the advantage.

Angling his wings, Sloan decreased his velocity. He threw Bastian a sidelong glance. *"I'm going low."*

Scales rattling in the wind, his commander nodded. *"You want company?"*

*"Nian?"* Sloan said, searching for night sky for the male.

*"Right behind you."*

*"Good. Get ready."* Seeing a break in the trees. Sloan painted a bull's-eye on the forest floor. *"Fast and furious, Nian. Wings tucked in tight right after I hit."*

Lightning struck, slashing across the dark sky.

*"Got it."* Golden scales winking in the storm flash, Nian snaked in behind him. *"I'll stay on your tail."*

With a burst of speed, Bastian took the lead. *"Two full fighting triangles, boys. Keep it tight. Do it fast. Take the rogues out before any can call for help. Give me time to breach the building and get into underground facility."*

A collective growl hit the airwaves.

Sloan bared his fangs. Excellent. Everybody was on board, claws out, lethal inclinations unleashed.

*"Gage, you're with me,"* B said. *"Need you to bust through any heavy-duty metal we encounter. I'll deal with anything electrical. We'll get in, get Azrad and the others, then get out."*

Mac, Forge, and Gage split one way.

Venom, Wick, and Rikar sliced in the other direction.

*"Quick, clean, and quiet,"* Haider murmured, silver scales blending with billowing grey clouds, making him disappear like a mirage. *"Surgical strike."*

*"That's the idea. Sloan—"*

*"Gonna burrow through fast,"* he said, five hundred yards from taking his flight subterranean. *"No one's going out the way they went in."*

*"Watch yer sixes."* Wind whistling through the link, Forge angled his wings, skirting around the edge of the three-mile marker. Good call. Total sneak attack territory. The trajectory would take him in behind enemy lines. He'd attack the Razorbacks before any of the bastards knew the Nightfury warriors were there. *"See you on the flip side, lads."*

His brothers-in-arms oorahed.

Sloan dove headfirst toward the ground. The clearing opened up. Focused on the center, he sent a continuous pulse like machine-gun fire into the turf.

Rock exploded. Heavy topsoil and chunks of clay blew sky high, streaming into a fountain of debris as he drilled a vertical hole into the ground. Jackhammering the bedrock underneath, he dug a channel straight into the earth.

The forest moaned as treetops thrashed. Wet leaves blew into his face. The air screamed, cutting across his scales, throwing contrails off his spikes as he tucked his wings against his sides and spiraled into the tunnel.

The mouth of hole closed around him. Dark became pitch black as the night sky disappeared behind him.

His eyes started to glow. Bright green light funneled down the side walls, washing over broken roots, half-chewed boulders, and sedimentary rock.

*"Hellfire. Earth dragon mojo,"* Nian muttered, stone and dirt pinging off his scales. *"Unbelievable."*

Ignoring his wingmate, Sloan measured the distance to the target. One hundred feet away, he changed the angle, shifting the trajectory. The vertical shaft turned, slanting before leveling out. He bent the tunnel until it became a horizontal tube. Chewing through granite, he pushed forward and, flying fast, blasted into the straight stretch.

Magic hissed. The smell of scorched rock infected the air.

Wings still folded, he touched down. Claws shrieking over solid rock, he put the brakes on. Dust kicked up, painting his dark scales white. Friction burned over the pads of his paws. Sliding sideways up the tunnel, Sloan bore down, muscles screaming, body torquing, eyes on the dead end.

His speed moved from spine-mangling to manageable.

Tucking his horned head, he rolled into a somersault and shifted to human form. Mid-flip, he conjured his clothes. A beat-up leather jacket joined his jeans and t-shirt. His combat boot soles slammed down. Surfing across granite, he stared at the spot his magic stopped drilling—where pale stone met the sheen and sparkle of blue-black *Blakeite.*

*"Goddamn it,"* Nian rasped, spinning out of control behind him. A thud echoed up the tunnel. The floor shook as he slammed into the curved wall, then stumbled sideways and landed on his ass. *"Ouch."*

Sloan didn't bother to ask if the male needed help. Despite the commotion (and all the cursing), the Archguard prince could look after himself.

Mumbling something about preferring the sky, Nian rolled to his feet.

Footfalls echoing through the quiet, Sloan walked toward the deposit of *Blakeite.* Stopping where the tunnel dead-ended, he ran his gaze over the smooth, dark stone, gathering more data, looking for weaknesses. Opaque in color. Solid in composition. Teeming with abundant earth energy. Dangerous, even to a warrior with his abilities.

Frowning, he reached out to touch it. An inch before his hand landed, energy sparked. He jerked, hissing as discomfort clawed up his—

*"Jesus-fuck,"* Nian growled behind him.

Reacting to the urgency, he glanced over his shoulder.

*"Start digging, Sloan. A rogue got away. A call for help went out."*

Shit.

Not good.

The absolute last thing anyone needed.

An SOS meant the entire Razorback pack would

mobilize and get airborne. More than likely Zidane and the kill squad as well. Sloan harbored no illusions —Ivar was in deep with Rodin and the Archguard. He took their money, profited from their connections, and did their dirty work, so...

Why not feed Zidane intel and help take out the Nightfury pack?

Not much of a question. One plus one, after all, always equaled two.

Ignoring the danger, Sloan pressed his hands flat against the *Blakeite*. Magic rippled from his palms. Starbursts undulated through the blue-black stone. Pain streaked up his arms. Gritting his teeth, he straightened his elbows and walked forward, beginning to chew through the mineral. No matter how agonizing, he needed to burrow into the complex under the cement factory, endure long enough to punch through to the other side. If he didn't, Bastian and Gage would end up trapped underground when the enemy arrived, and the Nightfury pack would be overrun in the sky.

Cloaked inside an invisibility spell, Zidane angled his wings. Cold night air rolled over his flank as he swung into a wide turn and made another pass over a house in an upscale neighborhood. Nice piece of property. Six acres of well-groomed lawns and gardens. Lots of green space around terraced patios that rambled down to surround an in-ground swimming pool.

Nice and tidy. Not the kind of place humans would believe a criminal hung his hat.

Zidane knew better. Having lived with his sire for over two centuries, he understood the true meaning of blending in. The best predators always kept up appearances.

Sweeping over the ornate front gates, he looked for a good spot to land. At the end of the long cobblestone drive lined by giant oaks, he found it. Folding his wings, he dropped out of the sky. Fire hissed in the rush, licking between spikes riding his spine. Smoke rolled off his scales. Halfway to his target, he snuffed out conflagration. No sense scaring the humans before he infiltrated the house and found what he needed.

Eyes trained on the ground, he adjusted his wings

and slowed his descent. His paws thumped down in the circular drive. Water jumped in the fountain depicting Zeus and his handmaidens. Stone pavers cracked beneath his talons. He watched the fissures run a moment, then sat down beside a sleek sliver sedan, wrapped his tail around his paws, and turned his attention to the house.

He snorted. Forget calling it a house. The three-story mansion made a statement, projecting imperialism and power with its pitched roofline and imposing stone façade. More sculpted patios out front, leading guests toward a grand staircase with curved banisters that swept up to huge antique doors with gilded lion-head hardware. Multi-paned windows set at equal intervals on all three floors gleamed in the lamplight. No shutters, but scrollwork was hand-carved into the lintels above each four-by-eight foot stretch of glass.

The absolute best money could buy. Six acres of manicured perfection. Not even a blade of grass out of place.

Only one problem with the setup—the twelve-foot stone wall enclosing the property. And if that didn't give it away, the armed guards patrolling the perimeter gave clear indication. The place might look good, but the house was not a home. It was a fortress designed to protect those who lived inside and intimidate anyone who didn't belong. A symbol of power. A warning. One an outsider had better heed if he wanted to stay alive.

The corner of his mouth hitched up. Gotta love the Bratva. Never stupid. Forever cautious. Always armed to the teeth.

Firing up mind-speak, Zidane reached out to his XO. *"I'm in. Wanna come take a look-see?"*

"Nyet," Yakapov said, his polite way of saying "fuck off" from his perch outside the main gate. *"I don't even know what we're doing here."*

*"Da, you do."*

He sighed. *"Don't know why you have a hard-on for this human. It's not as though he'll ever best you."*

*"I'm considering going into business with the asshole. Only smart I know more before meeting him."* Not information his XO didn't already know. Zidane was thorough. Always. He never left anything to chance. He'd done the same kind of due diligence before setting meets with the drug cartels.

Yakapov grumbled something no one should ever repeat.

Zidane bit down on a smile. *"Besides, I'm curious."*

*"You got fifteen minutes to appease it. After that, I'm digging you out by blowing the pretentious, idiotic-looking place sky high."*

Studying the architecture, Zidane tilted his horned head. Pretentious? Yes. Well done despite the ostentatiousness? No question. *"It's not bad, actually."*

*"Z—"*

*"Okay, okay. I know. Fifteen minutes."*

His friend snarled at him.

Zidane chuckled, then shifted into human form, conjured his clothes, and put his feet in gear. He didn't need fifteen minutes. But if he was going to meet Nicoli Antonov and do business with the Bratva, he wanted to know more about the human running the show. More than what Hinz had dug up online about the male, which—to Antonov's credit—wasn't much.

Moving off the driveway, he strode over scallop-edged patios to reach the front steps. The instant his boot soles touched down on the landing, he murmured his wishes. The alarm system deactivated.

Deadbolts snicked. One of the heavy wooden doors swung wide. Without breaking stride, he crossed the threshold, walked into the house, and...

Stopped cold.

"*Hovno,*" he muttered.

"*What?*" Yakapov barked.

Zidane blinked. "*Fancy just became distasteful.*"

"*So?*"

"*There's gold. Every-fucking-where.*"

The amount of gilding shocked him. Which was saying something, given where he'd grown up.

Mouth hanging half-open, Zidane gave it another once-over. *Kristus*, talk about crass. The place looked like a gold glitter bomb had exploded inside the entryway. Gold spindles on curved double banisters, one heading up to the second and third levels on his right, the other on his left. Gold hardware on every door and light fixture. Gold filigree brushed on the cornices and coating the coffered ceiling.

Needing a break, he glanced down at his feet. No luck there. Embedded in the dark marble floors, narrow bands of gold inlay wrapped around the exterior of the cavernous foyer, three lines deep, a foot from the edge of the baseboards.

Mesmerized, he shook his head.

Unable to see him inside the cloaking spell, a maid bustled past. Frowning at the open door, she muttered something about strange winds.

The locks clicked shut. Light footsteps tapped across the second-floor landing.

"Hey, Marsella?" a female called from upstairs.

The sultry quality of her voice sailed across his senses. Sensation prickled down his spine. His dragon half rose, attention rapt, hunger rising, forcing Zidane to pivot. His boots rasped over gold filigree as he turned. Slow and steady. No sudden movements, zero chance of him losing control as he glanced up toward the top of the stairs.

His gaze landed on the female. One look, and his brain scrambled, stealing his ability to think.

"Beatrice, what are you doing? You should be resting."

"I'm done resting." Moving slowly, as though in pain, the female stopped on the lip of the top step. "Have you seen my Pluta Booties? I need to leave for the Luxmore in twenty minutes, and I can't find them."

The maid said something in return.

Zidane didn't hear her. He couldn't hear anything as the female started down the stairs. Long, dark brown hair curling over one shoulder. Jade-green eyes in a stunning face. Dressed to kill in a black cocktail dress, feet bare, but... *Hovno.* Her bioenergy surpassed glorious. It was magnificent, so powerful breath stalled in the back of his throat.

Struck stupid, he stared at her.

Unaware of his presence inside her home, she continued down the stairs. Her bare soles tapped out a rhythm against marble treads. His heart followed suit, hammering the inside of his chest as she rounded the curve of the banister. The closer she got to him, the stupider he became.

Desperate to own an HE, his sire talked about high-energy females all the time, waxing poetic about their existence. Zidane had never believed him. Hard to do when he'd never laid eyes on what amounted to a unicorn for his kind. Yet here one stood, larger than life, proof positive his sire wasn't crazy.

Yellow flames flickered over the tops of his shoulders. Tightening the cloaking spell to remain hidden,

Zidane clung to his control, but...fuck, staying even was difficult. She was incredible, her aura a starburst of bright citrine and white, so potent the fine hairs on his nape stood on end, reacting to the charge in the air around her.

Saliva pooled in his mouth.

The maid kept talking. Something about a gym bag.

The HE stopped three steps from the bottom.

Less than six feet away. She stood just *a few feet away*. Within touching distance. If he reached out... If he stepped forward... If he just—

"Thanks, Marsella. Will you have Markov bring the car around?"

"*Si.* I will tell him. Would you like some ibuprofen?"

"Already took some, thanks."

"Beatrice," the maid said softly. "Your ribs. You really should—"

"No." Elbow tucked to her left side, Beatrice shook her head. "I need to get back to work."

*Beatrice.*

His nostrils flared. The name suited her. So did her scent—red roses with hints of cedar and smoke.

She turned to go back upstairs.

His dragon half nudged him. Surprise drained away. His muscles unlocked, allowing him to move. Eyes trained on her, Zidane set his boot on the bottom step. He needed to touch her. He needed to taste her. He wanted the skirt of her fancy-ass dress around her waist and her back against the wall while he—

Pain streaked across his temples as static invaded his head. A signal opened, blasting onto his mental screen.

Rocking to a stop, he kept his gaze on Beatrice and

flipped the switch. A link flared, plugging him into the Razorback pack's main line like an operator. Noise erupted through mind-speak. He picked up the panic. He heard the chaos, all the screams of pain and pleas for help. A deep voice he recognized came through next, issuing clear instructions.

Ivar, in command of his pack, sounding a call to arms.

Zidane tensed. The Razorbacks were on the move. About to spread their wings in full flight and come to the rescue of males in trouble. He listened a moment longer. The words tumbled into his head—Bastian, the Nightfuries, a secret facility found.

*"Yakapov,"* he growled, tearing his gaze from Beatrice.

*"Tell me."*

*"Nightfuries on the move,"* he said, then rattled off a string of numbers, providing his XO with the longitude and latitude.

*"About time."*

*"Everyone airborne. Now. I'll meet you in the sky."*

Spinning around, Zidane sprinted across the entryway toward the door. He growled at the deadbolts. Magic exploded out in front of him. Metal whined. Wood splintered, then shattered. The heavy door blew off its hinges, pinwheeling across the landing, out into open air.

The maid screamed.

Beatrice yelled for the guards.

The command in her voice made him shiver. Regret rose as he charged over the threshold. A shame the situation necessitated him leaving her behind, but he knew where she lived now. She wouldn't be out of reach for long.

The Nightfury pack, however, was a different matter. Now that the call had gone out, Bastian and his warriors wouldn't stick around. The bastards would close ranks, do as much damage as possible in the shortest amount of time, then bug out fast. He understood the MO, had used it more than once himself, so...

He'd come back and find Beatrice later.

Planting his boot on the outdoor railing, he leapt up and out. Halfway through the jump, he transformed, shifting from human to dragon form. Eyes painting the night with citrine wash, he unfolded his wings and rocketed skyward. Window glass rattled as he carved a path over the house. He needed to join his crew and get into fighting formation. The quicker he closed the distance, the sooner he'd get his claws on the enemy...and the faster Nightfury warriors would die.

The clicking woke him up. Spider tarsus and claws moving over hardwood did the rest.

Cracking his eyes open, Azrad assessed the situation. Mind foggy. Muscles relaxed. Location: ass planted on the edge of a couch cushion, legs sprawled out, feet under the coffee table, back of his skull against the headrest. He stared at the ceiling, letting the details filter in, taking in the most important one—the soft, warm weight of Kasi tucked against him.

Fast asleep in his arms, head under his chin, she straddled him, insides of her thighs pressed to the sides of his hips.

He drew a deep breath. The beauty of her sank in and...yup. Not a figment of his imagination. All real. Every astonishing inch of her.

She was so much more than he'd expected. Smart, funny, strong, and determined. A gift in many ways, one he never would've thought to want before meeting her. Which was saying something. He'd had a lot of time to think in prison. Days, weeks, months, and years spent yearning for a better life. In his quieter moments, holed up in the cave deep in the Siberian wilderness, he'd imagined so many things—being free, finding his older brother, learning the truth about his sire, how holding a female of Kasi's caliber would feel.

Weird how the fates worked. Years of deprivation had led him here, to this moment and the brilliance of her.

Rooted in her, he allowed himself to drift. No need to get up and get going. Nothing but acceptance, a quietness of spirit he'd never noticed before, though he noticed something else in the stillness.

For the first time in his life, he felt full, truly satisfied instead of grasping and greedy. The hunger that so often plagued him was gone. Contentment replaced it as his dragon half moved from ravenous to gratified so fast he struggled to clear his mind.

The realization whirled through him.

Mental cobwebs began to crumble, dragging him closer to acuity. Staring at the sea of white above his head, he traced the narrow lines in the ceiling. Strips of LEDs embedded in the plastic surface. Dimmed lights. No imperfections to be found. Nothing to raise his internal alarms, except...

His muscles flickered, making him shift beneath Kasi. His hands moved with him, stroking across her soft skin. Surprise rippled through him. He froze. Holy shit, he was touching her. Really *touching* her. Somewhere along the line, he'd slid his hands beneath her shirt, palms pressed to her bare back, fingers spread wide and—

"Fuck," he whispered, brain rocketing to the ON position.

Unhappy with the interruption, Kasi mumbled, then turned her head. Rubbing her cheek against his chest, she wiggled in his lap and tucked her face against his throat. Strands of blond hair trailed over his jaw. Silky skin slid under the heat of his hands. He held his breath, remaining perfectly still as sparks of energy tapped along his spine. Curiosity took hold, then shoved him over the edge, taking temptation for a ride.

Unable to stop himself, he caressed her. Light strokes. Nothing to disturb her as one hand drifted up her spine and the other slid down. Barely breathing, he explored, leaving a ghosting trail across her skin.

Quiet drifted through the suite.

He closed his eyes, enjoying the moment, knowing he shouldn't. An honorable warrior would wake her. A good male would slip out from underneath her. A respectful one would protect instead of touch, putting the necessary distance between him and her, then—

Her eyelashes flickered. "Azrad?"

"Yeah?" He looked at her from beneath his lashes.

Blue eyes closed, muscles relaxed, she was in no way ready to slide off him.

He swallowed, wondering how best to handle the situation. He'd never woken up with a female before. Didn't have a clue how to handle her or himself. Should he ask her to move or let her rest? Shifting her off him seemed counterintuitive, the absolute wrong thing to do. Primal instinct urged him to soak up every little bit Kasi gave him. And his dragon half? Shit. The bastard refused to move, was wallowing in the aftermath of a fantastic energy feeding. In all honesty, so was he, but...

Wasn't there protocol to follow after a male fed? Should he be doing something he wasn't? Was it all right for him to be prolonging the contact, instead of—

"Weird," she muttered, still sleepy.

"What?"

"I thought so before, but...weird. Seriously weird."

Not understanding, he returned his gaze to the ceiling. Safer territory. Looking at her while holding and talking to her would be the end of sanity as he knew it. "I'm thinking maybe the energy feeding fried your brain."

"Could be," she said, not moving. "Though that may not be a bad thing."

"No?"

"Nuh-uh. Never been this relaxed before. It's nice."

"Okay," he said, happy for her, but still confused as all frigging hell. "But if it feels good, why's it weird?"

"The other times...when he came into my cell, when he...put his hands on me," she said, so quiet he sensed the pain she tried to hide. "It wasn't... He wasn't...like you."

Her admission ripped him from his moorings. "He hurt you."

She dipped her chin. The tight nod conveyed a lot —confusion, embarrassment, shame.

Azrad clenched his teeth, fighting to contain the fury along with his outrage. The bastard. The *fucking bastard* had put his hands on her. Taken what didn't belong to him. Reduced her to a food source instead treating her with respect, like a vibrant female with the right to choose. To assert her will, say no, and leave unscathed.

Sliding his hands from beneath her shirt, he wrapped his arms around her.

"Why's it so different with you?"

"Because you were willing. You gave to me. I didn't take," he said, explaining it the way Terranon had to him.

He hadn't understood for years. The instant he

met the big male, his education began. Much older, a lot more experienced, Terranon knew things Azrad and Kilmar hadn't, still didn't, and never failed to share. He was a natural teacher, giving Azrad the knowledge he needed to move through the world. Thank the goddess. Without his friend's guidance, he would've made a lot more mistakes.

"That's all it takes?"

"Free will, *kazlita*. It's everything."

She shivered.

Taking a deep breath, he shelved his temper and shifted beneath her. His hands found her waist. He applied gentle pressure, urging her to sit up. She resisted, trying to hide. He murmured her name. With a sigh, Kasi complied and pushed upright. Her ass settled on his thighs. Not knowing what to do with her hands, she sat in indecision for a second, then set both on his shoulders.

Wary blue eyes met his.

Smart girl. She was tapped in, reading him, using the echoes of the energy feeding to gauge his mood.

He gave her a squeeze. "I need a name."

"Why?"

"His name, Kasi. Who is he?"

"Listen, I don't... He didn't—"

"Bullshit," he said, refusing to allow her to downplay the experience. Pain always faded. Memory blurred facts, healing wounds over time. She might not want to think or talk about it now, but he refused to let it go. She'd been hurt. He needed to right the wrong. Avenge her. Ensure she understood none of what happened was her fault. "I'm glad he didn't rape you. So fucking relieved, Kasi, I can't express how much. Not with words. Not with anything. But honey, Dragonkind has a code. We do not take a female, in any way, without her consent. Ever. He had no right to do what he did, and he's gonna pay for that. I'm gonna see to it, so...I want his name."

She chewed on her bottom lip.

His eyes narrowed. "Name."

She swallowed. "Denzeil."

"Anyone else touch you?"

"No."

"Okay."

"Okay," she whispered, turning her head, breaking eye contact as Scandela finished her journey from bedroom to living area. Sleek red skin flashing, she leapt from the floor to the back of the couch. Kasi smiled. "She's back."

"She's a fast climber. Even quicker on descent."

"She really is gorgeous."

His mouth curved as she admired his spider.

"Hello, Scandal," she said, leaning closer. "Hello."

Walking across the throw blanket folded over the back of the couch, Scandela paused on her way to him. Her front legs arched up. Connected to her, Azrad felt her test the air with the fine hairs on her forelegs. Eight eyes trained on the female he held, his spider clicked her fangs, greeting Kasi in the way of her kind.

Delighted, Kasi grinned at him.

Shaking his head, he reached out. Exhausted from her climb, Scandela accepted his invitation. Red blazed in a burst of movement as she jumped, landing in the palm of his hand. Knowing what his companion needed, he brought her to the side of his neck. The web on his skin transitioned from silver to black, revealing her favorite perch. His spider didn't hesitate. She crawled across his throat and settled into the middle of her web.

Magic hummed through him as she plugged into the energy he fed her, becoming one with his skin, flattening into what looked like a well-drawn, intricate tattoo.

Grabbing his chin, Kasi tilted his jaw up. A second later, the tips of her fingers touched his throat.

Disliking the vulnerability, he tensed.

Fascinated by his spider, Kasi ignored him. Eyes riveted to his ink, she traced the edges of Scandela's web. "That is so cool. How often does she come out? How often do you—"

*Clang!*

*Slam!*

A series of loud bangs knifed into the apartment. The floor shook, making the bookshelves rattle and standing lamps sway. A snarl echoed outside the door.

Gripping her hips, Azrad stood in one movement. Kasi jerked against him. Gaze on the entrance into the suite, he set her on her feet.

"Grab your shoes, Kasi."

"What's happening? What's—"

Metal groaned. Another clang sounded. A thin, bright line appeared above the doorjamb. Sparks cascaded around the narrow opening as someone cut into the apartment with the efficiency of a welding torch. Inferno-like heat rolled into the room. The smell of burning plastic suffused the air as the interior wall melted, oozing into white, stringy globs before hitting the floor.

"Azrad—"

"Shoes, honey," he said, keeping his body between her and the door.

Kasi scrambled into the bedroom.

Sparking embers stopped as whoever stood outside finished torching the wall. Another clang. More banging. A curse a second before steel shrieked and the door fell inward. As it slammed into the floor, a huge male dipped his head beneath the lintel and crossed the threshold.

Widening his stance, Azrad flexed his hands and raised his fists.

Shimmering with aggression, pale green eyes narrowed on him. "You hit me, I won't care a platoon of Razorback are on the way, I'll take the time to cut your balls off."

Unfazed by the threat, Azrad grinned. "Good to see you too, brother. Sent the signal over an hour ago. What'd you do—take a timeout for some tea before leaving?"

Bastian scowled at him. "This stunt... Fucking hell, Azrad."

"Worked, didn't it?"

"When we get home, no word of a lie, I'm kicking your ass." Boots cracking over the downed door, Bastian moved toward him. One second he stood ten feet away, the next he pulled Azrad into a bear hug. "Little brother."

Returning the love, Azrad thumped him on the back. "Not so little."

"No," Bastian said, acknowledging what everyone who met Azrad understood without being told. He was a warrior, born and bred. Nothing small about him. Pulling away, Bastian palmed his shoulder and looked him over. "You all right?"

"Solid."

"Good. Time to go."

Azrad nodded, then turned and yelled, "Kasi!"

"Coming! I'm coming!" Breathless, running shoes now on her feet, she raced out of the bedroom. "Ready."

He held out his hand.

She latched on, lacing her fingers through his.

Bastian's brow popped skyward.

"Don't give me any shit," he said, not wanting Kasi to hear whatever bullshit came out of his brother's mouth.

Amusement in his eyes, Bastian shook his head. "Blonds."

"B—"

"Looks like they run in the family."

"Let's move," he said, ignoring the idiotic comment, not knowing what Bastian meant, and not wanting to, either. He'd hammer his brother for teasing him later. Right now, he needed to free Kilmar and Terranon. After that, he'd kill the Razorbacks occupying the other suites and get the hell out of Dodge. Dragging Kasi behind him, he hauled ass toward the hole Bastian had punched in the wall. "What're we looking at?"

"Gage's freeing Kilmar and Terranon. The two Razorbacks are already dead."

"What about the girls?" Kasi asked, keeping pace with them.

"Unconscious."

She hissed at Bastian. "What the hell?"

"Necessary, *talmina*," he said, calling her "little one" in Dragonese. "They didn't fare as well as you. I was forced to knock both out with sleeping spells."

"Goddamn it," she whispered.

Hearing the pain in her voice, Azrad gave her hand a squeeze, but didn't stop. He strode over the threshold into a long hallway. He looked both ways. Black *Blakeite* floor, ceilings, and walls. Electrical cable and bare light bulbs. Two females wrapped in blankets, lying on the floor. Gage kicking into another apartment suite. He heard Terranon snarl in warning, Gage's rapid-fire explanation in response, then the sound of heavy footfalls.

Bronze gaze glowing, Gage exited the room.

Dark-skinned female in tow, Terranon dipped his head beneath the lintel. Left eye covered by a black patch, he met Azrad's gaze and tipped his chin. "You good?"

Striding toward him, Azrad nodded. "You?"

Steel whined as Gage began cutting through Kilmar's door.

"I hate being cooped up." Copper-colored eye burning with internal fire, Terranon bared his teeth. "I need to get into open air and kill something."

"Your lucky night," Bastian said. "Razorbacks are on the way."

"Good." Flexing his hands, Terranon glared at the Nightfury commander. "Exit strategy? How're we getting—"

A sonic boom echoed. An earthquake rocked the underground facility.

Walls, ceilings, and floor cracked, fissuring around them. Thick black dust billowed into the air. Everyone coughed as light bulbs popped like balloons. Sharp shards rained down. Ducking her head, Kasi gasped. Azrad cursed as another quake hit, blowing chunks of rock up the hallway.

"Holy hell," Terranon growled, fighting to stay on his feet.

Rounding Kasi with his arm, Azrad spun around, shielding her from flying debris. Glass and small stones hit him like shotgun pellets. Pinpoints of pain radiated down his spine. Gritting his teeth, he threw an incredulous look at Bastian. "What the fuck is that?"

"Not what, little brother—who."

He frowned.

Bastian grinned.

The nasty tremors grew stronger. The sound of heavy drilling reverberated. The subterranean structure whined, shaking as Bastian jogged past him carrying an unconscious female over each shoulder. Mouth half-open, Azrad watched him in shock, then put his own feet in gear and moved toward the end of the corridor. Kasi stayed on his boot heels.

Azrad grabbed Terranon on the fly, slapped Kilmar on the shoulder as he exited the suite behind Gage, and followed his brother down the hallway.

Toward a dead end. One comprised of solid *Blakeite.*

"Please tell me we've got a plan," Kilmar said as another tremor hit.

Stumbling sideways, Gage bumped into Kilmar. "Earth dragon mojo is—"

"Nasty mojo," Bastian said.

"You got one?" Terranon yelled above the noise.

Azrad frowned as a memory spun up from the depths of his mind. One of a male with dark skin and glowing brown, green, and gold eyes. Lethal vibe. Powerful magic. Quiet nature, down-to-earth attitude. A warrior with serious skills, the kind smart males didn't approach unless invited. He remembered meeting him the second time he met Bastian.

His mouth curved. Fucking hell. Brilliant. His brother was *brilliant.* A Dragonkind commander who'd chosen his warriors well, playing to each one's strengths, putting the skills the goddess gifted each male to good use.

Trying to put a name to the warrior's face, he thought back to the meeting. The one in the woods, when his brother told him he looked like their sire in dragon form.

Recall came to his rescue. "Sloan."

"Yeah—Sloan," Bastian said, stopping five feet from the dead end.

After transferring one female to Kilmar, Bastian placed the other in Terranon's arms. Excellent call. A mated male didn't tempt fate by touching females other than their chosen one, not unless absolutely necessary. Trapped underground with two unconscious HEs qualified as an emergency by any standard, but by handing off the pair, Bastian showed his loyalty, giving his mate the respect she deserved...all without her being present.

A solid move made by a solid male. Just another reason to look up to the Nightfury commander.

"Shit," Bastian said, looking over his shoulder, toward the other end of the hallway.

Gage snarled. "We're out of time."

Dragon senses contracting, Azrad searched for the problem. A little shaky after days surrounded by *Blakeite*, his magic realigned, coming back online slowly. His mental grid fired. Sonar flipped on, expanding perception. The slam-bang of footfalls echoed down from above. Multiple Razorbacks landing. A handful in human form on the move, boots slamming into concrete treads, running down the stairwell on a mission to intercept them and save Ivar's breeding program.

Azrad bared his teeth. *Shit* was right.

Letting go of Kasi's hand, he shifted into the middle of the corridor, putting his packmates behind him. One door into the hallway. No other entrances or exits. He flexed his fingers. Magic rampaged through him. Heat swirled in the center of his palms. He held on to the burn a second, allowing the power to grow, then raised his hands and flexed his wrists.

Gossamer-thin steel-infused threads shot from heels of his palms. Fine, sticky filaments flew through the air, then struck, sticking to the jamb and walls, crisscrossing the door, sealing the entrance into the hallway shut. A shot in the dark, worth a try if the cablelike threads kept the Razorbacks out. Or at least slow the bastards down.

The sound of drilling grew louder. The corridor heaved.

"Wicked," Gage yelled, legs braced to keep from losing his footing. "How long will the webbing hold?"

Good question.

Azrad had no clue. He always unleashed his spider webs in the sky, using the sticky steel strings to bring a male to ground or kill him in midair. Using his webs underground, against stone and steel instead of dragon scales, was a new experience. He'd never deployed his webs in the hopes of keeping the enemy out of somewhere he didn't want rival warriors to enter.

Meeting Gage's gaze, he shrugged, praying the high-tensile steel inside his webs held long enough for Sloan to break through. Otherwise, he'd end up with his back against a wall, fighting to protect Kasi and the others in what amounted to a kill box.

## 35

Pulling energy directly from the earth, Sloan pressed his palms against solid rock and walked forward. His earth dragon snarled. His magic churned, chewing through *Blakeite* at an unsafe pace. He should slow down. Determination pushed him forward, making him move faster, urging him to risk more.

He was already hurting, the pain so bad his insides heaved. Acid rolled over the back of his tongue. Gritting his teeth, he kept burrowing, refusing to acknowledge the danger, ignoring the risks.

He needed to punch a hole through the *Blakeite*. No time could be wasted. Razorbacks were swarming. He must open a back door, provide Bastian and the others an exit, before the enemy breached the hallway, forcing his packmates to fight in an enclosed space.

The pain didn't matter. The poison he breathed was nothing but a blip on his radar as the sound of battle bled through mind-speak. He should disengage from the link, concentrate harder, shut out the snarls and the clang of claws against scales, but he couldn't bring himself to block it out. So he listened in, knowing his brothers-in-arms had their talons full in the sky. The chatter was nonstop. The fighting brutal as multiple rogues converged on his packmates' location over the abandoned cement factory.

With a growl, Sloan pushed hard. Tremors shook the shaft he cut through solid rock. The ground beneath his feet rocked. Fine black dust billowed up and around him. Sloan coughed, but kept digging through diamond-hard stone.

Pain spiraled up his forearms. His lungs spasmed. Blood filled his mouth as he stumbled sideways.

Nian cursed. Strong hands grabbed Sloan from behind, keeping him upright. "For Silfer's sake, brother—stop!"

Ignoring the male, Sloan spun his magic, drilling faster. The conduit between him and the electrostatic bands flared. Minerals in the *Blakeite* sparked in warning. He saw Nian in the smooth, black mirrorlike surface. He turned his attention to his own face. Eyes glowing bright green, teeth bared, he snarled at his reflection.

Hands fisted in the back of his jacket, Nian growled in his ear, trying to pull Sloan away. Nice try, but the male had no chance of shaking him loose. No one, even a male as powerful as Nian, could force Sloan to disengage once he started burrowing.

Nian tried anyway. Wrapping his forearm across Sloan's chest, he yanked. And yelled. And shouted in Sloan's ear some more. He held firm, resisting his brother-in-arm's efforts to free him—to protect him... to save his life.

"Hellfire, Sloan! You're killing yourself. You need to slow down. You need to—"

"No time."

"Haider and the others might be outnumbered,

but they're holding their own. Take a beat. Take a breath, brother."

Sloan hissed as earth magic fluctuated. The powerful stream pulsated, twisting around his muscles and bones. His stomach pitched. Agony clawed down his spine.

"Sloan!"

"Go back, Nian." Breathing like a wounded racehorse, he bore down, chewing through another one hundred feet. "Get airborne. Help the others. I'm almost—"

Black rock split down the middle.

With a roar, Sloan fisted his hands, turning each into a jackhammer. Solid rock fissured into chunks. Huge boulders began to crumble. Artificial light bled through the cracks. The green in his gaze fractured into prisms, blasting streaks of color through the rupture. Choking on mineral dust, Sloan gathered the fractured pieces, storing each one in his mental vault, ensuring the tunnel stayed free of debris and—

The earth howled.

*Blakeite* rumbled.

Warm air met the blistering chill inside the tunnel, creating a violent vacuum. Wind buffeted him, tearing at his jeans, making his open jacket billow as the wall between him and his packmates tumbled down.

He caught sight of Bastian in the corridor.

"Goddamn fucking hell," he rasped, his relief so strong he swayed on his feet.

Stepping into the tunnel, his commander fisted hands in the front of Sloan's leather jacket. Blood in his mouth, Sloan folded forward. Nian cursed behind him. Bastian held Sloan up as debilitating pain took over, short-circuiting his brain as darkness descended, swallowing him whole.

## 36

Sloan regained consciousness like a badly wired light bulb. He kept trying to turn it on, but his brain misfired. His nervous system crackled as his muscles spasmed, joining the noisy, chaotic parade marching through his mind. All signs pointed to no-go, except for the one flashing RED ALERT across his frontal lobe.

His fingertips twitched.

Fighting to keep his eyes open, he blinked, then blinked some more until some of his thoughts collided, coming together only to bounce and move further away. Holy hell. Talk about brain burn. He needed a complete reboot. A pathway to stopping the brutal mental and physical upheaval.

Every time he reached for clarity, his mainframe went sideways, ping-ponging around inside his skull. Blink on. Shut off. Bounce in one direction, only to volley the opposite way the next.

The back-and-forth left a messy trail of mental debris, taking up vast stretches of runway inside his head. Scent, sight, and sound clashed, tumbling around until nothing made sense. Reaching for stability, he flipped on his sonar. Nothing happened. His mental screen stayed blank, throwing off static, forcing him to remain in the dark.

Not a good sign.

Worse for the fact he didn't know where the hell he'd landed.

Gritting his teeth, he tried to lift his head. Bad idea. Movement made everything worse—the pain, the amount of magical interference, the horrible metallic tang in his mouth.

He coughed to expel the bad taste. Black dust puffed between his teeth. He felt the gritty ooze clog the back of his throat. Heaving, he pulled the sludge from his lungs and spat out a gob of thick slime. Wetness hit a floor, a surface he couldn't yet see, but instinct told him was there.

Blinking again—and again—Sloan tried to focus. His thoughts shifted from blurry lines toward sharper edges. He needed to remember what the hell happened. He needed to get a handle on the damage and danger. He needed to get his dragon half on board and magic humming before rogues attacked, tore him apart, and he never woke up again.

With a groan, he flexed his fingers. Pain burned over his knuckles, up his arms, over both shoulders, down his spine to—

Sloan sucked in an agonizing breath. Thank the goddess. All his limbs appeared to be attached. *What else? What else? What the fuck else?* No immediate answers came back. Tightening his grip on reality, Sloan drilled down, searching for what he needed—more information, and fast.

Turning a series of mental dials, he tuned in. Jagged edges began to smooth out, helping him slip back into his skin. A sharp twinge across his lower belly. Sore muscles along with a raging headache. The crackle of too much earth energy vibrating in his bones. Little more than a vague impression as the mind fog blurred his sightlines, clouding perception.

Sloan reached for his dragon half. With a low snarl, he dug through the rubble, picking up the broken pieces, fixing the damage until he felt the twist of roving vines slither up from deep inside him.

Rising from the ashes, his dragon half uncoiled. Focus began to return. Staccato information machine-gunned through him.

Temples throbbing, Sloan clenched his teeth as intel streamed in, swirling into a murky cesspool, coming at him all at once. He hauled in the messy tangle, unknotting each string one at a time. As he straightened the threads, he took each jagged piece as it came, shelving what he could, letting the rest sail past.

Complete chaos, except for a trio of facts.

Latching on, he organized them inside his head. One, lots of movement along with the loud echo of hard, heavy footfalls. Two, the smell of scorched rock in the dusty air. And three, he was hanging upside down, being carried at a fast clip, with a shitload of visual interference blocking the usual clarity of his mental grid.

"Shit," he rasped, battling to lift his head.

"Don't move. Stay still," a familiar voice said.

Sloan blinked, struggling to place the heavy Czech accent and pissed-off tone, but...

His brain turned over. Mental acuity fired. His night vision sparked. Deep grooves winding around otherwise smooth, curved walls of the tunnel he'd cut through solid granite. Warriors hauling ass behind the one who carried him in a fireman's hold. Three females with the group, two being carried.

He glanced down at the boot heels kicking up dust beneath his head. "Nian?"

"You, my friend, are stubborn." Out of breath, Nian sprinted up the incline, heading for the vertical cave. "One hundred percent asshole."

Sloan grunted. "You crying over spilled milk?"

"I told you to slow the fuck down."

Whatever. The Archguard prince could be as pissed off as he liked. Didn't matter what he thought right now. "Got the job done, didn't I?"

"Yeah, and nearly killed yourself doing it."

Sloan coughed. No sense arguing the point. His condition told the story. He was nowhere near one hundred percent, but with his magic coming back on line, the effects of the *Blakeite* bled out of his system, making him more alert.

"Nian."

"What?"

"Put me down."

"You think you'll be able to stand?"

"I think I'm gonna kick your ass if you don't."

Gage huffed behind him.

Nian growled. "Ungrateful."

"Not true." Slapping his friend on the back, he shifted his weight. Nian slowed from run to jog. Sloan got ready to land on his feet. "I'm still holding *Blakeite* in my mental vault. Gotta get rid of it. Won't be able to fly if I don't. Also, I need to refill the hole before any Razorbacks follow."

"Five just entered the corridor."

"Outside the suites?"

Bastian nodded. "Moving toward the tunnel."

Bending his knees, Nian heaved Sloan off his shoulder. A wave of dizziness hit him. He teetered a moment before equilibrium returned. Balance set, he rolled his shoulders, settling back onto his frame. The group kept running, streaming around him, sprinting toward the vertical shaft at the top of the incline. Voices echoed up the tunnel.

His vision shifted from soft shimmer to intense glow. Green light washed over rock walls, throwing shadows as he listened to the rogues check each suite. Enemy males cursed. Boots tapped against the cement floor, echoing up the corridor. Timing his assault, Sloan waited until the Razorbacks entered his underground warren. Hearing the slam of heavy footfalls, he raised his arms, pressed his palms out, and conjured all the earth he'd stored in his mental vault.

Rock rumbled.

His magic roared.

With a snarl, Sloan started to backfill. Huge boulders and heavy soil blasted up the tunnel. Dense dirt and black dust billowed into the air. Moving his hands, he directed the flow, funneling the steady stream of granite and *Blakeite* back toward the subterranean complex.

The hole filled within seconds.

Rogues panicked. He heard the mad scramble. He listened as one or two made it out. Others got caught in the rage of swirling debris. Without mercy, Sloan rammed his hands forward, compacting the earth, cutting off the enemy's retreat, burying the enemy alive.

Feeling more and more steady, Sloan walked backward up the incline. The raging river of stone continued to flow. Like pieces in a puzzle, he placed each boulder, grain of sand, and speck of dust, interlocking the earth, ensuring no one could follow. The last of the *Blakeite* left his system. The excess earth magic in his blood surged, feeding his dragon half, super-charging his abilities.

Growling low, Sloan turned and sprinted into the vertical shaft. As he joined his packmates, the males in the group paused, mouths falling open. Gasps sounded as HEs backed away, shuffling behind the warriors still in human form, putting more space between them and him.

"Jesus." Cradling an unconscious female, Kilmar eyeballed him from ten feet away. "Fast recovery."

Azrad smiled at him. "Earth dragon mojo."

"Nasty shit." Black eye covering his right eye, good one trained on Sloan, Terranon adjusted the female in his arms. "Looking good, man."

Sloan snarled in answer.

Already in dragon form, claws buried in rock and damp loam, Bastian glanced down from his perch halfway up the wall.

Sloan looked up. Eyes narrowed on his commander, he switched to mind-speak. Static hissed through his head. *Plan?*

*"Kill everyone but our own."*

Good plan. No arguing with B's strategic prowess, but...

*"The females?"* he asked, taking in the rescued five, trying to ignore the fact the three who were awake looked away, afraid to meet his gaze.

Not a bad read of him, given the lethality he exuded with death-dealing earth magic in the mix, adding its power to his own. Even the blond shied away, moving behind Azrad, using the big male as cover.

Cursing under his breath, Sloan reached for control. The reins slipped through his hands, dialing up the murderous vibe frothing in the air around him. A low sound rumbled from deep in his chest. Everyone took a step back, moving further away from him.

The ground under his feet trembled. The quake spread, rippling up the sides of the vertical shaft. Rock tumbled down from above. Sidestepping falling debris, his brothers-in-arms growled at him.

Bastian murmured, warning him to lock it down.

With a nod, Sloan inhaled deep and exhaled long. B was right. He needed to get his reaction to the clusterfuck under control. High emotion never helped in tense situations. Worse, he'd already scared the shit out of females who'd endured enough.

Every time he looked at them, he thought of Theodora and how she would've fared under similar circumstances. Trapped. Defenseless in the face of Dragonkind warriors. In the hands of a mad scientist with no conscience and even less scruples. The idea made him sick to his stomach. Fate had done his mate a good turn, keeping her from crossing paths with Ivar before she fled her uncle and Seattle. The HEs surrounding him hadn't been so lucky.

His nostrils flared as he sucked in another breath. Goddamn Ivar and his breeding program. The bastard deserved to be taken apart scale by scale. The entire Razorback pack needed to be exterminated, for so many things, but mostly for the damage done to innocent females, ones now watching him with guarded expressions.

Sloan took another breath in. He pushed another out, clearing his lungs, settling his mind, downgrading his aggression from apocalyptic to manageable.

*"You all gonna stand there gawking at me? Or is someone gonna fill me in?"* Still furious, but more contained, he watched Bastian and Nian climb. *"Who's got the girls?"*

"*Us,*" Azrad murmured.

"*The tripartite,*" Nian said at the same time. Claws grinding over stone, he threw an amused look over his shoulder, nailing Azrad with shimmering opalescent eyes. "*The second we're airborne, they got one job—get the females to the safe house in one piece. You, Bastian, and I will cover their asses.*"

"*Tripartite?*" Terranon said, Australian accent rumbling. "*What the fuck's that?*"

"*You,*" Nian said, grinning down from his perch. "*And the boy band you got going on.*"

Good eye narrowed on Nian, Terranon growled, "*Boy band?*"

"*You looking to die, Nian?*" Pale yellow-green eyes flashing, Kilmar glared up at the male. "*Cuz I've been cooped up a while and need the exercise, not to mention the fun. Archguard prince or not, I'd be happy to—*"

"*Rip your golden scales off one by fucking one.*" Head tipped back, B's brother glowered at Nian. "*Put them in a shoebox, mail them back to Prague.*"

Baring fangs, Nian laughed. "*Bring it. No way you'll get your claws on me.*"

Bastian huffed. "*Not tonight, anyway. I might be persuaded to hold him down for you later, though.*"

"*Outstanding,*" Kilmar said.

"*Unfair advantage,*" Nian grumbled, amusement in his voice.

The blond cleared her throat. "Uh, hate to interrupt. I mean, I know you're probably having some secret, silent weirdo dragon powwow, but...can we go?"

Eyeing the female whose hand he held, Azrad raised a brow. "Weirdo dragon powwow?"

"You know what I mean," she said, full of fire and attitude.

"Kasi's right." Finished climbing, Bastian looked

over the lip of the hole. Midnight scales shimmering, he flicked his talons, clicking long, hooked claws together. *"Move your asses. Gage is already airborne. We need to follow. Get into the fight."*

Clear of the *Blakeite*, Sloan's sonar pinged, delivering information. He fine-tuned the signal. Chatter came through the line, giving him a grid. Two Nightfury fighting triangles. Both holding strong. Lots of snarls coming from his brothers-in-arms. Lots of bloodcurdling screams from rogues. The shriek and clang of claws meeting scales. The unmistakable whistle of fast flying as six Nightfury warriors maimed and killed multiple males, pushing the enemy further west, away from Sloan's position.

*"Go,"* he said, meeting Azrad's gaze. *"You three first. I'll follow you up."*

Piercing blue irises ablaze, the male nodded. *"Gonna fly south, away from the fighting, then zigzag west before going north toward Magnolia house."*

Sloan nodded. *"I'll be right behind you, but watch your sixes. I'll do my best to clear the sky, but one or two rogues might slip through."*

Giving Kasi's hand a squeeze, Azrad glanced at her. "Ready?"

"No," she said, looking petrified.

"Trust me." Magic heating the air around him, Azrad shifted from human to dragon form. Jet-black scales replaced human skin. Kasi jerked as he wrapped a huge talon with unusually long claws around her. She squeaked in alarm.

Wings pressed to his sides, Azrad curled his talons, caging her in his palm, then leapt up and started to climb.

Dragging his gaze from the pair, Sloan turned his

attention to Azrad's wingmates. *"B give you the address to the safe house?"*

*"Haider's code to get in, too."* Acid-yellow scales glinting, Kilmar set two females in the palm of one talon and followed his friend up the wall. Dragon scales scraped over stone. Sharp claws dug in, shaking debris loose. Dust billowed into the air. Severed tree roots and burned sediment tumbled down, pelting the floor from four stories up.

Sloan flicked his fingers. Falling debris froze, then disappeared into thin air. *"How much time do you need to get clear?"*

*"Five or six minutes to skirt around the fighting,"* Terranon said. *"I'll muffle our energy signals, keep the rogues from detecting our retreat."*

Sloan raised a brow. *"Can you spin illusions?"*

*"Nowhere near as good as Nian, but I've got some game."*

*"You a full-blown Metallic?"*

*"Copper dragon."*

*"Five minutes, then,"* Sloan said, impatience making him itch. He wanted to be airborne. He needed Azrad and his warriors to climb faster, but...*five minutes.* A blip on the wheel of time, but he knew what others ignored—time slowed when engaged in battle. One minute could feel like lifetime. Five often felt like forever. *"I'll make sure you have what you need to get clear."*

Two females in his paw, Terranon leapt straight up. His talons found purchase, digging in as he looked down. Six eyes, black as pitch, focused on Sloan. He blinked. Holy hell. He'd forgotten Terranon was hexa-eyed in dragon form—three eyes on each side of his head, though one was damaged. The contrast of the white iris against copper-colored scales corroded green at the tips was striking. So different from the metallic black of his five other eyes.

*"See you on the flip side, Sloan."*

*"Yup,"* he said, watching the Aussie reach surface level.

The second Terranon cleared the lip of the hole, Sloan unleashed the remaining loam and dirt. The doors to his mental vault wide open, he let earth stream from the centers of his palms. Boulders churned beneath his feet. Pressure built inside the tube. He cranked the valve, directing the rush. The river of rock geysered, catapulting him skyward like a champagne cork.

Dust turned to fresh air. Cold replaced the warm cocoon of wet earth.

Somersaulting into a backflip, Sloan cleared the treetops and transformed. Hands and feet turned to snow-white talons tipped by razor-sharp claws. His body lengthened beneath the spiral of spikes riding his spine. Dark brown, green, and gold scales flashing, he unfolded his wings. The triple tips of his scorpion-like tail sliced through violent wind gusts. Radar up and running, he searched the sky, found his target, then opened the door and let aggression out of its cage.

## 37

Angling his wings, Zidane sliced through a nasty updraft. Thick grey clouds swirled in his wake. Condensation gathered on his scales, but didn't stay, evaporating as yellow flames danced between the spikes along his spine. He inhaled, drawing smoke and fire into his lungs. The scent tunneled deep, preparing him for battle.

Dragon sense firing, he fine-tuned his radar and threw his net wide. He let it settle a moment, then pulled the strings. Information boomeranged, returning to him in bits in pieces. He knew his position—five miles from the fight. He understood the terrain—thick forest, high cliffs moving toward jagged mountain range, no humans for miles.

All fine and good.

The setup, though, bothered him. Something about the Razorback response wasn't right. Ivar's warriors were too frenzied, too reckless, approaching the fight in the wrong way, giving the Nightfuries too many opportunities to strike.

He smelled the blood in the air. Heard the clang of claws striking scales and the screams, along with the death rattle as warriors died. Who? From which pack?

No clue, but odds were Bastian and his crew were taking the Razorbacks apart, sticking around instead of bugging out.

Being outnumbered in open skies never made for a good game plan. The Nightfuries should've made like vapor and vanished long before now.

Tweaking his sonar, Zidane sifted through the information again. He read the current and all the signs. Horns tingling, he shook his head. *Kristus*, total chaos. Engaged in fierce claw-to-claw combat, Dragonkind warriors filled the sky. A huge group consisting of thirty-plus males. So many he couldn't distinguish one from the other. Razorback. Nightfury. He sensed the separation of packs, knew both occupied the sky, but—

A link into mind-speak sparked, breaking his concentration. His eyes narrowed, Zidane glanced at his first-in-command.

Flying off his right wingtip, Yakapov scowled back. *"Not good. It's a free-for-all."*

*"No pattern. Complete chaos,"* Montgomery muttered, emerald-green scales winking beneath weak moon glow. *"How're we supposed to tell who's who?"*

*"What the hell's Ivar thinking?"* Hinz asked.

Zidane grunted in answer. His usual reaction when dealing with Hinz. Too curious for his own good, the male did a great impression of a two-year-old. He never ceased with the questions. Who, what, why every outing, every minute of every day, all the freaking time.

Hinz raised an excellent point, though. What in the hell was Ivar thinking?

Engaging in the open air with skilled warriors was a bad idea. An ambush always worked better. But Bastian and the Nightfuries? *Hovno*, going head to head with the lethal pack was just plain stupid. Did the commander of the Razorbacks have a death wish, or was something else going on?

Ivar, much as Zidane disliked him, wasn't stupid. Which meant—

*"We need to get in there,"* Strecklin growled, yellow eyes flashing, blood-red scales picking up the glow. Aggressive to the point of self-destructive, he'd never met a fight he didn't like. *"Before the Nightfuries bug out."*

Lynhurst hummed. *"Been a while since I had blood on my claws."*

Zidane growled. Didn't he know it. Prague had been boring for years. Lots of Dragonkind to hate, no one to fight. His sire embraced the status quo, insisting on keeping the peace in public. In private, however, Rodin sometimes let him loose, sending him on missions to *benefit the cause.*

His sire's words, not his. Not that he cared.

Hush-hush or out in the open and in the Archguard's face, either option worked for him. But only if he flew out on a regular basis. The last time he got to kill anyone had been months ago...when Rodin sent him to eliminate the Belarusian pack.

Speed supersonic, Zidane blasted through the three-mile marker. His sonar pinged as fighting warriors picked up his unique energy signal.

Allowing his quarry to sense him might not be the best idea, but time was of the essence. The sooner he got up close and personal, sorted Razorback from Nightfury, the sooner he'd get blood on his claws.

*"Achan, Strecklin, Lynhurst—one group,"* he said, descending fast through thick cloud cover. *"The rest of you, follow me."*

His warriors growled in agreement.

*"Try not to kill any Razorbacks. I still need Ivar to co-operate."*

*"Don't know why,"* Yakapov said, sounding the way he always did—like a killer in search of prey. *"The sooner we kill the bastard, the faster we take over his pack."*

*"Patience, brother. I've got a plan. Stick to it."*

His first-in-command grumbled, broadcasting his annoyance.

Night vision focused on the flurry of activity ahead, Zidane ignored his friend and split wide right, searching for a way into the battle. He needed an opening, a small slice of space to enter without getting nailed by warriors in full flight. His gaze tracked north to the heaviest pocket of fighting. Turning his head, he scanned south and—

*"What the hell?"* he said, eyes narrowed on a section of sky.

Wavy, indistinct blur. Muted. Grey. Hiding in towering storm clouds, moving at a fast clip away from the battle. Unnatural. An oddity. The kind instinct always encouraged him to investigate.

*"Zidane."* Bright yellow hide winking, Yakapov looked in the same direction, following the blob across the night sky.

*"I see it."* Trying to get a bead on it, Zidane banked right, shifting course to intercept the anomaly. *"Monty, Warsaw—get in front of it. Yakapov and I are going over the top."*

*"See what's it's hiding."* Smoke wafting off his red scales, Warsaw snuffed out the fire streaking like a long-tailed comet off the tip of his tail.

Montgomery growled. *"Kill whatever's inside."*

Excellent summery. One hundred percent correct.

If what Zidane suspected was true, the Nightfuries' refusal to retreat made perfect sense. Bastian and his crew were protecting something—or someone. The longer the Nightfury commander stayed in the fight, the more time he bought those attempting to get out of the kill zone. Not a bad plan. With the Razorback warriors distracted by the tactic, Bastian's ploy might have worked—if Zidane hadn't showed up to rain on his parade.

## 38

Slicing along the ridgeline, Sloan banked into a hard turn. Contrails jetting off his wingtips, he blasted around a freestanding cliff, flying like a phantom in Azrad's wake. Almost directly below the males. Close to the ground. Following the rise and fall of rough terrain. Far enough away to go unnoticed. Close enough to come to the trio's aid if needed.

Thick with massive white pines, the topography dropped into a deep valley. Twin cliff faces rose, closing in on both sides. He went wings vertical, rocketing between jagged columns. Sheer stone faces quivered as he threaded the needle. Loose rock rumbled as shale leapt over the edge, tumbling toward the boulders sitting at the base of cliffs.

Weaving in and out, trying to keep up, Nian flew fast behind him.

Bastian split wide right, playing rover, tracking the battle in the skies above.

Dragon senses ablaze, Sloan monitored the situation. Nasty claw-to-claw combat, but his brothers-in-arms were holding their own. Pushing the enemy further north. Making rogues scream. Wounding many, forcing males to leave the fight before death came calling.

Killing Razorbacks might be the usual plan. But not tonight. Total annihilation took time, something they didn't have right now. Wounding as many as possible, forcing rogues to retreat instead of staying in the fight, was a better plan. The most expedient way to get Azrad, his warriors, and the females out in one piece.

Shadowing the trio, Sloan listened to the chatter. Heavy fighting. Rikar and Forge coordinating the Nightfury strategy. Calm. Cool. Collected. Unfazed by the number of rogues in the sky, each male called the plays, voices rising through mind-speak, ensuring the seven Nightfuries in the fight worked with one another as Exshaw shrieked, knocking Razorbacks out of the sky with the sound of his deadly battle cry.

The blazing cacophony bled through the link.

Pain scorched Sloan's temples. Goddamn. Even from miles away, Exshaw packed a serious punch.

The wren screamed again.

Sloan bit down on a curse.

*"Hellfire,"* Nian growled. *"He's frying my circuits. How the hell are the others fighting alongside him?"*

Good question. One Sloan couldn't answer.

Mac kept telling him he needed to connect with Exshaw, get close and embrace the pain. Something about downloading the unique energy signature the wren threw off like natural napalm. Toxic. Brutal. So painful warriors buckled, falling out of the sky the second Exshaw shrieked, and the mind-bending sound waves hit.

Which left him wondering why he should listen to Mac. Nothing but pain—and nasty headaches—came from spending time with the wren.

*"You two need to put in the time."* Spine aligned,

spikes rattling, Bastian came over a jagged ridge like a grim reaper. *"Once Exshaw trusts you, he'll inoculate you. Listening to him won't hurt as much."*

Nian grumbled under his breath.

Sloan understood. Enduring the kind of pain Exshaw dished out wasn't fun. Doing it until the wren decided to trust him would suck. Though he wouldn't argue with the results if the agony downgraded from catastrophic to—

His sonar pinged. Seven unique energy signals blipped on his radar.

*"Shit,"* Bastian said, crisscrossing over him.

Nian snarled. *"Trouble."*

Mining the signal, Sloan read the vibrations. *"Not Razorbacks. Kill squad or mercenaries?"*

Both good guesses. Hard to tell for sure. After years of fighting Ivar and his pack, he recognized the signals rogues threw off like pheromones. The seven warriors approaching read differently. Foreign. New. Not native to the western seaboard or Seattle.

Wanting more information, he sent his senses roving. His radar tightened the grid. He pulled on the cosmic threads, drawing all available intel into his net. Muffled signals came back, preventing him from breaking down the group into individual males.

Frustration thumped through him.

Folding his wings, he dipped, then sliced skyward. Rough landscape fell away, becoming dots beneath him. Magic rippled across the night sky. His horns tingled. He cranked the dial, tracking the unknown crew's trajectory across the night sky.

The seven cracked through the three-mile marker. Perception splintered.

Sloan frowned as nothing changed. The close proximity should've helped him dissect the group.

Static blew into his head instead, smothering clarity, making other realizations rise. The males flying fast in tight fighting formation were experienced, a warrior pack skilled enough to disguise and disrupt signals that should be clear.

*"My read's fucked. B—you got a better one?"*

*"Not yet. Need 'em to fly closer, but—"*

*"Got a problem."* Angling his wings, Nian split wide right. *"Crew just divided. Two groups. One headed into the fight. The other flying toward us. Azrad's been spotted."*

*"Time to intercept, two minutes,"* Bastian said, following the enemy pack's progress across the sky from a distance. *"Nian—illusion spell. Sloan—debris field. Treat 'em to a surprise. Slow the bastards down. Give my brother the time he needs while we crack their skulls."*

Sloan grinned, then searched the valley floor and rising ridgeline. Lots to choose from, no shortage of rock, downed trees, and other debris lying around.

*"Powering up."* Magic spreading like a heatwave, Nian built the spell. The sky flashed. Hot air funneled, warping the air around his golden scales.

*"Waiting on you."* Power whiplashed, streaming through his veins as Sloan connected to the earth. The ground trembled. Distant mountaintops rumbled. Wind picked up, spinning across the landscape. He suppressed the violent tornados, holding each back as huge boulders levitated, waiting on his command. *"Say when."*

Lightning dragon out in full force, Bastian dropped a net over the area. Electricity crackled, upping the voltage in the already supercharged sky. Thunder boomed. Lightning zigzagged, cracking jagged over thick forest.

Nian murmured a command.

The sky split. A vertical seam opened, slicing

through the clouds. Azrad and warriors swerved left, curving around the atomic disruption, disappearing behind the illusion Nian conjured.

"*Now!*" Nian yelled.

With a growl, Sloan unleashed hell. Violet twisters erupted from the ground, then went airborne. Ripped from the cliff side, taken from the valley floor, huge chunks of stone exploded into the sky. Controlling the churning chaos, he sent the storm of revolving debris sailing behind the illusion, hiding it from enemy view.

"*Holy fuck,*" Bastian said.

Nian hummed. "*Serious as shit...I wanna be an earth dragon when I grow up.*"

Ignoring the idiotic comment, Sloan charged into the pandemonium. Dirt and dead leaves lashed his scales. Giant boulders whirled over his horned head. Tucking one wing, he somersaulted up and over, slicing through swirling detritus. Bark flying, knotted roots spinning, a massive tree trunk sped toward him. He ducked beneath the log, whirled one way, then banked the other, whipping around the exterior of one of his tornados.

The storm snarled. Sand shrieked against scales as he hung like a ghoul inside the turbulence, riding the vicious wave. His prey came into view. Four warriors flying in a direct line toward him. His eyes narrowed, he watched and waited. Speed consistent. No deviation in formation. Staying on a tried and true flight path. Zero indication any of the males sensed his presence, the illusion, or the vicious maelstrom hidden behind it.

"*Ten seconds to splashdown.*"

With a curse, Nian dodged a flying branch. "*I'm staying out here.*"

*"Circle around the edge,"* B said to Nian. *"If any es-cape Sloan, we'll clean up."*

Focused on the lead male, Sloan flexed his talons. Aggression blazed through him. He started the count-down. Three, two, one, and...

The lead rogue slammed headfirst into the flying wall of rock. Dark brown, orange-flecked scales shrieked. Horns clanged against the stone. Jagged tips snapped off, spiraling out into open air as the dragon's neck whiplashed. A cut opened across his forehead. Blood splashed up and out. A stream of smoke puffed between his fangs as he lost consciousness. His wings folded. Fire swirling around him, the lead dragon plummeted.

Webbing billowing, the three behind him put on the brakes. Bright yellow scales flashing, one warrior tucked his head under and dove, trying to catch his leader before the male hit the ground. The illusion rippled, undulating into multicolored rings across the sky. The wall hiding him disintegrated, revealing the vicious shitstorm he controlled.

Hanging in midair, the blue dragon widened its eyes. The green-scaled male cursed and, black wings flapping, shot skyward, trying to get out of range. A wasted effort. Sloan was locked on the pair, sitting in the eye of the storm, in control of his environment.

Debris whirling around him, Sloan launched a frontal assault. Fangs bared, he flew straight toward the pair. The rogues squawked. Grabbing a boulder as it whirled past, he hurled it sidearm. A whistling sound cut through the air. Rock slammed against bright blue scales. Bone snapped. The male howled as the strike thrust him across the sky. Vibrant green scales flashing, the other warrior sucked in a breath, then exhaled. Venomous green fog shot from between his bared fangs. Toxic swill ate through the oxygen.

Somersaulting sideways, Sloan folded his wings. Gravity took hold. He lost altitude. The bilious cloud rocketed over his head. A tornado rolled beneath him. Using the funnel to stabilize his descent, he opened his wings. A nasty wind gust caught in his webbing. Muscles stretched. Pain streaked down his spine as he swung back around, snagged a flying tree trunk out of midair, and blasted out of the debris field. He revolved up and over the rogue. On the downward arch, timing it just right, he swung the white pine like a baseball bat.

Wood slammed against the underside of the green dragon's chin. His head snapped back.

The blue dragon took a swipe at Sloan. Sharp claws raked him, slicing across his hip, down his thigh and dug in. The enemy's talons sank deep. Blood welled on his scales. Agony bit. With a hiss, Sloan kicked out. The warrior's grip slipped. As Sloan shook him loose, the second rogue roared, ready to exhale again.

About to get hit, Sloan torqued into a spine-bending flip. Halfway through the revolution, he snarled. His tornados obeyed, rushing forward, eating the sky, destabilizing the air.

More cursing from enemy males.

*"Sloan!"*

Bleeding, pissed off, in pain, he snarled, *"What?"*

*"Get the fuck out of there,"* Bastian snapped. *"Azrad's clear. Rikar's called it. We're bugging out."*

*"Thirty seconds, B."*

*"Bug out,"* his commander growled. *"I can't get around the edge of the debris field. You're on your own in there. Get out. Now."*

A direct order. One Sloan wanted to ignore, but B was right. No matter how much he wanted to finish the pair of assholes now hauling ass in the opposite direction, giving chase wouldn't be wise. He'd been hit. Was leaking blood. The smart thing—the only thing—was to follow his commander's lead. He needed to return to the lair and his mate. Connecting with Theodora would provide what he needed—a steady stream of power energy. The kind that would heal his wound up tight.

*"Goddamn it."* Snapping his razor-sharp teeth together, he growled in frustration. *"I had 'em, B. Never seen the asshole, but I'm pretty sure Zidane was leading the pack."*

*"Dark brown scales with orange flecks? Citrine glow in his eyes?"* Nian asked, fury underpinning his tone. No need to guess why. He knew Zidane, hated him more than most—in and out of dragon form. The Archguard prince had spent years clashing with the male and his sire in Prague.

*"Yeah."*

*"Missed opportunity,"* Bastian growled, electricity crackling through the link, temper about to boil over.

*"Younger male with vibrant green scales, too. Venomous exhale. Scar on his face. Could've been Montgomery,"* Sloan said, adding fuel to his commander's fire.

Probably not the best play under the circumstances, but Sloan refused to hold his suspicions back. If Montgomery was the male he'd tangled with, the Scottish pack needed to know.

Dropping the tree trunk, Sloan banked into a tight turn, backtracking through the debris field. If Zidane and his warriors regrouped, keeping the storm between him and the enemy was a smart move. No way would the assholes be able to fly through it.

Glancing over his shoulder, he checked his position in the sky. Closer to Black Diamond than the safe house. Perfect. Azrad shared familial DNA with his blood brother. He also had the code. The protection spell shielding Magnolia house wouldn't give B's younger brother any problems, which freed him up to return home.

Favoring his injury, Sloan exited the maelstrom. Magic rippled around him, pulling debris across the sky in his wake. Not a surprise. Conjuring earth storms amped him up. It always took him a little time afterward to settle back into ordinary.

*"The whole kill squad."* Mourning lost opportunity, Sloan rocketed over the top of twin cliff faces. *"Could've ended Zidane and his brother in one go."*

Bastian came down out of the clouds. *"We'll get 'em, Sloan."*

*"Eventually,"* Nian said, chiming in from half a mile away. *"Sooner or later."*

*"I'd settle for sooner."* Having second thoughts, Sloan re-checked his sightlines. *"Maybe we should—"*

*"Live to fight another night."* Decreasing his wing speed, Bastian set up shop off his left wingtip and tracked the blood trail across his flank. *"How bad is it?"*

Tornado gusts buffeted Sloan. With a murmur, he spun down the wind. The powerful funnels dissipated, swirling into dust clouds on the ground. *"Still bleeding, but the wound's closing. I'll make it home."*

B grunted.

*"How about we head there now?"* Golden scales nothing but a blur, Nian blasted over the treetops. Contrails streaming off his horns, he settled on Sloan's

other side. *"Razorbacks are regrouping. Gage and the others are already out of range, waiting for us, so—"*

Sloan sighed. *"Live to fight another night."*

*"Damn straight,"* B said.

Sloan looked around, took in the boulders spinning around he and his brothers-in-arms, and gave in. Huge rocks fell out of the sky, cracked against bluffs, rolled down cliff faces and into the valley below.

Trees groaned. Dirt and loam swirled across the forest floor as Sloan dialed down his disappointment. Hoping and wishing never made things happen. Pragmatism was a better option. He needed to let go of the could've-beens and embrace reality.

Zidane and his warriors were gone. Sloan's side and leg hurt like hell. Pain and fatigue gnawed at his muscles as blood loss began to take its toll. The injury coupled with the absorption of too much earth magic and the effects of the *Blakeite* sapped his strength, making his head ache and wings wobble as he struggled to remain stable in flight.

He needed his mate. Craved her softness. Longed to hear the sound of her voice as he settled warm against her, so no sense acting tough or pretending he was all right on his own. A lie he liked to tell himself, but no longer could.

In a ridiculously short amount of time, Theodora had become his lifeline. The very center of his beating heart. Which left only one thing for him to do—give his female her due, accept the beauty she brought into his life, go home, and...live to fight another night.

Excellent advice. Something he would keep in mind as he took her to bed and immersed himself in the magnificence of his mate.

## 39

In the middle of an oversized gymnasium, Theodora watched her daughter pick up the plastic T-ball bat. Kid-sized, much like the rest of the equipment Daimler had conjured out of thin air an hour ago in Black Diamond's kitchen. All made of out vibrant colors—lime-green bat, neon-orange stand, gaudy purple bases accompanied by a bright blue baseball. The stuff of little-girl dreams. At least, her little girl.

Violet wasn't much for activities the world labeled "feminine." She liked to run. She enjoyed rough and tumble. She preferred to seek before hiding, tackle things instead of dressing them up, and sing rock songs from the 1970s instead of nursery rhymes.

Case in point? Violet stepping up to the hot-pink home plate while singing "We're an American Band" by Grand Funk Railroad.

Manning first and third, J.J. and Tania grinned.

Standing at second, Hope laughed.

Punching the center of her baseball glove, Myst bobbed from side to side in the outfield, playing the part, pretending Violet might hit the ball that far.

Evelyn crouched behind home plate, doing a great

impression of a catcher. Dark eyes sparkling, she threw Theodora a sidelong look. "How's she know all the words?"

Holding the ball, Theodora shrugged. "Anyone's guess."

And it was. How Violet remembered all the lyrics mystified her. Always had. Chalk it up as one of life's great mysteries. She loved her child. Theodora didn't need to understand all the ins and outs. She'd learned to stop questioning her three-year-old's freakish ability to recall lyrics after hearing a song once.

No need, after all, to dissect something that required no explanation—just acceptance.

"Mommy! The ball," Violet said, pounding the bat against home plate. Plastic met rubber. The *whack-whack-whack* echoed, bouncing off cinder-block walls.

Violet continued hammering. Sound boomeranged, rippling out only to come back as she set the ball on top of the stand. Millicent, J.J. and Wick's six-month-old American bulldog, froze, muscles quivering, eyes on the ball, waiting for her to send it flying.

Violet wound up and—

*Thwack!*

The blue devil flew. The dog burst out of the starter's gate. Violet laughed with glee. The bat hit the wooden floor. Dark curls flying, Violet took off running...in the wrong direction. Instead of heading for first base, she thundered after Millicent, chasing the puppy across the gym.

Someone chuckled behind Theodora. She glanced over her shoulder.

Laptop tucked under her arm, Angela said, "Got a minute?"

"Got a least ten. The chase is on...again," she said,

pointing toward the dog and Violet, knowing it would be a while before the ball made it back onto the stand. "You need something?"

"Sloan mentioned your sister."

"Yeah?"

Angela nodded. "His search pulled up more intel. I think we need to put a tracker on her cell and car."

The words echoed inside Theodora's head as surprise took her out of a spin. Her mouth opened, then closed. Her brow furrowed, she stared at a woman she barely knew, but had liked the instant she met her. Hazel eyes. Auburn hair cut pixie short. Athletic build, intense vibe, no-nonsense attitude, smart as all get out. No flies on Angela. The woman didn't stay still long enough to let shit rest.

"Do you think Bea's in danger?"

A guarded expression shuttered Angela's eyes. She tipped her head to one side, asking Theodora to step away from the game.

"Sure," she said, stripping the elastic out of her hair. A nervous habit, something that made her feel a little more in control as she raked her hair away from her face and retied her ponytail. "Evie, do you mind?"

Venom's mate nodded. "We've got Vivy, Theo. Go chat with Ange. See what's she found."

Dread pooled in the pit of her stomach as she refocused on Angela. "I'm not going to like it, am I?"

"No telling, but..." Angela flicked her fingers, indicating the island of blue mats spread out in one corner of the gym. "Come take a look."

"Sooner's better than later," she muttered, adopting Sloan's motto.

"Usually."

"I really hate this."

"I would too if it was my sister."

"Yeah," she said, bare feet tapping across the narrow-planked wooden floor.

Sitting cross-legged, Angela set up shop in the middle of a mat. Laptop balanced in her lap, she snapped the computer open.

Tense muscles tied in knots, Theodora sank down beside her new friend. Adopting the same pose as Angela, she leaned sideways to improve her view. Attention glued to the screen, she took a deep breath as Angela scroll through a bunch of files.

She didn't want to know. Really, *really* didn't want to see what Angela had dug up, especially without Sloan sitting beside her, but cowardice didn't become her. Not anymore. She'd run long enough. Turning a blind eye, creating alternate theories in order to avoid the pain, no longer served her. Sloan was right. Avoiding hard truths only made things harder. So...

Time to dig in.

Inhaling deep, she exhaled long and slow. "Sock it to me. What did you find?"

"Texts. A bunch of them from four years ago." Tapping the trackpad, Angela brought up a string of correspondence. "Between your sister and some guy. Went by Anthony Durant then. Goes by another name now."

Shock rang Theodora's bell. Buzzing filled her head. "What?"

"Beatrice deleted them. Did a pretty good job of covering her tracks, but Sloan's AI found the conversation. I could print it for you if you want to have—"

"No," she said, struggling to contain the pain as she read the first page.

Grabbing the computer from Angela, she set it in her own lap. Finger flicking over the trackpad, she scrolled through the rest. Disbelief rose before realization struck. Brutal. Undeniable. Betrayal at its most stark, making her want to vomit.

One hand pressed over her mouth, Theodora stared at the final message, then moved back up and read through the string again. It was all there, plain as day, written out in excruciating detail. Beatrice scheming with Anthony. His agreeing to an outrageous sum of money. The elaborate plan to sabotage Theodora's birth control. Beatrice's idea from start to finish.

Pain morphed into anguish. Her hands started to shake. She shook her head, unable to believe even though the proof couldn't be denied. "This can't be. I can't... This... Bea would never—"

"She did, Theo."

"But—"

"She set you up with this guy. None of this has been altered. These are her texts to Anthony at the time, and his back to her."

Heart hammering the inside of her breastbone, she swallowed the lump in the throat. "Why? Why would she do such a thing?"

"Not sure. Nothing I can find points to motive," Angela said, shifting from friend to cop. As a former homicide detective, she had the lingo down.

"I just... I don't even know what to... I love Violet, Ange. I love my daughter. Wouldn't trade her for the world, but...my sister...this? Why?"

Expression pained, Angela reached out and squeezed Theodora's knee. "I don't know. I'm so sorry. Maybe I should've waited for Sloan. Maybe I jumped the gun, but I just... I know you plan to meet Beatrice. Before you do, you need to be armed with this and... and, well..."

Angela trailed off.

Theodora got a bad feeling. "There's more?"

"I think, maybe, I should let Sloan—"

"Too late, Ange. You gave me this," she said, heart hurting, head aching, fury at her sister rising. "Give me the rest."

"I don't have anything concrete. It's more of a hunch."

"Tell me anyway."

Angela hesitated before she picked up the computer and set it in on the mat in front of them. Fingers flying over the keyboard, she opened another file. "It's not much."

"What is it?"

"A piece—a very small piece—of a report."

"Looks like something medical?"

"What I think too," Angela murmured, eyes on the screen. "Thing is, I think the report's about your uncle."

"Nicoli?"

Angela nodded.

"He doesn't go to doctors. Doesn't trust them."

"By the looks of it, this one came to him."

"He's sick?"

"Might be. No way to know for sure."

"But if he is," Theodora said, "he wouldn't go to a hospital like a normal person. He'd bring in doctors... get the best money can buy without anyone knowing. Receive the treatment he needs, keep the Bratva in the dark, stay in power."

"You know him, Theo. I don't."

"And Beatrice." Her eyes narrowed as the pieces started coming together. She knew her sister. Maybe not the extremes she was willing to go to get her way, but Theodora understood how her twin's mind worked. "She runs his businesses. Has her fingers in all his pies and gets off on the power. She's the heir apparent. If Nicoli dies, she becomes head of the organization, but the Bratva is a patriarchy. They won't accept a woman at the helm."

"A good working theory, but we don't know anything for sure. We haven't got—"

"I do." For the love Christmas, she was an idiot. Nothing else explained the fact she'd missed it. All these years, and she'd never once read the signs. "Bea's staging a coup. She began to lay the groundwork the day she fucked me over, ensuring I couldn't stay. I'm an idiot. A total frigging idiot."

"Hey. Listen—"

"I was entrenched, Ange. Adamant. Bea wanted me to go. Had been trying to get me to leave for over a year. I refused to go without her."

"Until she made protecting someone else more important."

Her throat clogged. Blinking away tears, Theodora searched the gym. Her gaze landed on her daughter playing tug of war with the dog. "Violet."

"Yeah," Angela said. "Violet."

"I'm gonna kill her."

"Who?"

"My sister!"

"Ah, well..."

Theodora's temper boiled over. She'd been duped. Lies had been told. Choices had been taken from her. Years of her life had been stolen. High crimes inside the sisterhood, all perpetrated by the one person she should've been able to trust without question.

Loyalty mattered. But so did the truth. Concepts her sister failed to grasp.

"I mean...God! Seriously!" Uncrossing her legs, Theodora popped to her feet. "She staged the whole frigging thing. What makes her think she has the right to—"

A tingle swept over the nape of her neck. The beginnings of a spectacular tantrum stalled.

Theodora frowned. "What's that?"

"The boys." Snapping her laptop closed, Angela got to her feet.

"Where?"

"Out in the—"

The signal intensified.

"Never mind," Theodora said, pivoting toward a set of double doors. "I got it."

Leaving Angela behind, she checked to see Violet was all right, then strode off the mats, across the gymnasium, and beneath the basketball hoop. Need driving her, she charged into the corridor, turned left, and—

Slammed into someone.

She reeled back a step. Big hands arrested her momentum. She tipped her chin up. Dark eyes ringed by shimmering green met hers. Her breath caught. Pleasure shivered through her. Cupping his nape with one hand, she caressed his jaw with the other and popped up onto her toes. She kissed him, welcoming him home. All instinct, no hesitation, greeting him the way she knew he wanted.

The brilliance of energy-fuse at work. The instant Sloan touched her, she understood what he needed. The bond she shared with him spoke plainer than words. He wanted her in his arms—close, comfortable, and connected. She drifted in the flow, relaxed into the moment, and gave him what he required, allowing the energy to flow. A buzz fizzed in her veins as she sensed his relief, along with his contentment, rise.

His hand landed on the side of her neck. The pad

of his thumb stroked over her pulse point. Gentle touch. Stunning pleasure. The sensual pull drew her in as he pressed his temple to hers.

Nestled deep, surrounding her, he sighed. "Theo."

"Hey," she breathed, running her hands over his shoulders.

Putting pressure beneath her jaw, he tipped her chin up. His eyes traveled over her face. "You been crying?"

"I've been pissed off."

"Your sister?"

"How'd you know?"

"Bond's taken hold, *mazleiha*. I'm rooted deep, tangled up in you."

"And what— That makes me easy to read?"

"Yeah," he murmured, walking backward. Up on her toes with his arms around her, she moved with him. "What happened?"

"Tell you later," she said as he half carried, half danced her down the hall.

His boots whispered across the concrete floor, the rhythm of his strides jagged instead of smooth. Not a whole lot different than his usual gait. A slight limp that would go unnoticed by most, but not her. She liked watching him move. Sloan was poetry in motion, a combination of athleticism and predatory grace wrapped up in masculine beauty. He moved smooth and sure—always. So the hitch in his step…

A niggle of unease sank deep.

Theodora tested the boundaries of their connection. It was powerful, complex, gorgeous in its intensity. She sensed the strings tying her to him—and him to her. Touchable, more real than anything she'd ever experienced, the hum of energy-fuse unfurled, unraveling inside her, helping her tune in.

Sloan growled. The soft sound rumbled from his chest, coming from deep inside him.

Murmuring back, Theodora trailed her fingertips over the sculpted ridge of his cheekbone, learning him, loving him, conveying her acceptance through touch. Sensation sparked. Perception narrowed. The connection flared. Prickles drifting down her spine, she turned the tables, used his tactics, and drew information through the link.

Impressions formed in her mind's eye. Nothing huge at first. The turbulent clash of emotion, a vague sense of something, but then...

A hint of pain came through the connection.

Her grip on him firmed. "Are you all right?"

"Wasn't before, am now."

"Sloan—"

She squeaked as his arms tightened around her. Hard muscles flexed. Her feet left the floor. He pivoted, took a few quick strides, entered a room, and kicked the door closed behind him. Suffering from a delayed reaction, she blinked. His eyes warmed with amusement. Her brain reengaged. She took a deep breath and—

He dipped his head and kissed her. No fooling around as he launched a sneak attack, turning her on so fast heat blistered through her.

Desire turned the screw, fogging her mind until all she saw was him. Forget about taking him to task for blatant manipulation. She'd nail him for that later. After he gave her what she wanted. After she gave Sloan what he needed. After the pleasure spiked and subsided, leaving the quiet beauty of contentment in its wake. Then, and only then, would she demand he tell her what the hell had happened, along with why he didn't want her to know.

## 40

H is computer screens flipped on, reacting to the energy surge in the Hub. Lights flickered overhead. The supercharged hum buzzed over his skin, overwhelming Sloan as he kissed his female. Her beauty blazed through him. The bond he shared with her activated. Her aura flared, submersing him in the glory of her white-hot energy.

With a groan, he slid his hands beneath her shirt and tapped in, slicing into the stream. The Meridian rose like a wave. Theodora reacted to him the way she always did, with blistering need and burning desire.

Out of control.

Hot as hell.

The female made and meant for him.

The one he hadn't believed existed until Theodora burst into his life. The disbelief seemed ridiculous. He watched his brothers-in-arms with their chosen females all the time. He understood energy-fuse, knew the bond was real, and yet...

Everything about his mate continued to surprise him. Her beauty. Her spirit. The way she reacted to him. Like him, she couldn't get enough. Every time he touched her, she lost control, which, in turn, threatened his. Each kiss dragged him closer to the edge. The way her hands moved across his skin shook his foundation. The tremor rumbled through him, making him want to dominate—take, control, pleasure her until she begged him for a break.

The urge struck with the force of sharpened claws.

Sloan snarled, resisted a moment, then wondered why. Theodora wanted him. She was his mate, so in tune with him she provided what he needed without hesitation. No matter how he came to her, she welcomed him. Hard fucking. Long, slow loving. Rough and tumble or gentle as hell. Didn't matter. She was his. *His.* No reason to hold back. No reason to move slowly. Every reason to take what he wanted, the way he wanted it, while giving her what she craved. Still...

He should probably take her temperature. Ask before dominating.

He inched away, breaking the kiss. "Theo."

She whimpered, protesting the separation.

"Baby."

"Stop talking."

He growled against her lips. "You want more?"

Breathing hard, she tipped her chin up.

"More, *mazleiha*?"

"I want everything. *Everything.*"

So be it. Question asked and answered.

"Gonna get rough." Baring his teeth, he scraped his canines across her cheekbone. With a hum, he licked over her pulse point, drawing nourishing bioenergy up through her skin. "Gonna feed while I take you. Gonna fuck you harder than I have before."

She moaned.

He spun her toward the wall. "Hands above your head, Theo. Palms flat against the wall."

"Oh, God."

"Keep them there. You don't move unless I give you permission."

"Shit."

Sloan grinned against her hair. Her eagerness unleashed him. He issued more orders. She surrendered, obeying without hesitation—spreading her legs wider, tipping her ass, granting him full access. She was desperate to fuck. He was deep in her energy field. The more instruction he gave, the more excited she became and...goddamn, Theodora was incredible. She liked the way he played, moaning as he stripped her down.

After tossing her clothes toward the table behind him, he ran his hands over her bare back and ass. Enthralled by her softness, he slid up and around, worshiping her curves, sensitizing her skin, pleasing himself while she quivered beneath his touch. He brushed his mouth over the back of her shoulder. He sucked on her skin. As she rasped his name, he caressed her hip, slid over her belly, then down and *in*.

Hot, wet, so fucking slick. She was so aroused, she coated his fingertips as he stroked her, circling her clit, bringing her up onto her toes. A warmup, the calm before the storm.

Her hands started to come off the wall.

"Don't move."

"Sloan," she said, hips rocking in time with his fingers.

Fitting his chest to her spine, he wrapped his other arm around her. His hand traveled across her belly, then up to curl around her breast. Close to orgasm, locked against him, she trembled in his arms. He held her still, stroking her sex, tugging at her nipples, his teeth against her skin.

She moaned, the sound half curse, half plea.

Sloan kept at her, upping the pace, immobilizing her, forcing her take what he gave her without moving. Tension rippled through her. Muscles quivering, she arched her spine. Dark hair tumbled around her face as the back of her head collided with his shoulder. Reaching up, he cupped her chin, turned her head, and invaded her mouth.

She whimpered against his tongue. Her core contracted around his fingers.

Deep in her energy field, he felt, heard, and tasted it as she detonated. Pleasure roared through her into him. Her body bucked. Her hands found the back of his head. The edge of her nails scraped over his nape. Snarling, Sloan murmured his wishes. Magic hummed. His clothes disappeared as he pulled her away from the wall. A couple of fast strides put him even with the table.

Fingers still buried inside his mate, he bent her over the edge and pressed her chest down on the wood. Kicking her feet apart, he entered her with one hard stroke.

Still in the throes of her first climax, Theodora arched. She keened his name, riding the pleasure as he rode her, Hard. Fast. Without mercy. Watching their connection, reveling in the feel of her as he held her down and fucked her.

So much heat. Untold beauty. All Theodora. The gift that she gave him.

Rippling around him, she started to come again. He rolled his hips, thrusting hard to her center. Advance and retreat. Strong rhythm. Devastating pace as he loved her and stroked her clit, shoving her over the edge.

"Sloan!"

"So good, baby. Fuck, but you're gorgeous."

"Ohmigod. Ohmigod. God, God…God!"

"More. Again, Theo."

"Can't. God, Sloan, I gotta… Oh, shit. I can't!"

"You will."

She mewled with each thrust, air exploding from her lungs each time his hips slapped against her ass. Sloan snarled as he watched her, sensing the devastating wave of ecstasy rise. Fuck, it was going to be huge. Mind-wreckingly, soul-stealingly *huge*.

Chest heaving, struggling to hold on, he buried his hand in her hair. Controlling her completely, he folded forward. His mouth found her ear. He nipped the lobe, listening her to come, feeling her hips roll, addicted to her spirit, in thrall to her body, in love with everything about her.

Bliss grabbed him by the balls.

The base of his spine tightened.

His rhythm broke, moving from fast and hard to wild and out of control. Pleasure sank its claws deep. Theodora gasped. Buried deep inside her, Sloan let the sound of his name on her tongue take him over. Tucking his face into the side of her throat, he groaned and thrust hard. Once. Twice. A third time, then settled, staying deep inside her. "Fuck, baby. My female. So beautiful."

Cheek resting against the tabletop, eyes closed, Theodora didn't twitch. She lay relaxed beneath him, chest rising and falling as her breathing evened out, then afterglow washed in and pulled her under.

"Okay?"

"Mm-hmm."

Nestled deep, split wide open, a wave of emotion hit him. His chest tightened. Just beginning to calm, his heartbeat picked up speed. Logic warned him to check his reaction. Instinct and his dragon half disagreed, pushing him forward.

Theodora deserved everything he had to give. His honesty. His devotion. The absolute best of him. Turning away, shutting down how he felt, was easy. He'd been doing it for years. But here, now, with her flush against him, Sloan refused to take the easy way out. He gave his mate her due instead, embraced the vulnerability, and put what he felt into words.

"I love you, Theo. Fuck, but I love you."

Muscles lax, tension gone, she sighed. "Ditto."

He blinked. Surprise lasted a second before amusement took over. He huffed against her skin. "Ditto? Did you just say *ditto*?"

Theodora mumbled something incoherent.

He grinned and lifted his head. Stroking thick locks away from her face, he caressed the apple of her cheek. Dark lashes spread like a fan on her skin, she didn't move. He traced the curve of her eyebrow, then the gorgeous slope of her nose. Nothing. Not even a twitch. Completely passed out. Bent over the table, deep in la-la-land with him still deep inside her.

His lips twitched.

Well, all right. Not completely unexpected. He should've guessed with the amount of energy she'd expended sleep was a possibility. Add three orgasms to the mix and his mate needed her rest.

She grumbled again.

He smoothed the crease between her brows. "Sleep, *mazleiha*. I've got you."

As she settled, he straightened and pulled out, leaving the warm cover of her body. Conjuring a blanket, he wrapped her in soft fleece and picked her up. He murmured. Magic swirled. His favorite jeans settled on his skin as she nestled into his arms. Careful not to jar her, he crossed the Hub, sat down in his chair, and tucked her into his lap.

Leather creaked beneath him. Motion sensors activated, bringing his system online. Code crawled across six different monitors. He swiveled in his chair, reached out, and tapped a command into his keyboard. Contentment moved through him as he settled into one of his favorite places inside the lair. Eyes on his screens, he pressed his mouth to the top of her head. His mate. So unbelievably precious. Thank the fates for doing him a good turn, 'cause he was lucky. So fucking lucky to have found her.

## 41

T he haze lifted a little at a time. Drifting in warm comfort, Theodora embraced awareness as it came. No need to rush or move. She was happy to float without the cerebral drag of surfacing too fast. Unusual for her. She liked hitting the snooze button—a lot—but never woke easy.

Most days her feet hit the floor before her brain registered the fact she stood upright. Force of habit. In her world, sleep meant unprotected, and being caught unaware always ended in trouble.

She liked steady. She liked certainty. Problem was, she'd never had much of either.

Unlike most people, she never closed her eyes at night and thought, *No worries, I'll just sleep in tomorrow.* Lazing in bed didn't appear anywhere on her agenda. Her itinerary included things like: looking over her shoulder, keeping a baseball bat by the front door and mace in her purse. Which meant she shouldn't be drifting in the warm current swirling around her. Shouldn't be luxuriating in relaxation and allowing her thoughts to come and go. Awareness, after all, arrived with movement—and open eyes.

Trying to jump-start her brain, she wiggled her

fingers and toes. Soft fleece brushed against the backs of her hands. More awareness trickled in. She cracked an eye open and...yup. Just as she thought. A blanket lay over her, soft and warm against her bare skin.

Another oddity. A renegade in her normally tidy world, the very anthesis of her regular routine.

She never slept naked. Nude didn't equal ready, and Theodora was always ready. To run. To hide. To grab her go-bag and get out of town. And still, self-preservation refused to press the panic button. Her finely honed senses left her to rest instead, wake in her own time as she shifted a little, becoming aware of the heat pressed along her right side.

She blinked, confused as the bare chest beneath her cheek registered. The mind fog lifted. Awareness rushed in, clearing the mental cobwebs, providing details rapid-fire. Holy crap. She wasn't alone. Wasn't even in a bed. She sat naked in Sloan's lap. Muscular arm wrapped around her, he held her secure, his body heat warming her, the steady beat of his heart heavy in her ear, his chin resting on top of her head.

With a hum, Theodora bent her knees and curled into him. Naked in Sloan's arms—outstanding. The absolute best way to wake up.

His arm tightened around her back.

Drawing a deep breath, she took him in. Spicy scent. Unbelievable heat. The echo of the delicious ache between her thighs. He'd warned her he'd take her roughly. And oh boy, had he ever, to stunning effect. She loved him gentle. But God, when he was bossy...

Her mouth curved.

Sloan was an amazing lover. He paid attention, discovering what she liked as he drove her wild. She wondered if she should be embarrassed by her loss of control, but...jeez. Hard to embrace shame when he made her come three times. *Three* to his one, in quick succession. Had to be a record. A glorious one she wanted to repeat over and over—then do it all over again.

Happy to stay right where she was, she listened to his heartbeat. The rapid click of typing broke through the cocoon. Theodora cracked her eyes open. Her vision blurred, then cleared, giving her a view over the edge of the blanket. She stared at his shoulder a moment, then resettled her cheek on his chest. Her gaze traveled over the enticing curve of his biceps, then down his corded forearm, coming to rest on his hand.

Broad palm. Scarred knuckles. Long, strong fingers. Perfection in motion as he sat, chair turned sideways, and typed one-handed.

Smoothing her hand over his shoulder, she shifted in his lap. The typing stopped. She tipped her head back. His hand slid up her spine. Cupping the back of her head, he brushed his mouth against hers. She kissed him back, responding to his slow, sweet, lazy exploration.

Watching her from beneath his lashes, he retreated. Just a little, keeping her close while his gaze roamed her face. "Good sleep?"

She hummed. "Violet?"

"With Hope and Forge. Building something with Lego."

"Lego?"

"Forge's a carpenter. His favorite thing to do is build stuff," he said, talking softly, keeping their cocoon intact.

"Out of Lego?"

Sloan shrugged. "Says it relaxes him. You should see the models he designs. Pretty cool. The trick is keeping G.M. from tearing them apart and eating the pieces."

"That happen often?" she asked, picturing Forge's son. Cute little guy. Incredibly alert and very agile. Seven months old, and he was on the verge of walking.

"Dragonkind infants'll eat anything," Sloan said, fingertips twirling in her hair.

"Babies of any species will eat anything." And she should know. She still had nightmares about some of the crap Violet put in her mouth as a baby. Enjoying the gentle tug on her scalp as Sloan played with her hair, she looked at his computer station. Six big screens mounted above a long stretch of desk. Two keyboards sitting on the scarred wooden top, one under his hand, the other further down in front of a small office chair. "You're working?"

"Waiting for you to wake up."

"Have you seen the text messages Ange dug up?" she asked, not knowing why.

God, she was idiot. She didn't want to talk about it. Didn't want to think about it, either. Every time she thought about what Beatrice had done, hurt surfaced. She wanted to be angry. She wanted to turn away, expel her twin from her life, and never look back. Problem was, ignoring the truth was simply another way to run. Something she'd promised herself—and Sloan—she wouldn't do anymore.

Keeping her eyes glued to one of his computer screens, she toyed with the hem of the blanket. She pleated the fleece, rolled the edge over, then folded it over again. "Did you?"

"I need you to look at me."

She closed her eyes. "I feel like an idiot."

"You're not an idiot."

"Easy for you to say," she whispered as he set his thumb beneath her jaw. He applied gentle pressure. With a sigh, she complied, opening her eyes to look at him. "Did you read them?"

"Yeah, baby. I read them," he said. "That the reason you were upset when I got home?"

Her throat clogged. "It sucks, Sloan."

"I know it does."

"You know the crazy thing?"

"What?"

"I keep trying to explain it away. I mean, that's crazy, right?"

"It isn't crazy."

"And you're super sweet, but I've seen the proof, read through those stupid texts twice, and here I am, still full of doubt. I don't want to believe Bea did that to me. I don't want to believe she's capable of that."

He murmured, the sound so full of understanding she lost the battle. Tears filled her eyes. She clenched her teeth, trying to contain the pain.

"She's my sister. My *twin*. I always thought we were close and now, I'm finding out it was all a lie. A carefully crafted illusion. Did I ever really know her? I mean, seriously—did I?"

"Theo," he said.

"She's a good actress. Theatrical. I've always known that, but *this*?" With an angry swipe, she brushed a tear away. "She's fed me nothing but lies. For years, Sloan. Nothing but *lies*."

"You still want to meet with her?"

"Want isn't the issue. I wanted to see her before. I *need* to see her now. She played me. Might still be doing it. I need to look her in the eyes. She won't be able to hide the truth from me face to face. Though..."

"What?"

"I may have to punch her first."

Amusement sparked in his dark eyes. "Wouldn't that be kind of like punching yourself?"

"Shut up," she said, wiping another tear away as he lightened the mood, bringing her back to baseline. God love him. He always seemed to know just what to say. "We're identical, not the *same*."

"Thank the goddess. I'd be fucked if you were."

A compliment. Big, bright, and beautiful, showcasing his ability of knowing what to say and when to say it. The skill was like a superpower, soothing her with acceptance. The kind she'd always wanted, but never believed she deserved.

"You're incredible," she whispered. "Apart from Violet, you're the best thing that's ever happened to me."

He closed his eyes.

Tracing his bottom lip with her fingertip, she watched relief move through his expression. He'd been bold while making love to her. He'd been braver afterward, going out on a limb, making himself vulnerable for her. Sleep had been close, but she'd heard him tell her he loved her.

"Totally incredible, honey. The best of the best."

"Baby."

"You know I love you too, right?"

"Fuck me," he said, voice thick with emotion. A green shimmer sparked around the edge of his irises, making dark brown seem darker. "You said ditto."

"I said ditto?"

He nodded.

"When?"

"After we fucked."

"On the table?"

"Yeah."

"Well," she said, smiling. "I meant it."

Shaking his head, he grinned back, then shifted in his seat. Jostling her, he pulled her cell phone out of his back pocket. She stared at the burner she used to talk to Beatrice.

He tilted it toward her. "Call her."

Nerves got the better of her. Chewing on her bottom lip, she hesitated to take it. He waved the pre-paid cell phone in her direction. A second passed, then two, before she inhaled deep, exhaled long, and reached out to take it.

Warmed by his body, plastic slid against her palm. She looked at the illuminated screen. "It's nearly two in the morning, Sloan. Shouldn't I wait until—"

"No. You call her now." Shifting her around, he lifted her up, setting her astride him. As her ass settled on his thighs, she wiggled, wedging her knees between the chair arms and his hips. The blanket slipped off her shoulders. He drew it back up, covering her as he said, "On speaker, Theo. I wanna hear everything she says."

Throat tight, she nodded.

"Tell her to meet you tomorrow night at the Luxmore."

Surprise rolled through her. "My uncle's hotel?"

"Yeah. Midnight at the Luxmore. Tomorrow night."

"I'm nervous."

"Act as naturally as you can. Keep it simple, as close to the truth without giving anything away. If she gets wind you know about the texts or the ambush at the cabin, she might refuse to meet you. We don't know what that asshole told her, so—"

"Markov?"

"The asshole," Sloan growled. "I want a piece of

him, but that's for later. Right now, you have one job—to get your sister to the Luxmore tomorrow night, yeah?"

"Yeah."

"Get to it, *mazleiha*," he said, sitting back, resting his hands on top of her thighs.

Phone cupped in her hands, she slid her thumb over the raised buttons. Sloan gave her a squeeze of encouragement. She started pressing the numbers. Thumb poised over the call button, she re-checked the number, making sure she hadn't misdialed, then hit go.

Beatrice answered on the second ring. "Theo?"

"Bea," she said, swallowing hard.

"Oh my God! Are you and Violet okay?"

"We're okay. I'm okay."

"Thank God. Thank God. You didn't show up. I was worried," her sister whispered, sounding so relieved Theodora didn't know whether to believe her. "Where are you?"

"I'm safe. I'm in a safe place."

"Are you in town?"

"Yes."

"Can you get to me? Can you get back to the—"

"I'm not going back to the cabin, Bea. It's not safe. I think Uncle Nicoli has guys waiting for me there," Theodora said, hoping Markov had lied about the cabin, praying her sister swallowed the story hook, line, and sinker. "He knows about Aunt Jean's."

"Shit." The sound of high heels clicking across stone came through the line. "Okay, listen. Here's what we're going to do."

Her sister paused.

Sloan shook his head.

Theodora took control. "I'm mobile. I've still got lots of cash. Did you get the IDs?"

"Got six ready to go."

"Okay, good. I'll come to you. Meet me at the hotel. Uncle Nicoli won't expect me to go there."

"When?"

"Tomorrow. Midnight."

"The Luxmore. Midnight. Tomorrow," Beatrice confirmed, forever efficient. "Not the lobby."

"Back entrance. In the alcove," Theodora said, making it up on the fly. "I'll meet you there."

"See you then," Beatrice said as the sound of her footfalls stalled. "Hang on a sec..."

A sound of a door opening and closing came through the line.

A soft thump, then...

"Sorry, Theo, someone's here. I've gotta go. You'll be okay?"

"I'll be good."

"Be safe."

"You too," Theodora said, then disconnected the call.

A sick feeling rolled through her. Closing her eyes, she dropped the phone and pressed her hand over her mouth. Sloan murmured. With a silent curse, she leaned forward and touched her forehead to his. His big hands moved over her back, soothing her with his touch, telling her everything would be all right. She wanted to believe him, tried to tell herself she'd done nothing wrong. Her conscience, however, begged to differ, accusing her of breaking a sacred rule by setting Beatrice up. No matter what she'd done, she was family. She was blood. A bond Theodora couldn't ignore.

Sisters forever, come hell or high water.

Loyalty mattered, but love meant more. So...

She needed to find her way past the betrayal and forgive. Being angry was all right. Beatrice had earned her fury, but she also needed help. Their uncle corrupted everything he touched. Beatrice had never been immune. Which meant Theodora must take control, rein her in, and drag her away from life inside the Bratva. But Beatrice was stubborn. She wouldn't see reason without serious change in perspective. Sad, but true, leaving her no other option but to bait the hook.

The only thing left for her to do now was hope Beatrice stayed true to her word and showed up at the Luxmore.

## 42

Cloaked in magic, monitoring for enemy activity, Sloan tilted his wings, banking into a smooth turn above the Luxmore. Lots of bright lights shining up from below. Glitz and glamour showcased by elegant circular drive fronting a bank of glass doors. A brisk north wind rippled over his scales as he watched cars pull in and swing around the drive. A sleek Maserati. A couple of low-slung Mercedes. A gunmetal-grey '69 Mustang, pristine condition. And bringing up the rear—a canary yellow Lamborghini, engine purring as the owner waited in line, five down from the valet station.

*"Fuck, I love this place."* Gage said, flying off Sloan's right wingtip, bronze scales gleaming in the Luxmore's glow. *"Perfect place to boost cars. Add to my collection."*

Nian threw him an outraged look. *"You've got more money than you know what to do with...why not just buy them?"*

Gage shrugged. *"Stealing from humans is more fun."*

Rolling his eyes, Nian shook his head.

Silver scales winking, Haider chuckled.

"*A little focus, assholes,*" Sloan growled. "*My mate is in the mix tonight.*"

The Metallics grunted in agreement. At the same time. As a unit, as though the three males shared one brain. Any other night, Sloan would've found the close-knit group spooky. With Theodora on his back, protected by the warm air bubble he'd enclosed her in, Sloan didn't give a shit about the trio's ability to finish each other's sentences. He wanted the males focused and aware, ready, willing, and able to do damage, not distracted by each other and humans with expensive cars.

Scanning the Luxmore's roof, Sloan whirled into another turn. No humans milling around. Lots of space for him to land. Angling his wings, he set up his approach. Theodora shifted on his back, small hands wrapped around the spikes behind his horns, flying with him instead of fighting the flow.

She was a natural. Beautiful to watch as she leaned into each turn.

Adjusting the tether holding her secure on his back, he reached out with his mind. Her vital signs streamed on to his mental screen. Steady heartbeat. Even breaths. No longer nervous but settled in, relaxed and comfortable, enjoying the ride.

Fine-tuning his sonar, he pinged his packmate. "*Ven...you inside yet?*"

"*In position.*" The thump of boots across tile came through the link. "*Wick's at the back entrance. I'm headed to the mezzanine. Lobby's jumping. Lots of humans in tuxes and ball gowns. Fancy fundraiser of some kind.*"

Spreading his wings, Sloan reduced his speed. "*All part of the plan.*"

"*Cover?*"

The best kind. Humans liked to party. People plus

alcohol equaled lots of chatter and confusion. The late hour, the fancy setting and high-powered guest list all worked in his favor. At least, he hoped. Nothing about the situation spelled steady, but Theodora needed closure. He wanted to give it to her. A goal born out of selfish intentions. He wanted her settled, not mired in the past. So yeah, he might be giving her closure, but in doing so, he'd get what he needed in return—Theodora out of her old life and safely ensconced in the new one he and his pack provided.

*"I'll keep Theo cloaked until she meets with Beatrice."* Hanging like a ghoul over the Luxmore, he folded his wings. Gravity dragged him out of the air. His paws thumped down on the rooftop. Steel groaned. Industrial-sized AC units clanked. Claws scraping over light gravel, he crouched like a cat and scanned his surroundings. *"The second I step away, though, she'll be—"*

*"Vulnerable,"* Wick growled, helping in the usual way...one word at a time.

*"Yeah."* Not an ideal part of the plan. Sloan didn't like any of it, hating the idea of leaving his mate unprotected, even for a few minutes. Though he'd stay close, cloaked and concealed. Far enough away to give Theodora some privacy, but close enough to intervene if the situation went sideways. *"Big crowd. Lots of distraction, less focus and attention. Easier for my mate and her sister to slip away unnoticed."*

*"All right."* Increasing his wing speed, Gage blasted overhead. The roof shook. Gravel jumped, becoming wedged in between Sloan's talons. *"Time to post up. Let's—"*

*"Get this party started,"* Haider said, cruising in Gage's wake. *"The sooner she talks to her bitch of a sister, the sooner you're on your way home and Nian and I will get some action."*

Venom laughed. *"You're in luck, H. Plenty to choose from in here."*

*"Outstanding. Haven't fed in days. I'm hungry as hell,"* Nian murmured. Revolving into a holding pattern over the Luxmore, he frowned at Sloan. *"Are you going to shift or what?"*

Sloan wanted to say, "Or what?" Turning around and flying home sounded better. Much safer. More prudent for Theodora. Nothing but heartache awaited her inside the Luxmore. He'd read the files and longed to protect her from the hurt, but some truths needed to be learned up close and personal. *Closure.* The entire reason Theodora wanted to see her twin face to face. A noble gesture, sure, but also a lost cause. He knew what Theodora suspected, but didn't want to admit—Beatrice was in so deep nothing less than a miracle would pull her out.

One of Theodora's small hands left his spike. A death grip on the other, she shifted sideways. Fabric rustled against his scales. Long hair tumbling in a dark wave, she leaned over to look at him. "Thought we were going in the back way."

"Change of plans."

"Diversion?"

"She'll expect us to come in that way, Theo. We're not going to give her the upper hand."

"Bea doesn't like surprises."

"I don't care."

She huffed in amusement.

He sighed.

Earth magic puffed from his nostrils as he spoke. Green and gold shimmer flew like confetti. Theodora gasped in delight. Watching her smile, Sloan transformed. The rapid shift from dragon to human form popped her off his back. With a squeak of surprise, she flew into the air. Feet planted on the ground, gaze glued to her, he conjured his clothes. Jeans, a long-sleeved Henley, and his favorite leather jacket settled on his skin as she stopped going up and started to come down. Stomping his feet into his boots, he snagged her out of midair, spun around, and set her on her feet.

She laughed.

Cupping her nape, he dipped his head and kissed her. "Ready?"

"As I'll ever be," she said on a quick exhale.

Straightening her clothes, she ran her hands over her outfit. Dressed for the occasion, she looked stunning in a pair of wide-legged dress pants, turtleneck sweater, a leather blazer, and stiletto boots with pencil-thin heels. All in black. Modern and sleek. Sexy as all fucking hell.

Adjusting the diamond-drop pendant around her neck, she looked up at him. "Do I look okay?"

"Good enough to eat."

"Well," she said, "I'm sure you'll do that later."

"Count on it."

She smiled.

Grinning back, he palmed her waist, lifted, set her on the concrete walkway. Hand curled around hers, he led the way toward a steel door that exited onto the roof. He murmured. Locks clicked. Security sensors turned off. The door swung wide. He towed Theodora into the stairwell.

Fresh air shifted to warm and dry as the door slammed shut behind him. Blue numbers painted on cinder-block walls gave him the lay of the land as he spiraled deeper into the Luxmore. His mate kept pace, holding his hand, heels clicking on concrete treads, nerves jangling as he stopped on the third-floor landing.

"Theo."

"They can't see us, right?" she asked for the umpteenth time. "No one can see us?"

"I've got you covered, baby. Hold my hand, stay close to me, and you're invisible to human eyes." Setting his fingers beneath her chin, he turned her face in his direction. "That being said, if shit goes south, I'm hauling you out of here. Whether or not you talk to your sister."

She took a big breath, exhaled, then nodded. "Go."

Magic simmering around him, Sloan tightened the cloaking spell and murmured his wishes. The door opened. The smell of heavy perfume hit him as he stepped into a wide hallway. His boot soles sank into plush carpet. He looked both ways. Empty corridor. Low light coming from fluted wall sconces. Two options—turn left or go right.

Holding the architectural plans to the Luxmore in his mind, he veered right. Footfalls silent, he walked down toward the mezzanine. Human chatter drifted up the corridor, growing louder with each step he took. The click of glasses sounded. The scent of lemon mixed with gin registered as he exited the hall and entered a wide-open space.

Ruby red eyes snapped his way. Back to the wall, arms crossed over his chest, Venom tipped his chin in greeting.

Sloan nodded back and kept walking. Dragon senses roaming, he glanced at his watch. Twelve fifteen a.m. Perfect timing. Not too early. Just late enough to ensure Beatrice made it to the rendezvous point first. Approaching the top of the staircase, Sloan sensed Venom rolled in behind him. He stopped at the curved railing with an intricate steel banister and looked down from three stories up.

A party was in full swing inside the grand lobby. The crème de là crème of Seattle society framed by Art Deco opulence as waiters dressed in black tie weaved through the crowd.

So not his scene.

Although no one could argue with the décor or the obvious comfort. A *grande dame* built in the 1930s, the Luxmore epitomized elegance. Black-lacquered, smooth columns stood sentry along pale walls, rising to meet the soaring ceiling painted with interesting geometric shapes in muted orange, sharp grey, and white. Graceful lines. Stylish furniture. Welcoming atmosphere. A building he'd gotten laid in well and often over the years.

Good memories, but he had better ones to make with Theodora now.

His mate gave him everything—love, acceptance, the kind of connection he thought he'd never have, but somehow managed to find. A quirk of fate? Being in the right place at the right time? The Goddess of All Things intervening to correct a mistake? Maybe. He'd never know for sure, but the shift in life circumstances gave him hope, brought him peace, returning what had been lost—a mate and a child after having suffered the loss of his son.

He still mourned Simeon. It didn't matter that his infant hadn't survived. His son had been the love of his life for so long, he would never let him go. But he had Theodora and Violet to care for now. The past no longer hurt as much, so instead of doing what he normally did inside the Luxmore—picking a female to fuck for an hour or two to help him forget—he turned his attention to the humans, searching for Markov and Nicoli Antonov in the crush.

Not finding either, he fired up mind-speak. *"Wick—anything?"*

*"Russians."*

*"Russians?"* Venom asked, setting up shop beside Sloan at the railing.

*"Lots of 'em."*

*"Fuck,"* Sloan growled. *"Beatrice?"*

*"No sign of her,"* Wick said. *"Ambush. No fucking doubt."*

Venom cursed. *"The sister's slime. Total frigging trash."*

Ignoring his friend, Sloan drew Theodora in front of him, trapping her between the banister and his body. *"You checked the alcove?"*

*"Empty. Lots of eyes on it, though,"* Wick said.

*"Lots of eyes in here, too."* Gaze on the lobby, Venom left his side to walk down the length of banister. Assessing the crowd, he paused to point at males below. Sloan did the same, holding Theodora close as he surveyed the human horde. *"Dressed to blend in—guests, waiters—"*

*"One of the bartenders, too,"* Sloan said, clocking the male with gang ink peeking above the collar of his dress shirt, busy pouring vodka into a martini glass, eyes moving over the guests, scanning the entrances and exits. *"Waiting for Theo to show up."*

Wick snarled.

A muscle twitching in his jaw, Venom pivoted, pace slow, still focused on the crowed, making his way back to where Sloan and Theodora stood. *"You clock Markov yet?"*

*"No,"* Wick replied.

*"Goddamn it,"* Venom growled, ruby-red gaze beginning to glow. *"Total bust. I need to get my hands on that guy."*

"Theo..." Pulling her back against his chest, Sloan set his chin on the crown of her head. "See anyone you recognize?"

Strung tight, Theodora grabbed his forearm with both hands. A tremor shook her. Her knuckles went white. "Yes."

"Who?"

"The gang's all here," she said, her voice whisper-thin. "Bea must've told him."

"Your uncle?"

She nodded. "He's at the bar."

Sloan snapped his gaze toward the curved antique bar in the lobby. He scanned those sitting on the plush, low-backed stools. It took him a moment, but he found Antonov.

Dressed in an expensive tuxedo with crisp lines, the asshole held court. Elbow perched on the gleaming hardwood at the end of the bar, cuff pushed up, Rolex on display. Tumbler full of amber liquid in his other hand. The center of attention, a king on his throne as a cluster of males vied for his favor.

Theodora didn't need to point the bastard out. Sloan saw the family resemblance. Dark-haired. Green-eyed. Same bone structure, bolder, masculine, but just as striking as Theodora's.

The self-important asshole. Down there, playing king of the castle while he waited for his niece to walk into his trap.

The urge to rip Antonov limb from limb rampaged through Sloan. His dragon half snarled. A burst of powerful energy crackled down his spine.

*"Not a good idea. Power down, buddy,"* Venom murmured, interrupting the magical tantrum. Not a bad idea. The best course of action, given the damage Sloan could do if he let loose. He'd level the place, reduce the Luxmore to a pile of rubble. *"You want, we'll take Theo home and come back. Got Markov on my hit list, and Nian and Haider plan to stay anyway, so—"*

"It's official," Theodora said, cutting Venom off without knowing it.

Stuffing rage back in its box, Sloan glanced down at his mate. "What's official?"

"I'm done. Finished." Making a hoarse sound, she dragged her gaze from her uncle and turned in his arms, resignation in her expression. Grief already surfacing through the hurt. He saw it all, every ounce of pain she tried to hide. "She set me up. *Again.*"

"It sucks, baby."

"I'd like to go home now."

"I need to kill your uncle first."

"Not worth it, Sloan."

*"Mazleiha—"*

"I'm part of your world. Violet and I...we're part of your world now," she whispered. "You told me so."

"I did. Never doubt that you are, Theo."

"If that's true, then this...him...none of it matters. Nicoli no longer factors. Neither does my sister. I wanted to bring her with me. I hoped she'd..." Her voice broke.

With a soft growl, Sloan set his mouth against her temple. His touch steadied her. She nestled in, accepting the comfort he offered.

She drew a shaky breath. "A pipe dream, Sloan. Her. Me. The two of us together as a family. It's never going to happen. Beatrice made her decision four years ago. Now I have to make mine. As much as it hurts, I've gotta wipe the slate clean. For me. For Violet. I'm starting fresh...with you."

"I'm sorry, baby. I'm sorry your sister—"

"Not your fault."

"I thought by bringing you here, I could make it better."

"You make everything better. No way I'd be here without you." Slipping her arms around his waist, she pressed her cheek to his chest. "I mean...literally. My sister had me shot, remember?"

"Goddamn Markov," Venom grumbled, watching, listening, showing no shame. "I really need to kill that guy."

"You mind?" Eyes narrowed, Sloan threw him a warning look. "Private moment."

Arms crossed, hip leaning against the banister, Venom shrugged. "Sorry to say it, buddy, but if you want one of those, get behind a closed door."

Sloan clenched his teeth. The urge to hit Venom surged inside him, the need so strong his knuckles tingled. Total pain in his ass. Nice try at deflection, but...Venom wasn't sorry. A skilled eavesdropper, the male never apologized for intruding. He made an art form out of sticking his nose into everyone's business.

Gaze steady on him, Venom grinned.

He scowled. "Maybe I'll skip Antonov and settle for ripping your head off instead."

Clearly trying not to cry, Theodora laughed.

"See," Venom said, completely unrepentant. "Your mate doesn't mind."

Sloan didn't agree. Theodora was holding on by her fingernails, trying to be brave as the truth began to crush her. He felt her pain, understood the sorrow that threatened to undo her. Losing her sister like this might not be as final as death, but it came close. Being unable to save Beatrice from herself was a hard pill for his female to swallow. Even without asking, he knew Theodora blamed herself.

Crazy making, to his way of thinking.

She owned no part in the destruction Beatrice left in her wake. Human. Dragonkind. Didn't matter. Everyone made their own decisions, then lived with the consequences.

Fresh wounds, though, rarely listened to reason, so he'd wait. Bide his time. Be patient. Talk it through with her, watch, listen, and learn. Guide his female to clarity. Help her navigate the messy tangle of emotion until she came out clean on other side.

Her breathing hitched.

"Let it go," he murmured, refusing to let her bury the pain. He'd done it for years, stuffing the anguish deep down, trying to forget. Nothing but sorrow and frustration lay in that direction. He knew the road well, had traveled it so many times he'd worn grooves in the pavement. "Don't hold it in. Let it go, Theo."

"I hate this," she said, voice thick with unshed tears. "I hate it for her. I hate it for myself."

"I know."

She lost the battle, and tears tipped over her bottom lashes. "Please take me home."

With a nod, Sloan moved to do as she asked. She needed an outlet, a safe place where she could scream at the unfairness and come to terms with the extent of her sister's betrayal. He could give her that—all his patience, all his love, every bit of his compassion.

Heart breaking for her, watching her tears fall, Sloan gathered her up. Holding her safe in his arms, he didn't bother retracing his steps. Cloaked in an invisibility spell, he took the stairs instead. Magic rolled in front him. The throng parted, clearing a path as he crossed the lobby and walked under Antonov's nose, then out the front door, leaving the Luxmore and her asshole of an uncle to his narrow little life, helping Theodora bury the past and leave the ugliness behind.

## 43

## Night of the Meridian realignment — T-minus one hour

A roll of painter's tape in her hands, Theodora turned full circle. Her bare soles rasped over polished concrete. Her mouth curved as she surveyed her new pottery studio. Good bones. Wide-open space. Still in its infancy.

A wall of untrimmed folding doors opened into a courtyard, currently blacked out by magic to keep the sunlight out. Plaster-skimmed, unpainted walls. Baseboards not yet installed. Vaulted ceiling and raw timber beams stretching overhead. Nothing much to recommend it, except the brilliance of eleven hundred square feet of untapped potential.

And boxes. Lots and lots of unopened boxes. Each full of supplies not yet ready to be unpacked.

Stacked against the far wall, the mountain of unearthed equipment Daimler ordered for her rested in what would eventually become a small office with a sliding pocket door to keep the dust out. The place she'd keep her computer, an area to take photos of her work, and do any and all business-type things—invoicing, ordering, packaging, and shipping. Different work zones. The pinnacle of organization and efficient workflow.

Daimler's idea, naturally. The Numbai was a master of décor and a field marshal when it came to setting up systems. He made suggestions (that really weren't suggestions at all), helping her mark off each zone on the floor. Green tape for her ten-foot-long worktable under the skylights in the center of the studio. Blue to indicate where her throwing wheel would sit. Purple for the glazing station. Yellow for the damp room. Red for where the gas kiln, electric kiln, and air compressor would go. Regular old masking tape for the army of metal rolling racks with interchangeable ware boards with dedicated sections for greenware, bisqueware, and fired, finished pieces.

Perfection in planning. All laid out in precise, straight, two-inch lines. A fantasy factory about to be brought to life.

Now, all she needed was walls.

Tapping a roll of tape against her thigh, she made the rounds again, moving from zone to zone, testing the flow, visualizing what her studio would look like when all the furniture sat in place.

"Zone!" Violet shrieked from out in the corridor. "Cats can't be purple!"

Sloan chuckled. "You sure?"

"I'm sure to be sure to be sure," Violet said with great authority. "Maybe pink, though. I'll ask Lulu."

Sloan scoffed. "She won't know."

"She will too! Lulu knows everything."

"Everything?"

"*Everything.*"

Biting down on a laugh, Theodora glanced toward the double doors into the aboveground lair that stood open. She smiled as the pair came into view. Carrying Violet on his hip, Sloan turned into her studio. His boots left the hardwood in the corridor, thumping onto polished concrete as he dipped his head beneath the lintel and crossed the threshold.

Her chest grew tight. The corners of his eyes stung.

A normal reaction for her when it came to him. Every time she looked at him, she couldn't believe her luck. The beauty of him, inside and out, awed her. Overwhelmed her. Made her so grateful she drew a deep breath, trying to steady the chaotic clang of emotion.

God must really love her.

As good an explanation as any for the gift of him in her life. Sloan was a miracle made real. The man she would've dreamed about, had she known the possibility of him existed. Until he came to her rescue in the woods, she hadn't *believed*. Not once. Her upbringing had killed her ability to dream big. But now, watching Sloan become father to her daughter, possibility and opportunity lay everywhere. In a matter of days, he'd opened her eyes, thrown the doors wide open and changed the landscape of her life. In a single stroke, he'd made her realize she should've held on longer, dreamed bigger, imagined harder, instead allowing the idea of *the one* to slip away.

*The one* didn't mean perfect. Sloan was far from that, and so was she. What she'd needed for years, and never gotten, was the man perfect for her—until now. Until him.

"Hey," she said, smiling at the pair.

Dark eyes full of laughter shifted to her as he set Violet on her feet.

A perturbed look on her face, she put her hands on her hips. Suffering the indignity of being carried by one ear, Lulu whipped backward, then swayed forward. "Mommy."

"Yes, honey-bunny?"

"Zone thinks cats are purple." Violet tsked. "Silly."

Sloan grinned.

Smiling back, Theodora smoothed an errant ringlet off Violet's forehead, then pointed to a plastic container sitting next to the boxes. "Chalk's in the bucket, honey. You want to draw on the floor?"

"Hurrah!" Violet yelled, and, with a quick pivot, raced across the room, Lulu flapping behind her.

Theodora watched her daughter go.

A strong arm slipped around her waist. Sloan's mouth touched her temple. She closed her eyes as contentment drew pleasure up from deep inside her. With a sigh, she settled in, fitting her side to his, enjoying his heat.

"*Mazleiha?*"

"Mm-hmm?"

"You wanna tell me why there's a material witness warrant out for you in New York?"

She blinked. A second later, she tipped her head back. Gorgeous brown eyes met hers. A red file folder appeared in his hand. He waggled it in her periphery and raised a brow.

"New York, you say?"

"Oliva Cartwright ring a bell?"

One of her aliases. The last one she'd assumed while working at Umbridge, Carter, Stern. It felt like forever ago, decades instead of days.

She pursed her lips. "Well..."

"Well, what?"

"I may have...ah..." She paused. He waited, holding her gaze as she smoothed her hands over his chest. "...started criminal proceedings against the managing partner at my old firm."

His brows popped up. "What the hell does that mean?"

"I copied documents proving my boss was embezzling from client trusts and, ah...sent them to the U.S. attorney for the Southern District of New York."

"By mail?"

"Well, yeah. It's not like I could walk them through the government's front door. They would've asked questions. Ones I couldn't answer without blowing my cover."

"Fucking hell."

"I couldn't stand it, Sloan," she said, feeling the old tension rise. "I didn't do anything before...didn't go against my uncle at all. Not once before I ran. He's hurt so many people. If I'd have spoken up, taken what I knew at the time to the police—"

"You'd be dead."

She sighed. "Probably. But the thing with Umbridge? I saw a chance to right a wrong. Fix what Memphis couldn't, help her out by doing the right thing."

"Memphis was your boss?"

"She's a good person."

"She doesn't exist."

"What?"

"I checked, Theo. Her digital footprint is well-crafted. Good enough to convince most, but Memphis Alexander is a ghost, just like you were."

"But..." She shook her head. "I've been to her house. Met her wife and sister. She's got two dogs!"

"All a façade."

"Well," she said with a huff, pissed off her former boss-slash-friend had lied to her. Which was totally hypocritical. It wasn't as though she'd been a fount of honesty while working for Memphis. Hell, she'd lied every day about the simplest thing—her freaking name. "Doesn't that just twist shit sideways."

"Little bit," he said, bobbing the file in his hand. "So, this warrant."

Watching Violet draw a clowder of purple cats on the floor, Theodora waved her hand, dismissing his concern. "The U.S. attorney has all the proof she needs. Umbridge left a paper trail. Easy to follow once you know where to look. She doesn't need me to testify to anything."

"Good." Red card stock flashed as he flicked his wrist. The file sailed into a trash bin sitting next to the door. "About tonight—the realignment."

"You haven't changed your mind?"

He shook his head. "I know you don't want me to, but I'm going to lock down with the others."

Disappointment struck like a fist. She breathed through the pain.

He'd already talked to her about the realignment and what the flex of electrostatic bands ringing the planet meant. Told her what he planned in bed, after making love to her, and explained his reasons. And yet an undeniable yearning rose inside her, one so strong she had trouble seeing her way past blinding need. She wanted everything Sloan had to offer. The complete package. *Everything*. All of the beauty a life with him promised.

Battling the craving, she drew a steadying breath. "I want another baby, Sloan."

"I know you do, and I'll give you one. More than one. We've got plenty of time," he said, talking sense, the way he always did. "But it's too soon for us. I want time with you and Vivy before we bring an infant into our lives. Once she's settled, totally comfortable, we'll give her a baby brother."

"Is this about Simeon?"

Pain pooled in his eyes. It always did when he spoke about his newborn son and the fact he'd lost him before even getting to hold him. Eleven years hadn't lessened his regret. His memory of the day Simeon died hadn't dimmed. Time provided distance, but withheld closure, ensuring some pain stayed sharp and never faded.

"Honey," she whispered, cupping his cheek, trying to comfort him.

"I'm not gun-shy, Theo."

"Okay."

"I'm already a sire. The instant you and Vivy came into my life, I became one."

"Yeah."

"Yeah," he said, soft and sweet, making her heart beat faster. "I love you. I love her. I'll love the babies we make together."

God. This man. The wonder of him never ceased.

Tucked tight against him, she fisted her hands in the back of her shirt.

"I'm asking you to be patient, *mazleiha*," he murmured, mouth pressed to the top of her head. "I'll get us there. Got nothing but clear skies and a beautiful life ahead of us."

That sounded amazing. The best, given she'd live it at his side. "Nothing but clear skies."

"And a beautiful life."

"Thank you, honey."

"For what?"

"Being who you are." Holding him, being held in return, she swallowed her tears. Happy ones, unlike the others she'd shed in her life. "I love you, Sloan. So much, sometimes it takes me by surprise, and I think you can't possibly be real. Then I look up, and there you are—the man made and meant for me."

His arms contracted around her. "Goddess, Theo. My love for you is intense, bright, so fucking beautiful, baby, it's blinding."

Her breath hitched. "Clear skies."

"Nothing but beauty," he murmured as Violet started singing.

"Bed of Roses." A Bon Jovi favorite. A new one in her daughter's growing compilation of eighties rock bands.

Giving Theodora a squeeze, Sloan smiled against her temple. "Freakishly accurate. She hit the nail on the head with that one."

Theodora chuckled. Leaning away, she met his gaze as Violet's voice rose and fell on the chorus. "How soon do you need to go?"

"The boys are already gathering."

"Outside the vault?"

Sloan nodded. "Azrad, Kilmar, and Terranon just arrived."

"Want us to walk you down?"

"Yeah, baby," he said.

She shivered, enjoying the tingle his deep voice gave her, then wrapped her arm around his back, slid her thumb through his belt loop, called to her daughter, and did as he asked—settled into patience as she walked with him out of her studio, straight into the elevators and underground lair.

Not hard for her to do. Acceptance came easy in the end.

Sloan was right. They had time. Nothing but clear skies and a beautiful life ahead of them.

# ACKNOWLEDGMENTS

Sloan and Theodora's story took me by storm. I struggled in the beginning. None of the words came easy at first. Everything felt out of focus, but then Sloan and Theodora made their presence known, and the pieces in what seemed like a broken puzzle aligned. In an instant, the details came fast and furious, making me to scramble to keep up. In the end, the mad dash was fun. I hope you think so too and enjoy every of second FURY OF AGGRESSION as Sloan and Theodora take you on another wild ride into the Dragonkind world.

I'd like to say a huge thank you to Christine Witthohn, literary agent extraordinaire. You've always believed in me. I'll forever love you. We make a great team.

Thanks as well to Tanya and the wonderful team at Oliver Heber Books. You gave me the extra time I needed to fit all the jagged story pieces together, lightening my load along the way. Thank you a thousand times over. It's amazing working with you. I'm so grateful to be part of your crew.

To my family—you're the best. Love you to the moon and back. I couldn't do it without you.

# A NOTE FROM THE AUTHOR

Thank you for taking the time to read Fury of Aggression. If you enjoyed it, please help others find my books so they can enjoy them too.

**Recommend it:** Please help other readers find this book by recommending it to friends, readers' groups, and discussion boards.

**Review it:** Let other readers know what you liked or didn't like about Fury of Aggression.

Follow me on Facebook, Instagram and Bookbub to get all the latest news.

Sign up for my Newsletter and get exclusive VIP giveaways, freebies and sales throughout the year.

Book updates can be found at www. CoreeneCallahan.com

Thanks again for taking the time to read my books! You make it all possible.

# ALSO BY COREENE CALLAHAN

**Dragonfury Scotland**

Fury of a Highland Dragon

Fury of Shadows

Fury of Denial

Fury of Persuasion

Fury of Isolation

**Dragonfury Bad Boy Shifter Series**

Fury of Fate

Fury of Conviction

**Dragonfury Series**

Fury of Fire

Fury of Ice

Fury of Seduction

Fury of Desire

Fury of Obsession

Fury of Surrender

Fury of Destruction

**Circle of Seven Series**

Knight Awakened

Knight Avenged

**Warriors of the Realm Series**

Warrior's Revenge

# ABOUT THE AUTHOR

A native Texan and former history teacher, award-winning and internationally bestselling author Alexa Aston lives with her husband in a Dallas suburb, where she eats her fair share of dark chocolate and plots out stories while she walks every morning. She enjoys travel, sports, and binge-watching—and never misses an episode of *Survivor*.

Alexa brings her characters to life in steamy historicals, contemporary romances, and romantic suspense novels that resonate with passion, intensity, and heart.

Keep up with Alexa
Visit her website
Newsletter Sign-Up


More ways to connect with Alexa

9 781648 391408